"UTTERLY
MAGNIFICENT."
—*New York Times*
bestselling author
COURTNEY MILAN

DISCOVERY
of DESIRE

SUSANNE LORD

"BEAUTIFULLY WRITTEN,
DEEPLY ROMANTIC,
AND UTTERLY MAGNIFICENT."
—*New York Times* bestselling
author Courtney Milan

*Previously in the
London Explorers series*

In Search of Scandal

SUSANNE LORD

**Escaping the brutal reaches of Tibet is one accomplishment,
but escaping the snare of love is another entirely…**

"A wounded hero, a feisty, vivacious heroine, intense emotions,
and a vibrant voice mark Lord as a talent to watch.
Readers seeking a powerful and poignant story that satisfies both their
hearts and minds are sure to put this high on their TBR pile."

—*RT Book Reviews* Reviewer Top Pick ★★★★⭑

DISCOVERY of DESIRE

SUSANNE LORD

sourcebooks
casablanca

Published by Sourcebooks Casablanca, an imprint of Sourcebooks,
Inc.
P.O. Box 4410, Naperville, Illinois 60567-4410
(630) 961-3900
Fax: (630) 961-2168
www.sourcebooks.com

Printed and bound in Canada.
MBP 10 9 8 7 6 5 4 3 2 1

One

Mazagaon Port, Bombay, December 1850

SETH MAYHEW WOULDN'T CALL IT A CURSE.

But a man on his 13th sail couldn't help but wonder.

Damned if he hadn't lived this before. From where he stood on the deck of the HMS *Isabella*, Bombay might have been Brazil. The same briny stink of the harbor. The stray dogs nosing the pier. The carts, the cargo, the cries of the dockmen—all agitated and out of sorts like the arrival of a fifteen-hundred-ton steamship somehow took 'em by surprise.

It was just like every port in Brazil. Like a remembering. Like the start of every other expedition that had ever failed.

But Seth wouldn't call it a curse.

This time, he wouldn't dare.

Under his boots, the ship steadied entering the still waters of the harbor, same as the clippers he'd sailed to Santos, Recife, and Paranaguá had done. After three months at sea, he had that same urge to jump the rail, to swim for shore, to race on dry land as far as his legs and lungs would carry him.

Christ, yes, Bombay might have been Brazil.

If not for the hundred love-starved bachelors waiting in welcome.

"You ever seen a sorrier sight 'n that?" Eddie, the young cabin boy from Dover, slouched on the rail beside him and spat overboard. "All them hot-arsed English come for a look at our girls like they was buying cattle. A man's meant to have dignity. If it was me, and I was wanting a wife, she'd not see me standing down there."

Seth could say nothing to that. He'd be the first man forward if he could afford to keep a wife. But he was only an explorer, and this expedition held no promise of profit.

"It's a queer sight, I give you that," he said.

"Them black suits don't make no sense for India," Eddie said. "Or them silk chokers and beaver hats."

"Well, there's an English gent for you. Like they're strolling the Strand." Seth eyed the mob, envious of their tailored suits despite the heat. "Shows why they're here, I suppose. For a first look at Englishwomen fresh off the boat. These men'll not be going native—not in their dress and not with the local women."

"No sense in any of 'em," Eddie snarled.

Seth had to grin. Only a shirttail lad of sixteen could muster that level of scorn. "None I can see." He elbowed the lad gently and winked. "But then, I've always been democratic where women are concerned."

He thought that was clever enough, but Eddie

only scowled down at the mob like all forty-four ladies onboard were his kin.

Seth sighed. "Cheer yourself, lad. East India's been shipping our girls here for a couple hundred years to wed their men, and that won't be changing today."

"No matter to me. Wasn't one that didn't chuck me a shoulder if I said a word to 'em."

"You know those ladies couldn't fraternize with the likes of us. They have to keep their reputations, not arrive all sullied. Besides"—he lowered his voice—"their mums likely warned them about sailors like you."

That was said in jest, but Eddie puffed up. "There's truth in that, I suppose."

Erasing his grin, Seth nodded manfully and let it alone. The boy was of a tender age. He'd not yet learned the kind of girl he might win. Hell, if a seaman's life was all the boy had ahead of him, he'd not be marrying at all. And Seth knew himself that wasn't a hope that died easy.

The ship listed and the grim thought scattered. The tugs were nudging the ship into its berth, inch by maddening inch.

Seth gripped the rail and pushed his body up and down as he waited, relishing the burn in his shoulders. He'd found all sorts of ways to take his exercise these months at sea. Seemed the only way to keep from chasing all the questions in his head in a circle, like: Was he too late? Would Bombay prove the curse?

Was Georgie still alive?

He gripped the rail tighter and kept on.

Down on the wharf, a fair number of the men held up name signs. There might be distant family and fiancés among them for the lady passengers. And for him, hopefully one translator.

Tom Grant was supposed to meet him, but damned if Seth would find him easy. The man may be fluent in three Indian dialects and supervisor of an East India Company plantation, but there was no knowing if he was clever enough to bring a sign of his own.

Seth pushed off the rail and patted his coat pocket. The letter crinkled in answer.

"Well now, lad." Seth picked up his bag and shook Eddie's hand. "This is good-bye. Safe travels. And don't you go ruining any of these women before they get a chance to get themselves wed." He winked at the boy. "After that, they're fair game."

"I won't." Eddie's smile faded. "And…good luck finding your sister."

Surprised, Seth stared down at the boy. He'd only told a couple of his bunkmates.

The boy shuffled his feet. "I wondered why you was sailing on account of your not looking like a Company man. I thought you might be a soldier, but soldiers don't book steerage and eat mess with the crew." He shrugged, shrinking farther into his shirt. "I didn't tell nobody. I just wondered."

"It's all right, lad." Seth patted him on the shoulder but the boy didn't raise his head. This was why he'd wanted it kept dark. Knowing such things was nothing but a burden. "Thank you, Eddie. And don't worry. I'll find her."

And he *would* find her. Finding was what he did.

With a final wave, Seth hiked his bag onto his shoulder and headed below deck to the gangplank—and saw he wasn't getting off this damn boat as quick as he'd hoped. The four dozen ladies were queued to disembark, so he retreated a step.

So these are the venture girls…

He'd not seen the women the entire sail—hoped not to see them at all. Booked steerage as he'd been, and not allowed aft of the paddle boxes, it had been impossible anyway.

No, he didn't want to see them. Their bonnets and ruffles and ribbons were too much of England, of home. Most of them would never get back.

And some wouldn't survive the year.

On the wharf below, the bachelors hushed with anticipation. With this welcome, wasn't any wonder these ladies did the long sea to marry. In England, men with the blunt to keep a family were worse than scarce.

The women at the back of the line turned to examine him—worn boots, secondhand suit, overgrown hair. The speculation in their eyes dimmed and he tried not to mind.

"Afternoon, ladies." He put on his best smile.

Some dropped their gazes, some pressed against their corsets like they'd forgotten how to breathe. All of them were scared-looking.

No, he didn't want to see this.

Beneath their pale skin, Seth saw the prettiness. He couldn't help it, even when his heart wasn't in it. Well. Georgie always did call him the Worst Flirt in the Midlands. But that had never been accurate.

He'd always been the best.

"Don't I hear the gentlemen's hearts cracking from here," he teased, and the women giggled nervously.

"Careful not to smile at 'em, ladies, or you'll start a stampede."

The girls laughed more easily, a few of them blushing.

Damn their fathers. Did they even know what their daughters would face here?

The gangplank connected to the quay with a hard clang and the bonnets swiveled around. It was time. Slow as a march to the gallows, the ladies shuffled across the plank and stepped onto the dock.

And then matters went ass over elbow.

Eager bachelors swarmed the ladies. Stevedores shoved the Indian servants aside. Ragged beggars—some missing limbs, some crawling on the ground—pleaded for coin and food.

"*Sahib…*"

The instant Seth stepped foot on land, a clawed hand tugged at his sleeve. He followed the wiry arm to the bent head of an old man.

"*Sahib*," the old man pleaded.

Automatically, Seth reached for a few copper *paisa* but a white hand shot out to stay him.

"You mustn't give them anything," a mustached man said. "It only makes them more aggressive."

Aggressive? The old man couldn't stand straight and had an eye cloudy with cataracts. Seth gave him a silver *anna* instead.

The crush of bodies swayed him, but he'd never been afraid of people. The venture girls, however, were huddled as close together as their wide skirts allowed.

Indian servants shooed the beggars away. Black-suited Englishmen corralled the ladies like sheepdogs. A rumbling din of male voices advised the ladies, consoled them—*badly*, it seemed—and underneath it all, a calm, crisp voice…

"Ladies?"

A woman's voice. Sweet and low and nearly swallowed in the fray.

Maybe it was because his explorer's senses were honed to seek the rare, the anomalies in nature, but Seth trailed that voice to a venture girl twenty feet away. She wore a trim white jacket and green skirt with starry, white flowers all over it. Her sun helmet concealed all but a bit of brown hair.

"Ladies, as no one has told us yet what to do, if you are to be met by someone, would you move to this end?" She gestured and the ladies shuffled to do her bidding, obedient as soldiers.

Seth jerked to follow, then paused. *He* was to meet someone. Should he wait with them?

A small wave of her hand and the ladies leaned forward in attention. He did, too.

"And the others can wait here for Captain Travers," she said. "He will accompany you to the customs house." The women sorted themselves, fear in every pair of eyes clinging to their officer.

Seth dragged in a lungful of air that didn't ease the tightness in his chest. Wasn't any of his business.

And wasn't a thing he could do to help.

He turned to plunge into the crowd, but then the little officer spoke again.

"We are here, ladies," she said gently. "And we are fine."

The words were plain, but it was like she'd hushed the whole world. He didn't want to, but he looked again. The venture girls stood in two close circles, their small valises and parasols clutched to their chests, and watched the chaos around them with wide eyes.

But they kept their chins up now.

For the first time in months, a real smile curved his lips. People needed someone to depend on. Like those ladies depended on that little officer.

And she *was* little, at least to him. She wouldn't stand any taller than his chin and his hands could span her waist. But little or not, she wore that dainty, braided jacket like a captain of the Eleventh Hussars. There wasn't a wrinkle on her skirts or wayward crease in its folds. And that straight spine was all the sight he had of her—she didn't fidget and she didn't turn.

Composed, capable, orderly-like. He'd drive a woman like that to Bedlam.

But he fell a little bit in love with her anyway.

He was bumped from behind. The mustache-man angling for a closer look. "Give the ladies their breathing room, mate," Seth said. "They might like a bit of time to repair themselves."

The man swung about. "You traveled with them, didn't you?"

"I suppose."

"Did you learn any names? Which are the prime articles?"

"The prime—? Hell, I don't know."

The man turned around to survey the girls. "Not that I expect them all to be handsome. They couldn't find a husband back home, could they? But taking an ugly wife…" He grimaced, then squared his shoulders. "I mean to have one, just the same."

Seth stared down at the man and muttered, "There you go, mate. Words to set a lady's heart aflutter."

Irritated, Seth waded against the stream of bachelors closing in on the ladies. Wasn't any of his business.

The men holding signs had formed a line and were shuffling toward the ladies to be claimed. They obeyed the little officer, too. His translator might be among them, so he read his way through the crush. MISS EUNICE SIMMS…MISS LOUISE ALPERT—

Ah, here! CLAIMING WILLIAM REPTON AND—*and?*—MISS W. ADAMS.

The man holding the card eyed him suspiciously. So this was his translator. Brown hair, spectacles, younger than he'd expected. But he looked clever. He'd do.

"Tom Grant?" Seth asked.

"I am. You're Will Repton?"

Seth grinned. "For your purposes, I am." He shook his hand. "I'm Seth Mayhew. You'll be working for me instead."

"I—"

"This explains it." Seth handed him Will's letter. "Will couldn't leave England on account of his being leg-shackled and expecting a little baby. But Georgie's my sister after all, and the orphan in Tibet is who she was after, so I'm here and Will's not. It's all a bit Hamlet-without-the-prince, but there it is."

Tom Grant blinked behind his spectacles. "*Who* are you?"

Maybe he just *looked* clever.

"Seth May—" He never was skilled at explaining. "Read the letter, mate."

Tom Grant passed the sign to him, cracked open the letter, and began to frown. That frown wasn't how Seth wanted to start their partnership, but the man had agreed to the job, and would be earning a hell of a salary for the effort.

But Tom's expression wasn't growing any happier as he started page two.

"That letter explains it all." Seth flapped the sign against his thigh, *waiting*. "'Course it was Will who raised the funds to sail here hoping to—"

"To find the lost orphan. I know," Tom said, his voice dropping to a grumble. "Another survivor of that massacre." He didn't bother looking up from the letter—which was damn provoking.

"You don't think the baby survived, do you?"

"I think Will Repton survived a nightmare, and I think he needs to believe he wasn't alone."

"That baby lived. My sister crossed into Tibet to search for her."

That stopped Tom's reading. "Right." He lowered the letter a fraction to push his spectacles higher. "Sorry. The latter is true enough, in any case. So when you lost communication with your sister, you persuaded Will to let you come in his place?"

Seth nodded. "Would've gone off my head not being able to search for Georgie."

Tom's frown deepened, and he went back to staring at that letter like he was hoping the words would change.

It was good that Tom's help had been secured in advance. Finding another translator wouldn't have been easy. Seth's rank as an explorer-for-hire wouldn't open any doors with the Company men. Even when he'd been under the employ of East India, they hadn't treated him much better than a mule driver.

Or the mule.

Tom flipped the letter over and started reading from the beginning. *Again.*

With a sigh, Seth dropped his bag at his feet to wait—and remembered the sign: CLAIMING MISS W. ADAMS. Tom Grant was collecting one of the venture girls then.

W? The man couldn't write her name in full?

Wasn't any of his business.

Meaning to be helpful, Seth held the sign high and waited.

❧

"Mina!" Emma clutched her arm. "I see him. I see your Thomas Grant."

Mina's stomach rolled. Thomas was here. Of course he was—of course he *would* be. If only the ground would steady. Her sister's sudden grab had nearly toppled her. Ninety-nine days on a boat and she couldn't seem to lock her knees.

Mina reached into her skirt pocket and squeezed the stone in her hand. Through her lace glove, the quartz was as cool as if it still held the weather of England within it.

Emma's blue eyes shone—and that was nearly all Mina was sensible of. Distantly, Mina felt the sun on her neck. More sharply, a bead of sweat trickled to the small of her back. *Too warm…*

Emma had suggested she wear her green dress

to meet Mr. Grant—the pattern of starry woodruff reminded Mina of home and it was the finest of her day dresses. But it was too warm. Especially with the cholera belt—no, the *healthful* flannel cummerbund she wore.

Oh dear, all her gowns would be too warm…

"Mina?" Emma's eyes narrowed with concern.

"Yes, you…you see him?"

Emma stepped close, her voice dropping to a whisper. "I *knew* you had to be as nervous as the rest of us, for all your managing ways."

"I'm not managing," Mina protested weakly.

"He's very handsome. He looks every inch the protector he's meant to be."

Dear Emma. Mina tried a smile. "He does?"

"Remember how kind he is being. You are not yet betrothed. He wishes to give you your choice of husband."

A choice. She'd never wanted one. Better—and safer—if the marriage were settled. "That is kind," Mina repeated numbly. "He *is* kind. His family assured us he is. And he *is* my choice, as he'll keep me close to you."

"Mina…you don't have to marry him if you don't wish. Truly. I would understand. If he's not—"

"Oh, Emma." The sadness in her sister's voice swept away her stupid nerves. Mina hugged her younger sister, who stood taller than her now but still clung like a child. "We are staying together." She added a smile to her voice. "And our fiancés will be kind and gentle and will love us the moment they meet us. How could they not?"

Emma nodded and smiled brightly, but Mina wasn't fooled. Not with Emma clutching her as if afraid to let go.

Please, God, let both Thomas Grant and Colin Rivers be gentle, decent men.

Mina pulled out of Emma's hug to look into her face. "Remember what your Mr. Rivers wrote in his letter to you, Emma? 'I will not see you unhappy…'"

"'Not for worlds and worlds,'" Emma whispered, her grip easing. "Thank you, Mina. I would be so afraid if not for you."

"We'll always be together, so neither of us need be afraid." She linked her arm through Emma's and turned to face her future. "All right then. Let's see this Mr. Grant."

She swept the crowd for brown hair and a serious face to match the likeness Thomas's mother had shown her, but those who might have been him held no sign for her. Emma's head was turned, seeking her own gentleman in the crowd, so Mina let her alone.

A tall man in the group, the tallest man, drew Mina's eye again and again. He wasn't a gentleman—he wore a rather coarse coat—and his wide-legged stance was a markedly different posture than a gentleman's. But his form was decidedly male. Very male shoulders and very male arms that swelled in ways she'd never seen—until she realized those solid bulges straining his sleeves were muscles.

His dark-blond hair was swept haphazardly from his tan brow and the choppy ends brushed his shoulders. Many streaks of his hair were so bleached of color they were nearly silver.

No, not a gentleman. From his build, he must be a laborer—and a steel-strong laborer at that. Yet there was something so endearing about his face. Something so friendly. His wide mouth was curled in a grin and his eyes crinkled as if he was accustomed to squinting against the sun. He seemed utterly undisturbed by the disorder about them.

"What do you think, Mina?" Emma asked. "Is he not handsome?"

Mina jerked to attention. "Right. Where is he?"

"Mina, you're staring at him."

Emma pointed toward the blond giant and Mina's heart lurched in her chest. The card said...but the man... Impossible. *Impossible*.

"That isn't him," Mina said. "Mr. Grant has brown hair."

"The sun must have lightened it."

"No." She read the sign again. "Emma, no. Does he look like a botanist to you?"

Emma's lips opened to speak, then shut in a considering moue. "Well. We know the Punjab region is wild and remote. A superintendent of a plantation there might require skills beyond horticulture for...well, discouraging bandits." She eyed him. "Or...wrestling things, like that animal we read of, the rhinoceros."

He must be six feet or more. And fourteen stone. Mina nodded absently. "Yes...wrestling."

"They are native here. Perhaps the rhino is a nuisance in the garden. Like rabbits."

"Yes...wrestling...rabbits."

He dropped the card and bent to retrieve it, flashing a backside sculpted by hard muscle. Mina's heart lurched and she turned away. This was all wrong. He was...*handsome*.

But Emma did not look away, her jaw dangling. "I think him very attractive, Mina. And he looks quick to laugh. I think merry men make the best husbands."

Sweet Emma. Trying to bolster Mina even though her own stranger was somewhere in this swarm of men. And if they did not suit, what choice did Emma have? What choice did any of the Adams sisters have?

Especially Mary, who had made the worst choice of all.

Mina steeled herself and turned back around. And her legs wilted again at the sight of the man.

No. *No.* Mr. Grant had sent for a wife, not a sweetheart. And she was an excellent housekeeper, resourceful and economical. And she would never be severe with him—she would be a restful companion. Surely that was what he wanted...? A woman of congenial mind...?

"You're right," Mina said. "He does look kind." And manly and swaggering and experienced, and not at all given to dull, domestic spinsters like her. He was going to be disappointed. Or worse.

His letter had promised her the husband of her choice—but those were merely words in a letter.

What if he did not choose her?

Two

TOM GRANT FINALLY LOWERED THE LETTER. "I CAN'T help you."

The hell? An arrow of uncertainty pierced Seth before he yanked it out and stomped it to the ground. "Sure you can," Seth blustered over his tightening nerves. "I'm your employer."

"Repton was my employer, and the man had six years' experience in Asia and the Indies."

"And he hired a man who spoke Marathi, Hindi, and Bengali. Same as what I'm needing."

"You need more than me, Mr. Mayhew—"

"Call me Seth."

"The scope has changed entirely. Repton needed a bit of translation help, a few introductions. You need… *what*?" Tom looked at the letter. "An investigator to track your sister? A guardian to cross into Tibet?"

Confused, Seth looked the spectacled man up and down. "You think I'd hire a botanist as a guard?"

Tom held up a hand to silence him. "Do you understand I can't leave India? I've got my work and commitments and—*give me that sign.*"

Commitments? Seth kept the sign high and out of reach, needing Tom's full attention. "Maybe you're not understanding our arrangement, Tom." He spoke slow and careful so as not to be misunderstood. "You're hired and paid for. I'd say your commitments start and end with me, don't they?"

"*Hello?*"

A woman's voice sounded from about a foot below him, so Seth took a deep breath before looking down. Beneath a straw bonnet were big, brown eyes, white skin, and the most kissable mouth he'd ever seen. If she wasn't the prettiest—*wait*. Starry flowers on her dress. The little officer.

Well.

Tom needed a moment to come to reason anyway.

Seth smiled down at her. The lady blushed in peach. "Now who are you meant to be, pretty?"

Her brows rose. "I'm Wilhelmina."

His smile widened. "All right then."

She pointed up. "You have the sign."

Tom Grant pushed forward. "Miss Adams."

Adams? Seth read the sign again. "Oh, *W*. Adams. For Wilhel—"

Tom ripped the card from his hands, and Seth looked from that sign to her. Wait—*she* was the one Tom was claiming?

Tom doffed his hat. "Welcome to India, Miss Adams. I'm Thomas Grant."

Her head swung around, her eyes huge. "I... Oh... yes, of course you are."

Seth leaned down to whisper in her ear. "I know. Wasn't what I was expecting either."

"Do you mind, Mr. Mayhew?" Tom said.

But he couldn't mind Tom Grant now. Wilhelmina Adams had a grip on the pocket of her skirt, and was breathing through lips the palest shade of coral he'd ever seen. She wasn't as composed as he'd thought.

Careful not to startle her, he dipped his head toward the lady again, catching a trace of English rose and warm woman. "He won't call me Seth," he whispered. "But you will, I hope." He winked and her warm, brown eyes cleared and focused on him—and she was composed again. Yes, she was a rare one.

And she wasn't any of his business.

He straightened away from her. "My apologies, miss. You go on and make Tom's acquaintance now. I'll not interrupt."

He crossed his arms and waited—nice and polite, considering he'd just learned he'd be sharing his employee with the lady—but she stood gaping at him until Tom drew her aside and got on with the business of getting acquainted.

Seth turned to give them their privacy. Besides, he had a new city to learn, and that cinnamon smell was some kind of food, and finding Georgie was going to take every bit of his attention.

So he wouldn't pay Tom's venture girl any attention.

Looking at her wouldn't take much attention. None at all, really. He turned back around. The flowers on her dress—he knew they were sweet woodruff. He only ever saw those in the woods behind his cottage. Already knowing a thing didn't take any attention.

So it didn't take any attention knowing she was a lady from the ground up—and beautiful in a way that would last. And quiet and thoughtful, too, if those eyes were anything to go by.

No, she didn't take any attention at all. Because he already knew a woman like that would never pay any attention to a man like—

You have the sign.

The hell? He huffed a laugh and shook off the echo of her words. No, she wasn't any of his business. But damned if he didn't stand up straight when she turned to face him.

She didn't seem to know where to look. His chest, his neck, his shoulders. Like she was reconciling his size but was still puzzled. That wasn't new. He'd reached six feet by the time he was sixteen and had gained a few inches in the years since. He knew— better than he wanted—that he was too big for most women. Even normal-sized women, like Miss Adams.

Actually, she might be a stone shy and an inch short of normal-sized.

Her eyes finally met his. Hadn't he always been partial to brown eyes?

"We haven't been introduced, sir," she said. "I am—"

"W. Adams." Seth grinned. "Despite appearances, I learned to read. Tom must not have had enough sign to write 'Wilhelmina,' but 'Mina' is likely what you're called anyway, isn't it? I'm called Seth. That's not short for anything, if you wondered. Seth Mayhew's my name. You might have gleaned that already, as Tom was slow in providing it." He ducked close to her again. "Try not to hold that first impression against him, pretty. I'm thinking he's the nervous sort."

Her startled eyes shot to his and a flare of desire
heated him.

Desire?

Well. Damn awkward.

He stepped back, stumbling over his bag. That close,
those warm, brown eyes pulled on a man. She might
have taken a bit of his attention there.

But she *was* pretty. Even more than the usual.

Mina reached for the hand of a blond who hovered
behind and pulled her forward. "May I present my
sister Emmaline? Emma, *this* is Mr. Grant and this is
Mr. Mayhew."

Emma shared a look with her sister before murmuring, "I'm pleased to meet you both."

The blond sister was comely too, but Seth wasn't all
that inclined to take his eyes off Mina.

"I don't suppose"—Miss Emma smiled tightly—
"that is, I'm to meet my fiancé, Colin Rivers. Mr.
Grant, I wonder if you see him?" The smile thinned.
"I don't believe he brought a sign."

*Hell. This business of ladies marrying gents they'd
never met.*

Tom Grant shook his head, looking at the dozens
on the dock. "I'm sorry. He was only recently trans-
ferred to my province. I don't know him by sight—"

"COLIN RIVERS!" Seth bellowed into the mob.

The men standing nearest to Seth flinched and
swung to face him, their shoulders up at their ears. His
voice was a big one, so the volume might've been a
bit...alarm-raising, he supposed. Seth nodded an apology and then bracketed his mouth with his hands. "IS
THERE A COLIN RIVERS HERE?"

The mob looked around, checking the faces of their neighbors. A grumbled "good Lord" and "What the deuce?" answered, but the rest shook their heads. Even the women looked afraid of being accused the missing man.

This Rivers wasn't here. The bastard made his woman sail all the way to India and hadn't bothered to meet her.

Seth turned back around. Tom's head was lowered. So was Miss Emma's and she was blushing. Like they were embarrassed. Like *he'd* embarrassed them. Had he?

Well, what else should he have done? He crossed his arms and tried to keep searching.

But suddenly, Mina had all his attention.

She was up on her toes, scanning the crowd, unembarrassed, and with all the purpose in the world contained in that straight-backed bundle of womanhood. And it wasn't just that her profile was beautiful, like something he'd see on a tin of lady's face powder or a painting.

No, it wasn't that. It was like the surprise of discovering a night-blooming orchid in the tangle of a jungle. Like discovering something so rare—*knowing* it was rare, knowing he'd never had a hope or a dream before of seeing such a living-and-breathing prize close enough for him to touch. And there wasn't another prize like her ever to be had.

And, no...he wasn't at all inclined to take his eyes off her.

She dropped down to her heels and nodded at him. "Thank you, Mr. Mayhew. That needed doing."

Well. Now *he* was blushing.

But that was nice, being looked at by a lady that wasn't laughing at him. Women never took him serious—even when he meant them to.

Tom cleared his throat. "I think we're assured Mr. Rivers is not present. Any number of things can delay a man in India. I've arranged rooms for all of us at Benson's Hotel. I'm confident Mr. Rivers will call in the next day or two."

The women didn't look confident.

Behind them, the venture girls and a caravan of trunks were moving toward a two-story building that managed to look both British and Indian at the same time. The customs house, then. Some of the women had been claimed and walked beside their gents. The men beamed; the ladies didn't. Their expressions ranged from weepy to weep*ing*.

Seth turned from the sight. They weren't any of his business and Georgie was counting on him. He had to keep his thoughts nailed to the ground.

Tom Grant would help with that. Outside of expeditions, where Seth had a decade of experience and hard learning, organizing matters wasn't easy for him. It never had been. Planning was easier with people—and Seth needed a lot of people to find his sister, especially these Company men, at every turn.

Puffed up and superior as these gents were, Tom would have to help with them, too.

Mina and Tom were talking close. Closer than before. Tom even let a smile crack that sour face of his, and she had a blush on her cheeks.

You have the sign—

"We ought to be going," Seth called.

Mina turned to him and then caught sight of the women leaving the wharf. "Oh, we mustn't miss saying good-bye." And with a little hop, she and Emma hurried after the ladies.

And Tom was frowning again.

They followed the ladies, but Tom wasn't exactly inviting Seth's company. Seth pondered the man's silence along with the sway of Mina's skirts. "So who is she? Your intended?"

"Yes," Tom grumbled. "*No*—not yet. She's—"

"You call her Wilhelmina?"

"I call her Miss Adams."

"Wouldn't she be called Mina?"

"By her intimates, yes."

"Intimates?" He grinned. "You mean like her intended?"

Tom frowned harder. "Mr. Mayhew—"

"Call me Seth. You might want to secure that one fast, mate."

"She's come to marry. It may as well be me." Tom's jaw tightened like he regretted his words. "Her late parents and my mother shared a mutual friend. I've promised to look after her until she chooses a husband."

"And if she fancies another?"

"I'm not going to force the woman to marry me."

"Decent of you." Seth grinned. "Damn awkward though, eh? Hell, a lady like that might hook herself a commissioner." A scarlet coat walked by. "Or a cavalry man. Or one of the viceroy's aides—they're the gentry here, right? Or even a governor. That'd be a feather bed, wouldn't it?"

Tom stared straight ahead.

Seth waited, but the man wasn't saying anything. He cleared his throat. "Not meaning to cast a mercenary light on it, but a widow of a commander gets a hundred pounds a year *for life*. If I were a woman, I'd be angling for one of them. A hundred-pound-a-year man, even dead as mutton."

"Not to cast a mercenary light on it," Tom grumbled.

Seth sorted his words for what he'd said wrong. *Hell*, how was he to get the man on friendly terms?

Mina looked back at them, like she was afraid they'd disappear. Something tightened in his chest at that look, but Seth nodded and gave her a wink. She stumbled and turned quickly back around.

And to hell with friendly terms.

"*Christ*, Tom, we both know fevers here can kill a healthy man in twelve hours." Seth unbuttoned his coat with more patience than he was feeling. "Better if Mina found a husband on the next boat to England. Or one already in the infirmary, provided he's due a widow's pension."

That made Tom stumble. "India's not an easy place, but not so bad as that. Here in Bombay, Malabar Hill is as English as Mayfair and the Society twice as rigid."

"Well that sounds damn awful."

"I'm saying there are six thousand English here. Will Repton wrote that your expeditions were in Brazil. You adapted, I assume. People adapt."

"*Adapt*," he muttered. "Sure they adapt, if they're like me—built like a gorilla with a head like a rock. Not been ill a day in my life. Don't even get seasick. I keep down any food, drink any water, and watch

while men—damn near my size—turn down their
teacups. Some adapt." Ahead, Mina pressed a handkerchief to her neck, and Seth cursed under his breath.
"But you'll not tell me India's any place for a little
Englishwoman like that."

Tom looked at him. "Those women made the same
passage as you. They drank the same water, ate the
same food, but they traveled knowing they'd never
see home again." Tom shook his head. "You may be
strong, Mr. Mayhew, but this is a new world. And
over here, mighty is as mighty does."

Mighty.

Women weren't meant to be mighty. They weren't
meant to sail and marry strangers, like Mina was planning. Or cross into a hostile country and disappear,
like Georgie had done. Women weren't mighty; his
sister wasn't—

No, Georgie wasn't mighty. And she was lost, and
Seth needed Tom's help to find her, so maybe he'd
shut his damn mouth and not debate the matter.

Ahead, the Adams sisters linked arms, their wide
skirts flouncing as they walked. Two Indian women,
dressed in saris, stopped to watch them.

"I heard some of the native people think our
women have tails on account of their skirts," Seth said.

Tom actually smiled. "I've heard that, yes."

Seth studied him. "You know…you're not ugly
when you smile. You might win Miss Mina's hand
after all."

There went the smile. "Thank you. Listen, Mr.
Mayhew—"

"Call me Seth."

"I want to help you find your sister. God knows you've a task ahead of you. It's just…I wasn't expecting *you*."

"I know it. I wasn't expecting to stand about and watch you woo a young lady."

"I'd rather you not watch."

"It's damn awkward."

Tom stopped walking. "A man needs a wife in India, and money to set up housekeeping. I counted on Repton's—or *your* money—but working with you… I can't *leave* Bombay. At least not until I marry Miss Adams."

Seth considered all that. Every odd time, he remembered to consider things slow and careful. It wasn't natural, so it usually took a minute. "*If* she marries you, right?"

Tom took a long, deep breath, his nostrils flaring. "That's right, Mr. Mayhew. *If*."

Seth crossed his arms, planted his feet wide, and surveyed the scene around him. He couldn't read the writing on the bales of cotton piled on the dock. For every English word, there were a dozen in Hindustani. Hell, he didn't know where he'd get his next meal and he was always hungry.

"I need your help," Seth said, thinking aloud. "And my plan was to start in Bombay. I'm not needing to travel until I know where I'm to go. I need information from someone in East India to tell me the whereabouts of the Milford Expedition—the crew my sister was with, may *still* be with—and I need to post letters by the fastest means possible through India. The running men who deliver the mail, what are they called?"

"The *dak-wallah*."

"Right, them."

"Or you could use carrier pigeons, the pigeon post."

Seth grinned and punched Tom lightly on the arm. "*Pigeon*. I knew you had a sense of humor in you. But I think I saw a spider crawl out your mouth when you used it."

Tom winced, rubbing his arm. "That wasn't a joke."

"Here's what I'm thinking, Tom. You help me now, and when the time comes to leave Bombay, well…you'll be wed if you put on some haste. It's a tidy sum. It'll set you up nicely for a wife. Maybe even Mina." Seth smiled. "I'd call her *Mina*."

Tom stared, then turned to stomp toward the customs house. "You'll call her *Miss Adams*."

Three

"PROMISE TO WRITE, MINA. EVERY FORTNIGHT."

Outside the customs house, Mina hugged Anne and blinked rapidly to dry her eyes. All the venture girls had grown as close as sisters onboard, but Anne had become her best friend. And she was leaving Bombay any moment.

Around them, the streets were snarled with coaches, carts, and carriages. The venture girls clogged the avenue, their portmanteaux borne away by coachmen who seemed to no more regard the freight upon their backs than they would a pashmina shawl.

"I promise." Mina shut her eyes against the pandemonium. "Now you promise, because you must tell me everything of your new home."

Anne nodded, breathed deep, and stepped out of their hug. "Dharmapuri is so remote."

"There will be other wives there, and they'll love you. And your Mr. Abbot seems a very good man." Though the widower was at least twenty years older than he alluded in his courtship letters to Anne. A man of his years, to be stationed in the *mofussils*, as they called the rural areas here, seemed a little unusual. Perhaps a little unpromising.

Anne wiped her tears and searched Mina's eyes. "This *was* the right thing to do, wasn't it?"

The right thing? Who could say? Anne might have stayed in Lewisham with her greengrocer father, daily surrounded by all manner of costermongers—many of mean dispositions, many whose wages were paid directly to pub owners, most with no aspirations to home and family.

Yes, Anne might have stayed, just as any of the venture girls might have stayed to wait and pray for a man of some education and suitable income to present himself.

And she likely would have waited forever.

Even she and Emma, orphaned four years now, might have stayed with what little family that remained to them: an aunt already living a threadbare existence with the care of Mina's four younger sisters. Two more mouths to feed…and they all might have starved.

And there was Mary in London, of course.

Of course, Mary.

"It was the right thing, Anne," she said softly. "Never doubt that."

Anne looked to where Mr. Grant stood overseeing the packing of the luggage onto a carriage. "I'm so glad you and Emma conspired to live near one another. To wed men who are to work together was so clever."

"Not so clever. Geography is no real challenge when one is willing to marry in the junior ranks, as we are."

"I had hoped to meet Emma's fiancé before—*oh*. Is that him?"

Mina swiveled to look and, disappointed, she shook her head. Mr. Mayhew was stacking his trunks by Mr. Grant's carriage. He seemed to feel her gaze and straightened with a question in his eyes. When he smiled, her mind momentarily blanked.

"No, that is"—*who exactly* was *Mr. Mayhew?*—"an acquaintance of Mr. Grant's. I don't believe he's very eligible. We've not yet found Mr. Rivers."

Anne's fiancé, Mr. Abbot, approached with his hat in hand, his smile wide. Thank God he seemed safe. "Miss Trager? Are you ready, my dear?"

Anne smiled back. "Indeed, Mr. Abbot." She gripped Mina's hand, but didn't turn her head to look at her. "Good-bye, Mina," she whispered hoarsely, and hurried to join her fiancé.

Mina braced against the pain swelling in her chest as Anne walked away.

She would see her again. She would *someday*. And her other friends, the unclaimed women, would stay in Bombay with her. For a time.

But so many were leaving. Emma and Theresa were hugging good-bye. Susan waved to her one last time before ducking into a carriage. Olivia's face was hidden by the handkerchief she held to her eyes the moment before turning the corner and disappearing from sight.

Leaving. Dispersing. The flotsam and jetsam from the steamship *Isabella*. What was the mariner's law? Flotsam could be claimed by the owner; jetsam belonged to no one but the Lord...

"Are you ready, Miss Mina?"

Mr. Mayhew's deep voice surprised her. Ready? Had he been waiting for her? "Pardon me?"

He straightened, his massive shoulders squaring, and she sensed that he *had* been hovering. The notion brought the strangest pang of pleasure. It was nonsense—Mr. Mayhew knew nothing of her, cared nothing for her, but at the moment, the proximity of his strong body soothed her. It was a rare sensation, a man's presence. Or was it a man's...*protection*?

"Tom Grant is packing our carriage for the hotel," he said.

"*Our* carriage?"

"Are you ready?"

His slow smile lit his face and, oddly, that was enough to end the soothing fantasy. Mr. Mayhew would aim that smile at every woman he met, as well as it worked. And he held her gaze too long. A gentleman wouldn't, would he?

Still, a woman would be so fortunate—

She blinked, realizing she had been staring stupidly back. "I did wonder, Mr. Mayhew, are you a friend of Mr. Grant's?"

"We have business together. Let me tote this for you." He pulled her valise away, and she squeaked in alarm, stopping herself in midgrab for the bag that held nearly everything she owned.

"Truly, Mr. Mayhew, I can manage."

"I know it. I'd wager a lady like you is capable of managing quite a bit." He sent a grin back to her over his shoulder, not breaking his stride. "Look how fast you found yourself a man eager to tote your bag."

"I… Thank you." She followed her valise—and Mr. Mayhew—toward the carriage. *Their* carriage, apparently.

Mr. Mayhew was so large, the people in his path gave way without pause. In his wake, her way was clear, though she had to closely follow the broad shoulders as the bodies filled in quickly behind them.

"We stowed your trunk already," Mr. Mayhew said.

They had? How different India was. Men packed her luggage, carried her bag, and hovered as she parted from friends.

"I didn't see a trunk for Miss Emma," he said.

"My sister and I only needed one." To her shock, tears stung her eyes and she blinked furiously to dry them. How foolish of her. They had everything they needed. There was nothing more to bring.

Mr. Mayhew didn't say anything for a moment, and she dabbed her eyes dry in case he turned.

"You ladies are more clever than me," he said, "to learn that lesson on your first passage. Better to outfit yourself once you arrive, when you better comprehend the climate. I hear the tailoring is reasonable here. Maybe not if you're oversized like me, what with all the extra materials and labor entailed in covering my amount of nakedness—sorry, I don't mean to say 'naked,' but the dressmakers wouldn't get all twitchy at the prospect of your figure, would they? Sorry, I don't mean to say 'figure,' but looking like you do, they might pay *you* to model their wares for 'em."

Mina frowned at the barrage of words. And then her breath hitched in her throat. Mr. Mayhew wasn't just a flirt.

He was kind.

The realization did not help the tenderness of her heart. Mr. Mayhew would have guessed how difficult the circumstances were for her and Emma. How they would have to rely on their husbands for anything new to wear.

She had to swallow before she could speak. "I've heard that as well. About the tailors' costs, that is."

She kept her gaze on the back of his coat, the wool rubbed and worn into little pills at the seams. Secondhand clothes for him, as well.

Who was he?

Voices rumbled all about them, so she lifted her chin and aimed her question at his ear. "What sort of business do you and Mr. Grant—"

"Wouldn't you be a picture in one of those saris?" He grinned at her over his shoulder.

A young Indian woman stood a few feet away, her lithe shape draped in shimmering emerald, the gold embroidery glinting in the sunlight. "So beautiful," she blurted in happy surprise.

He turned his head to wink. "If you don't buy yourself one in ruby-red silk, I will. And don't think I wouldn't add a dozen gold bangles for each arm."

Ruby red? Her smile surprised her, and it seemed to have the same effect on Mr. Mayhew, for he stopped so suddenly to face her, she bumped into his chest. A hard chest beneath a layer of warm, soft cotton. He smelled of coffee.

She took a fast step back.

"That was the first smile I've seen on you," he said. "You could knock a man over with that, Miss Mina."

She took another step back, unsure what to say. But when had she ever been sure with men? "I don't own anything red. I'm not that brave."

Something softened in his eyes. "I'm thinking red would suit you." His gaze dropped to her mouth. "Or maybe coral like your…" His lips pressed shut.

Like her what? Her face burned. She wasn't used to this—not any of it. She wasn't used to Bombay and attentive men, and now even Mr. Mayhew was uncomfortable. His tanned cheeks were reddening.

In the corner of her vision, Mr. Grant was scanning the crush of bodies. For her, presumably. She side-stepped Mr. Mayhew so hastily, her skirts threatened to twine about his ankles and he lifted his boots clear.

Stupid, Mina! She breathed deep. What a coward she was. Overwrought and overwhelmed and ridiculous. It was hardly Mr. Mayhew's fault that she wasn't accustomed to men speaking with her.

She peeked over her shoulder. Mr. Mayhew loped behind her with her valise in his large hand, his head down.

He had teased her to try and make her laugh. A kind flirt. And he was right—she hadn't smiled once. For Emma, for her own future, she did so now.

Mr. Grant was watching.

❧

Seth put Mina's carpetbag on the carriage floor where she could keep watch over it. He hadn't missed how those big, brown eyes followed the bag when he took it from her. Now, he understood why. The trunk he'd already stowed for her was so small it wouldn't hold more than his boots and a few bricks of tea. And she shared that trunk with her sister.

"Thank you, Mr. Mayhew," Mina said.

Not trusting himself with what he might say—not the way he was feeling, all disordered—he gave her a wink and moved to the rear of the carriage.

The coachman and Tom's servant—"bearers" they called them here—were struggling to load one of his trunks onto the tip-wagon that would follow them to the hotel. The smallest of his supply trunks weighed more than the Adams sisters combined. He waved off the servants and hefted the trunk onto the platform, the wagon creaking under the weight.

Behind him, Tom and the ladies were silent. Not a one of them seemed to know who or what to look at. Damn awkward business.

"Do you need any assistance, Mayhew?" Tom sounded desperate for a chore.

"No need." And just to play the devil a little, Seth added, "You just stay there and entertain the ladies."

If Tom gets to marry Mina, let him work for her.

"Are you going on a long trip, Mr. Mayhew?" Emma eyed the large, wooden trunks he was strapping onto the wagon.

"Not sure, yet. So I brought all the supplies I travel with," he said. "Blankets, candles, field glasses, a crossbow, whiskey, lead, gunpowder, rifles, and such."

The Adams sisters stared at him.

"The whiskey's not for drinking," he hurried to add. "It's for cleaning wounds."

"Wounds?" Mina whispered faintly.

"What is it that you do?" Emma asked.

"He collects plants." Tom ushered the women into the carriage. "Ladies, I'm sure you're fatigued. Shall we proceed to the hotel?"

The women looked at Seth and his trunks again before Tom handed them inside. Seth moved to join them, but Tom signaled him back to the rear of the carriage.

Seth sighed. Right, Tom was under the impression they had business to sort. "That Mina's a rare one. You're a lucky man."

"You *do* agree the scope has changed?" Tom paced behind the wagon.

"I suppose I'm lucky, too, as you need my money to marry her."

"I don't speak Mandarin or Cantonese—"

"It'd be a shame to lose a woman like her on account of not having the funds."

"How would I even manage a passport outside of India?"

Seth grinned—not that he was feeling at all amused. "How many proposals would you wager she'd get the first week?"

Tom stopped pacing and gripped his temples. It took a minute before he spoke. "All right."

"Is that your yes?"

Tom gave a short nod.

There was never a doubt Tom would hold to their agreement, but Seth was relieved anyway. He wasn't accustomed to forcing matters—or not being liked, now that he thought on it.

"This won't be easy," Tom said.

"I know it."

"Your sister could be anywhere, and what if she's—"

"What if she's dead?" The words scraped his throat. Tom's head reared back. "*No*. I wasn't thinking that—"

"I'll find her. I always find what I'm looking for. Six expeditions for East India, and there wasn't a hardwood, medicinal, or palm seed I couldn't find."

Tom nodded and stood a little straighter. "Profitable, were you?"

"For them." He shrugged. "The prizes I collected for myself never came out right in the end. The seeds wouldn't sprout or the roots rotted in the Wardian cases during the crossing. The one orchid that fetched me enough to buy a home... Well, that home came with a surprise list of repairs that'll take me years to cover."

"But six expeditions?" Tom asked. "Surely there was something of value that remained?"

Seth's jaw tightened, but he held Tom's eyes so the man could read the answer there. "You don't believe a man can be cursed, do you?"

"Of course not."

Seth grinned. "Then we'll get on well enough."

Tom started for the carriage door. "It's damnable luck, though, Mayhew."

"I know it."

"Let's start in the morning," Tom said. "We can meet in the hotel lobby."

"I've no plans tonight. Was hoping to eat someplace if you were available."

"I'm with Miss Adams tonight. The ladies are to sit up at the Byculla Clubhouse to meet all the East India men and their wives. Plus all the bachelors, of course."

"Sit up?"

"That's what they call it here—dinners, balls, recep-
tions. Whenever a new ship arrives, the ladies *sit up* for
three or four evenings in a row meeting everyone in
Bombay Society. It doesn't take much longer than that
for them all to be claimed."

"Seems an opportune time to meet some Company
men."

"It's invited guests only. And, trust me, not the
appropriate time or place. We'll start early tomorrow."

Seth nodded, but he'd never been one for taking
direction nor did he have much truck with propriety.

His sister was lost, and tonight was as good a time
to start as any.

Four

"I'M AFRAID WHERE I LIVE IS NOWHERE NEAR AS GRAND as Bombay." Thomas handed Mina her lemonade and sat beside her on the Byculla Clubhouse terrace.

It was the first time Thomas had alluded to a possible future between them. And she detected little happiness behind the words.

"I don't require grand living," she blurted.

Oh dear, that sounded desperate. And blunt. She added a smile and tried to keep it from wavering as Thomas studied her by the ballroom light flooding the terrace.

Well...let him look. It was to be expected, wasn't it? She folded her hands in her lap and submitted to his inspection.

Thank goodness they were now outdoors. The ballroom had grown oppressive with the blazing chandeliers and hundreds of East India men, officers, and exported ladies circling one another. She loved all those ladies, yet the one dearest to her heart was sitting alone in their hotel room.

"Emma so wished to come," she said. "During the

sail, we heard of the assemblies here. We were told, outside of Delhi, there are no rooms finer."

"I hope she is well tomorrow. Not that I am surprised by her megrim after this day."

She lowered her eyes—demurely she hoped. It was only a small lie, anyway. Emma's head was fine. There was no megrim, only Emma's unfabricated hope that the absent Colin Rivers would find her easiest at their hotel.

"It must be overwhelming," Thomas said. "Your first night in India and forced into Society."

"Oh. Not at all. This reception is very—" She cut off at Thomas's skeptical look and smiled. "A bit overwhelming, yes. Especially as the Society I come from is far less distinguished. I do not recall any gentlemen's clubs with marble ballrooms in Chesterfield."

Thomas smiled. "I don't recall them in Edwinstowe, either."

He really did have a nice face. Though it was difficult to see his eyes past his spectacles. Is that why it was so difficult to talk with him?

"I visited Draper's Hall while on my tour of London," she said. "The stairwell here very nearly rivals that one. My eldest sister lives in the city and"—and Mary was not to be discussed. Not yet—"and that was the grandest place I had ever visited."

Thomas nodded. "I've never been."

Another silence. Indian crickets seemed rather louder than English ones.

What if he chose another? There was no contract. She and Emma had to stay together. "Do you miss home, Mr. Grant?"

She regretted her hasty words instantly. He sat back in his chair, his smile fading.

"There are moments I miss England a great deal." He set down his glass, his voice bleak. "But India is my home now."

Oddly chastened, she swung her gaze to the manicured gardens. Beyond its confines, a city square teemed with local people carrying their bundles. Barefoot. Backs bent. Perhaps hungry. *Were* they hungry?

She had read of the poverty here. In the days to come, would she feel it as well? Just as she had with Mary? The world was not so large if Bombay could recall her to Bethnal Green. If the line between those who ate and those who starved was so thin as to be invisible.

At the far corner of the square, a group of young Indian men were laughing. A ball—a cricket ball—was being tossed into the air and caught. They were moving toward the club, and as they drew near, her gaze centered on one man. The single white man.

The rather tall, remarkably broad-shouldered—"Is that Mr. Mayhew?"

Thomas's attention was already aimed at the cluster of bodies circling the man. His lips thinned. "I believe it is."

"Did you expect him?"

Thomas wiped a hand over his face. "Not at all."

"Oh."

Mr. Mayhew intercepted the tossed ball, and in an instant, four other men clambered atop him to get it back and he was forced down to his knees.

"*Oh!*" Alarmed, she sat forward, straining in the dark to see. "Is he all right?"

Thomas waved an annoyed hand. "He's fine."

Mr. Mayhew roared a laughing curse, but Mina did not look away lest he find himself pitched upon again. With five younger sisters, it seemed she'd been born to keep watch. "I did mean to ask the nature of your work with him."

"I did intend to tell you later." Thomas shifted in his chair, a flush rising on his cheeks. "But as he is apparently joining us, perhaps now is the time. I was hired by a Will Repton of London to help him prepare for an expedition. Simple help. Translating letters, purchasing supplies, whatever was needed. But rather than Mr. Repton, I was given Seth Mayhew in his stead."

"Why Mr. Mayhew?"

"The expedition is to find a lost woman and child. It's Mayhew's sister that is lost."

Surprise and sadness hit her at once. "How awful for him." Mina looked back to Mr. Mayhew, still tussling with the young men. "I would never suspect he was under such a strain."

But then, a smile could disguise a great many things. And perhaps flirtation was the most distant conversation of all.

"And the missing child is his sister's?" she asked.

"Actually, no. The child is an orphan. Her parents were French missionaries, murdered this past Christmas at their mission. A horrible massacre, in the borderlands between China and Tibet."

Dear God. "And the child is with Mr. Mayhew's sister?"

"He believes so. Georgiana Mayhew was a botanical

illustrator on a nearby plant-collecting expedition. She was en route to find the child. I suppose they thought me a logical choice, being superintendent of a Company plantation that cultivates the collected plants."

"So you have information that may help?"

"Very little. I'm not apprised of an expedition's progress until the specimens arrive at my door. Actually, your sister's fiancé, Colin Rivers, will be of more help, as he's positioned higher in the agriculture department." Thomas shook his head. "It will not be easy, in any case. There's been no communication from Georgiana Mayhew in many months."

Her heart sank further. "Finding them seems so…" *hopeless*.

"Improbable, yes. He sailed all this way for a sister." His smile twisted wryly. "Just as *you* did."

Her head reared up. "I… That is, I did not—"

"It's fine, Mina." Thomas covered her hand. "You didn't wish your sister to come to India alone. Your devotion to her is commendable."

His hand was warm, and the vise on her chest eased. "I *do* want a family of my own, Mr. Grant. And I sincerely appreciate this opportunity to know you."

He squeezed her hand. "Won't you call me Thomas?"

He really did have a nice face. "Yes. Thank you, Thomas."

Mr. Mayhew's deep voice rumbled faintly on the air. He was waving good-bye, but the young men fell back slowly, as if reluctant to let him go. The streetlamps burnished his hair gold. He had long hair for a man, yet it suited him. The mane evoked images of rugged Vikings and medieval kings, and by appearance alone, all the forces of destiny should bend to his will—to deliver a lost sister to him.

A sister who could be lost nearly…*anywhere*.

She turned to Thomas. "Will you need to accompany Mr. Mayhew on his travels? Beyond Bombay?"

Thomas slid his spectacles higher on his nose. "Perhaps not. Not immediately, I shouldn't think."

Was that an answer? If Thomas left Bombay, how long would he be gone? Would a marriage be settled before then? Would Thomas and Mr. Mayhew be in danger?

Thomas rose from his chair as Mr. Mayhew made his way to the entrance of the club. "I fear I must intercept Mr. Mayhew. He is not expected this evening."

"Not expected?"

"He holds no invitation."

"No—*oh*." She surged to her feet and made for the entrance. "Will they turn him away? They will not be too unkind, will they—?"

"Uh…Mina?"

Vexed by the delay, and confused that Thomas was not hurrying beside her, she turned to look back at him.

"Might I deliver you to one of your friends?"

It took her a moment to understand his gentleman-like offer, and she barely managed to hide her cringe of embarrassment. Thomas would not like her if she acted too managing—Emma was always accusing her of that. But she and Thomas were meant to become acquainted. They ought not separate.

She smiled—flirtatiously, she hoped—and tried again. "You are kind to want to spare me any unpleasantness, but I would much rather stay with you, Thomas…?"

"Oh. Well." He smoothed his coat and offered his arm without delay. "Yes. Certainly, then."

That worked?

That worked. She breathed a sigh of relief as they walked through the ballroom in the direction of the entry hall.

Mr. Mayhew must already be at the door. Perhaps the butler would not embarrass him. The man had enough to bear without—

Thomas's hand flexed on her arm to slow her step, and only then did she realize how fast she walked. Guiltily, she checked Thomas's profile, but he pretended no notice. He was such a gentleman. So reserved. A lifetime may not be enough to know him, while Mr. Mayhew had winked at her. Four times. A man like him—

And there the thought ended. What did she know of men? She didn't even have a brother. Mr. Mayhew winked and teased and smiled—at her, of all women— but he was a flirt. And, at worse, a distraction. As much for Thomas as for her, it seemed.

In the entry hall, Thomas stopped so abruptly, her skirts swayed. At the door, the Indian butler, with hand raised, was blocking Mr. Mayhew from entering.

But it rather appeared he was trying to hold off Mr. Mayhew's words.

"…devil of a time finding this place." Mr. Mayhew smoothed his hair with both hands. "Had to stop and buy some of those fried pies on the street. Samosas, you call 'em. Awful good. Do you know the ones I mean? Hope I can find those little women again, had themselves a red cart and a monkey. You wouldn't know if they'll be there tomorrow? It doesn't matter. But then I met a few lads watching a cricket match who understood my English, as I'm not clever enough to speak Hindi, and they pointed me here."

Mr. Mayhew's easy smile was in place and his coat pocket bulged with papers, ruining the line of his suit. Not that *this* suit was well constructed, either. It seemed rather boxy to accommodate his shoulders.

His gaze landed on Thomas and he raised a brawny arm to wave. "There's my mate." He pointed to Thomas. "*Tom! Tom Grant!* Tell our man here I'm expected."

Thomas's face was stony but he nodded to the puzzled gatekeeper. "He's, uh, newly arrived."

Mr. Mayhew patted the butler on the arm. "I'm sitting up tonight. Or whatever you call it."

The butler's head cocked. "Sitting up? You are not a female, sir."

"He's not sitting up," Thomas said. "He's—"

"Hello, Miss Mina," Mr. Mayhew called. "You're looking pretty as a bowl of oranges."

She managed a small wave. "Good evening, Mr. Mayhew."

His grin widened as he looked her over in her gown. "A man could get used to a picture like that. Look at her, mate." He clapped a hand on the butler's shoulder and turned the dazed servant about to face her.

Her cheeks must be red as a radish—

And did Mr. Mayhew just tell the butler she had a tail?

The butler's face cracked with a smile. He bowed, and to her astonishment, let Mr. Mayhew pass.

"Good man." Mr. Mayhew patted him on the back and strode over to her.

But…he has no invitation. She had only a second to brace against the heat of his body, the towering height and smiling eyes before he swept up her hand. Her senses assailed, it took her a moment to feel the callused hand holding hers. Then she realized he wasn't releasing it.

"Miss Mina, after we parted at the hotel, I was thinking of you and it struck me all at once. I found an orchid with your coloring beside the Rio Gurupí. Do you know where that is?"

His eyes crinkled so deeply at the corners. Had she ever met a man whose eyes did that? She blinked. "I don't. Is that in South America?"

"Brazil." Mr. Mayhew turned her about, placed her hand on his hard arm, and walked her back down the hall.

She looked back at Thomas, whose expression was pained as he followed them. "Oh, I—"

"East India sent me there as a surveyor," Mr. Mayhew said. "But I had a talent for finding plants—no, that's not accurate. Had a talent for not dying. She was the best beauty I ever found."

"The orchid?" she said.

Mr. Mayhew nodded. "A slipper orchid, with petals dark as chocolate, and glossy like your hair, and a little slipper labellum that was coral, like your lips. She was hiding in the moss of an old, gnarled tree— where's Tom?"

He stopped to haul Thomas over to stand in front of her and peeked around him. "Tom here being the dead wood—and when I came upon that flower, it was like finding a jewel."

"Are you finished, Mr. Mayhew?" Thomas asked.

"Better than a jewel." Mr. Mayhew set Thomas aside, his handsome face looming over her. "Like a magic, little sprite."

"You were a plant hunter," she said. "How wonderful."

He smiled wider. "The botanists named her *Catasetum phantasma* after I told them the story. *Phantasma*'s Latin for 'sprite.' It's more for 'ghost' or 'spirit,' they tell me, but had I known you then, I'd have told them to name her 'Wilhelmina.'"

She bit her lip against a befuddled frown. Men never teased her. She did not inspire them to. He was truly kind. Even with all that must be worrying him, no one else had ever bothered to make her feel she was the only person in the room before—

Oh dear. The man *was* distracting.

She sent a smiling glance to Thomas, but her embarrassing blush was all due to Mr. Mayhew. "No one has ever likened me to a flower before, Mr. Mayhew."

His eyes narrowed, studying her. "That doesn't make any sense at all. But that orchid wasn't just any flower, Miss Mina. It was the finest God ever created."

She stilled as he lowered his head to talk just to her. A move he'd done before that tripped her heart.

"And I fear, all the rest of my days, I'll never be given such a gift again," he said.

His words surprised her to silence. Big and blustering

as he was, she thought him incapable of doubt, of depth. Even his sea-green eyes conjured shallow waters. But just at the moment, she couldn't look away from them.

"I wasn't expecting you tonight," Thomas said, breaking the spell.

Mr. Mayhew straightened from her and looked into the crowded conservatory. "I thought I might introduce myself to a few Company men. If you point me to a likely man or two, Tom, I'd appreciate it."

"They won't be receptive to hearing of your sister," Thomas said.

Mr. Mayhew stiffened, his eyes narrowing as he shot a sidelong glance to her.

"She knows," Thomas said. "I told her about Georgiana."

"Did you now?" Mr. Mayhew's jaw tightened, but the smile he turned on her was warm, if a bit regretful. "Don't worry on none of it, Miss Mina. It's all a bit of a mucker, but tonight, these men will help me learn where Georgie's crew is."

Thomas shook his head. "I don't think—"

"Look what I had printed up." Mr. Mayhew pulled one of the papers out of his pocket and smoothed it on his broad chest, creasing it more.

But he winked at her while he did it.

Mr. Mayhew showed her the poster. "It's my sister's likeness—which is a fair rendering I think, not that I'm that fine an artist—including her last known location, the crew she was with, where people can find me, and my reward for information about her." He watched her face as she read. "Did I forget anything?"

"Appreciated" was missing a *p* but all else seemed in order. "I think it will serve very well, Mr. Mayhew," she said.

He smiled wider. "It will, won't it?"

The sketch of Georgiana had been carefully, *lovingly* rendered. "Your sister is very beautiful."

"She is, but you could never tell her that." Something like regret shaded his eyes. "It's been a few years since I've seen her. But I'm thinking she couldn't have changed much."

Years traveling, exposed to the harshest elements of nature…Georgiana would undoubtedly be altered. But perhaps a sister would always be seen more with the heart than the eyes. At least that would be true for her and Emma, as they'd never see their sisters in England again.

"No, I'm sure she hasn't," she said quietly, returning the paper to him. "Her crew is still afield?"

"Maybe, maybe not," Mr. Mayhew said. "They may be lost, too."

His voice throbbed in her like the bass chords in music, so there was no missing the hitch on "lost." And there was something familiar about his voice…

Mr. Mayhew pulled out the thick roll of his posters and tugged at the hem of his coat, which only slightly improved its appearance.

"Will you send telegrams, Mr. Mayhew?" she asked. "To the East India offices in Calcutta? If the Milford Expedition is still collecting plants, they'd need to requisition money for supplies, wouldn't they?" She turned to Thomas. "Is there a department for traveling botanists, Thomas?"

"Yes, I believe so," Thomas said.

Mr. Mayhew smiled at her questions. "I don't think in straight lines like that. When forced to, it fatigues me no end."

His smile didn't waver, even with that unflattering admission. But she suspected that Mr. Mayhew's constitution was happy and agreeable. And that reminded her of Missy.

"My youngest sister is the same," she said. "Her mind leaps from one thought to the next like a frog. And so does her conversation."

"A frog, is it?" Mr. Mayhew said. "I wager that's charming coming from a sister of yours. From me, people think me beefheaded."

She started to protest, but he took her elbow and guided her to a quiet alcove. She looked back at Thomas, who followed with a resigned shake of his head.

"Telegrams is tomorrow, since the office was closed today," Mr. Mayhew said.

She nodded. "At this time of year, what sort of work would plant collectors be doing?"

"Now there's the perfect question, Miss Mina. This might be the time for collecting seed, depending on their location." He led her to a settee and sat beside her, leaving Thomas to collect a chair from several feet away to sit. "Tom Grant would know better than me which terrains are in seed."

"As I'm right here," Thomas said in a wry tone, "I'd say the lowlands of the eastern Himalayas."

"Perhaps Georgiana's crew is already in India? To wait for a growing season?" Mina turned to Mr. Mayhew for a reply, but his eyes roamed her hair, her bosom, her lap. Was he not attending? "Mr. Mayhew?"

His head lifted and his ocean eyes crinkled again. "I'm listening, Miss Mina."

Fresh heat flooded her face.

"India's definitely a possibility." Mr. Mayhew leaned back, stretching a long, thick arm along the back of the settee behind her. She leaned away as far as she might in an effort to keep her countenance.

The nearness of his body heated her, and there was something electric tingling under her skin with every look, every low, reverberating bass chord in her ear. It was the oddest feeling. It was…attraction.

She was attracted.

Oh no.

His hard thigh shifted to rest against hers but he seemed unaware of the contact. "The fastest way of knowing where she is, is with them gents in there." He slapped the roll of papers in the palm of his hand and rose, the settee creaking with a sound like relief. "Wish me luck." He winked at her.

For the sixth time.

"Wait, we should—" Thomas reached to stop him, but Mr. Mayhew was already striding through the arched doors to the conservatory.

Thomas wiped a hand over his face. Was that a habit of his? Was he easily irritated?

"This is not how things are done," he said. "Especially with men like this."

No, it wasn't proper. Not at all. And he didn't even have an invitation.

They followed Mr. Mayhew's path and stood in a

corner of the glittering conservatory. He was easy to find. His head towered over the others, and he was talking to an older gentleman dressed in tailored black and white. The man might have been a director of East India by the careful arrangement of his watch fob strung across his well-padded stomach and his elegant stick—which he held clutched in front of him as Mr. Mayhew advanced, pressing the poster at the man until he accepted it.

Mr. Mayhew swung about and caught the next man in sight, his poster already thrust forward.

"Will you excuse me?" Thomas said. "I really must stop him."

"What will you do?" She cringed at her school-marmish tone. "That is…Mr. Mayhew is only attempting to gain information of his sister."

"And perhaps allowances will be made because of it, but men of this rank—well, tonight they're rather intent on making the acquaintance of the newly arrived ladies."

Mr. Mayhew's posters were held by half a dozen men or more, most giving it no more than a second's glance. And the men now pointedly kept their backs to him if he approached. One poster already littered the floor.

"Yes, I see," she whispered.

Mr. Mayhew saw the discarded poster and bent to pick it up. The confused look on his face when he rose stabbed her heart.

"Please, Thomas, go and help him. He's—"

Thomas looked at his sleeve—where she had grabbed him.

What am I doing? She removed her hand, stunned by her reaction. "I…sorry—" Oh God, she'd forgotten. She was under close scrutiny. She must be more biddable, more—

"Of course. At your service, Mina." Thomas bowed his head and marched to the rescue.

But her heart was pounding. For the first time that evening, she had seen Thomas's eyes very clearly behind his spectacles.

And the doubt within them.

Five

"MIGHT NOT HAVE BEEN THE BEST TIME." SETH DIDN'T look at Tom's face. At least Mina wasn't with him.

"Tried to tell you," Tom said.

"I know it." Seth shrugged, but it didn't lessen his embarrassment. Bloody Company men. They never gave him the time in London, and they were the same in India. Not even when he'd made them tens of thousands of pounds. And not even now, when a woman's life was concerned.

And he'd started the night excited—happier than he'd been in months—over all the help he thought he'd get. Damn stupid of him.

"These men care for nothing tonight except the Fishing Fleet," Tom said.

"The what?"

Tom pointed with his chin into the conservatory. "A ship full of ladies, *fishing* for husbands. You've not heard that expression?"

Seth shook his head, frowning. "No. Doesn't sound fitting, anyway. Or nice." He folded his papers into his pocket. "We can start in the morning, I suppose. I hope you know a man or two that might be more cooperative."

"One or two, but they'll make it understood that I'm overstepping. Bombay may as well be London for men like us."

"Like me, you mean."

"Like us, Mayhew."

Tom's words were so bitter, Seth paused in his turn for the door.

Tom raised a brow. "Why do you think I'm out in the Punjab?"

"The plantation—"

"I started in Calcutta, at the gardens. The Punjab isn't Calcutta. It's not Delhi or Bombay or Madras. It's the *mofussils*. Three years out there because I dared to question my superior." Tom looked dispassionate as he surveyed the room, but when he spoke, his words were hard as steel. "Society *is* twice as rigid here, Mayhew. But damned if they'll turn us out with your sister missing. They may treat us as expendable, but they'll learn we're not."

Despite Tom's troubles, warm relief smothered Seth's anger. Tom *was* going to help him—and not just because of the money. He patted his new ally on the back. "That's damn right. You might deserve a wife after all. Maybe not Miss Mina, but a wife."

Tom shook his head, but a grin tugged at his lips. "Now that you mention her, do you have to flirt with my intended?"

Seth's heart plummeted—and it surprised the hell out of him. "Your intended now, is she?" His words came out too loud, so he grinned and blustered through. "She's accepted your offer then?"

Tom's mulish pout was answer enough.

Seth grinned in earnest, but his relief was damn stupid. Soon enough, Mina would have any man of her choosing. And that man wouldn't be some wandering explorer without a spare shilling to his name.

Tom scanned the room. "I wonder where she's gone to?"

If Mina were mine, I wouldn't be all that likely to misplace her. Seth pointed to where she stood with a group of ladies beside a potted sago palm. "There. In that pink frock, she looks like a fancy teacake." And with that milky skin, he had a strong urge to lick her. "She's a beauty, that one."

"You've made clear you noticed, you realize?"

Confused, he dragged his gaze back to Tom.

"Yes, she's lovely to look on." Tom studied him. "Listen, Mayhew—"

"Call me Seth."

"I'm sorry to disappoint, but Miss Adams is here to meet a husband. And that will likely be me."

Seth laughed but it came out weak. "I know it. Hell, every lady in here knows I can't offer them anything by way of a future."

"Certainly you can. I just meant—"

"I tease too much, maybe, but I never led a woman to believe I could take on a wife and family. Besides, Miss Mina is too fine for the likes of me." Seth crossed his arms and feigned interest in the crowded conservatory.

With the ladies so fresh and pretty, every man in here had his head on a swivel. Yet nothing in their faces showed how the men had got here. They were comfortable, proud, believed they were entitled to a wife and children. Believed they could support them.

Nothing showed, but Seth always recognized the certainty—because he never recognized it in himself.

A throbbing started in his head and the candlelight stabbed his eyes. Not enough food—that's why he was getting muddled. Men and their suitoring were none of his business. His business was finding Georgie, and that wasn't looking too easy a task with the Company men ignoring him.

And he was suddenly damn tired.

"I suppose it was a waste of my time coming here," he said.

Tom's silence confirmed that and Seth swallowed another dose of shame. "Will you say good night to Miss Mina for me?"

"Certainly. We'll start early tomorrow."

Seth buttoned his coat and from the corner of his eye, saw Mina hurry toward them. It was too late to avoid her. Had she seen how the Company men had treated him?

"Mr. Mayhew?" Her voice was a little breathless. "You are not leaving?"

Would he see her again? He'd have no cause to. The thought made him feel...not lonely. Just alone.

But because he didn't know of anything he could do about it, he did what he always did. He took up her gloved hand and smiled down at her. And her eyes were sherry lit by candlelight, and the blush on her cheeks as wondrous as a peach sunrise over the Atlantic, and the beauty of her face was the surest proof of a God and his angels that Seth would ever, *ever* need.

And there wasn't a thing the Worst Flirt in the Midlands could say but "Good-bye, Miss Mina."

Her lips parted, but she seemed to change her mind and only smiled a little. "Good-bye, Mr. Mayhew. You and your sister will be in my prayers."

She pulled her hand away and the loss left him cold and swaying on his feet. Yes, he must be damn tired.

"I'll see you out," Tom said, then turned to Mina. "Will you excuse me, Mina?"

She might have nodded but Seth didn't look again. He busied himself with his gloves and headed to the door with Tom.

"There's a man here tonight who might be willing to help," Tom said.

Seth blew out a breath. "Might, huh?"

"Fallon's his name, a clerk I've had dealings with. He's been given permission to wed recently, so he's likely about. I'll say hello, but it won't do to bring up all the particulars tonight. If we go through the correct channels—be proper, patient, even strategic—we might get the information we need."

Seth's doubt sank deeper. Proper, patient, strategic. Wasn't his nature at all.

Tom asked the doorman to call a victoria for him, and they waited in the entry. A gentleman and his richly dressed wife passed by without acknowledging either of them.

When they were past hearing, Seth grumbled, "I spoke to that gent earlier. Said he'd do what he could. Wished me luck, even. Must've forgot me in the last quarter hour."

"Frightfully short memory."

"Bloody Company men," Seth muttered, then remembered Tom. "No offense."

"None taken."

Out of the corner of his vision, a lady's head bobbed out from the door of the conservatory to peek at him. It was just a flash of a little face and bouncing ringlets, and when he looked, she was gone.

Two other faces appeared from around the door to gawp and disappeared just as fast.

Seth blinked. No, those women wouldn't have anything to do with him. But Tom was looking in the same direction. Suddenly, a half dozen ladies popped from around the door to look at him and stood whispering behind their hands.

And right in the middle of them was Mina.

She broke away from her friends and hurried toward him. And a lightning bolt of energy coursed through his body. Seth propped his hands on his hips and grinned as she approached. "There's nothing better than the sight of a pretty lady coming to—"

"Would you give me one of your posters, Mr. Mayhew?"

"Uh...all right." Seth fumbled with his roll of papers. *It wasn't the best compliment he'd ever given but—*

"Did anyone offer to help you?" she asked. "Did you make any connections?"

He tensed with embarrassment. "Me and Tom are getting us a strategy. Proper channels and all that."

Her lips pressed into a thin line, and Seth could have sworn she grew an inch with the straightening of her spine. Mina took the poster and hurried back to her friends.

She didn't say good-bye this time. And she didn't turn around.

He shuffled back to the door. "You'll speak to Fallon then, Tom? That clerk?"

But Tom wasn't with him. He stood watching the women with a bemused look on his face. "Huh."

"What?" Seth followed Tom's stare. The ladies were craning their necks to look at Georgie's poster.

Tom smiled slowly. "I think Mina just found you a way into the East India Company."

The ladies took out dainty pencils and notebooks to copy from his poster. And then it all became clear.

It became damn perfect.

The Fishing Fleet. *His* Fishing Fleet. Forty-four friends of Mina's. Forty-four potential wives of Company men.

Men who'd do anything to prove themselves worthy of marriage. Like help find a wee orphan and a lost Englishwoman.

Seth laughed in surprise. "*Damn me.* I think I love that woman." Seth patted Tom on the back. "I'm back to thinking you don't deserve her anymore."

But Tom laughed with him.

"Got myself a fleet of ladies now, Tom." Seth rubbed his hands together. "Better go meet the reinforcements."

"Wait, Mayhew."

Seth pulled up. "Now what am I doing wrong?"

"You can't approach those women without an introduction."

"Miss Mina will—"

"A *formal* introduction. It's not Mina's place, and her friends won't like it. These women have to appear all that's proper. These early days are crucial for the unwed ladies."

Damn. Why didn't he know any of these rules?

Three more women joined Mina. Forty-four allies...if he used Mina. If he admitted he needed her help. Well...*hell*. He didn't have time for stupid pride.

Besides, she knew what he was. And what he wasn't.

"Going to have a quick word with Miss Mina, Tom." Seth held up a staying hand. "I'll be back directly."

To his surprise, Tom didn't follow or try to stop him. It was the alarm in Mina's big, brown eyes that slowed his step. She handed Georgie's poster to a lady next to her and hurried to him.

No, there was nothing better than the sight of a pretty girl coming to talk to you. Especially if that girl was composed, capable, and orderly-like—and blushed whenever you looked at her. Which he enjoyed doing more than he should.

"Did you wish to see me, Mr. Mayhew?"

"Every waking moment, Miss Mina." He grinned. "Wanted to make the acquaintance of your friends—I know that can't happen—but I appreciate your telling them about Georgie, which is the best notion and one I never would've thought of.

"Involving the *wives* might've been a bit of Lysistrata-without-the-war, but the venture girls are better. Tom's Mr. Fallon was all the plan we had. Do you think we might give the ladies a few more of my posters?"

Mina squinted at him. Damn, he was talking all over the place. Like that frog she spoke of.

"Is Mr. Fallon the only connection Thomas has?" she asked.

Clever Mina. He nodded.

Her squint relaxed, but he could almost see her brain flipping through all his words. "You know *Lysistrata*, Mr. Mayhew?"

He shrugged. "We've a theater where I grew up. A good one."

She smiled a little, so he moved closer. Having a fine lady to himself was nice. Tom Grant would be collecting her any minute.

"I saw lots of theatricals," he said. "Shakespeare and that Aristophanes gent and Scribe. And melodramas, too, all the bloody ones like the *Red Barn Murder*. But I liked the old plays best. The players were good, too. People said they weren't good enough for London, but they were. And real fine for Matlock."

She stared at him, her pretty mouth dropped open with what looked like surprise. A very pretty mouth. And the most kissable—

"You're from Matlock? I'm from Chesterfield."

"You're not! My mates live there—the Douglas boys. And me and Freddy Kent went to the public school together."

"Fred's sister was my friend." She shook her head, her eyes widening. "I thought there was something familiar—it wasn't your voice; it was your speech at times. East Midlands."

He winced a little. "I med a right codge of it then, m'lover, if'n you know'd 'ow I spake."

She giggled and clapped her hand over her mouth. "Oh, enough, Mr. Mayhew. You mustn't give us away."

He smiled because he'd finally made the little officer laugh, but she didn't know how hard it had been to correct the way he talked. One schoolmaster had corrected it with a switch of rowan tree, when he bothered trying to teach him at all.

His father's speech was worse—pure Black Country. As a boy, Seth hadn't understood him. And the man hadn't stayed long enough for him to learn.

"I'm sorry, Mr. Mayhew," she said, still smiling. "It's actually rather wonderful to hear again."

He'd never known brown eyes could shine with all that gold in them. They might have been reflecting the glow of a fire. "Is that so?" he murmured.

And though he'd not told anyone, he wanted to tell her. Wasn't anyone to tell, really—no one that wouldn't laugh at him.

He dipped his head closer to speak just for her hearing, and her eyes were still glowing. "I, uh…I bought myself a bit of land just west of there. That orchid I found, that Wilhelmina orchid, sold for a good amount, and I bought as much land as I could. Near a thousand acres. Not all of it worth farming—some oats maybe, but I'm thinking sheep, an orchard, a kitchen garden, too."

"You have land in Derbyshire?"

Her eyes grew huge and he felt damn near ten feet tall. So he wouldn't tell her the bit about how Old Man Hartwig had said the hedgerows were dead and the cottage roof would fall in so it was good Seth had a head like a rock. But Hartwig was just a cranky, old pinch-fart.

And he wouldn't tell her the rest of it. How even though he'd sold the prize orchid for all that acreage, he couldn't afford to make the repairs to all the buildings that stood on that land.

But Seth wouldn't call that a curse. Because if he

did, that meant he was doomed to fail in this expedition, too.

And that meant he wouldn't find Georgie alive.

He shook his mind free of that hellish thought. "And it's, uh…it's got a handsome stone cottage, too. It needs mending, though, and a hedgerow that's not been trimmed since the Romans, but I'll be fixing it up. Eventually—*soon*. Real soon."

She nodded quickly. "A home needs all sorts of maintenance. I tended my family's garden. I would so enjoy that employment again."

He grinned and waited for her to continue. But she wasn't saying anything. He shifted his weight. And shifted back. And her smile was…*encouraging*?

Did she *want* him to talk more?

Well.

He cleared his throat. "I've a plan on that cottage, of course. My Wilhelmina orchid was described and sold, straightaway, but I found lots more prizes than that. Had them in seed, though. Some of the prettiest flowers you'll ever see, and lots of practical plants, too. My best mates have those in England; they're looking after them for me. They're plantsmen, cultivators.

"I had over a dozen orchids that I shipped, too, but I'm not sure if they're new discoveries. But if they are, and they sell for a good amount, I'll have the money to fix up all my outbuildings, the stable and washhouse and granary."

He paused, checking her eyes for glazing or puzzlement. He grinned when he saw neither. "And if those seeds are viable, I'll be able to marry, too. And keep a family."

"That sounds really perfect, Mr. Mayhew."

And the way she said it, he believed she meant it. Would Mina have herself a little garden here? "It does, doesn't it?" he murmured.

"And your land? What is it like?"

He smiled, seeing that landscape in his head. "There's a stream that flows right through this flat valley and into a grove of birch that might be out of a painting. And the grass all around it—green and soft and cool, like it was begging you to take off your boots and sit down for a picnic."

"Is there a footbridge? My favorite walk was across the Hipper River and there was a bridge of stepping stones across the water."

"Stepping stones, eh?" For the first time in his knowing her, Mina's face went all soft and wistful and he wasn't about to disappoint her. "I'll build one just because you said it."

She blushed deep. Maybe Miss Mina liked his compliments, after all.

And didn't he like looking at that face? Maybe because she seemed to like what she was seeing, too. Even if he wasn't a gentleman. He could almost pretend there was something there that wouldn't mind kissing him.

Damn…

"Why is it we never rubbed shoulders till we found ourselves here?" he said.

"Fate, I suppose," she said softly.

Fate. He never had any use for it.

Georgie's face looked at him from her missing poster. "I had a thought to go over and introduce myself to your friends."

That worried look sprang to Mina's face again.

"But Tom tells me it's not done," he said.

"You mustn't think they don't want to help. It is just that they're aware a man like you will distract them."

"I didn't plan on any distracting." Mina's face was getting that peach blush again, which was distracting enough.

"No, of course you don't. But they are here to meet potential husbands."

"I know it." A bit of lace peeked from her sleeve and he tapped it. "What's this, Miss Mina?"

She pulled it out and gave it to him. "A handkerchief. It is only that—"

"Did you stitch these little flowers?"

"I did, yes. But the women—"

"Bluebells, right?"

"Yes. Only that you could sway the ladies from their purpose if—oh, thank you"—she took back her handkerchief—"well, I think you understand what I'm trying to say."

She'd stopped talking, and when he looked up, her brown eyes were scanning his.

"Mr. Mayhew?"

So damn pretty. He grinned. "I'm listening, Miss Mina."

She squared herself in front of him as if she wanted to wrangle his full attention. She had it, but he didn't mind her placing herself just so.

"It is just that you mustn't distract them with your masculine wiles."

The hell? He roared with laughter—something he'd not done in longer than he could remember. "My wiles, is it? No one's accused me of such before. I thank you. What wiles might those be? My frog brain?"

"Your brain is fine."

She sounded almost angry, and it made him like her all the more.

"You possess many attractions," she said.

"Attractions?" He rubbed his jaw, damn curious what Mina would say. "What might those be?"

"Well…" Her gaze drifted to his…chest? Belt? Shoes?

"You possess a very handsome form," she said so low he had to bend his head to hear.

Handsome? He looked down at himself. And it was a long way down. Hulking, maybe. "You don't mean my constitution? Or something in the way of stamina?"

A question flickered in her eyes before she blinked it away. "I…I don't wish to speak of stamina, Mr. Mayhew."

Now she wasn't looking at him at all. "Why don't you call me Seth?"

That worked. She looked at him over her burning cheeks. "I don't think—"

"And I'll call you Minnie."

She blinked. "My friends call me Mina."

"Am I your friend?"

"I don't know. Aren't you?"

"Not sure," he said. "Who calls you Minnie, then?"

"No one."

He grinned. "Good."

She started to speak, then looked to be weighing his request—just like a lady would, just to be nice and polite.

"*Minnie* makes me sound small," she said.

"I know it. But I could carry you around in my pocket, couldn't I?" He crossed his arms and winked.

"Stop that, Mr. Mayhew. That is seven times now."

He didn't know what she was saying there. He shook his head, chuckling. "I don't know about wiles, Minnie—"

"*Mina.* Or Wilhelmina, or—"

"I don't know any other way to talk to women except with a little teasing. It might do me a harm to try. Georgie always said I was the Worst Flirt in the Midlands."

Whatever he said seemed to sober her, and she dropped her gaze. "Yes." She threaded her hand around his arm. "Shall we return to Thomas?"

Disappointment swept over him, but he stood straighter anyway. It was a rare thing to escort a lady anyplace. Even if it was only across a room. "So, Miss Mina, as I'm not proper, will you speak for me?"

"You're not improper, just distracting." She shook her head a little. "I've offended your feelings—I'm sorry. You and your wiles are blameless, so you mustn't be uncomfortable if the ladies imagine you an object of attraction."

An object of attraction…? He considered that. "No. I've no objection to that."

She shot him a confused look, and his heart softened seeing the peach tips of her ears. The woman could blush there, too. But she'd not answered his question. "So would you? Speak for me?"

She raised her chin and looked him straight in the eye. His little officer again. "I will do everything I can to help you."

Ah…damn. He *was* a little in love with her.

Someday, he might meet another lady as fine as her who wouldn't mind marrying him. A lady who'd be such a credit to him that people would think twice about seeing him as just a laboring man. And they'd live in a house with a library full of books she'd probably already read, and a pianoforte their children knew how to play. Someday. If he wasn't cursed.

She shied from his gaze and looked into the conservatory. At Tom.

She pulled her hand from his arm. "I understand you and Thomas were invited to the picnic and snipe hunt tomorrow at Vehar Lake."

"I heard that, but it's not likely we'll attend with all there is to do."

"Could you both come along after your work is done? I had hoped to see Thomas."

He huffed a surprised laugh. "You do speak plain, Minnie." And damn if it didn't hurt his feelings. "Tom and me, we have telegrams to send, and plans to make, and that Mr. Fallon to meet."

"The carriages do not leave until eleven." She planted herself square in front of him again, her head tilted back to look straight at him, and he was caught by those big, brown eyes. "Please, Mr. Mayhew?"

Well…*hell.*

"The hunt would not be a bad use of your time," she said. "If you spend the forenoon on your planning and letters, the rest of the day could be employed reminding others of your search."

Seth bit back a sigh. Mina was making sense. It wasn't as if he could go haring off to all the corners of Asia without information. Patient, polite, proper channels, and all that.

"That sounds real fine, Minnie." And it *would* be fine. It was going to have to be.

"And you'll bring Thomas?" she asked.

"I'm thinking Tom will want to be anywhere you're at."

"Do you think so?"

Her eyes were shiny with hope and he raked a hand through his hair. Damn awkward. She needed Tom for marrying and Seth needed him to find Georgie—anywhere that might be. Once time came to travel, nothing would stop him from taking Tom with him. Away from Mina.

There wasn't but one solution he could think of: Tom had to wed her.

So he'd better do it damn soon.

Six

"DO I PERSUADE YOU I AM A GREAT HUNTER?" THOMAS said by way of greeting, posing beside the carriage that would take them to Lake Vehar. "On yet another *shikar* for rampaging beasts? Which I find only mildly amusing, of course."

Mina smiled, examining his sporting ensemble from his pith helmet to his boots to his holstered knife. "Good afternoon, Thomas. And yes, you do look the proficient."

"Ah, good, as I've only ever hunted quail. *And* I'm a sorry marksman."

Emma poked the handle of his blade with a frown. "Truly, I'm going on an Indian *shikar*. I suppose the drive will allow me to see something of the country-side so the day will not be a complete waste."

"A waste?" Thomas asked.

"No one in the family shoots," Mina explained. "Emma is particularly averse."

"Ah." Thomas handed his gear to his servant. "Killing God's creatures is a favorite pastime among Company men. Unfortunately for them, snipe is on offer today. Frightfully hard to hit; they fly in a corkscrew pattern when flushed. There'll be a great number of sullen men at the end of the day."

"I hope you're right," Emma said.

Thomas chuckled. His mood seemed much improved from yesterday. Already the conversation was easier. Perhaps she had been anxious for no reason. Thomas had sent for a wife—she was assured he wanted one.

Whether he wanted her was yet to be determined.

At the least, this second day together provided a facade of familiarity. She had no talent for rapid rapport, a necessary skill in women exported for marriage. Four friends had accepted offers after their first interviews yesterday. And those from perfect strangers.

"Has Colin Rivers sent word?" Thomas asked.

Emma huffed a breath. "No. Not a word, note, or telegram."

Thomas frowned in sympathy. "I'm sure he is desperate to get here. Shouldn't be much longer. Laxman?" Thomas called to his bearer, who was climbing down from the carriage. "Where is Mr. Mayhew?"

"I believe he is en route, *sahib*," Laxman said. "I certainly did see him buy food from the bazaar."

"Are you sure that was him?" Thomas asked.

Laxman bowed his head. "Mr. Mayhew is not easy to mistake, *sahib*."

"I'm so glad you and Mr. Mayhew were able to join us," Mina said.

"He won't be if he's late." Thomas scanned the street. "But I'm hopeful this may be a productive afternoon. The men may be more amenable to helping

Mayhew if meeting him on the hunting field. But then"—he frowned at a thought—"they'll all have their shotguns."

"I think it wonderful that you are helping him," Emma said. "Is there any news of his sister?"

"Not yet," Thomas said.

"Mina is helping, too," Emma said before Mina could warn her to silence. "Our friend Julia is engaged to a political agent in West Bengal and he is very keen to inquire. He promised he would. And Edith's gentleman, also. Mina has secured so many promises of help that we're sure to—"

"We mustn't raise hopes, Emma," she said.

Thomas met her eye for an instant but his look was unreadable. "I'm sure we are grateful for the aid."

With those cool words, Mina's doubts returned. Should she not have extended herself on Mr. Mayhew's behalf? Any woman, any *person*, would be sympathetic, wouldn't they? "It was the work of a moment, really."

"Yes, well," Thomas murmured. "Your friends may do far better than us." He opened the door of the carriage, one of a dozen waiting outside Benson's Hotel to carry the venture girls the short distance to the lake. "Ladies?"

Mina could think of nothing to say, so she took his hand silently as he handed her into the carriage. But he didn't join her, continuing to wait on the pavement for Mr. Mayhew.

In the dim carriage, she took a steadying breath. Helping Mr. Mayhew might have been a mistake. Did Thomas think her distracted by the explorer? Did he doubt her regard? Was Thomas waiting for her to somehow encourage his offer, or was she free to just…*accept* an unspoken one? And with Colin Rivers delayed, should she commit to him at all?

Or was she driving herself mad for no reason?

"That's quite a blade, Tom." Mr. Mayhew's deep, laughing voice sounded from outside the carriage. "I thought this was a snipe hunt. You expecting to wrestle a panther?"

"All right, all right," Thomas said. "I have no need of the knife. But it rather completes the outfit."

"Should I grab my poleax in case we encounter a flock of pigeon?"

"You're late," Thomas said, climbing into the carriage.

"I know it." Mr. Mayhew appeared framed in the door of the carriage wearing a safari hat. "But only by a minute. I couldn't inconvenience these pretty women. Good afternoon, ladies."

The brim shaded his eyes so all Mina could see was his hard jaw and the tilted smile of his lips… She had not really noticed the shape of his lips before. They were fuller than she realized. A mouth built to smile and taste. And talk, too, she supposed. He stretched his thick arms overhead to lean against the carriage door's lintel, and his powerful chest tapered dramatically to lean hips and a trim, flat stomach.

Oh dear. He *was* distracting.

Emma must have been similarly affected. She sighed. And rather lengthily. "We weren't waiting. Perhaps a moment, but that is not any wait at all. I mean, it's quite all right, Mr. Mayhew."

Mina smiled with real amusement. But really, a

woman would have to be blind not to be attracted. And deaf. And she could not touch any part of Mr. Mayhew, not with those muscles. Yes, she'd have to be altogether insensible. Perhaps dead.

"Good afternoon, Mr. Mayhew," she said.

Mr. Mayhew pushed back his hat and his sea-green eyes latched on hers and—drat him—that triggered a strange quiver in the pit of her stomach. He smiled the slowest, loveliest smile.

And then, of course, he winked at her.

She turned to look out the window, and then stupidly hurried to pull back the curtain a moment later. She had never been so affected by a man. And the timing was truly terrible.

He wasn't entering the carriage. A small hope lit within her. Perhaps he had changed his mind; perhaps he wouldn't come?

"Ladies, if you'll excuse me." Mr. Mayhew stepped back from the carriage. "I thought I might ride up on the box, get a view of the city."

"*Nooo*, Mr. Mayhew." Emma leaned forward in her seat. "You must not deprive us of your company."

"It pains me to refuse a pretty woman, but I don't think I can listen to Tom hold forth on all his rousing tales of chicken hunts."

"*Quail*." Thomas shook his head but he was grinning. Perhaps the men were becoming friends after all.

Mr. Mayhew's eyes glanced off Mina's before he pulled his hat brim low and closed the door. What was that look? Why would he not ride inside—?

Oh. He didn't wish to intrude on her time with Thomas.

Oh! And after she had forestalled their work today. Without Thomas, how much would he accomplish? There were scores of Company men to ingratiate himself with today. To be seen arriving on the box would be embarrassing. Was she that callous to his situation? And to wish him away…

"Mr. Mayhew?" she called.

He stopped, his hand on the door. "Yes, Miss Mina?"

Thomas sat still and watchful, but she pressed on. It was only right and sensible. Besides, the faster she proved her impartiality to handsome explorers, the better. "Won't you join us?" she said as lightly as she could. "The box will not be comfortable."

He searched her face. "No, I—"

"Get in, Mayhew." Thomas slid over. "There's room enough. Even for you."

He hesitated a moment, then doffed his hat, the carriage tipping as he climbed in. Mina angled her knees to the side to avoid his long legs, and he smiled in apology. Which was adorable.

She frowned hard at the thought. *Fine.* She was attracted—that hardly mattered in her circumstances. She could sit here and converse like the sensible woman she had been all her four and twenty years, and he would soon be persuaded that his winks and wiles and flattery were wasted on a woman like her.

Perhaps he was already done flirting with her. "And how was your morning, Mr. Mayhew?"

"Full of smiles knowing I'd be seeing you, Miss Mina."

No, he wasn't done. "Well, I… Thank you. And productive too, I hope?"

"We sent telegrams to the Calcutta and Delhi offices, and a couple letters back to England in case Georgie was trying to reach me. And here's a stroke of luck—Tom's mate, Mr. Walpole, will be at the hunt—"

"Not really a mate—" Thomas said.

"—so that's a door opened. There's no knowing how many gents Tom will be introducing me to today. Right, Tom?"

"*One* gent," Thomas said. "I know one."

"The men will be curious over you," she said. "And inclined to be friendly, I think."

"That's what I'm hoping, Miss Mina."

The carriage jerked to a start and she aimed her gaze out the window. Mr. Mayhew looked out at the same view and somehow even that felt intimate. She turned toward Thomas. "How often do you travel outside of Saharanpur, Thomas?"

"In the past year, once."

"And where did you go?"

Thomas looked confused by the question. "Oh, *here*. Bombay's my only trip this year. The year before—no, it's nearly two years now, I trekked a bit west, deeper into the Punjab, but was struck by a mild bout of dysentery. Might have been a parasite. But by and by, I returned to the plantation and the *babu* sorted me out in a few months."

Months?

Emma leaned forward, her eyes wide. "I understand most English outside of the cities contract malaria within the first months, often in the first weeks." Her eyes widened. "Or the cholera or typhoid or dengue or blackwater fever or—"

"And what is a *babu,* Thomas?" Mina asked, squeezing Emma's hand.

"A doctor."

She smiled. "Oh."

"*Of sorts.*" Thomas tipped his head, thinking. "He's not so much a doctor as a…*medic*…or *therapeutist*?"

Her smile slipped. "Oh," she said more quietly. She sat back in her seat. Mr. Mayhew watched her so she busied herself with smoothing her skirt.

Thomas opened the window curtain wide and sighed. "A fine day."

"Yes." She faced Thomas—but he faced the window.

She held Emma's hand tight and tried not to worry over the fact there was not yet a ring on either of their fingers. She had to be patient. Thomas was a gentleman and would not rush an intimacy between them that would be unnatural. And yet…

And yet he seemed to have no more feeling for her than she did for him.

"You have a kitchen garden up there, Tom?" Mr. Mayhew asked.

The question surprised her. Mr. Mayhew had been oddly quiet. Even now, his brooding stare was aimed at her lap.

"A kitchen garden?" Thomas asked. "Yes, the plantation is home to over three hundred men and their families so there's a rather large one."

"What did you grow in your garden, Miss Mina?" Mr. Mayhew didn't raise his head. "Potatoes? Turnips? Did you grow any flowers?"

"My garden? Yes, all that, and oats and onions and

my mother's peas and—" Her voice broke with some surprise emotion and she dropped her eyes.

What was the matter with her? Hot tears blurred the sight of her lap. And no one was saying anything—

"You grow English vegetables up there, don't you, Tom?" Mr. Mayhew's voice was loud and gruff in the close space.

"We do," Thomas answered quickly. "Indeed. Many, uh, many of the same."

"Good," Mr. Mayhew said. "And probably a fair number of plants the ladies wouldn't know of. I had my first Bengal quince yesterday. Looks like a grapefruit on the outside, but it doesn't eat like one."

Thomas's gaze was heavy on her, so she blinked the moisture from her eyes and raised her head. "A Bengal quince? I shall have to try one." She could barely hold Mr. Mayhew's gaze, as deeply as he looked into her eyes. But at last, he gave her a small smile.

Thomas sat forward in his seat. "I will find you one tomorrow, Mina. I did not wish to bombard your stomach with too much of the exotic. Unlike Mayhew here, who fears no food."

"Have to sample what I can, when I can," he said.

"Indeed, Mr. Mayhew," Emma said. "Once you find your sister and quit India for good, you will find nothing so novel in your garden."

"No, likely not," Mr. Mayhew said. "But when I'm back in Matlock, I'll be well content imagining the Adams girls of Chesterfield tending to their eastern gardens."

"An eastern garden," Mina murmured. "I should like one, I think. What would I grow in it?"

Mr. Mayhew leaned back against the squabs, his eyes not leaving hers, and said quietly, "Anything you want, Miss Mina."

His eyes crinkled, and it struck her they would always do so. In happiness and sorrow, and even compassion, like now. Lulled by that gaze, she remembered what was true: She was in India and she would stay here. And she would *live* here.

But she could have a garden again.

She smiled her thanks to him, and he winked at her. She took a bracing breath of air scented by the sea, and everything was clear. She was here forever, as was Thomas. And they could make a life of respect and civility toward one another. Because it wasn't love that mattered.

After what happened to Mary, love never would.

⬥

Seth leaped out of the carriage. "Now there's a lake!"

He spoke too loud, exited too fast, but damned if he didn't need to be out of that carriage. Nine miles should have been an easy distance, but not in company that included Mina being sad. Not when he couldn't say all he wanted.

Not when there wasn't a thing he could do to help.

It wasn't his place to help Mina from the carriage, either. He moved aside so Tom could hand the women down.

Mina's lips parted at her first sight of Vehar Lake, the water wide and blue and bordered by a range of long, green hills that seemed to stretch without end. The sun was warm and the prospect the finest he'd seen in India. Would it be enough to spirit up a venture girl?

She strolled to the front of the carriage to pet the horses and his eyes followed, lured by the marvel of her little waist, nipped in by her skirt, and the filmy white blouse hugging the sweet curve of her breasts. Her dark hair was shiny as glass in the sun before she tied on her bonnet and hid all that prettiness from him.

But for all that was so calm and composed on the outside, Mina couldn't hide the trouble showing in those big, brown eyes of hers. And in the carriage, it had nearly made him haul her onto his lap and hold her.

Tom said she'd come to marry, but that wasn't the whole truth. Wasn't even most of it. What was clear was that *Emma* was the one committed to wed. With Tom and Colin Rivers working together in the Northwest Province, Mina must have come because she wasn't about to let her sister be alone.

No, India wasn't any place for an Englishwoman.

"Mayhew?" Tom was at his shoulder. "I asked what you hunt?"

He steered his attention back to Tom and caught the knowing look in the man's eye. He knew he watched Mina too much, and Tom was being patient with his interest. For now. There was no understanding the man. Hell, Tom didn't seem to be courting her at all.

What had he asked? "Ay? No, never hunted for sport," Seth mumbled. "Isn't a pleasure outing for me anyway."

"There may be something useful to be had from Walpole," Tom said.

"Maybe, but he's just a clerk. We know a man higher in requisitions."

"Not one keen to help."

Seth nodded grimly. "We're here—we'll talk to Walpole. Just remember why *you're* here. You need to win over Miss Mina."

"It's been one day."

"And you better work on that powerful charm of yours. Hell, Tom, what was all that talk of dysentery?"

Tom stared. "What? She asked—"

"She asked for a nice story about your travels in-country, and you give her tales of bowel disorders."

"That's what happened."

"Minnie doesn't want to be here, might even be afraid of being here, and you're not helping with all your talk of sickness. Hell, *I* couldn't think of anything to say. Not even a bit of nonsense to make her smile or blush."

"It's not your concern, Mayhew."

"I know it," he growled. *Damn idiot.* "But if you want to marry her, go and talk to her. And leave off stories of the ass-stinging blister flies you have over here."

Tom mumbled something under his breath but stalked over to Mina. The smile she gave Tom hit Seth like a blow to the gut—but that was all right. Mina needed settling first. Once the search for Georgie took them out of Bombay, at least Mina would be safe.

Seth walked in the other direction. A dozen carriages had arrived before them. Ladies unrolled straw mats higher on the hill and arranged the picnic, while the servants unpacked the carriages and herded the dogs.

The men inspected their rifles for the benefit of the women, while Seth studied the men. Even on a snipe hunt at the edge of Bombay, the gents wore English suits.

He'd never owned any suit—let alone a sporting suit—that fit as fine as those the men were wearing. He pulled down the hem of his coat and straightened his hat. In London, Will Repton had given him the name of his tailor, but he couldn't afford such things. Mina would never see him in anything good.

Damn stupid of him to be thinking on it.

Mina, Emma, and Tom joined him, and Seth looked at the lake, the hills, the dogs—nearly twisted his head off looking at anything but Mina and Tom standing arm in arm.

"Look, Mayhew." Tom pitched his voice low. "The one in the green waistcoat is Mr. Walpole. You might not want to outshoot him."

"No danger in that," he said. "Didn't bring a gun."

Tom squinted at him from behind his spectacles. "No gun? Why not? You own several."

What did he do wrong now? "They're for traveling."

Tom blinked. "You're at a hunt."

"I told you—never hunted for sport."

"Huzzah, Mr. Mayhew!" Emma cried.

Was Mina as pleased with him? She was admiring the view and there was no deciphering from that small smile if she approved of a nonsporting man or not. "I *can* shoot, of course," Seth said. "And fish. *And* ride—I stick on a horse real tidy."

Mina turned a puzzled gaze on him.

Well…right. Damn awkward thing to be mentioning just then.

"No gun," Tom grumbled, his stare screwed on him. "Don't think you'll loll about among the ladies, Mayhew. You'll stay with the men, even if you aren't hunting."

"I know it," he mumbled.

"And no pulling out Georgiana's poster unless the conversation turns in that direction."

Seth frowned and just managed to stay his hand from pulling Georgie's poster out of his pocket. Tom may not credit him with much of a brain, but there was no cause to be scolding him in front of Mina—especially when Seth only agreed to come to give Tom a little time with her.

Mina didn't seem to be listening anyway, her eyes intent on her friends. The venture girls waved and smiled at each other. And nodded and pointed and shook their heads, communicating women's matters silently.

"Shooting cannot be to everyone's taste," Mina said distractedly, smiling at a couple strolling toward them. "*Oh look*, here is my friend Beatrice."

Seth grinned at the false surprise. Even Beatrice's brows rose at Mina's big welcome.

"Hello, Mina." Beatrice presented the gent with her. "May I introduce Mr. Hodges to you all?"

Introductions were made and the ladies did the pretty, saying all the civil things ladies said, leaving the men to stare blankly at each other and nod.

Hodges turned toward him. "Mr. Mayhew, I understand from this enchanting creature"—he patted Beatrice's hand—"that you require information from John Company."

Seth perked up. "I do at that."

"I can offer an inroad into that prickly territory, I daresay," Hodges said. "Let's not disturb these gentle ladies with our talk. Come along, Mayhew."

Come along? Seth corrected the frown on his face and followed. *Come along*...like a damn dog. But he sent Mina a grateful nod for the help.

When they'd removed themselves from the ladies, Hodges took out his card. "Call on me tomorrow. We'll discuss the matter of your sister."

Seth grinned. "I appreciate that—"

"What's this I hear of a missing Englishwoman?" A thin gent with an ivory stick demanded loudly as he joined them, but he appeared to be posing for a redhead who looked ready to swoon with ecstasy at the man's question.

And suddenly, Seth was in a circle of gents proclaiming themselves the only possible solution on the matter of the missing Georgiana Mayhew. Voices were rising, too, but Seth collected cards as fast as he could reach for them. *Damn me, a productive day, after all.*

"Attention!" A stout man in tall boots shouldered his rifle and waved his arm, ending the men's posturing over whom was best positioned to gain information and rescue Georgie. "The snipe are nesting in the dry rice paddies just around the bend of this hill. Ladies, as I'm sure you wish to see the men shoot, we must all come upon them silently so as not to frighten them off before the dogs set them to wing." He tucked his chin coyly, holding a plump brunette's eye. "So none of your giggles, Hester."

The ladies giggled and a few men frowned. Married

men, likely. If they were keen to shoot, they'd come on the wrong day. Today was all about suitoring.

"Should the ladies not wait here, then?" Mina asked.

The giggles died and the venture girls all turned to look at her. Mina looked from one stricken face to the next. "We'll frighten off the snipe." She used her smallest voice. "Won't we?"

The man with the rifle smiled sheepishly. "Oh my dear, what fun is there in that? You must walk with us, ladies. At a suitable distance for your safety, of course."

The women relaxed into smiles and sidled next to their men. Mina and Emma stayed with Seth as Tom collected his rifle and kit from the carriage.

He chuckled at the blush rising on Mina's cheeks and bent to whisper in her ear. "You don't know how to flirt at all, do you, Minnie?"

She took a fast step from him. "Evidently not, Mr. Mayhew."

His heart cracked and the grin slipped right off his lips. And he didn't miss her glance at Tom, either. Well...*hell*. He shouldn't have done that. He was embarrassing her. He didn't even own a proper sporting suit.

"You're right of course, miss," a man said from behind them.

Seth turned to face him but the man's smile was aimed wholly at Mina. Wait—green waistcoat. *Walpole*.

"There's no sense in having a big, noisy party scare up those snipe," Walpole said.

"Thank you, sir. I have no experience with hunts." Mina lowered her lids and smiled shyly.

Seth had never seen her do that.

The man bowed to her. "My apologies. I am Earnest Walpole, miss. Please excuse my boldness. I fear I offend you."

"Not at all," Mina said. "I believe we may have a shared acquaintance in Thomas Grant?"

Walpole turned a questioning eye on him and Seth shook his head. "Not me." He pointed to Tom at the carriage. "There's your man."

"Ah, yes." Walpole promptly redirected his attentions to Mina and Emma in his pursuit of a comely wife. "It really is only sensible to separate the men and ladies." He leaned close to Emma as if sharing some great pearl of wisdom. "I've learned to take only one silent servant and my cleverest bitch when shooting snipe."

His smile showed all his teeth. How the hell was this Walpole going to help him again? "You must be quite a gunner," Seth said dryly.

Walpole shrugged, looking pleased. "The snipe are smaller and swifter here than back home, but in truth, I never enjoyed the hunt better than in Ireland."

"I've often heard the Irish countryside is very beautiful," Mina said.

Walpole's leer slid over to her. "Indeed. So you would be quite at home there, Miss Adams."

Seth's eyes narrowed, but that *was* a good compliment. A little fast, maybe. He cleared his throat a bit too loud—a bit too stern maybe, because Emma arched a warning brow at him.

Right. He may need this Romeo.

"You flatter me, sir." Mina slipped her hand around Walpole's elbow. "I have never been to Ireland." She aimed her perfect lips at Walpole's ear. "I wonder if Mr. Mayhew has?"

Maybe she knew a *little* about flirting. She was standing too damn cozy with the gent, in any case.

And where the hell was Walpole looking?

"Mr. Mayhew is an explorer and has traveled extensively," Mina said. "Though I daresay his mission here is the most vital journey of them all."

Seth cleared his throat again—it sounded more like a growl—but Mina didn't even spare him a glance. Hell. She'd vowed to do everything she could to help, hadn't she? But he sure didn't want this kind of help.

Walpole held Mina's gaze, evidently not caring where Seth had traveled or why. "Yes…well. A man might do well to explore closer to home."

Mina shook her head. "Yes, but Mr. Mayhew—"

"Every young man of spirit should see Ireland," Walpole said. "But the bogs make some snipe hunts frightfully treacherous."

"That so?" Seth said. "Why's that?"

Walpole spoke over his shoulder at him. "The bogs, man. Put a step wrong and you'll be good and gone." He chuckled smugly. "Unless you learn to throw yourself, er, sideways, of course."

Walpole's voice had lowered as he leaned toward Mina, like he was suggesting something *sideways* with her.

"And why's that?" Seth demanded.

Walpole's chuckles faded, and he turned to face him. "Because, Mister…Mayhew, is it? The bog can support the weight of a man if he's horizontal."

"Why's that?"

Mina was giving him a pointed, panicked stare, but this time Seth ignored *her.*

"*The peat*, Mr. Mayhew." Walpole smiled, but it looked strained. "And then, of course, you must learn the correct way to throw your gun off." He turned back around and covered Mina's hand with his own.

And Seth couldn't stop himself. "And why's that?"

Walpole's back stiffened. "Because the gun might—Mr. Mayhew, for the sake of variety, could you pose a question that doesn't begin with 'why'?"

"I suppose I can," Seth said.

"Excellent."

"How come you have to learn to throw your gun off?"

Walpole faced him. Seth returned the challenge in the man's eye. And doubled it. The gent blinked first and seemed to understand.

Because he took his hands off Mina.

Walpole turned his attention to Emma. "Miss Adams, I believe I see the refreshment table and feel a sudden need for a drink. Will you join me? If you are not"—he looked at Seth—"otherwise engaged?"

Emma's eyes were wide but she was quick to nod. "Yes, of course. Thank you."

Walpole shot him a dark look, offered Emma his arm, and left Seth alone with Mina.

Who wasn't looking happy with him, either.

Seth turned away because he was probably looking like a stubborn, pouting ass. It was damn stupid of him. She was trying to help. Mina wasn't even his to—

You have the sign.

He snorted a hot breath.

"You have quite an interest in Irish bogs," she said.

No, she wasn't happy. He shrugged. "I ask more questions than people expect."

"And why's that?"

Hell. He ground a clod of dirt under his boot. "Maybe because I don't look clever enough to be curious."

Nothing? He checked to see if she was looking at him. She was, but she wasn't one to huff or roll her eyes or screw her face up like most women after they'd gotten a little familiar with him. She wouldn't like him teasing her, either. Or trying to bluster away how he'd behaved. She took things seriously. Took him seriously, he supposed.

And he didn't know how to be with a woman like that. "Minnie—"

"*Mina.*"

"I don't need Walpole, and there wasn't any persuading him either, so you don't need to be behaving like that. I wouldn't object if you were using your wiles on me, as I'm aware I'm not to be encouraged, but not some third-rate bachelor like Walpole."

"Mr. Mayhew—"

"Call me Seth."

Her cheeks were turning that pretty peach color. "No matter your feeling for East India men, you must endeavor to secure their cooperation."

"I don't have any feeling for them, good or bad. But I don't need to see some gent behaving like he deserves you just because he bought his way onto the Company payroll, or he's got some connection that put him behind a desk wearing bespoke suits—"

She caught his wrist, and even roused as he was, that surprised him into looking down at her.

"Mr. Mayhew, you must be more deferential, even if that pains you. They are all too aware that you are more interesting and accomplished a man than they are. They will not like to help you if you remind them of that."

The hell? He stared at her, but she looked like she believed what she was saying. And before he could puzzle out her words, she let loose of his wrist, hiked up the hem of her skirt in a fist, and swept off to a group of her friends.

The woman wasn't any of his business anyway.

But she was right about helping Georgie. Why didn't he know what was right before doing everything wrong?

He doffed his hat to comb back his hair, and positioned it back on his head careful and straight. Mina was only half-right about those gents. They didn't like his sort; they never had—but they'd tolerate him so long as he remembered his place.

So it was damn stupid of him to always be forgetting it.

And now Mina was mad at him.

He stomped toward the hunters, but they kept company with the ladies. They'd not welcome him just then. He sorted the calling cards he'd collected and stuffed them deeper in his pockets. He'd call on every one of them tomorrow, but today he'd start with that gent in the agriculture department.

After wandering to watch the servants load the rifles and ready the dogs, the men began separating from the ladies and retrieving their guns from their bearers, making a big show of inspecting their weapons.

Except for Tom Grant, who was suddenly in a hustle to get to Seth.

"Walpole just hauled me through the coals over you," Tom said. "Don't count on any help from him."

"I know it."

"Why the devil—?"

"Because he was poaching Mina."

Tom's laugh was harsh, and the anger simmering under Seth's scalp erupted. "You'll be sorry if she chooses another."

Tom shut his eyes and held up his hands. "*All right.* The ladies are coming. Calm down your feelings."

"I'm thinking you're a little too calm, Tom." But Seth could say no more with Emma and Mina approaching.

"The hunt is about to start," Emma said in a voice already mourning all the fallen snipe.

Mina moved to stand beside Tom, and damned if Seth's stupid heart didn't sink lower.

The men veered into the dry rice paddy, cut low now that the growing season was done, and the ladies walked a little behind on higher ground. The dogs were let loose, the snipe took wing, and the first volley of shots was a waste. Not one bird was hit.

"I knew I wouldn't stop one," Tom mumbled.

"You're shooting too fast," Seth said. "Wait until the bird's higher in the sky and less scared, not twisting to evade a predator."

Walpole was listening and smirked at his words. "A surprising observation from a man with no gun."

"Never hunted for sport," Seth said, aware that everyone was suddenly listening. Including the agriculture gent.

"No?" Walpole handed his gun to his bearer to reload. "I'm rather unclear why you *are* here, then, Mr. Mayhew. Perhaps men of your situation are unaccustomed to pursuits of skill and concentration. Perhaps you are gratified only by more immoderate pastimes."

Seth clenched his teeth. He couldn't say anything to that. He wasn't exactly sure where the insult was in those words, but it was there all the same.

Walpole would like him to tug his forelock and retreat to the line of servants, but Seth found himself looking at Mina instead. Composed, capable, orderly-like Mina. And she looked right back at him like she shared every thought in his head.

And damned if that didn't make clear as crystal what an ass Walpole was.

The men moved quietly to their next position. The hunters stood and waited, and the dogs were released. The reeds rustled as the snipe exploded from their nests, whirling into the sky. Shots rang in his ears; the birds continued to climb—save for one that jerked oddly.

Walpole's bird.

"You winged her," Seth called to him.

"Why isn't she falling?" Walpole said.

"She's crippled," he said. "Finish her."

Walpole raised his second gun and then appeared to reconsider. "I'll not hit her now. It's getting near fifty yards. Look how she's flying."

The wounded snipe frantically dipped and rose in no pattern that could be predicted, and the men murmured in agreement, as the ladies whimpered with little sounds of sympathy.

"At least try," Seth hissed. But Walpole just flushed red, staring at the sky.

Hell. Seth reached for Tom's extra gun, raised the rifle to his shoulder, sighted the flailing bird, and shot it from the sky. The late boom silenced all the voices. Even the dogs turned in a confused circle, seeing the bird fall so far in the distance.

"Capital shot," a voice mumbled behind him. But no one else said a word.

Walpole shouldered his rifle, turned, and stomped off. The Company men pretended no notice of the departure and avoided looking at Seth at all.

Ah…damn. Of course they wouldn't. Walpole was one of them. And Seth wasn't but a laborer in a secondhand coat.

Mina frowned, for the bird or him, he couldn't tell. But she had a worried crease between her brows he didn't like at all.

Thomas gaped at him. "You said you never shot for sport."

"Not for sport," he muttered, handing Tom his gun. "I hunted plenty. On expedition, we had need of fresh game."

Birds were flushed once more but not one was hit, and the men quickly lost their enthusiasm for the shooting.

"Ladies," the stout man who'd addressed them earlier signaled for their attention. "Alas, the Indian snipe is dev-ilishly hard to hit." His eyes snagged on Seth but darted away. "So…shall we return to the picnic ground?"

The party headed back. Seth left Tom and Mina alone to their courting, and walked beside one gent after the next. But try as he might, there wasn't a man who swapped more than three words with him now. The man in agriculture didn't let him come within ten paces.

He shouldn't have bothered to come. It was clear he wasn't a Company man or a gentleman or even a soldier. The only way someone like him would get information would be to pay for it.

He prepared a plate and retreated from the party to sit alone on a hill overlooking the lake and began to eat.

"A lovely prospect, Mr. Mayhew."

Startled, Seth looked up as Mina kneeled gracefully to balance her plate and sit beside him. He wiped his mouth with a handkerchief and swallowed, but couldn't think of anything to say. She waved Tom and Emma over and they sat, too.

Confused, he stared at her but she pretended no notice. He looked back at his food. Mina wouldn't let him sit alone.

Damn me. A lady from the ground up.

No. A *defender.* That's what she was and what he'd seen the first time he looked at her. A lady who'd defend her friends against a mob of bachelors. And a sister from a strange, new world. And even a hulking six-foot-three explorer from a whole tribe of East India Company men.

A lady who chose a side. And she was on his. Somehow he knew that more than he knew anything else.

Wasn't much that shut his mouth, but gratitude must be one because he ate in silence as Mina, Tom, and Emma talked.

After a time, the voices of the party changed, grew faint.

"Appears the picnic is over." Tom rose and helped the ladies to their feet.

The carriages were being packed and the dogs shooed into their wagon. Seth stood and wiped the grass from his trousers. "I suppose we better—" He cut off at the sight of Tom whispering in Mina's ear.

Well. They were meant to be doing that. And it was about time Tom got on with it. Maybe Tom would settle their marriage tonight.

Seth slapped his hat on his thigh, pretending to knock the dust off it. "You three go on back without me." He started to plod down the side of the hill. "I got a ride back with a gent I spoke to after the hunt."

"Who?" Tom asked, stalling him from his escape.

"The man's got an interest in South America," he said. "He offered a seat in his carriage. Wants to hear about my time in Brazil."

Tom looked confused, but he nodded. Thankfully, he didn't press for a name. "Good. Let's hope he has some influence in the Company. I'll see you in the morning."

Tom and Emma headed to the carriages with the rest of the party. But Mina paused, that worried crease on her brow was back. "I didn't see you talk to anyone."

He waved her off. "Go on now, Minnie."

She started to leave, then turned back. "Will I... I *will* see you again, won't I?"

Seth smiled. *The little officer…still trying to keep her soldiers in rank and file.* "I'd not leave Bombay without saying good-bye to you."

Her face looked pale but maybe it was a trick of light. "Will you promise me?"

The soft words winged his heart and spun it. Just

like that little snipe. "I promise," he said quietly. "Go on now, Minnie. Tom's waiting."

Her hand clutched the pocket of her skirt. Seemed she did that when she wasn't sure about things.

"I'll see you again, I think," she said. "There's a zoo outing on the eleventh. Thomas has promised to come. You'll come, won't you?"

A tired sigh escaped him. "A zoo, is it?"

She nodded. "I'd like to see you."

And that was a direct hit. "I'll try, Minnie."

With a final plea in her brown eyes, she turned to catch up with her sister and Tom.

Seth walked toward some carriages and out of her view. Then he kept walking until he was hidden from everyone and found a boulder to sit on and wait. He wouldn't be asking anyone for a ride. There wasn't a man here who'd welcome him in his carriage while they were courting. Besides, nine miles was an easy distance when he was used to walking more than thirty a day on expedition. And the exercise would keep his mind quiet.

He couldn't think right now about how he didn't fit with any of these marrying men, or the mistakes he'd somehow made today. Or how maybe the only curse there really was, was one he'd brought on himself with every stupid choice he'd made. He couldn't think on that. Not now.

He couldn't think how he might not be enough to save Georgie.

Seven

"FOR AN ANIMAL THAT COULD CRUSH US, HE LOOKS friendly," Emma said.

The zoo elephant did indeed seem to be wearing a smile. He almost seemed to be winking at them.

Mina said nothing as she took in the sweet animal. As a social outing, the Bombay Zoological Gardens was a perversely fitting locale for the Company men to examine the female wildlife on display. The cages, the landscaping, the wide promenade—a picturesque habitat for the unclaimed venture girls.

Mina frowned seeing the small group of ladies and Company men strolling ahead of them. Such a small group of ladies now. Their population was rapidly declining. Facing extinction, actually.

The elephant nodded his ponderous head as if agreeing.

"He is a dear thing, isn't he?" Mina said. "So placid and amiable. And mammoth. The drawings in the *Illustrated News* hardly did justice to his size."

A moment of contemplative silence passed before Emma said, "I wonder how Mr. Mayhew is faring."

Mina smiled, squeezing Emma's hand. "If Mr. Mayhew *were* an animal, he might be an elephant."

"While my Colin Rivers would be that neckless hyena," Emma said. "The one with the mange."

Mina eyed her sister. "I had not wanted to broach the subject of Mr. Rivers but—"

"Then why are you?"

She started carefully. "You threw your hairbrush at the mirror this morning."

Emma shrugged. "My hair has been impossible. The humidity is provoking."

"And the hotel deskman?"

"He knows how anxious I am. Why must I queue each and every time to inquire after my letters?"

"Because—"

"And why *are* you broaching the matter? *You* are not yet engaged and it's been eight days. You might keep your concern for your own marriage."

Her own—That stung, but Mina kept her tongue between her teeth. Emma knew very well matters were not as simple as all that. Not when so much hinged on the absent Colin Rivers.

But of all her sisters, Emma had the quickest temper—

"I'm sorry," Emma mumbled. "I'm horrid."

And the shortest-lived one. "No, you're distressed."

Emma swatted at the netting of her hat. "What if he does not come, Mina?"

Swallowing the usual panic that question bred, Mina kept her voice calm. "Then I will speak to Thomas."

"He won't want his wife's sister in their home."

"Then we begin again, that's all. We find two new bachelors living in the same district."

"But if Mr. Rivers—"

"We must give him a reasonable amount of time, and no longer."

"A month more?"

Poor Emma. She cared for her letter-writing beau more than she would admit. "A fortnight, I think."

Emma fell silent, her gaze on the ladies strolling with the Company men ahead of them. "I know you're right. The best bachelors have already been claimed. I just wonder… Mr. Rivers *did* pay my bond to sail. And we are contracted to marry. Is a fortnight a fair amount of time?"

"Could you bear to wait longer?"

"No…I suppose not," Emma said quietly.

"And we cannot afford to wait, Emma." Mina didn't want to frighten her younger sister, so she said this as lightly and as simply as she could. That always seemed to work best.

A quiet moment passed before Emma spoke. "I heard Mr. Rivers sent his last communication from a post in the Upper Mekong River Valley."

Surprised, Mina looked at her sister. "Who told you that?"

"Alice. Yesterday, Sarah said that Vicky heard the news from the wife of a director."

"How long ago was the letter sent?"

"Months ago. He's drawn funds from his accounts since, but no one has seen or heard from him." Emma stared at the ground. "Do you think something's wrong, Mina? They tell me that region is dangerous, the borderland between Tibet and China."

The borderland…where the massacre occurred.

Where Georgiana Mayhew had traveled. "I don't know, Emma."

"He did write lovely letters," Emma said softly.

Mina linked arms with her sister.

"Mina." Emma tugged her arm to gain her attention. "What's the difference between an Indian elephant and an African one?"

"I don't know."

"About three thousand miles."

Mina stared at Emma. "Goodness. Was that a joke?"

Emma's blue eyes glinted with the faintest humor—a valiant humor. She hugged Emma's arm. They *would* stay together. She had not sailed all this way to abandon another sister.

They continued their walk, slowly pacing after their party as they neared the monkey cages.

Mina checked her timepiece. Where was Thomas?

"He's just late," Emma said, guessing her thoughts. "Thomas has much to do with Mr. Mayhew."

"Yes." Would Thomas bring Mr. Mayhew? Did she want him to? Part of her wished to believe she and Thomas would be engaged by now without the distraction of Seth Mayhew. That Thomas's attention would be hers, and he would promise to shelter Emma because there would be such an understanding between them that there would be no need for her to plead for her sister.

And yet the other part desperately wanted a happy ending for Mr. Mayhew and for Georgiana.

A happy ending for them all.

"I think that is why Thomas has not made his offer," Emma continued. "He knows he has neglected you these first days."

"Perhaps it's better he has not. Not without Colin Rivers secured."

"I think that makes him a very superior sort of gentleman, Mina, allowing us this time to wait."

She wasn't at all convinced of his motivation. "Yes, he's very"—*what?*—"pragmatic."

Emma frowned but smoothed her countenance immediately. "Then he is perfect for you. Two such pragmatic, managing people—"

"I'm not managing."

"—it hardly seems fair. You ought to marry a complete wastrel and rehabilitate him."

"And if our children resemble the wastrel?"

"Then you will rehabilitate them, too. You always did take care of everyone. Not that Thomas will ever need such help."

The words struck Mina cold. That was true. She would be a resourceful, economical wife.

To a man who required one.

They wandered nearer the monkey exhibit, lingering behind their friends who strolled with Company men. Would the ladies remember to ask after Georgiana Mayhew today? She would have to remind them again. Perhaps she might meet some of the gentlemen herself?

"You *do* like him, don't you, Mina?"

"Yes, of course. Mr. Mayhew is very likable."

Emma slowed her step. "I was speaking of Thomas."

Oh…stupid. "Yes, of course. I like Thomas as well."

Emma raised a brow and waited.

Well, what matter if she knew? Mina sighed. "It is just…sometimes I have the strangest feeling with Thomas. He doesn't seem willing to take me into his confidence at all. It's as if he were already claimed by another." She reached for the pebble in her pocket, the stone's smooth contour so familiar. "If we wed, we need to be friends, companions. It doesn't matter if he loves me but—"

"*Mina!*"

Emma's admonishment was immediate, but there was no conviction behind it. And that broke Mina's heart. Because Emma knew it was the truth.

"We left our sisters, Emma. Our home. Love doesn't matter." She squeezed Emma's arm. "We learned that dearly from Mary, didn't we?"

Emma's eyes clouded with sadness. Ahead, the ladies giggled at something one of the gentlemen said, and Emma leveled her chin. "One week, Mina. Not two."

Mina understood. There was only ever one man on Emma's mind—for all the turmoil he was causing. Colin Rivers had one week to reach Bombay.

Tears pricked her eyes and she turned to hide her face. Emma might possess the quickest temper in the family, but she also possessed the most rigid code of right and wrong. Even if Mr. Rivers returned before Wednesday next, she might never forgive him this offense.

"India is a large country," Emma said. "Full of Englishmen desperate for English brides. Whomever one of us chooses, wherever he lives, there will be an available gentleman for the other."

"Yes." Everything will be all right. Mina knew that.

When she was feeling brave, she even believed that.

"We are falling behind." Emma nudged her forward.

"Yes—" She cut off at the sight of two men walking toward them. Thomas and Mr. Mayhew. The men had their heads together as they approached, their expressions serious. Still in the midst of their planning, then. Recognizing them in their hats would have been difficult if not for Mr. Mayhew's broad shoulders and long, easy stride.

Thomas wore a crisp pith helmet that was the very picture of British India. And Mr. Mayhew, in his safari hat and slim, low-slung trousers—*Oh, honestly*. She ought to be able to *look* at the man without her body heating so stupidly.

But evidently she *had* wanted Thomas to bring Mr. Mayhew. She'd had no assurance he would come, and as invulnerable as he appeared, not knowing what his sister might be enduring had to be awful.

Mina shook off her reverie and smiled at Thomas, her future husband—God willing.

"Good afternoon, Mina." Thomas nodded to Emma. "Emma."

"I'm so pleased you were able to join us," Mina said. Mr. Mayhew doffed his hat and stood back, a small smile on his lips. "And how have you been, Mr. Mayhew?"

"Sadder than the tears of a puppy without the sight of you, Miss Mina."

Her cheeks warmed, but in her relief in seeing him, she didn't mind. "Really, Mr. Mayhew, you will swell my head. You must stop your flattery."

"Yes, Mayhew," Thomas said dryly. "*Stop*."

Mr. Mayhew nodded to Emma. "Miss Emma, aren't you looking well?"

Emma beamed, her cheeks blushing. "Oh, thank you, Mr. May—"

"What's this little monkey, then?" Mr. Mayhew turned to peer into the cage. "A gray langur? Looks like my Uncle Fred except his side-whiskers are a bit tidier. The monkey's, I mean."

Emma deflated without a better compliment of her own.

No, Mina did not understand men at all. Emma was the most beautiful of all her sisters. Mr. Mayhew's flirtation was as disordered as his conversation. And already, he was studying the party of Company men.

"Tom, know any of the gents up there?" he asked.

A look of surprise flashed across Thomas's face. "The one with the beard. Turnbull's his name. He's usually in Calcutta. He's secretary to the agriculture board of directors."

"An important gentleman, then," Mina said.

"He'd have access to information of Georgiana's crew." Thomas held Seth's eye. "We were in Calcutta together for that unpleasant bit of time. I'm not the man to make an introduction."

Confused, Mina waited for an explanation, but Mr. Mayhew simply nodded, rocking on his heels. The man seemed to constantly be in motion. He dipped his head down to hers. "Who's that lady with him, Miss Mina?"

A warm fragrance of shaving soap enveloped her. He really had to stop talking in her ear like this. "That is Amelia Radcliffe. She knows of Georgiana. She was at the Byculla Club that night."

He nodded, his eyes sharp and intent on the

company ahead, and she tensed with excitement for his opportunity. But when he turned to meet her gaze, his sea-green eyes crinkled warmly and all he said was, "That hat is awfully becoming on you, Minnie."

The words were too low for anyone else to hear but she blushed to the roots of her hair. "You are a terrible flirt, Mr. Mayhew," she whispered.

He grinned and straightened from her, and she concentrated on cooling her heated face—which was impossible, as he wouldn't look away. "Emma and I visited the shops on Rampart Row this morning. Our *sola topees*, that is what they call sun hats here, were recommended. As were these tinted glasses for the sun."

"But how will I see those pretty brown eyes?"

"Look, Seth, a baboon," Thomas said dryly.

Mr. Mayhew winked at her. "Got no time for monkeys, Tom." And without another word, he fitted his hat and strode in the direction of the Company men.

Thomas wiped a weary hand over his face. That *was* a habit of his, then.

"Do you think Mr. Turnbull might help?" she asked.

Tom sighed. "I'm not hopeful."

"But how could anyone refuse to help him?" Emma said, sounding decidedly smitten.

"He has no real connections," Thomas said, not understanding that was meant as a rhetorical question. Absently, he offered Mina his arm, and she took it with a smile that he did not notice. "And worst of all, many Company men have secured their brides in the days since the *shikar* and feel no need to honor their promises to lend aid."

It took her a moment to comprehend, then anger spiked in her. "*Who* has not?"

Thomas's brows rose with mild amusement at the question. "Shall I provide a list?"

"A list?" she breathed in horror. How could Thomas smile at a time like this? "There are so many?"

"Well—"

"Then, yes, a list would serve," she said. "Emma and I can inform their fiancées of their conduct and inconstancy."

"Indeed." Emma huffed. "Are they men, or are they weathercocks?"

"Well…uh," Thomas stammered in the face of two, suddenly indignant women. "I suppose I could write up that list."

"*Today*, Thomas," Emma demanded pointedly.

"If you please," Mina added, in apology for Emma's passion.

"Yes, of course," he murmured.

Frustration simmered just beneath her skin. Thomas should not be so cavalier. And those so-called gentlemen…she would never understand men.

"Mayhew's made progress elsewhere," Thomas said, his tone placating. "He's been interviewing many of the locals who've accompanied British and French expeditions before. He's secured quite an impressive crew if the day comes to leave India."

Mina tensed. "Could that happen soon?"

"There is not much more we—*he*—can accomplish in Bombay." Thomas looked straight ahead.

We.

The plummet of her stomach broke Mina's stride.

She gripped the pebble in her skirt pocket till the rough edges left her palm throbbing.

Coward! Thomas did not *say* he was leaving.

But it was time. She must speak to him today about Emma, about their future, as it seemed unlikely he ever would. She notched her chin higher.

They strolled in silence behind Mr. Mayhew as he paced beside Amelia. He flashed his smile at the lady, and she dipped her head subtly. But the quick turn of Amelia's head invited no familiarity and Mr. Mayhew did not press. He took off his hat and raked a hand through his hair, doggedly trailing the men who ignored him.

Horrid, *horrid* East India men.

Her heart ached for him, for herself, for Emma, but she could not afford to act defeated. Thomas was the man she needed to marry. Especially if Colin Rivers returned.

She forced her gaze back to him and smiled. "Have you ever seen a rhinoceros, Thomas? Emma and I laughed because—"

"*No,*" Thomas groaned.

Mina stiffened at the blunt word, but Thomas's attention was not on her. Mr. Mayhew had sidled up to Secretary Turnbull, who was pointing out the baby warthogs to Amelia.

Mr. Mayhew leaned on the railing in front of the cages, and crossed an ankle behind him. The wide vee of his back and muscled backside quickly caught the admiring glances of the women and stirred the men into all manner of fidgety posturing.

Oh no. Masculine wiles.

Poor Mr. Mayhew. He really had no idea how to conduct himself with this company.

Mr. Mayhew grinned and said something to Secretary Turnbull, but the man merely arched a superior brow and turned his back.

Vile man. Why did Thomas not *do* something? Why didn't Amelia?

As if hearing her silent scold, Amelia whispered in her gentleman's ear. He patted Amelia's hand and then turned to Mr. Mayhew. The men shook hands and wandered a few feet to converse. Thank goodness. Perhaps there would be help today after all.

"Forgive me, Mina." Thomas smiled down at her, his attention restored. "I was distracted."

She dragged her gaze from the scene and focused on Thomas. She smiled into her own reflection in his spectacles.

They walked and talked. The conversation was easy, but not at all one of intimate acquaintance. Ahead, Mr. Mayhew finished his discussion with Secretary Turnbull, but when he saw her and Thomas walking arm in arm, he pulled low the brim of his hat and turned, sauntering in front of them.

Would he not rejoin them?

"…the rainy season is far worse in the south," Thomas said.

"I see," she murmured stupidly, unable to think of anything to say. Thomas would not like a wife with no conversation. But this was unnatural. Mr. Mayhew's search for Georgiana was of vital importance and they spoke of the weather.

The cluster of men and ladies ahead diverged from

the cages, their attention caught by a crowd forming a large circle.

"Where is everyone going?" Emma asked.

"Appears there is an entertainment about to begin," Thomas said.

They approached the ring of spectators and Mina jerked with surprise. An Indian lion was crouched and pulling from his handler's chain. A low growl sounded from the animal's lowered head, but the poor creature didn't move. It almost seemed frightened.

A crack in the air made her heart leap into her throat. The handler's whip swung a second time but she was no more prepared for the sound. The lion reared back on its hind legs and roared, startling the onlookers.

But the lion's teeth looked odd. And his paws swiped at his own collar rather than the whip. The crowd gasped, but an uncomfortable relief seemed to settle over them at the lion's show of spirit.

"This is horrible." Emma started forward but stopped, knowing better than to distract the handler at the other end of the dangerous animal.

Thomas's face was grim, and Emma turned her back. Mina's own body trembled with disgust but Mr. Mayhew…

Mr. Mayhew didn't look away. He stood with his arms crossed over his chest, his face stony. She might have thought him disinterested if his gloves weren't stretched taut over his knuckles.

The handler bowed, the lion dropped its head, appearing resigned to its captivity, and the crowd applauded. Mr. Mayhew's face, even in the shade of his hat, had turned pale. The next instant, he stalked off and disappeared around the corner.

Her heart pulsed sickly in her chest. What was the matter?

She looked to Thomas and Emma, but they hadn't seen him leave. She mustn't—she *shouldn't* worry. She had to let him alone, not jeopardize her match, her future—"Thomas?"

His name spilled from her lips before she fully knew what she meant to say. His brows rose in question, and she swallowed against the block in her throat.

"Mr. Mayhew has left," she said. "Would you… might you go after him and see that he is all right?"

Thomas searched the crowd.

"No, he's gone. In that direction." She pointed, but Thomas only looked down at her.

"He must have remembered an errand, Mina."

"He looked upset."

"I'm sure he's fine," Thomas said. "Mayhew's not a man sensitive to upset, and he has much on his mind."

Frustration spiked in her. "Yes. He does." She willed him to see the plea in her eyes. Would he not help? Even for her sake? Even after eight days of this stupid, *interminable* waiting for Colin Rivers, for him, for some…for some *reassurance*?

But she did not have the power to command him, as a woman loved might have. Her heart sank. "I…I would like to be sure."

But Thomas's stare was predictably, horribly unmoved.

She was so tired of waiting. Tired of pretending any of this was normal. Tired of feeling so…*alone* in this. She withdrew her hand from his arm. "Mr. Mayhew has shown me only kindness and encouragement from my first moments in Bombay. I feel I owe him the same."

"Mina—"

"I'll return directly. Please stay with Emma." And before Thomas could say another word, she hurried to find Mr. Mayhew.

God, was this a mistake?

The slow-moving crowd hindered her search at every turn but no one seemed to notice her chase. *There.* Mr. Mayhew stood again near the monkey cages, his arm braced against the trunk of a tree. He stared at the ground but the nearer she drew, the more she doubted he saw anything at all.

"Mr. Mayhew?"

He lifted his head. "Minnie?" He looked behind her. "Where's Tom?"

"Are you leaving?"

The realization she was alone seemed to irritate him. "No, I was…" He shoved off the tree and, in two long strides, was beside her and taking her elbow. "I'll walk you back. Tom'll be wanting you."

No he doesn't—

He steered her around, his grip gentle but firm. Obediently, she walked with him but the heaviest sadness descended on her heart, slowing her feet. "I didn't like how they chained that lion," she said quietly.

His stride faltered and he came to a stop. But he kept his face turned from her. "Did you see what they did to him?"

As low as his words were, she had to strain to hear him. "The chain?"

"They filed down his fangs and took out his claws."

Her stomach lurched before she could blank the picture from her mind. "I didn't know they did such things."

"They do as they please." His voice was nearly a growl. He unclenched the grip he had on her. "And he has to let them. A beast wouldn't know better, so they think it don't matter."

"Mr. Mayhew—"

"They take away everything. Anything they can take, they'll take. But you don't make it so he can't protect his family or provide—you don't take that away. *It's damn—!*"

The words quit abruptly but the roar reverberated through her. His broad chest heaved and his muscled arms ended in two massive fists.

But her feet moved toward him anyway.

He jerked when she drew close but stood still. The only movement in his body was the flicker of a muscle in his jaw. "I don't—" He clenched his eyes shut. "Sorry, Minnie, I don't mean to be using that language with you."

"I know," she whispered. His fist was large and heavy so she held it with both hands. And that was all she could do. Because she *was* a coward. She couldn't hold him or dare comfort him with anything more, because she was a coward and she couldn't lose Thomas and yet…

And yet she'd followed him here.

His fist eased open between her hands, but he didn't let her go. His fingers laced through hers and held tight. The strength and the warmth in his hand might have been wrapped around her heart. She waited, unable to move. Unwilling to move. Beneath the shadow of his hat, his eyes were closed and his chest rose with slow breaths. Once…twice…three times—

A langur monkey shrieked and his eyes flew open. He pulled his hand from hers and rubbed his brow.

"It's all right," she whispered.

He huffed an embarrassed laugh. "Sorry, I shouldn't…" His eyes followed the restless monkeys, a grim smile on his lips. "There's monkeys and there's gentlemen, and there's them in-between."

"Don't say that!" She caught his hand and hugged it against her breast, and his brows crashed down in confusion.

"Minnie—?"

"You have no right to say that. And I am *not* laughing."

A tempest darkened his face, his ocean eyes fathomless. "Then you're the only one." With his hand held against her, all it took was a curling flex of his arm and she was pulled to his body.

"Maybe this'll make you laugh." His eyes crinkled, but she didn't like them this way. "You want to know what Turnbull said to me back there? He said he'd spare some time for me when he's back from his wedding trip. In *April*. If he wasn't busy, if there wasn't another matter claiming his attention. *That* made me laugh."

"I can speak to Amelia—"

"*Another matter*—like Georgie wasn't any sort of matter at all. What sort of man would say that? Like my sister didn't matter? How am I supposed to wait—?"

"*You're not alone here!*"

He blinked, and the storm in his eyes broke. Hot pants of breath laved her face, but his hard wrist relaxed.

She didn't know why she said that, but the words would not be held back. "You are not alone, Mr. Mayhew," she said softly. "Please don't ever feel you are alone in this, that there is no help. I'm with you."

His eyes drifted to her chest as if suddenly aware she held his hand pressed against her.

"And…and Thomas and Emma, too." Her voice shook. "We're all--"

Slowly, he spread his fingers open, over her breast, and her nerves tightened—but his fingers didn't linger. They slid higher, brushing her collarbone, until his palm flattened against her. On her heartbeat.

"Mr. Mayhew—"

"*Seth.*" He raised his eyes from his hand, from her heart, and she was caught by the plea in them. "My name's Seth, Minnie."

The need in his deep voice—undemanding but raw and deep—sent a tremor through her. It was the same need mirrored in her own heart. For him.

For him, and not Thomas.

The instant the thought crossed her mind, he saw it. Whatever showed—betrayal or hopelessness or wanting—he saw it. And it terrified her, because the storm in his eyes raged to life again.

She should move. Her heart was pounding—he would feel that. "We should return—" But her step back was denied by a large hand on her back. He pressed her close, their hands flattened between them. His heartbeat hammered against her now.

"Miss W. Adams," he murmured. He angled lower,

dipping beneath the brim of her hat, his lips hovering at her brow. He nuzzled her hair and breathed deep, and that slow smile bloomed across her temple. "Why are you on my side?"

The bristle of his whiskers pricked her cheek and it was the only sensation she could name. Her head was heavy, swimming. His lips moved closer, slowly, softly, until her eyelids fluttered shut against the sight of him. Warm lips pressed the corner of her mouth. And lingered.

Her heart pounded. Or was it his? Held tight against his chest, his size, his heat and strength overwhelmed. And his mouth was crowding closer.

A small, strangled gasp escaped her and his lips parted, but not to cover hers. They shared the warm, wet air between them, intimate and perfect and dizzying.

It was not a kiss…not a kiss…

It was more.

His hand slid higher to cradle her neck. "Minnie…"

His voice rumbled deep in her core. Even pressed against him, she strained to feel more. The hard ridge of his hip, the lean stomach, the powerful thighs. All of her vibrated deep and low with a sort of electricity.

She clutched the back of his coat, the fabric stretching over his hard back. He was so hard all over—

He moaned, "God, Minnie."

And his lips covered hers. A strong tongue pushed past her lips and tasted her, savored her. His arms tightened and his kiss deepened. The possession so complete, so *right*, her body swayed. Like on the ship…on the sea…and Seth had the sign—

Her lids blinked open. Seth. Not Thomas, not…

The ground rushed back under her feet, steady and solid. Seth's hand tightened on her neck with a low, desperate sound. His kiss lightened, lifted, until his mouth hovered and their panting breath mingled.

Seth…this was Seth. Ocean eyes. They could be so blue—

There was some question in his eyes, but she was frozen. He turned his head. "I… That's enough," he rasped, his voice low and gravelly.

His body retreated so suddenly, she swayed and reached for balance. He caught her arm and pulled it through his, and then they were moving in the direction she had come from. The air cooled her body, and she hated it. She wanted his arms.

She stumbled on the pavement, only then realizing how she was hurrying to keep up with him. "Mr. Mayhew?" But he stared straight ahead. Was he angry? Was he—?

That's enough.

Shame flooded her. He had been angry and anguished over Georgiana. And no one had helped him; she had not helped him.

"I'm sorry," she breathed. "I did not—"

But his arm slipped from beneath hers, and she sailed forward without him, toward Thomas and Emma, where they stood with the group. She swung around and instinctively moved to follow—

"Mina?"

She froze at Thomas's voice. Mr. Mayhew disappeared around the corner. She breathed deep and licked her lips, soft and tingling from the kiss.

Her first kiss.

She could not think of that now. Steeling herself, she turned. Thomas and Emma watched her with puzzled looks.

"What was the matter?" Thomas asked.

The matter? "I…" She averted her eyes. "Mr. Mayhew was feeling unwell."

Thomas said nothing and she forced herself to meet his eye. Her face would be flushed, but there was no help for it. She steadied her voice. "I was worried, with the strain he is under. And all that's new."

Thomas tilted his head, his eyes masked by the glare of his spectacles. "You needn't worry so. I'll be with him. Tonight and tomorrow and every day until matters are sorted." After a moment, he approached and offered his arm. "You are softhearted, Mina, but Mayhew would tell you himself: he's an extremely resilient man."

No, not so resilient. But Seth *did* have Thomas. He wasn't alone, not really. And she…she would do all that she safely could.

And she would not think how small that sounded.

Emma's face was wan and confused, and Mina nodded with what she hoped was reassurance. She would not forget again—not *risk* again. They were no more than jetsam on the sea. Alone and vulnerable until claimed by a husband.

Other winds may propel her toward Mr. Mayhew, but Thomas was the man she had sailed to marry.

Starting now, she would correct her course.

Goddamn it, what the hell was he doing?

Seth couldn't leave the zoo fast enough, or far

enough, behind him. A narrow alley weaved to his left, and he turned down it blindly.

Why the hell was he kissing Mina? Kissing her when she had another man waiting? Why did he want her? How was that supposed to help Georgie? How the hell was he going to find her without help from East India? Without any goddamn help, he couldn't, he wouldn't find—

The thought slammed him like a club to the gut. Bent double, he struggled to get air into his lungs. *Christ, Georgie, I'm sorry. I'm so sorry. Just stay alive. I'm coming, I swear it.*

His lungs were burning. Why couldn't he breathe? *Stay alive, Georgie.*

He'd made a little progress today. Secretary Turnbull... They'd been introduced. He'd said he was willing to meet. But not in April. They'd meet tomorrow—he'd try to meet him tomorrow. It wouldn't be too late.

He slammed his fist into his thigh—*it couldn't be too late*—and again, and again. Anything to stop all the damn questions in his head—

You're not alone here...

Mina.

You are not alone.

The memory of her voice slowed his thoughts, sorted them. Seth's body, his brain, clung to her. The soft, warm body fitted against his, and the beat of her heart under his palm. The smell of her perfume. She smelled like roses, like a garden in summer. She was— Christ, she was sweet. She'd tasted so sweet.

She'd come looking for him, worried for him. Like a wife would...

His hands fisted the fabric of his trousers where they rested on his thighs. A wife wasn't any of his business. He pushed up and stood straight, pacing forward, one foot in front of the other.

Mina wouldn't think too long on it. It hadn't been a long kiss. He'd wanted to kiss her longer, *could've* kissed her longer, but she'd changed. Her body went stiff.

Shame sizzled under all the other regrets he was feeling. She had gone all stiff in his arms. No, it hadn't been much of a kiss. Maybe it was barely a kiss to her.

Except it was like no kiss he'd ever had. He'd had damn few in his life, though.

A young boy hurried toward him, his teeth dazzling and his black eyes shiny as Whitby jet. Seth slowed his step. "Hello there, lad."

"Memsahib, you are like *Bali*, like *Mahabali*." His hopeful smile widened, even as his palm opened and hovered under Seth's nose.

Seth shook his head and despite everything, despite his blood still coursing hot in his veins, he chuckled at the boy's beaming face. It was either that or cry. The lad's clothes were rags.

"*Mahabali*, is it?" He fished in his pocket for a few coppers and handed them over. Then added an *anna*. "I'll pretend that's some sort of compliment as I don't know any different."

The boy beamed, shaking the fist that held the coins in the air. "Thank you, *sahib*, thank you. You are *Mahabali*."

"That's all right, lad."

The boy turned and dashed off on his thin legs.

"It's all right," he breathed, though no one was listening.

Seth followed and found himself on a long, bustling street teeming with mules, buggies, and a horse-drawn omnibus. The boy wasn't anywhere to be seen. Market stalls stretched along either side, offering live chickens and vegetables, and red and orange and yellow spices, and copper pots and calico and khaki.

And everywhere he looked in the bazaar, women and children crouched on the ground, ignored by everyone, even the stray dogs. Most didn't bother to find themselves a bit of shade, but sat under the full force of the sun.

Christ, Bombay might have been England. The England he knew, anyway—where men abandoned their families.

Mina had a man that would take care of her. Hell, what was he thinking, kissing her? If Tom had seen…

Seth heaved a centering breath. It was past time he let Mina Adams alone. He'd already lost his mum and hadn't kept Georgie safe. He had no business being alone with Mina, or wanting her.

He wasn't a man that took care of things.

Eight

"APPEARS THE MAIL SHIPS ARE IN." THOMAS GESTURED toward the port beyond the window, and Mina obligingly took in the familiar view. From her seat in the restaurant, she could see only the towering masts of the clipper ships. The carriages lining the street blocked any sight of the sea.

"Yes, Apollo Bunder is such a bustling port," she murmured.

Emma didn't look up from her lunch. "And we see so much of it every day."

"I do like the curry here." Thomas smiled politely.

Mina was beginning to rather dislike that particular smile.

"That's because you're English," Emma said. "You know all these restaurants lining the port are the most accommodating to English palates. Mina and I take nearly every breakfast, tiffin, and supper here, with that same view every day."

Mina barely attended the conversation. Today, it seemed she could not without her throat squeezing shut and dread whipping her heart to racing.

Fourteen days since she and Emma had arrived—
"Are you not hungry, Mina?"

Her head jerked up at Thomas's solicitous inquiry.
Automatically, she reached for her napkin. "Yes, indeed."
She returned his polite smile with one of her own.

Fourteen days, and no Colin Rivers. And no offer
from Thomas.

Fourteen days. And each time she'd broached the
topic with Thomas, he assured her there was no need
to rush matters. No *need*. She had been so stunned by
his deflection, she had only managed to nod. And the
second time, panic stilted her words. And the third
time he put her off…

The third time had been humiliating.

The hand in her lap clenched the pebble in her
skirt pocket with painful force. Such a *gentlemen*. So
reserved. Speaking of restaurants and mail ships and the
weather as if she were merely a tourist. There was still
one topic they could speak of without any discomfort,
so she pounced upon it. "Thomas, did you tell Mr.
Mayhew one o'clock?"

He checked his timepiece. "I did. Though he'll
likely be late."

"Yes, Emma and I are often lost in Bombay."

"Mayhew doesn't get lost. He gets friends. His
sense of direction is excellent from his years of survey-
ing unmapped terrains. He just can't seem to walk a
city block without getting drawn into conversation. I
don't know why—the man's Hindustani is appalling.
But the man has a passion for conversation. He could
talk the hind legs off a donkey."

She smiled through her strained nerves and straightened

the letters she had collected from her friends and their gentlemen, all promising information on Georgiana. The number of letters had surprised Thomas, but she and Emma had worked hard to enlist the venture girls to press their suitors. "I'm so eager to know if there is something useful here. I hope he hurries."

And she had missed him so much more than she'd expected. And wanted.

A memory of his kiss flashed to mind and sparked a blaze beneath her skin before she could banish it. Did he regret kissing her, seeing how affected she had been? Would a flirt give kisses freely and expect them to be received in kind? Her red face would not do, in any case.

"We have not seen Mr. Mayhew since our visit to the zoo last week," Emma said. "Is he well?"

"Tolerably, I think," Thomas said.

And that was all he offered. Mina swallowed a gasp of frustration. "And there has been no information at all from the Company?" she prompted.

"Very little from the Company." Thomas frowned. "Unfortunately, we posted signs in the marketplace with a reward for information. More money than most of the local people see in a half-year's work. Seth paid a great deal of money for information, much of it false. It was not the best thinking."

She stiffened in her seat. "It is not Mr. Mayhew's fault that there are unscrupulous people in the world."

"No, Mina, I blame myself as well for that decision. But Mayhew is increasingly desperate. I'm afraid he may start acting more rashly, and his funds are dwindling."

Mina fidgeted with her *chapati*. She really had no appetite.

A tall shadow darkened the door, and her heart jolted in her breast. Mr. Mayhew swept off his hat and ducked inside. It seemed he never allowed her time to brace for his presence. Standing beside the table, his hips were level with her eyes, so she had to look a long way up to see his face. And those sea-green eyes.

"Hello, Miss Mina." He nodded to her but his eyes darted away. "Miss Emma, Tom." He didn't sit, his hands worrying the brim of his hat.

"Sit down, Mayhew," Thomas said. "I can't imagine you're not hungry. They have a *pav bhaji* here you'll like. You can eat it like a sandwich."

"We have that appointment at the registry office."

"They're not open for an hour. Sit down."

He hesitated a moment before he sat. His fingers drummed the table. The skin across his cheekbones was taut, reddened by the sun. And there were new lines at the corners of his eyes.

"I am so glad to see you, Mr. Mayhew," she said. "You are often in our thoughts."

His fingers drummed faster and he faced her with a half smile that didn't touch his eyes. His gaze was too restless to meet hers. "Thank you, Miss Mina. You're in mine as well."

Look at me. Or…flirt with me—anything.

But he didn't flirt. He didn't say a word. The search must not be going well at all.

Mayhew is increasingly desperate—

She pushed the letters on the table toward him. After all that Thomas and Mr. Mayhew had done, what help could come from any of the venture girls? "Some of the ladies have collected letters for you, Mr. Mayhew."

Their eyes latched again for an instant before he reached for the letters. "Would you mind if I…?"

"Of course not."

He cracked open the first letter and began to read. A weighty silence descended on the table.

"I'll order you *pav bhaji*, shall I?" Thomas said.

Mr. Mayhew frowned, his eyes on his letter. "Ay? No, Tom. No thank you."

"You've never refused a meal with me." Thomas sighed. "No one is fooled into thinking you know how to eat here. Your system of pointing at any odd food from the street vendors will get you in trouble one day."

Frustration and fear filled Mina at the thought. He'd lost weight; his cheeks were hollow.

"Shall we order him something?" Mina whispered in Thomas's ear, so as not to interfere with Mr. Mayhew's reading. "He looks thin."

Thomas studied him with a frown. "I suppose I hadn't noticed—"

Seth lowered one of the letters he'd been reading. "This one says the Milford crew is headed to Calcutta. They're expected there by the sixth of January." His eyes met hers and, at last, a real smile stretched across his lips. "The last we heard they were still in interior China and they hadn't surfaced for months."

The clamp on her heart eased. "It's helpful information, then?"

His eyes were bright. "If Georgiana's with them, that's where she'll be." He combed a large hand through his hair. "It's the best tip we've received." He looked at Tom. "The sixth—that's just under three weeks. How do we get to Calcutta?"

Mina's smile faded. He was leaving.

And Thomas would leave with him.

"Well…" Thomas fidgeted with a letter. "We might take a bullock train as far as Aurangabad. From there, a carriage has to be hired to Sambalpur. There used to be a coach to Kharagphur and we could likely hire a seat."

Thomas wasn't looking at her—no, he *wouldn't* look at her.

"And from Kharagphur?" Mr. Mayhew prodded. Thomas and Mr. Mayhew passed some sort of silent communication.

Mr. Mayhew looked out the window to the street, then pushed to his feet abruptly. "Excuse us, ladies. I'm needing to speak to Tom outside a moment."

Mina didn't even nod. Her eyes followed the men as they walked out the door but, in truth, she saw nothing.

She was making a new plan.

❦

"Marry the woman, settle her with her sister, and let's go." A fiery blade twisted in Seth's gut. "What's taking you so damn long anyway?"

"We've not left yet. I told you I wouldn't leave Bombay until—"

"I know what you told me. But I need your help to get to Calcutta, and I sure as hell won't risk missing the crew on account of your not settling matters with Minnie."

"That's none of your—"

"It *is* my business. I"—*I had the sign*—"I've been patient, Tom, and reasonable, when I don't need to be."

Tom took off his spectacles and rubbed his eyes. "It's only been two weeks. It's not fair to her. Rivers hasn't shown for Emma. I promised her a choice."

"She's chosen you!" The force of his voice propelled Tom a step back. "Damn it, Tom. Do you see her seeking out other men? She's been loyal to you, even when she's helping me. You'll not find another better than her. Christ, if it were me, I'd have married her the second I saw her."

Tom let out a breath that seemed to shrink an inch off him. "She's not—"

"Not what?" he growled.

Tom put on his spectacles and stared grimly at the ocean.

The hell? What man wouldn't want her unless... "Are you not inclined to women?"

Tom's head snapped around. "*What?*"

"Women? Do you not like women?"

Tom blinked. "No. Christ, Mayhew. I like women. Marriage is complex—"

"I know it."

"—and I would never want to hurt Mina."

"Then what—?" A new anger rose. "Do you have yourself another woman?"

"No."

"You heartsick for another?"

Tom hesitated a second too long, and Seth tightened all over. "Christ, you are," Seth growled. "Why the hell would you send for Minnie? If you weren't willing to marry?"

"I *was*. I was willing." Tom didn't speak for a time, and then took a long breath. "There was a woman. Constance."

The fury ignited in Seth and he spun away before he put a fist in Tom's face.

"She's in England," Tom called after him. "*Hell*, she's *married*. There's no reason I shouldn't wed Mina—"

"*No*," Seth roared, surprising himself with the certainty of his objection. "No." He stalked back to Tom. "Minnie deserves better."

Tom's jaw tightened. "I know she does."

Tom looked so damned pathetic, Seth forced himself to breathe. "You're saying you can't wed her?"

"*Christ*." Tom wiped a hand down his face. "I think that *is* what I'm saying."

Something cold was spreading through him. "What do we do?"

Tom faced him. "She needs a protector. You agree with me on that. We have to find her another husband."

The fury flooded him again. After she'd come all this way and how scared she'd been. Was there even a man in India who deserved her? "You got someone in mind?" he asked through clenched teeth.

"Not yet. I'll need time."

"Time? Hell, Tom. We don't have time."

"A couple weeks."

"*Weeks?*" His rage was turning to panic. Tom held up his hand for calm and Seth swatted it down. "We got a couple days, maybe."

"All right," Tom said. He narrowed his eyes, appearing to be calculating. "Give me…*ten* days."

Seth stared, shaking his head. "Six."

"Seven."

"*Four.*"

"You're supposed to go *up*! Dammit, Mayhew." Tom rubbed his temples. "To get to Calcutta by the sixth… we'd need a fortnight to get there. We could spend five days here in Bombay. And there'll still be time to get there by the sixth. Come on, man. This is her future—"

"I know it!"

"You like her, too, I know it—hell, *she* knows it. Let's do all we can to find Mina a good man."

A good man. How the hell was he going to do that when he wanted her himself? When he wanted to take her home—

Home.

He looked at Tom. "We could find her a man headed for England."

"She won't leave her sister."

Right. *Damn!* "Then we'll find two."

Tom scoffed. "Two men bound for England? In five days?"

He couldn't think on the odds of that. Not just now. "Minnie deserves the best bachelor in India."

"I'm not sure the likes of us can find him."

"I can." He leveled his chin. "I can find anything. We'll find a man who'll never give Minnie a day's trouble. One who won't be chasing other women and hurting her feelings. Stable and secure and dull as a dead horse—you would've been perfect, except for that business of pining over a married woman."

Tom frowned, but said nothing to oppose the idea. Wasn't a thing he could say—especially if he wanted to keep his teeth—because Seth damn well knew the best man for Mina. A man the least like himself as possible.

And they only had five days to do it.

❧

"Thomas is not going to marry me," Mina said.

Emma dragged her gaze from the sight of the men outside the restaurant window. "What?"

She folded her napkin beside her plate and closed her reticule. "Could we leave, Emma?"

Emma's eyes went wide. "No. Why?"

"Thomas doesn't wish to marry me. We aren't suited."

"But…but you *are*."

She stood and picked up her hat. "He would have offered by now, Emma. Would have assured me somehow that we would be safe. Please, let's just get our things." Outside, Mr. Mayhew's jaw was clenched, his eyes boring into Thomas. "*Please*, Emma."

Emma hurried to pick up her things. "But shouldn't we stay and—"

"Thomas will return with the same, thin smile he always smiles and ask to speak with me in private— perhaps ask to walk with me—and he'll apologize and beg my forgiveness and it will be dreadful and demeaning."

Emma stood, her parasol and hat clutched to her stomach. "What if Colin returns? What if you're wrong?"

She wanted to be wrong, wanted to do anything to

protect Emma, but she wasn't wrong. She held Emma's eye until her little sister saw the conviction there.

And like two twin blue flames, the temper flared in Emma's eyes. "It's not fair," Emma spat, shoving her gloves into her reticule. "First, Colin Rivers and now *this*. Do men have no honor?"

Thomas and Mr. Mayhew walked back into the Apogee restaurant, their faces wary, and the slow, sick roll of her stomach nearly drove her back to her chair.

Thomas surveyed the scene, his face guarded. "Mina? I wonder if we might speak in private? Perhaps go for a walk?"

A walk. Oh God—

"No!" Emma threw down her napkin. "No! She will *not* go for a walk!"

Oh dear.

Emma swept her skirt clear of the table and stomped to the door. There was nothing for Mina to do but follow. She hurried to collect her reticule and fold her napkin—

"*Mina.*" Emma called from the door, sounding weepy and exasperated now.

I'm coming, she mouthed, smiling apologetically at the other diners. The restaurant was rather more full than she'd noticed. Not at all skilled in dramatic exits, she shuffled past the chairs and tables more carefully.

"Mina, wait." Thomas looked at her blankly. "Where are you going?"

Her legs threatened to collapse beneath her but she faced him. "You're leaving Bombay."

Thomas swallowed, and that was confirmation enough. His hands hung at his side. "Mina—"

"When?" she asked.

"*Mina!*" Emma hissed from the door, which she held pointedly open.

"Five days," Mr. Mayhew answered for Thomas, his gaze steady on her. "I need him with me in Calcutta, Minnie. If I'm late, if I miss the crew by a day, an hour, I'd have to follow and I don't know how far I'd get without Tom."

Her heart ached—for him, for her. How had it come to this? And she searched Thomas's eyes one last time. *Say I should wait. Say we'll marry and we'll take care of Emma. Say you'll be gone a week or two and you'll be back.*

But Thomas wasn't saying anything.

She turned for Emma. Her sister would cry in a moment, so she hurried. And when she reached her, her sister's grip was so tight...

Oh God...both of them jilted. No—*unclaimed*. Jetsam.

The thought was mad. Perhaps this whole scheme was mad.

She escaped the restaurant, dragging the salt-soaked air into her lungs. Row upon row of carriages blocked her way across the street to the pier. Clutching Emma's hand, she walked unseeing down the pavement.

"What will we do, Mina?"

Emma's voice quavered with worry, her temper apparently extinguished by fear. Mina ground to a stop and smoothed her countenance, but the most horrible hopelessness dulled her sister's blue eyes. Mina had seen that look in another sister's eyes.

It was the same look in Mary's when her sister had confessed she'd sold her body to feed her son.

"We'll be fine," she said, her voice blessedly steady despite her heart banging against her ribs. "Everything is fine."

"Miss Mina?"

She and Emma turned their heads at Seth's loud voice. "*Bother it*," she breathed.

Mr. Mayhew was gaining upon them quickly with his ground-eating stride. "Minnie, I'm needing to talk to you."

And Thomas hurried right behind him. "Mina, please, I have to—"

She flung up her hands to silence them. "*Hush*." Like children, they stopped and gaped. But at least they were rendered speechless. She checked the faces of curious passersby as they watched. Some shred of reason telling her she couldn't put a step wrong now. Not if she was to find a new husband. Not if they were going to survive.

Hiking her reticule up her wrist and with a straightening tug to her blouse, she walked to the men. "There is no need for this display."

"Won't you let me explain?" Thomas asked.

"We did not suit. That is explanation enough," she said. "I'll write so we may settle the matter of your bond."

"I don't care about—"

"*I* care." She closed her eyes and composed herself. "I care, Thomas." A fifty-pound bond was no pittance. The hotel was paid through the month. Once they paid Thomas back, what would they have left?

Thomas paled under the white glare of his spectacles, but Mr. Mayhew's focus was unwavering. "I need a minute with you, Minnie," he said. "Tom can take Miss Emma back to the hotel."

Confused, she looked at Mr. Mayhew. "I don't see what there is—"

He ducked his head near hers and now she was the one startled to silence. "Just a minute, Minnie," he whispered. "Please?"

Mr. Mayhew was as grim as she'd ever seen him. And he was too thin. And he'd not eaten the *pav bhaji* she'd ordered for him.

"Fine," she said. "One minute, and you will see there is no cause for your concern. Will that do?"

She expected a simple yes, but his eyes narrowed in consideration.

"I probably shouldn't have said a minute." He crossed his arms and pursed his lips in thought. "I'm thinking I'd like your attention for fifteen—no, twenty-five minutes." His eyes narrowed even more. "That's if you aren't saying much back, which you aren't likely to do—*twenty* minutes should do."

She bit back a frustrated sigh. "That's—" But it wasn't ridiculous. It was nice. And courteous. And she'd had more than enough of dithering and indecision.

And she appreciated Mr. Mayhew for that small comfort. As looping as his thoughts were, he was not bent to vagueness. She rather detested vagueness. "Yes, twenty minutes is fine."

She nodded to Emma, who stared as if they were both idiots. Thomas offered his arm but Emma ignored the gesture, turning up her nose and flouncing off in the direction of Benson's Hotel, leaving him to follow like a servant.

Emma and Thomas disappeared around the corner, and she could delay no longer. She faced Mr. Mayhew, and frowned at the baldly pitying look on his face. "I don't require pity. And I don't blame you for taking Thomas away, Mr. Mayhew."

He tipped his head to the other side. "Why aren't you calling me Seth yet?"

Bother the man. Even now, his eyes crinkled.

She marched toward the harbor rather than standing stupidly about on the pavement. And she feared she might start to cry if she didn't do something. His heavy boots crunched the gravel behind her, his long stride leisurely compared to her stupid escape to the dock's railing.

She stopped shy of the rail. Why did she come here? The glare off the sea stung her eyes. And England was at the end of all that water. She turned her back to the sea.

"I'm thinking you might blame me, Minnie, so I wanted you to know the truth." He gripped the rail to lean close and look into her face.

"I don't blame you."

He watched her carefully. "I didn't tell him. About the kiss I gave you."

She almost laughed. As if jealousy would play any part in this. "I know you didn't," she said. "I think I always knew Thomas wouldn't marry me. Before we met, I thought we would suit. I *hoped* we would. Every night on that interminable sail, I hoped."

Mr. Mayhew frowned and nodded.

"We should have suited. Both our families were of modest means but respectable. And I have some education. Enough to suit a man employed by East India."

"I know it. You'd be a perfect wife."

"And he's from Edwinstowe. Did you know that? Our villages are only a few miles apart." She shook her head. "So stupid of me—as if that mattered at all."

"It matters. I'm from the Midlands and we rub on fine, don't we? There are plenty of gents likely from the Midlands." Mr. Mayhew turned to a group of English lingering by the pavilion. "Excuse me, gents. You lot are English, aren't you?"

The men nodded dumbly.

"Any of you from the Midlands?" He waited. "No one?"

"Please, Mr. Mayhew, it is of no account," she protested weakly.

"I'm trying to persuade this beauty there are gents here from her corner of the world she might marry."

A hopeful hand shot up. "I'm from Swindon."

Mr. Mayhew shot him a narrow-eyed stare. "And that's nowhere near the Midlands, is it?"

To her utter shock, a smile tugged at her lips. "Thank you, Mr. Mayhew, but this isn't necessary."

"Swindon," he muttered, shaking his head.

"It's fine." She took a breath, jamming her hand into her pocket to hold her pebble. "I thought matters were arranged, that's all. I can make a new plan."

He scanned her face, as if checking for the truth there. "Tom's not the man for you," he blurted, and then frowned at the ground. "He's not, on account of his being in love with a woman he knew before you met. And I know it wasn't right to send for you and get your hopes fixed on marrying when this other woman's got him raked all fore and aft." He frowned harder and ground his boot over a clod of earth. "But when a man meets a woman that fits him…a woman he can't stop thinking about, that's no common thing. A man can't forget a woman like that."

A woman that fits him…

She'd sailed ninety-nine days and she didn't *fit* him. And she thought *she* was sentimental. In her pocket, she squeezed the pebble in a punishing fist and yanked her hand out to toss it. Useless, foolish thing—

Mr. Mayhew caught her hand before she could hurl the stone into the sea. "What do you have?"

She jumped, startled by his sudden grab. His hand engulfed hers, the callused fingers strangely gentle and drawing her hand toward him. She unclenched her fist and dropped the white, quartz pebble into his palm. "It's nothing," she whispered. "It's from my garden in Chesterfield." The last day…that last time…

"You got yourself a charm."

She shook her head vehemently.

His gaze was heavy but she didn't dare look into his face. "It's pretty," he said. "Like a diamond before it's all cut and polished." He held it out for her, but she didn't take it.

"It's no charm. And it's nothing near a diamond."

A moment of silence passed, and he slipped the pebble into his coat. "Minnie—"

"Mina."

"You want to see what's in my pocket?"

She looked up at him and he pulled out a small notebook that looked almost comical in his large hand.

He handed it to her. The red leather was worn at the corners and the book resisted closing, as if the pages had been read again and again.

And on each page, poetry scrawled with a careful hand. *We are such stuff as dreams are made on… The fault is not in our stars, dear Brutus, but in ourselves…*

Mr. Mayhew's head was turned in the other direction, his hands restless on the rail.

She doth teach the torches to burn bright. Was this his… charm? *She doth teach… Romeo and Juliet.* She breathed deep, and something a little like peace settled over her. "I like Shakespeare, too."

His cheeks were flushed when he turned to smile down at her and take back his book. "I saw those plays but didn't understand half of them. I mean, I understood but not as much as I was meant to. Until I got to Mr. Elliot's and read them a few times. He was a neighbor who had himself a library. He didn't mind my borrowing his books and dictionary. And even then"—he shrugged, fidgeting with the book—"well, Shakespeare couldn't help but write like he knew how."

"No, I suppose he couldn't. Do you have a favorite?"

He smiled and thumbed through the book. "This one: 'There is a tide in the affairs of men which, taken at the flood, leads on to fortune. Omitted, all the voyage of their life is bound in shallows and in miseries.'"

"That's nice. I've never heard that before."

"*Julius Caesar.* Saw that one in Ripon with Georgie. It's my favorite."

"Is he writing of fate or destiny?"

"I'm thinking it's the opposite, which is why I like it. Opportunity is what it's about. And boldness.

We're on that flood Shakespeare wrote about, Minnie. We're going to find you a better husband—one richer and set to return to England."

She shook her head. "I can't return, Mr. Mayhew."

"I wish you'd call me Seth."

"Emma is—" Her voice sounded without a bit of life so she breathed deep. Their fingers were entwined. When had Mr. Mayhew taken her hand? She pulled but he wouldn't release her.

"Your hand was looking heavy, Minnie, so I thought I'd hold it for you."

She had to smile a little at that. He was incorrigible. But when she expected to see him wink at her, his ocean eyes held something determined in their depths. Almost as if he believed finding her a husband, and a husband bound for England no less, was his responsibility.

He really was the kindest man.

He held up his little book. "'On such a full sea are we now afloat. And we must take the current as it serves, or lose our ventures.'" He winked. "Right, venture girl?"

"You would use Shakespeare against me?"

He grinned. "If I can." He pulled her hand through his arm and they started to walk.

Carriages clattered up and down the street. The sun was different here, the air salted, the blue of the sky, the clouds…all different. The Hindustani letters challenged her eyes to comprehend even as the English translation tracked alongside them.

"You won't ever feel like you belong here, Minnie."

His words stabbed her. Was she so easy to read? She looked at him and he gave her a sad smile.

"You'll make some friends," he said. "They may even love you like family, but a part of you will always be back in Chesterfield, just like a part of me will always be back in Matlock and a little bit of me is back in Brazil. You travel enough, you leave pieces behind everywhere you go." He looked at her. "I'll be leaving quite a bit with you, I wager." He smiled, his eyes roaming her face. "I suppose there's only one place in all the world where you leave your whole heart." He squeezed her hand and gave her a wink.

And suddenly she was afraid she didn't know where her heart was.

They entered a large square, with market stalls all around selling all kinds of goods. *This must be the Crawford Market near the native town.* But there were English ladies and their servants all around, wearing the same sun hats as hers. But she wasn't the same as them. Those women were married. Safe.

A cold sweat formed on her back. Under the sun, her skin prickled with cold. *Thomas will not marry me… He really will not marry me.*

"Mary," she whispered.

Mr. Mayhew dipped his head. "What's that?"

She looked at him, confused. Then realized she must have spoken aloud. He watched her carefully, but she could not tell him of Bethnal Green. The children left to starve. Or sold to baby farmers. The whores, and the drunkards and thieves. And Mary and Sebastian living in all that.

And Mary selling herself.

"Nothing." She shook her head. Desperate not to

remember that now, she moved to a stall of painted pottery. Most were in vibrant red and gold but one serving platter had a pattern of thistle and vines that was masterfully rendered. Mina traced the design with a light finger. "This is beautiful. It feels like home somehow, doesn't it?"

Seth picked up the platter, studying it. "Looks like the thistle we had in the county, remember? I used to practice sketching them. Georgie always trailed after me, wanting to draw them, too. Wanting to make them pretty. I told her pretty wasn't important in science. If you draw true, then pretty works itself out." He frowned. "And she had a talent for drawing truer than I'd ever seen."

"She's more than an illustrator, then."

He returned the platter to the table. "She's an artist. A good one. I never thought…"

"What?"

"I never thought it would lead her here, get her lost. I never would've let her pick up a pencil."

His voice had never sounded so devoid of life. "That isn't your fault."

"Our da left us when Georgie was seven. She must've been thinking I might do for a replacement. She needed a father—no matter how poor a substitute she was getting in me."

"I'm sure you were a loving brother."

He shrugged tightly. "I left her, too. I was eighteen. Wasn't any work except the lead mine. I was too big to work in the mill. And I had a chance to sail to Brazil. It wasn't all that profitable—not for me, anyway. East India took most of it—but I was able to send Mum and

Georgie a little. Mum was at the mill until she passed of the black lung."

"I'm sorry," she said quietly. "How old was Georgiana?"

"Eighteen. And all alone because I was so far from home." He took a deep breath. "Everybody's got to bear troubles, eat their own peck of dirt, make peace with losing and loss. Adapt, I suppose. Georgie and I were good at adapting by then, so maybe leaving England didn't hold all that much fear for either us. A bit unnatural for a girl. I never thought she'd ever leave England, though."

Her heart sunk heavy in her chest. She wanted to hold him, but she didn't dare, so she hugged his arm. "You're going to find her."

Mr. Mayhew smiled down at her, but the corners of his mouth were tight. "I will, Minnie. I'm sailing with that current now, aren't I? Leading me to Calcutta and the Milford crew."

She forced a smile and nodded.

"But we're with you five days, Tom and me," he said. "And our aim is to find you the best bachelor in all of India. A man worthy of you. We'll even find a gent for Emma since this Colin Rivers hasn't come up to the scratch."

Colin Rivers, and now Thomas. And Mr. Mayhew thought he would find them both husbands in five days.

"We'll find you a decent man," he said so softly he might have been speaking to himself. "We'll find a man who's ready to provide for you and your children. Who'll never leave you or let you go hungry."

His jaw was firm. He truly believed that.

What did it matter, so long as she knew the truth? Men liked to pretend to be in control and strong and capable. They pretended, and all the while they denied women the right to earn their own livings. Except in the basest, most degrading ways. Like Mary.

And like herself and Emma, exporting themselves to India for this bizarre bridal market. Society was perverse and unnatural, but there was no changing it. She may as well try to change the tide.

Men liked to pretend. Even with his kind heart and good intentions, Mr. Mayhew did not have the right of it. He raged at the chaining of the lion.

But it was the lioness that fed the pride.

They arrived at the hotel and she withdrew her arm from his. But before he could open the door to the lobby for her, she put a hand on his arm. "Mr. Mayhew, thank you for offering to find me a husband but I don't need your help."

"Minnie—"

"And I don't want it," she said as clearly as she could. "Go to Calcutta with Thomas, and find Georgiana. I have to find a husband, Mr. Mayhew. And I'm afraid all you would be…is a distraction."

He stared at her but said nothing as she slipped into the hotel.

Nine

THERE WERE FEW SIGHTS IN THE WORLD THAT SHOULD have pleased Seth more than the circle of fine, tea-drinking ladies in the lobby of Benson's Hotel—mainly because he was the lone male within forty paces.

But there was one little officer who wouldn't welcome the infiltration of their ranks. And she was the only one he was infiltrating for.

She'd called him a distraction.

Well. Fine, then. She'd been distracting him plenty, too. But he'd been grateful to focus on a task before setting off to meet Georgie's crew in Calcutta. A man ought to be able to hold more than one thought in his head without it turning him in circles.

He pulled out his paper with the names of possible husbands for Mina and pulled down the hem of his coat. Only four days left, but he'd made good progress yesterday. He'd been eager to share his list, but Mina hadn't been in her rooms yesterday evening. Should he try talking to her now? With all the venture girls about her? Would he shame her?

He sidled nearer. The ladies were all so fine. Their

backs didn't even touch their chairs. Probably discussing lady matters like frocks and blends of tea and fripperies like ribbons.

"There would be no annuity upon his death, only a hardship grant of forty pounds," a lady in a sky-blue dress said to Mina. "So I think not, Mina. Did you call on Mrs. Mayne, *and* did she receive you?"

Mina nodded. "The second day. After calling upon Mrs. Chester."

"Excellent," another lady said. "And did you leave another card at Government House?"

"I did not."

The ladies fell silent, their faces wrinkling in deliberation. Mina's head swiveled from one lady to the next. "Should I have done? Is it too late?"

"The matter is not irreparable but a call should be made this afternoon. Mr. Oswald is yet unattached. Samantha, what were Mr. Oswald's credentials again?"

A lady—evidently Samantha—snapped open her notebook, thumbing through the pages. "Richard Oswald or Henry Oswald?"

"Richard."

Samantha flipped the page. "Oswald, Richard. Born in East London. Age thirty years. Four hundred eighty a year. Currently sharing a residence in the city with two servants. His health seems excellent and prospects in the company—" She frowned. "He was not advanced last year."

A disapproving silence settled upon them. Mina sighed. "He does not seem eligible, then?"

Samantha patted Mina's hand. "There are others—"

The ladies cut off as Seth took a tentative step forward. He smiled and, thank God, the ladies smiled back. They normally did, but his confidence had been knocked around of late.

"Good afternoon, Mr. Mayhew." Mina wasn't out-and-out smiling, but she'd never embarrass him.

"Good afternoon, Min—Miss Adams." He nodded at the ladies. "Ladies. I don't mean to interrupt." Well… propriety be damned. "I was hoping I might sit?"

Mina blinked but gestured to a chair. "Certainly, Mr. Mayhew."

A smiling woman reached for the tea tray. "We were taking our tea. Will you have a cup?"

He nodded and eased his weight onto the delicate chair. This was a country for flimsy furniture. "Yes, please. I'd be much obliged." The teacup didn't fit his hand all that well, either, but he pretended taking tea with ladies was a common enough occurrence. He crossed his leg, then uncrossed it. "I should introduce myself. I'm Seth—"

"Yes." The tea pourer smiled. "We know who you are, Mr. Mayhew."

Right. 'Course they would. He cleared his throat. "I couldn't help but overhear your talk of that Oswald gent. In fact, I had some ideas of my own. Of eligible men for Miss Mina."

The ladies turned to look at one another, then settled back in their seats. Mina's blush worried him, but it was too late to stop now.

"By all means, Mr. Mayhew," one lady said. "Do share."

They smiled at him like a child reciting his letters.

DISCOVERY OF DESIRE   149

"Well...there's Mr. Clevenger. He's a learned man, with the East India College. He seems—"

The ladies flipped open their little notebooks, cutting him off. They were shaking their heads.

"Mr. Clevenger was denied a transfer to Delhi," one lady murmured.

"He suffers from recurring gout," another said.

"I heard it was dropsy of the lungs," said another.

The blond tsked. "He does not even keep a horse."

"And yet overfond of the races, I understand," another said.

All the ladies heads rose in unison to face him. Seth checked his notes again. "Uh...I thought the Clevenger gent applied to return to England?"

A woman to his right checked her book. "Yes, in... October. The application was denied last week."

He blinked, reading the woman's log over her shoulder.

"It's fine, Mr. Mayhew." Mina smiled at him. "Really, you mustn't trouble yourself."

"Er...well." He reached into his pocket and unfolded his notes. "There's a man by the name of Wharton—"

Heads dropped. Notebook pages flipped. One lady found him fast. "Wharton, Richard. Six hundred a year."

A chorus of considering mumbles at this promising fact until...

"No. He has three children with a local woman."

The ladies shook their heads. One pressed her lips thin. "That will not do. Carrying the cost of two households."

The women looked at him for the next name.

"Well, uh." He gulped his tea. "I met an officer by the name of Thomas Tilden?"

"Thomas Tilden of the Forty-Ninth Native Infantry? Or of the Ninth Lancers? Tilden of the NI is in his thirties, the other in his forties."

He didn't know with a certainty. He should've asked. But the ladies—save for Mina, who was smiling with sympathy—were waiting. "The Lancers, I think. A stout man. Looks real smart in his colors."

A blond lady didn't even need to consult her notebook. "Tilden of the Lancers. It is rumored he is not sound."

"Not sound?" he asked.

A silence descended. A little brunette leaned forward, her mouselike voice lowered to a discreet whisper. "Physically, Mr. Mayhew. He applied for the invalid list last month. A *French* sort of affliction."

Oh God. The man had the pox? And he'd chosen him for Minnie?

"Thank you for your suggestions, Mr. Mayhew." Mina moved to sit beside him, opening a notebook across their laps. "They're all very good thoughts. But the ladies have put forward other names."

Mina unfurled a sheet of foolscap that stretched over both their laps. There was a grid.

"We think Henry Block in the Bengal Civil Service is a most promising gentleman. He is well positioned for advancement and is recently widowed, which explains his availability." She pointed to another row. "And in the same province, Captain Ravenshaw is in command of a Native Infantry regiment and his commanding officer is Samantha's future father-in-law, who assures her he is a man of great expectations."

"And he is handsome as well," the tea pourer added.

"Oh yes, terribly handsome," another lady said.

Jealousy flooded him, but he relaxed the scowl on his lips and nodded.

Mina folded up her bachelor chart. "If those men will do for Emma and me, then we will reside in the same province. Do you think they sound acceptable, Mr. Mayhew?"

Seth shrugged. "Have you not met them?"

"No."

"Are they going back to England?" he asked.

"No."

"But—"

"There is an assembly at Government House this evening, which I hope to secure an invitation to. Though I failed to deliver my calling card upon arrival. If I do so this afternoon, I may yet be accepted."

"You will, Mina," the blond assured her. "And you must remember all we've told you to gain the gentlemen's notice."

"Gain their notice?" Seth turned to look at Mina. "What's that mean?"

Her brows rose innocently. "Nothing," she squeaked. "Nothing really, only that there are a great many ladies who will put themselves forward, and I am not adept at…flirtation."

His heart was sinking fast.

"We will help you, Mina," one lady said, giggling.

"For the ball, you must wear the lavender, the one

off the shoulder," said another. "And rouge would not be frowned upon."

"And you must smile and hold the gentleman's gaze at every opportunity," said another.

"I don't think I can be that bold," Mina said.

"It is essential," the mouselike brunette said. "You must allow it is essential. Do you not agree, Mr. Mayhew?"

Rouge? Off the shoulder? What was he agreeing to? "I like lavender—"

Mina stood, as did all the other ladies. He lurched to his feet. "You're going?"

"I really must," Mina said. "If I am to call at Government House before two o'clock, I mustn't delay. Thank you for your assistance. A male perspective is most helpful."

"But…all right—"

Mina and the ladies sashayed off, their chatter all about Mina's dress and hair and something whispered about her *bosom*.

The hell! He had to find Tom and discover where this Government House ball was.

Mina wouldn't just choose a husband without him, would she?

Ten

"EMMA, THIS DRESS DOES NOT SEEM DARING TO YOU?"

"You look beautiful, Mina. Lavender becomes you so well."

"I should have worn my shawl." A ridiculous statement. No one would pay her décolletage any mind. The ballroom of the Government House was massive, and scores of women filled the space—with nary a shawl in sight.

Emma lowered her voice so as not to be overhead. "You are not used to the neckline, that's all. You disguise your figure too well. You always have."

Mina ignored the urge to tug her dress high over her bosom. Life in Chesterfield did not include formal balls—and never a gown as revealing as the one she wore now. But perhaps a lady *did* appear to full advantage in such a dress. And she needed every advantage.

Emma noticed someone and stiffened. "Mr. Block is behind you. His waistcoat is a houndstooth pattern in navy and green."

Mina turned, discreetly studying the man swirling his whiskey. "He does not look recently widowed."

"He looks aware that he is most eligible."

Mr. Block caught their study and flashed an enormous smile to them.

But his smile didn't crinkle his eyes.

Emma was caught by Genevieve and pulled into a circle of their friends. Mina started to follow but a hand touched her arm.

"Minnie?"

She turned, and there stood the man she was unfortunately always thinking of, with his deep voice and tilted smile and large hands that were always fussing with something. Tonight it appeared to be a long seedpod.

"Mr. Mayhew?" He was so handsome in his suit, and with his golden hair combed into a sleek queue, her heart whimpered before she could steel it. "Good evening. I did not expect to see you here."

"Neither did anyone else. I wasn't invited."

She checked if anyone had overheard. "How did you—"

"In all my days, Minnie, I've never seen anything as beautiful as you tonight."

A terrible flirt…and yet she still blushed down to her bosom. She really should have brought her shawl. "Thank you, Mr. Mayhew. And you"—*my goodness, the man's shoulders*—"you look very handsome this evening."

His grin broke into a smile. And that was adorable.

"Thank you." He wiped a big hand over his smile but didn't manage to erase it. "It's not so easy finding a good coat, my height being unnatural. You wouldn't understand, being normal-shaped." His eyes swept her from tip to toe, stopping on her bosom before leaping back up to her face. But they dipped down again before darting up toward the ceiling.

Her corset was suddenly suffocating, and she surreptitiously checked her décolletage—oh.

Oh. From his high vantage point, he might be seeing even more of her than others.

She held her chin up, trying for an air of nonchalance in the matter of all her exposed parts. "What is that in your hand, Mr. Mayhew?"

He didn't seem to hear her for a moment, and then raised his brow in question. "Ay?"

The word was a tug on her heart. Pure Midlands in that. She pointed to his hand, and he presented the pod he was holding in his massive hand.

"Don't know," he said. "Wanted to ask Tom. Saw it on my way here."

"It isn't familiar to you?"

"I'm not all that skilled in identifying trees."

Confused, she searched his face but he only smiled down at her with the usual kind, appreciative light in his eyes. "Are trees not your specialty, then?"

"I'm no botanist, Minnie." He dropped his gaze. "I studied for a certificate in horticulture, but East India mainly needed a man to journey into the jungles and collect anything that looked useful. And who wouldn't die. That was probably the more important skill—the not dying. But I had a talent for finding the useful, too. I probably overlooked a bit that was valuable, but not much."

She shook her head. "No, you wouldn't have."

He looked into her eyes as if gauging the truth in

them, which confused her until his eyes crinkled with something like pride.

He caught her hand and gave her the seedpod. "What they don't tell you in the Company is to talk to the native peoples. I don't know why they don't—it's the best way to find the medicinals.

"Once, I was in a village off the Rio Cupijó—that's in Brazil—and I saw the tribal women shaving the bark of a tree and steeping it in hot water. They used that for their digestive troubles, so I sketched the tree and leaves, took myself cuttings and seeds, and sent it back to the company with that note. The tribal women had no fear of me and seemed to want to share all their skills." He winked at her. "I think they thought me some sort of novelty. Like a talking ape."

"I doubt that very much." She studied him, bemused that Mr. Mayhew, a plant collector, wasn't a botanist and yet… "I think you must have been very good at your work."

He shrugged, but his smile grew. "The Company never complained." Something sobering flickered across his face. "They said they couldn't pay me what a real botanist might earn, one that read science and botany at university. But they said any new ornamentals I found, I could keep."

"Like your slipper orchid?"

His grin returned. "My *Wilhelmina* orchid."

"That flower bought you a home."

"Bought me the land, anyway, didn't it? The best beauty I ever found. Spent the last farthing on the land, which I found wasn't the best thinking."

"No?"

"I should've kept a bit aside, for all the repairs and setting up that's needed."

"I see," she said. Land would be terribly expensive to maintain, and it seemed Mr. Mayhew had not set aside a reserve of funds to do so.

His face was flushed, his gaze aimed over her head. "But I told you of those other orchids and ornamentals. They arrived in London just when I was to sail. I don't know if those plants survived the crossing, but my mates, the Skinner boys, will do all they can. I won't know for months if those seeds were viable."

The prospect was full of risk. As kind as he was, she could never marry a man like him. It was not in her nature to bear uncertainty. Though an explorer would always risk, and do so with ease. Except... looking at Mr. Mayhew now as he spoke so quietly, she somehow doubted he was easy with such a chance future himself.

She handed him back his seedpod and smiled. "You'll sell all your other flowers, too. And set up your land and cottage, and marry and have your children."

"You think so?"

He looked at her so long she had to drop her eyes. And yet, she answered truthfully when she said, "I do."

He chuckled. "Do you want to know how I found most of the flowers?"

"How?"

"Climbing. The treetops and cliffs. I wasn't ever afraid of any height, and climbing's how you find all the treasures. That's where you find the plants that don't mind the variability of English weather. Hardy little flowers. Clinging in places you don't think a plant would dream of taking root. A flash of scarlet in a meadow is already known to the world. Only one simple as me would crawl up the ledge of a cliff so narrow he'd have to do it on all fours. Stopping every foot or so, praying that vertigo you only get when you're staring down four hundred feet of granite will pass."

Her heart pounded at the thought. She clutched his arm. "You mustn't ever do such a thing. Not ever again."

He looked at her hand on his sleeve. The last time she'd touched him, he'd kissed her. She slipped her hand away.

"I've been talking about myself all this time, Minnie. And I know that's not a topic of any lasting interest."

"I like your stories. Most men don't talk to me as you do. They don't know what to say to me, or I to them."

"Why not?" His eyes followed the arc of her headdress. The silk flowers and vines dangled from her temples and ended in glass beads, which, to her alarm, he captured between his fingers.

"I...I don't know," she breathed. "I think I'm too serious."

He moved closer, his eyes sweeping her face. "You're not *too* anything. You're just right," he murmured. His finger played with her hair ornament. "What's this little sprig of ribbons called, Minnie?"

That crooked smile...it might have been a harpoon in her heart. Trying to ignore the radiating warmth of his hand, she shrugged. "It's just a bit of decoration. To match my dress."

His eyes locked on hers. "You're all the beauty a man can take and you go and add a frame like this." His voice deepened, the words thrumming beneath her skin. "Not even Shakespeare could describe how you look tonight."

Oh dear... She should move. She should *breathe*.

His finger touched her cheek for a moment, and he released her gaze to watch where he touched her. Instantly, his gaze sharpened and his hand dropped from her. He straightened from her and only then did she realize how close he'd been standing.

Had anyone seen? Emma was in conversation, and no one seemed to pay the least bit of attention. She cleared her throat. What had they been talking about? "You are always full of compliments, Mr. Mayhew—"

"Why don't you call me Seth?"

She had to smile at that. "Why don't you call me Mina?"

"Everyone calls you Mina."

He was incorrigible. "You *are* a terrible flirt."

"I never flirted with you, Minnie."

She covered her lips, but a laugh escaped. "A flirt *would* say that."

His eyes narrowed, studying her. "I don't flirt with you, Minnie. I never have. I can't say you ever flirted with me, either."

Her smile vanished and she tore free of his intense gaze to check her ear baubles, smooth her skirt— *anything* to derail his attention. "I'm told I must engage the men with conversation, but I don't know how. Do you have any suggestions?"

He shrugged, looking irritated by the question.

"With these gents?" He propped his hands on his hips to survey the room. "Men like to feel useful. Just ask them for advice you don't need."

"That's not what I was told."

"See—that's wrong, what you just did." He grinned. "What did the venture girls tell you to do, to lure a man?"

Lure a man… How had she come to this? She breathed deep. "They said I ought to touch the gentleman on his arm—which I did not mean to do to you, though I realize I just did. Truly it was not meant to…"

"Seduce me?"

"Yes. I mean, no. Not meant to."

He frowned. "I know it," he grumbled. "What else?"

"They said I should walk to display my"—*figure*—"my dress."

His eyes crinkled with mirth. "Your dress, is it?" He dipped his head to speak close. "Shall I tell you what draws a man's eye, Minnie?"

His deep voice sent tremors down the back of her neck, so she nodded quickly.

"Happiness. You're already easy to look on, but a happy woman is easy to be with. Makes the man think you'll forgive him for all the mistakes he's sure to make."

She bit her lip against a smile. Which made Mr. Mayhew's gaze drop to her mouth and go still.

"Do you care to know what holds my eye in particular?" he murmured.

"Not happiness?"

Odd how Mr. Mayhew could somehow seem so

shy. He looked at her as if deciding whether or not to tell her. "I don't know what to call it, but I know it when I see it. My mum had it. She'd been left with two babies and nothing else—but Lucifer himself couldn't have led her on any path but the one that saw us warm and fed.

"Some might say that was just a woman being practical, but it was more. It was defending who you love, no matter what was testing you. A woman like that..." He smiled sheepishly. Shy again, but proud, too. "Who wouldn't love a woman like that?"

"She was formidable," she said.

"Damn me," he said quietly, as if realizing something. "She *was*. She was mighty." His eyes roamed her face. "She was like you."

Her lips parted to scoff, but she caught herself at the look on his face. To imagine her brave or *mighty* was astonishingly mistaken. "I'm not at all."

She feigned interest in the ballroom, but when she turned back around, Mr. Mayhew's eyes still watched her. She clasped her hands, rather than crossing her arms and shrinking into herself. Men did not look at her like that, and when Mr. Mayhew did...she actually didn't mind at all.

But she rather felt like she might need to drop to all fours to keep her balance.

His warm hand came to rest on the small of her back. "Why don't you go on now?" he said gently. "I wager that Captain Ravenshaw and Mr. Block are counting the seconds till they can know your name."

The strangest pain shot through her heart. This was impossible. *He* was impossible.

With a final look at his sea-green eyes, she turned for the deep waters of Bombay Society.

⤞

There was nothing worse than seeing a woman you wanted for yourself walk toward another man.

A long spiral of hair had slipped from her pins and bounced behind her ear. He wanted to catch it, comb his fingers into all that brown silk, and hold her just so. Just at that perfect angle to kiss those warm, full lips again and watch those brown eyes melt and close. Then she'd go soft in his arms so he could kiss her in earnest. Kiss her the best way he knew how.

He rubbed the seedpod in his hand, needing something other than her to look at. It didn't help that his roger had been stiffening in his pants all the while he was near her. Damn if she didn't have a body to match that gorgeous face of hers. But there'd be no more kissing or touching her.

She was meant for a Company man.

"Mina is in fine looks tonight."

Seth started at Tom's voice, and turned to find him holding out a glass of wine. "You're a damn puzzle, Tom, you know that?"

"Still in a pleasant mood, I see." Tom drained his wine and started on the glass Seth refused. "When do you plan to forgive me? It's been two days."

"I know it."

"I told you why I can't marry her. Several times now, in fact."

He shook his head and grumbled, "You could have married her. You earn a good living. You've got some sense. You're not out gambling or catching diseases or keeping a harem of women like some maharaja."

Tom brooded into the distance. "I shouldn't expect you to understand. Hell, Mayhew, no man's going to be right enough for her, is he?"

Christ, he was getting turned around—because deep down he *did* understand Tom not being able to marry, not when he was in love with someone else. "Where've you been, anyway?"

"Asking after that Captain Ravenshaw. The Fishing Fleet had his credentials right, but I've not found one man that likes him. He sounds like a pompous ass from many accounts."

"Could be sore feelings, couldn't it? Envy over his post?"

Tom wiped a weary hand over his face. "Yes, perhaps that's it. Didn't know how difficult finding a husband would be."

"Wouldn't have been if you'd kept your end of the bargain," he couldn't help grumbling.

Tom's jaw tightened. He set his empty glass down hard and turned on his heel. "I'm going to ask after that Block fellow."

"Good," Seth ground out. He wasn't ready to feel any charity for Tom. Might not be for a long time.

Seth tensed. The lady named Samantha was walking Captain Ravenshaw over to Mina to be introduced. The captain's red coat was real smart, crossed all over with gold braids and buttons, and his black boots were outfitted with brass spurs. And he had good, curling hair. Styled neat as Prince Albert's. For a pompous ass, he wasn't a bad-looking gent—

Wait, where were they going? The man was leading Mina out of the ballroom. That probably wasn't any of his business.

But it didn't take half a second to decide to follow anyway.

Mina hadn't let the captain take her far. They stood at the other end of the crowded hall. Seth edged closer and kept enough of a distance not to be noticed, but he heard them well enough.

"Chesterfield, you say? In the Midlands?" Ravenshaw laughed. "I've no idea. Where is that near? And tell me a town a man might know of."

Seth gritted his teeth. *Pompous ass.*

"Do you know Clay Cross or Bolsover, Captain Ravenshaw?" Mina asked.

Ravenshaw snickered and shook his head.

"Sheffield, then?"

"Yes, Sheffield, of course," Ravenshaw said. "So smack in the middle, is it, then?"

"Yes." Mina said in her soft, calm voice. "In the Midlands."

Ravenshaw smiled, his eyes lingering on her breasts. "This is a lovely gown, Miss Adams." He edged closer to her. "And you are lovely in it."

"I… Thank you."

"Shall we seek a *kala juggah* for ourselves?"

"What is that?"

He chuckled. "A useful addition to your vocabulary, I daresay. A *kala juggah* is a private place, arranged near assembly rooms for, well…*privacy* and sharing secrets, whatever is desired. And I should like us to be better acquainted."

"Can we not become better acquainted here?"

"We really can't."

Mina clutched the pocket of her skirt. "I should not leave my sister long."

"Nonsense. A man and a woman cannot hope to know each other without more intimate conversation." He traced her bare shoulder with a gloved finger and Mina, startled, stepped backward.

That was all Seth could stand. "*Excuse me.*" Seth didn't bother to subdue his voice and the ass ducked his head in alarm.

Ravenshaw popped straight back up. His brass spurs jangled as he pivoted, and the hand he propped on his hip sent his scabbard off-kilter. "What is it?" The captain didn't bother to subdue his voice, either.

Seth bristled at the tone and sized up the man. His hair was slick with pomade and the ends of his mustache were waxed into stiff needles. No, he wouldn't do at all.

And the bastard shouldn't have touched her.

An icy anger was flowing through his veins, so Seth turned his back on the stuffed uniform. "Minnie— Miss Adams, I've come to collect you."

She blinked at his offered elbow, which hovered under her chin. "Collect me?"

Would she refuse to leave with him? She might at that, and it'd be damn awkward. Angry as he was, it was a relief when she took his arm.

"Of course, Mr. Mayhew," she murmured.

Ravenshaw wedged his head between the two of them. "Hold your steam there, man. I was talking to her."

He turned to growl, but Mina squeezed his arm. "Excuse me, Captain," she said. "I'm afraid I forgot a previous engagement."

Ravenshaw frowned, his mustache drooping. "A previous—?"

"Geography lessons, mate," Seth grumbled, before staring down at Mina, who returned his look with a warning in her own as he led her back to the ballroom.

"Was there an actual reason you came to collect me?" she asked.

"Didn't like him."

Mina sighed but said nothing. *Good.* She was in agreement, then.

She shifted her hold on his arm to walk closer. She didn't seem to notice she'd done it, and something in that little adjustment stopped the words he was preparing to spout about her wandering off with pompous asses.

Mad as he was, he shouldn't like that little touch so much. Shouldn't like that she had to reach a little to place her hand on his arm. Or like knowing he could protect her against men like Ravenshaw—or any man for that matter. For the next three days, at least.

Then she'd have to protect herself.

That thought stretched every one of his nerves. He secured her hand more fully about his arm, pulling her closer. Mina was so small. Her head barely reached his shoulder, and he could lift her with one hand if he had a mind to.

Even her skin was delicate, protected under all her bonnets. Would a man like Ravenshaw be mindful of how easy her skin would burn in India? Or how her rose scent would draw mosquitoes? Or how she had to be handled delicately, even if she was crisp, composed, and orderly-like? Maybe even more so because of it. Mina might have the bearing of an officer, but he knew she liked being reminded she was a woman.

She stopped at the edge of the ballroom. "We need to talk, Mr. Mayhew. Outside would be best."

Outside? Well…hell. She wasn't looking at him, and she didn't appear all that bothered. But then, Mina never looked bothered. That didn't mean she wasn't wanting to snap his head off.

They maneuvered through the crowded room onto the terrace, but the company here was as lively as the one inside. And that was no wonder, with the view. The stars shone and the ocean glinted under a full moon.

"Pretty night, isn't--" But there wasn't any air left to finish his words. By moonlight, Mina's skin gleamed like pearl, and her brown eyes were soft and liquid. They'd melted like that when they'd kissed.

Christ, she was a beauty. She'd be the perfect wife for any of these men—*You have the sign.*

He was jostled from behind. Damn, they were never alone, *ever.*

"Mr. Mayhew, you cannot—"

"Not here," he said hoarsely. And, before she could question him, he gripped her hand and led her past all the milling couples and down into the garden. In the corner of the landscape, a grove of banyan trees, with their low canopy, smothered the lamplight. Like a dark forest or a…a *kala juggah.*

Like a damn good idea.

"Mr. Mayhew—"

"*Seth.*"

"Where are we going?"

A couple sauntered by, but they were the only ones to pass. He and Mina would finally be alone. And he'd look into her eyes again. Maybe for the last time.

"I mustn't go far," she said.

Mina's hand flexed in his—he must have squeezed it. He relaxed his grip and Mina stumbled, holding him tight now to keep her balance. Her head was down, watching the ground as she nearly ran beside him to stay abreast.

Christ. He slowed his step. "Minnie—sorry. I'm sorry."

Her pretty headdress slipped, and with her free hand, she fumbled with a pin to secure it. She glanced sharply behind her. "I shouldn't be this far from the others."

A strange ache cramped his chest. He stopped and breathed deep. God, what was he doing? She couldn't do this, couldn't be seen with him like this.

"Are you listening to me, Mr. Mayhew?"

She never called him Seth. Not even now. Because Mina was sensible and kept her thoughts in a straight line. And she could turn all that common sense and straight thinking on him like the swing of an axe.

Or just the shutting of a door.

Mina wouldn't be led astray, not from the path of knowing what she had to do. It was damn stupid of him to take her from company, to want her alone, to…to *panic* seeing her with another man.

But he'd never been one to think in straight lines.

Even now, words and feelings and pictures of home and Mina, and Tom, and Georgie swelled and crashed like waves in his head, and he couldn't hold one still. They tumbled over each other and rolled away again.

"I'm listening. I'm sorry, Minnie." He stood still, the two of them exposed in the middle of the garden. "Go on and say what you were wanting to say." He squared his shoulders. "But the captain wasn't right for you, laughing at where we're from. Like *he* comes from better. And he wasn't respectful, with that talk of *intimate conversation*. And what was he wearing spurs for anyway?"

Mina's upturned face was beautiful and composed. As usual.

He *would* drive a woman like her to Bedlam. He'd forever be saying and doing the wrong thing, being out of pocket, embarrassing her. She deserved a man she didn't have to manage and apologize for. And Mina would've known that the instant they met.

The shame of that cooled his temper better than a dousing of ice water.

"This isn't proper, Mr. Mayhew." She pulled her hand from his and he had to let her loose. But she curled her hand around his elbow, like a lady.

"I know it. So ye can give me your tidy doing off"—he cringed at his ignorant speech—"I mean, you can scold me here. If you're of a mind to."

But Mina didn't say anything. And she suddenly looked different. Still like the little officer she was but…harder.

"There's some sort of summerhouse over there," she said.

Within the cluster of trees, a faint structure took shape in the shadows. A walled gazebo, remote and secret. "I see it."

"Is that where you planned to lead me?"

Miserable, he nodded. But Mina dropped her hand from his arm and marched toward the trees.

"Minnie?" Now what? He started after her, ducking a little like that would help his oversize carcass not be seen. "Minnie?"

She kept walking.

"Minnie, no," he hissed. "It's not respectable."

"You had no fear of ruining my reputation pulling me across the lawn."

"But—"

"And you are hardly a rogue, Mr. Mayhew, much as you would like to pretend."

Was that supposed to be some kind of compliment?

"And it appears I need to make something clear to you, so while no one is looking, please put on some haste." She walked faster and disappeared into the summerhouse.

Well…*hell*. He scanned the lawn behind him—she was right; nobody seemed to be watching—and ran to duck in after her.

The room was a small octagon, the walls patched with panes of colored glass and pierced with carved openings that streamed the garden light into the dim room in delicate shapes and jeweled shards. She faced him with her shoulders back and chin high. Little diamonds of emerald and gold light played on the mounds of her breasts, which he was trying hard not to look at—and failing.

This wasn't romantic. It *wasn't*.

"Mr. Mayhew, I appreciate your wanting to help me, but you mustn't interfere again."

Mr. Mayhew. Like she didn't even know him. "You didn't like that Ravenshaw, either."

"That is not the point. I must marry."

"I know it. But you don't have to marry the first gent that offers. You can choose. That one wasn't even soldierlike *or* a gentleman. And what about liking the look of the man? Are you even partial to dark hair? Or side-whiskers?"

"His appearance is of no importance."

"You can't want to marry an ugly man."

"Not every man is handsome."

"I want you feeling something for your husband, Minnie."

She threw her hands up and huffed an odd, squeaky sound, and he stared in surprise. He didn't know she did that. But if that was all the vexation he caused, maybe that wasn't so bad, was it?

Her hands dropped back to her sides, but they were clenched into fists and her eyes were closed. "I know you are trying to help," she said. "But love is not my concern."

His heart sank. She sounded like she meant that.

"You must devote your attention to helping Georgiana. She needs you."

"And you're saying you don't."

She opened her eyes, and looked at him without a word.

No, she didn't need him. And she was right not to, but knowing she was right didn't make it hurt any less. He rubbed his eyes, careful to catch the wetness there. "You think that Captain will do? Or that Henry Block?"

"I don't know. I don't know if *I* will do for him. But that is *my* task—not yours or Thomas's, or even my friends, with all their lists and rankings."

"There's a ranking?"

"I am the one on offer here, not them. That ballroom is my marketplace—"

"Minnie—"

"—so please let's *not pretend* I have any real choice in the matter. Unless you wish to add to my humiliation."

Christ. He caught her hand. She pulled at his hold but he couldn't let her go. "Minnie—"

"We should return."

"Wait." What the hell could he say? He probably had something in his book. If he could just keep her a minute more, he might help—

She stayed his hand from opening his notebook. "There is no Shakespeare here. Not in this. And nothing at all that poetry would serve."

He stared at her hand, too embarrassed to meet her eye. He wasn't smart enough even to use his own words. "I just thought…"

"I know."

She moved closer, and even in the dark, he could see the soft brown of her eyes.

"I know," she whispered. "Thank you. No matter whom I choose, he will not be as kind and compassionate as you." She smiled a little. "Or as handsome, sadly."

Christ, she was such a lady. Saying things like that

to him, like no one ever had. And she was brave and beautiful and smelling of roses and sunshine. Like England. Like home.

"Minnie, won't you even try to leave India?"

Her lids lowered and his heart cracked in two. There wasn't anything he could say to persuade her. No way to rescue her.

And then she rose on her toes, her sweet weight leaning against him. Soft lips pressed against his cheek, and his body tightened and fought against every emotion that kiss stirred.

"Please, Minnie…" He didn't recognize the hoarse rasp of his voice, or have any control over his hands sliding around her slender waist and holding her against him. He wouldn't rest his cheek on her fancy headdress, so he bent lower to nestle against her neck.

And her lips were at his ear, whispering, "The minute I saw you, I wanted to choose you."

He clenched his eyes tight and wrote those words into his heart. He'd write them in his book and read them again and again. He hugged her tight and she hugged him back. Only her round breasts resisted his body sealing against hers but, *ah, Christ*, that was fine. The valley of her slim back and the swell of her backside fit the palms of his hands as if he'd sculpted her body himself.

"God, Minnie…" He moved to kiss her. And she stopped him with a hand over his lips.

He clenched his eyes against the pain in his chest. Christ, it hurt. She wouldn't let him, and he wanted to feel that again—the way their first kiss was a surprise, and then it wasn't. Because he knew, he *knew*, she was going to be special. But she didn't want him, didn't want his kiss—

Her hand slid from his mouth and touched his eyelids. And then she pulled him the rest of the way down. And the instant their lips met, he was whole again.

And it wasn't a surprise at all.

There wasn't a kiss in his life he would ever count as more natural or tender. Mina's body was made to be loved by his. And he'd be gentle. He'd never be anything but gentle with a lady as precious as this.

His tongue coaxed the seal of her lips apart and with a groan, he plundered the sweetness there until his body began to quake and demand more. He tore his mouth away and gasped for air. "God, Minnie. I was the first to kiss you, wasn't I?"

She pulled at his neck, straining for his lips. "The first."

With a groan, he sealed his lips to hers again. He'd wanted to hold her like this the moment he saw her, the very moment they met—*You have the sign*.

No, he didn't believe in fate. Fate wasn't—*Christ*... the way she kissed him, the way she held him—

Or was it opportunity? *On such a full sea we are now afloat*—

Did he sail this current? If he didn't... What if he didn't? Without Mina, would his life be stuck in the shallows? In misery?

Could he do this? He forced his eyes open. Mina clung to him. Her sweet, lush body was a fire threatening to burn every thought in his brain to ash. He wasn't ready, but would she trust him? *Would she have him?*

The possibility slammed into him and his head reared back, breaking their kiss.

Mina's eyes were unfocused, soft with desire, and that look set the flames roaring into the sky. His whole body was swollen with wanting, his roger strained against his trousers, but he had to think.

"Minnie?" He waited for her eyes to focus. "Could you have me?"

Her breath didn't follow any sort of rhythm and her brows knit in confusion. "Have you?"

He swallowed against the damnably thick lump in his throat. "Yes." His heart was pounding and he was suddenly afraid of her next words. But his little officer wouldn't ever shy from anything.

"I don't understand," she said. "Have you... To *marry*? Did you ask me to marry you?"

That lump wasn't going anywhere. But Mina *did* talk plain; he knew that. He'd talk plain, too.

"Yes. The second thing, the marrying." His voice was a stupid croak, and he cleared his throat roughly. "I'll work. Every day, I'll be up with the lark. And I'd work hard to take care of you and we'd be together; we'd be home—I'd give you my home. I don't have much, but I might, once I meet with the Skinners, and I promise, I'd never leave you or our children. I never would. I'd never want to. I'd always be with you—which may not be all that appealing, now that I'm hearing it—but I'm saying I'll be faithful. I'd never go loose on you."

She stared at him. And his heart stopped when tears welled in her brown eyes.

"You should put me down," she said.

Down? Her eyes were level with his. And he was standing upright. He had to look to know he'd picked her up to kiss her. Carefully, he set her down but couldn't bring himself to let her go. "Minnie, if you're to be had, I'll have you." Why wasn't she saying anything? "Will you have me?"

She backed away as far as the little room allowed, till her back was at the wall. "I wish it had been you."

His heart stilled in his chest, and it made every word she spoke too loud and too clear.

"I wish it had been you—*really you*—holding my sign on the dock that day." She shook her head. "You were the most beautiful man I'd ever seen, and the kindest, and you make me feel pretty like I've never—"

"You're beautiful."

"But you're not ready."

"I—"

"And you're not safe."

The breath rushed out of him. *Safe?* Mina didn't trust him. He couldn't push a word past his lips if his life depended on it.

"You have no employment. Your search for Georgiana may take weeks, or months, or *longer*. And it will be perilous and…you will return to England, and I cannot leave Emma, even if she marries, I will never leave her."

"But I—"

"I can't. I feel too much with you, and I must keep my wits and reason about me."

He struggled to keep his voice even, but failed. "Maybe you love me, then?"

"Love doesn't matter."

A tear raced down her cheek and he started for her. If he could just hold her… He couldn't say the right words, but if he could touch her…

But her arms held him away. "No. You don't even know me. You called me brave."

"Minnie—"

"You don't know me at all." She shook her head. "If you did, you'd know I could never marry a man like you."

And before Seth could say another word, Mina pushed past him and out the door.

Eleven

SETH LOCATED MINA IN THE CROWDED HOTEL LOBBY right away. He couldn't help it anymore. She lured his explorer's eye—she was too rare a prize not to. Mina was having her tiffin at a table full of other venture girls, but it had to be done. Tomorrow, he and Tom would leave Bombay, and there wasn't much chance he'd ever see Mina again.

Had she found a man yet? It had been a couple days. Maybe that Henry Block had come up to the scratch. He was older, but there was good to be found in a man who'd lived a little life. And Block was stable. Safe.

Not like him.

His stomach rolled again and a cold sweat formed on the back of his neck. *Hell.* Must have been that *masala* he bought for his rice. But he couldn't recall a day he'd been sick off food. He should lie down, but he'd not get another chance to see Mina. And he had to say good-bye, wish her happy, leave her alone—

I could never marry a man like you.

Pain cramped his gut and his eyes watered. "Christ," he muttered, his teeth grinding. He was never sick.

Mina's eyes lit on him and worry creased her brow. The next moment, she was on her feet and hurrying toward him. Despite it all, he smiled. His little officer. Wasn't any hesitating when she had a purpose, when she was caring for someone.

"Mr. Mayhew? You look pale."

His stomach uncoiled a little. "And you're looking perfect, Minnie."

"Sit down."

She tried to push him to the settee against the wall, but he grabbed her hand. "I was needing to speak with—"

"I'll sit with you."

Good. But he didn't let go of her hand until she followed him down onto the settee.

"What's wrong?" she asked. "You're unwell."

"No, I'm"— he smiled to reassure her—"I'm feeling right again." He wet his lips, but his whole mouth was dry. "I'm thinking I can't ask you outside or someplace private." Not after asking her to be his wife—not now. It had to be here, in the middle of all these damn people.

He ought to be efficient like Mina. Give her the money. Say good-bye.

"So, I…I'll get on with it," he mumbled.

Her dress was pale yellow today. And it suited her. "That's a pretty dress." And he could've sunk into the ground at the sadness of those words. Because he never saw her in anything that didn't suit her, and he wanted to—wanted to see her nose red with a cold, and her hair tangled from sleep, and barefoot in her night rail. But he'd never see her like that, never have the right to see her like that.

"Thank you, Mr. Mayhew."

She looked eager for him to get on with it, but damned if he could. "Is that Henry Block—?"

"Nothing is decided. Emma is still—" She lowered her head. "He seems very kind. You'd approve, I think."

"Does it matter if I approve?"

Her face shuttered. Christ, what the hell was he saying?

"Nothing is decided." She didn't look at him. "But you mustn't worry. Emma and I will be fine."

"You don't need to say things like that to—"

"*I* need to say them, Mr. Mayhew." Mina met his stare, and for the first time, Seth noticed the faint shadows under her brown eyes. "What else would you have me say? You are leaving tomorrow. What else do I say?"

His stomach clenched again. "I can't… You already said it. I can't give you what you need. I'm not safe enough." Seth couldn't look at her. Mina's fingers curled into fists on her lap. "It doesn't matter, Minnie. I've never been that smart—"

"No—"

"—or one for good manners like Tom. Even if I had all the money in the world, you're better off without me."

A choked sound came from Minnie, and her breath jerked as if she was going to speak but he couldn't bear to hear what she might say.

"How are your finances?" he blurted.

Ah—damn. This whole good-bye was a disaster. He smoothed the cringe from his face. She *was* better off without him.

"I know it's not proper to ask, but I was thinking you and Emma must have expected to be wed by now—"

"Thank you…Mr. Mayhew." She touched his arm, silencing him, that light hand like a dagger straight to his heart. She was always a lady. And she was still on his side. "But I am not your concern."

He stared at his hands. "I wouldn't say that, Minnie."

"I wouldn't ever want to be."

He heard every word she was saying but didn't understand any of it. *Minnie.* That stubborn, proud, little chin dared him to kiss away her resistance, to let him take care of her just for a little while, just for now.

She straightened on the settee like she was preparing to leave. He ripped the envelope from his coat pocket and thrust it at her. "You need to take this."

She surged to her feet, but he caught her wrist so she wouldn't run off again. "Please, Minnie, this is enough for you and Emma for a year. I need to know you'll be all right. I can't say good-bye and leave you without knowing that." She shook her head and wouldn't look at him. A tear glistened in her eye and his heart cramped. "Christ, Minnie, don't."

"I won't take that from you." She pulled out of his hold. "Good-bye, Mr. Mayhew. Say 'good-bye' now. Think of me only so far as it brings you pleasure, and I will pray for you, and pray you find Georgiana quickly."

"Good-bye?" He shook his head, catching her hand. *God, please don't let it be real. I can't be cursed. You're taking Minnie but let me find Georgie alive. Just give me that.*

Minnie tugged at his hold, but he couldn't let go. Not like this. "Minnie, wait."

Miserable as he was, he was surprised to feel anything but his own trampled heart—but they were being watched. And with a focus that had him rising to his feet and setting Mina behind him.

Lurking in a shadowy corner at the end of the lobby, an Englishman watched him.

Seth blinked, trying to correct the sight, trying to bring the man into the light that surrounded everything else, but the dark figure resisted—his boots, his black neck cloth, even his close-cropped hair checked the light like dull steel.

From this distance, there was an intense stillness about the man. Wasn't a doubt in Seth's mind that he saw everything in this room. That stare wasn't aimed at Mina. Had it been, Seth might've charged the man.

Mina saw him, too. She wiped a tear from her cheek without looking away. "Do you know him?"

Seth shook his head, not taking his eyes off the stranger. The dark man started for him—and damned if the shadows didn't shift with him, a streak of night against the pastel, sunlit canvas of Benson's Hotel. The man's arm hung rigid at his side, but the set of his shoulders seemed to be daring Seth to notice it. Or he might have been in pain.

The man stopped a few feet away and angled the right side of his face from them. The man kept his distance almost as a…as a *courtesy*. Before he'd turned, Seth had glimpsed an ugly scar running from the man's ear, down his neck, and under his collar. The wound must have been given the same time it had taken a nick of the man's ear.

With his scars and shadows, it was hard to look on

the man. But when he spoke in a low, gravelly voice, he had Seth's full attention.

"Are you the man looking for Georgiana Mayhew?"

"I'm her brother. Who are you?"

"You can call me Rivers."

Mina's breath caught behind him, and Seth took a hard look at the man. No, it couldn't be. "What's your full name, mate?"

His face turned a fraction, his eyes narrowing with question. "If it matters at all, Colin Rivers."

Ah Christ.

Mina swept forward and Rivers shied from her—not with fear. Like a stallion stamping its hoof at a grating mouse.

"My sister is Emmaline Adams," she said. "She has been waiting for you."

Rivers revealed nothing. Mina might not have spoken at all.

She hitched her chin higher. "Were you injured? Why did you not send word?"

"I beg your pardon, miss." Rivers spoke softly to Mina, but every word seemed to strain him, scratching and scraping on every launch of breath. "I don't know any women named 'Adams.' Mayhew, do you want my information or not?"

Seth took Mina's arm and pulled her from Rivers. "Go on, Minnie."

Thankfully, Mina didn't protest. With worry in her eyes, she nodded and left. From the corner of his vision, Seth watched her return to her friends. He only hoped Mina would return to her room and keep Emma there. Better if Emma never met this man.

Ignoring the pull to follow Mina, Seth faced Rivers. He said he had information, and something told Seth to listen to the man.

Rivers slid his stare across the crowded room. "Can we speak in private?"

"Here's private enough."

The man shifted his weight, his lips thin and white at the movement. Rivers didn't use a crutch, but his body must not be sound. Seth pointed to a bank of empty chairs against a far wall. "There."

Whatever the man's injuries, he moved swiftly and soundlessly. "I understand there's a reward," Rivers said as they walked.

"Twenty thousand for the orphan by the name of Aimee Bourianne to London—"

"I don't have the child, only information on George."

Seth's hands were like ice of a sudden. Georgie was called 'George' by the men who knew her. "Fifty pounds for information that's not false."

"It's not false."

Rivers lowered to his seat, his knees slow to bend. Seth joined him—but he kept a chair between them.

Rivers kept his eyes trained and alert on the lobby, not looking at Seth as he spoke. "I joined your sister, George, and a Chinese translator by the name of Xiang in Jiazhong. That's on the border of Tibet and China. They were buying provisions for a trip into Tibet."

Seth gripped the seat of his chair, pushing back against the avalanche of questions. "When?"

"June."

June. Seven months ago. "What brought you there? Why did you join them?"

"I was after the orphan myself. Heard a man who'd survived the massacre wanted to find the child."

"Right. The man's name is Will Repton."

Rivers listened without a flicker of feeling in him— until Seth uttered Will's name.

And then the fury blazing in Rivers's eyes set Seth back in his seat.

"Will Repton," Rivers growled softly. "Why he believed she lived…" His lip curled with a sneer. "How he got that money…"

"My sister…?" Seth prompted.

Rivers swiveled a burning gaze back to Seth. "George, Xiang, and I found the orphan. Alive."

Seth didn't dare to breathe. Like doing so might change the words coming from the stranger's lips.

"The baby was young, weak, but of course we took her. They traveled too slowly. I needed to be elsewhere, so I left them outside Tezpur, India. I told them to wait until I returned."

"And?"

The scorching gaze cooled. "I returned a week later and learned Xiang had been killed—and a woman with him." Rivers held Seth's eye. "I assume the woman was George."

The words hit him like a boulder. "Georgie…"

A woman laughed somewhere in the lobby, shrill and piercing, even as a tempest swirled, sped, *roared* in his head. "How?" he croaked.

"Robbed. Stripped of their possessions. No one knew anything of the child."

Georgie…I was too late. Georgie…I'm sorry—I did this. It was my curse.

Christ, he couldn't breathe. The room was too bright. He dropped his head in his hand. It was shaking. He was shaking. Maybe Rivers was wrong— maybe it wasn't her.

Seth raised his head. Focused on Rivers. Tried to see a falsehood in him. But the man looked straight back.

"Who are you?" Seth asked. "Why should I believe you?"

Rivers reached into his coat pocket and pulled out a small glass vial and a book. "I took these. *Before.* George had them in her portmanteau."

The glass tube was filled with a blue pigment, a paint pigment. "That isn't hers."

"It's hers."

Seth picked up the book, an artist's journal. "No, Georgie didn't use—" The cover fell open.

And all the breath fled his body.

A sketch of a pink camellia filled the page, but in the corner was a familiar mark—one Georgie would scribble to prepare her brush, to spread the paint on the bristles. A connected *M* and *W*. It didn't look like anything but a random scribble.

Unless you knew the artist's last name was Mayhew.

Seth did the same thing.

With hands that shook, Seth turned the pages. Her talent had grown over the years. He could almost feel the velvet on the petals of the violet. "Can I keep this?" Seth asked, his voice hoarse.

Rivers sat still as stone as Seth fought to control the tremor in his hands, but now he nodded once. "It's yours." Rivers rolled the glass tube in his palm. "Why did you say this isn't hers? This was in her bag."

Seth shook his head, swallowing hard against what was blocking his words. "Years ago, Georgie…she bought a supply of ultramarine. For painting. She vowed never to use anything else but that or azurite. My sister…she's particular about her materials. Already that pigment is fading."

Rivers unstopped the cork and lowered his head as if to smell it.

Seth held up a hand. "Don't. It's likely not fit to be breathed."

Rivers stopped up the tube and returned it to his pocket. He skirted Seth with a glance. "I am sorry. I liked George."

Seth smoothed the cover of her journal.

Rivers cleared his throat gruffly. "The fifty quid?"

The fifty—? Right. Seth breathed deep and sat up straight.

"The information's not false." Rivers handed him a card. "I wrote the name of the Bengal commissioner of Upper Assam. Man by the name of Jenkins. You should be able to confirm my information easy enough."

Seth nodded, shoving the card in his pocket.

"My direction is on the card." Rivers stood. "I'd appreciate a note when it's confirmed, or I'll call on you again. Are we done?"

"Mr. Rivers?"

Seth and Rivers turned at the woman's voice.

And Emma glared up at her intended.

Mina and Tom were coming up fast behind, so Seth

pushed to his feet. "We're done, Rivers. But you owe the lady an explanation."

And before anyone could question him, Seth turned and escaped the hotel.

❧

What had Mr. Rivers said to Seth? His skin had been ashen. Mina stared after Seth's back, but she could not leave Emma alone with this man. Colin Rivers faced Emma, and Mina wanted to haul her sister back. Without Seth, Mr. Rivers was far more intimidating. He was not as tall as Seth, but his shoulders were just as broad. Dark, hooded eyes studied Emma from a stony, arrogant face.

But Emma's fury was more than a match for the man's menace.

"Where have you been?" Emma didn't stop advancing until she was toe-to-toe with the man. "What happened to you? Did you not understand I was to arrive?"

His eyes narrowed and the confusion on his face appeared genuine. Perhaps the man was not impenetrable after all.

"Emmaline Adams, I presume?" He rasped her name softly, and it was a sound like something long dormant and little used. And more than a little...astonished.

Emma's eyes flashed and her cheeks flushed red. "Who else would claim you?"

He didn't move an eyelash, but Mina could have sworn a flicker of admiration softened his stare—but the light was suppressed in an instant.

"And what are you to me?" he asked.

Emma flinched as if struck. "I am to be your

wife." The words hung in the air between them as they stared.

No, Emma would not marry this man. Mina put her arm about Emma's shoulders and tried to pull her away, but her sister would not be moved.

Mr. Rivers's eyes shifted to the door. "I have no knowledge of any wife. I'm not the Colin Rivers you seek."

"Are you Colin Pierce Rivers? Deputy director of agriculture in the North-Western Provinces?"

He held very still.

"We are betrothed," Emma said. "You paid my bond to sail here. You wrote me letters. You—"

His head swung about. "What letters?"

"How *dare*—" Emma gripped her reticule, her knuckles white. "You *know* very well what letters."

His jaw tightened as he scanned Emma once more. "I am ignorant of any marriage scheme, Miss Adams, and I have no intention of taking on a wife. You'll forgive me." With a curt dip of his head, he turned on his heel and made for the door.

Emma sobbed, and before Mina knew what she was doing, she followed the broad back of Mr. Rivers. He'd reached the door before she managed to catch the man's arm. His right arm didn't swing from against his side as a normal arm would, but was unbending as steel beneath her fingers. "How dare you speak to my sister like that?"

He stopped abruptly, his eyes scanning the room behind them over her head. "There is no need for hysterics, Miss Adams."

"Hysterics?"

"I will not wed your sister and all the better for her." He unhooked her hand gently from his arm. "I just informed Mr. Mayhew that his sister is dead, so perhaps you might maintain the proper perspective."

All feeling rushed from her body. "Dead?"

"Your sister Emmaline will have no difficulty in securing a willing husband. No one that beautiful would lack for admirers. Good afternoon to you."

The man stalked out of the room, and Mina struggled to keep her legs beneath her. Georgiana was dead.

And Seth was alone.

Thomas and Emma appeared at her side. Emma's skin was ashen. "That was him—" Emma's voice broke halfway through. Like a fever, Emma's tempers always left her shaken and weak after they'd run their course. "Did you see him? That was him and he was hateful."

"He was, dear. He was cruel." Mina hugged her tight, as much for herself as Emma. "You will not marry him."

"But…his letters. He promised." Emma wrapped her arms about Mina, her breathing ragged, and watched the direction Mr. Rivers had departed.

Mina looked to Thomas. "We must return to our room."

Thomas jerked to action, putting an arm about Emma's shoulders. "Of course. I'm at your service." Thomas looked around. "Where has Mayhew gone to?"

A sob rose in her throat and threatened to choke her. "I don't know." She locked eyes with Thomas. "I don't know. But we must find him."

Twelve

THE MOMENT SETH RETURNED TO HIS HOTEL ROOM, he knew it was a mistake. He should have kept walking. The streets had been dark but at least there'd been life—dogs in the alleys and bodies huddling in doorjambs and turning in sleep, exposed under the Bombay sky.

The room was a mistake.

It was quiet as a crypt.

Where could he go? What could he do? It was the middle of the night, and he'd just come from walking all over the city. He stared at his bedroll on the charpoy platform. How could he sleep? His head was aching.

Georgie's journal was in his hand. Still in his... He should put it down. Light a candle. Put a cleft on the fire. Drink some water. Did he have anything to drink? He could try to sleep or...or maybe he should go out and walk again. He could—

A soft knock sounded on the door, and Seth turned as if he could see through the wall.

"Mr. Mayhew?"

Thank God…thank God…Minnie. He hurried to the door, his chest tight and burning. The light from the hall illuminated his room. He should light the lamp…but he was so relieved to see her face, he froze in place.

In the dim light, her lips worked into a warm, loving, *sad* smile, and for the first time that night, hot tears stung his eyes. He turned his head before she could see.

"You changed your dress." He frowned. Damn foolish thing to say. Now she'd know he wasn't right.

"May I come in?" she whispered, her gaze flickering up and down the hall.

Quickly, he stepped aside, even knowing he shouldn't. Closing the door plunged the room into darkness. "I'll…uh." Damn, he couldn't find words. He pointed to the mantel and lit the lamp, holding Georgie's book under his arm.

A gentle hand landed on his arm and the book was slipped from him. "Let's put this down."

He watched Georgie's journal be carried to the table and set down. Standing in the center of the room, Mina passed him again to light the fire. "I should do that, Minnie."

"I have it."

In moments, the fire crackled and grew, and she took his hand to lead him to a chair at the table. "Why don't you sit?"

He only had the one chair. The room was too dark for company, for a lady. "You shouldn't be here." But he couldn't put up more of an argument than that. When she pressed him into his chair, he didn't resist.

"It is all right. Emma is asleep and no one saw me come. I came earlier, but you weren't here. I'm glad you're back." She put a kettle on the hob over the fire.

"I don't have any tea," he said. "Sorry, Minnie. Don't have much of anything to eat. I have some mustard, I think."

"I brought tea. And jam and bread. Well, naan."

A jam pot was placed in front of him, along with three pieces of the flat bread the native people ate.

"That is an explorer's trick, isn't it?" she said. "Jam or mustard can make any food edible."

A small smile curved her lips and he clung to the sight. "What did you make of Colin Rivers?" He needed to know. The man almost seemed a specter now—no, all of it seemed a nightmare. One he couldn't wake from.

"At first, I thought he was trying to deceive us," Mina said. "But it's obvious he's endured some trauma. He claims to know nothing of his agreement to marry Emma. She will not marry him in any case."

"Good, that's good," he murmured. Mina poured tea from a kettle he didn't recognize. "Did I have a teapot?"

"I brought this with me. Will you try to eat?"

Obediently, he ate in silence. Mina bustled about the cupboard, arranging the kettle and teapots and dishes. *Turn around, Minnie.*

He carried his cup to his bedstead, freeing the chair for Mina to sit. The tea warmed him, released the tension in his back and shoulders, and made him calm. Calmer than he'd been in hours. "He said he knew Georgie. He had her sketches."

"May I look at them?"

He nodded and Mina picked up the journal and sat beside him on the bed. "These are beautiful drawings." After a moment, she asked, "Are you certain this belonged to Georgiana?"

"Do you see that *M* and *W* on most of the pages?"

She didn't look up. "Yes."

Fresh pain surged in his chest. "He said…said she'd been robbed and killed in Burma. He said he wasn't there—"

Mina's arm slid around him, her body warm and bracing as the tea. He breathed deep and dared to look at her. No tears. Thank God, no tears. He couldn't bear those right now. "I'll send a telegram to the Assam commissioner in the morning."

"That's a good idea. Nothing is certain. Nothing confirmed."

Hot tears flooded his eyes and he turned his head to hide them. Soft cotton was pressed against his eyes to dry them. Mina's handkerchief.

Embarrassed, he huffed a laugh and took the little square. No use pretending.

"It's normal to be afraid for her," she said.

His little officer. Straight-thinking, plain-speaking Mina. He could breathe again, but his tears wouldn't stop. But it seemed all right to let them fall with her. He never cried. Not since he was a lad.

She stood and, instinctively, he caught her wrist, nearly hauling her back.

"Shall I refill your tea?" she asked quietly.

He let her go, embarrassed to look at her as she moved to the fire.

"I think you should sleep," she said.

Mina handed him another steaming cup, which he drained. The tea might've been the only heat in his body. She drew the curtains closed and he clamped down on his shredded nerves. She'd leave him and he'd go back to his pacing, back out to the street maybe, until sunrise—*what did she say?*

He looked at her. "Ay? I didn't... Did you say something?"

She smoothed her hair, though it was neat as a new pin. "I could stay here with you. If you would like...?"

Stay? Stupidly, he looked down at the bed. He wanted her there, wanted her to stay, wanted not to be alone with that journal.

"Yes." He cringed at how loud he answered, how desperate he sounded, but he couldn't take it back. "Stay. Please."

She clutched her skirt pocket, and it took a moment before she spoke. "Let's sleep, then. There is nothing more we can do tonight."

"No." That made sense. It made sense.

She turned quickly, and there was no need to say anything more. Pins were plucked from her hair, and small, white fingers released a thick braid to sway down her back.

Maybe he shouldn't be watching. He looked at his lap as her skirts rustled. She shouldn't be here. If she was seen—

But she was always on his side.

"Mr. Mayhew?"

His head shot up and the smile she gave him was bashful.

"Will you undo my top buttons?" She presented her back. "This neckline is not comfortable for sleep."

He lurched to stand. Mina was even shorter in her stockinged feet. She slung her braid over her shoulder before he could touch it. There wasn't much to do, only a few buttons. But he memorized the line of her neck, the delicate whorl of hair at the nape of her neck. He'd draw that in his book…

"Thank you," she murmured.

It seemed abrupt when she stepped away from his fingers, but he wasn't moving with any sense of time. And Mina was efficient about things. Hairpins were stacked at one corner of the table with her necklace, her shoes arranged on the floor directly beneath them, the lamp had been turned down.

She was so beautiful with her hair down, like an angel. His fingers curled into his palms, wanting to touch her.

Christ, his head was muddled. He turned his back, took off his waistcoat, and unbuttoned his collar. That was enough—she wasn't undressing and he wouldn't either.

She folded down the blanket and lay down. Without a word, he followed her into the bed. And lying beside her was easy. So easy. Her rose scent was different now, richer, darker, like liquor. *Pretty Minnie…so close, just inches away*.

She faced him, her lids heavy and her hair so dark and soft against the pale sheets. "Seth? Close your eyes."

It took him a moment to speak. "You said my name."

Her hand found his under the blanket, their fingers threaded together. She edged closer. "Close your eyes."

"I can't." The faint firelight bathed her in a haze of light. He didn't want to see anything else, didn't want to dream anything else. "I can't close 'em."

She stroked his hair back from his brow. "All right." She inched closer, and it was so easy, so right, when her head rested on his chest.

And this was like nothing he'd ever felt. This woman, so small and light on his chest, her hair the softest silk under his chin...

Just for tonight, he'd take her comfort—a wife's comfort—even if he didn't deserve it. He'd never deserve it now.

I was too late, Georgie. I'm sorry.

He held Mina's hand on his chest, her fingers cool in his. "Are you warm enough?"

"I am," she whispered.

His head swam with exhaustion. "Are you comfortable?"

"Yes. Are you?"

His body was heavy, and her hair... "Roses..."

"Hmm?"

Mina's roses were in the air. Soft skin. She was warm. His lids grew heavy, his eyes closed.

And he dreamed of home.

❦

Mina came awake in an instant and knew exactly where she was. This dark room was Seth's and this was his bed. This was his arm he'd slung around her waist. And his body pressed against hers.

But this couldn't be her. She didn't recognize this woman. She didn't break rules. She didn't risk. Even sailing to Bombay to marry Thomas had calculated in her favor.

She had to leave. Right now.

Seth's deep, even breaths tickled the hairs on the top of her head and the tension in her body eased a notch. He'd slept. At least he'd slept.

He rolled, and his hug drove her into the mattress and pinched her lungs. The man's weight was nothing to trifle with. Carefully at first, then with more effort, she extricated herself from beneath his hold and slid off the bed.

"Minnie?"

"I'm here," she whispered quickly from where she stood by the table. His low, gravelly voice would be heard in the hall.

The blankets rustled and the bedframe creaked. "Are you leaving me, then?"

The sad words gave her pause, but she stuffed whatever she was feeling down with all the very urgent reasons for getting out of his room before she might be discovered. "The sun is rising." She adjusted the drapes to allow the smallest sliver of light in.

He swung his legs to the floor and sat up, rubbing a hand over his eyes. Bent over his knees, his head hung from his massive shoulders. The sight arrested her, but she couldn't tarry. She pocketed her hairpins, slipped on her shoes, emptied the tea into the slop bucket—he could keep the jam.

He hadn't moved. Was he asleep again? Holding the teapot, she ventured closer and set a hand on his shoulder. "Seth, lie back down."

He caught her hand and rose, a solid wall of man,

heated and powerful, but always so gentle. His size did not sway her anymore. His heart had beat against her cheek, and he'd held her hand to sleep. There was no flirtation or bluster in him now.

Not now. Perhaps not for a very long time.

"I don't want to leave," she said softly. "I'm sorry—"

Her neck was cradled by a big hand and, in the next instant, a warm mouth covered hers. Surprised, her lips were rigid—cool and unmoving as the teapot in her hands. But Seth pressed gently and she relaxed against him, resting a hand on his hard chest. And that was all. A kiss of comfort. For him. And for her.

I'm so sorry, Georgiana…

She had come to his room as much for her as for him. Life in Bombay seemed possible when he was near. Somehow, he could offset so much of what was wrong and frightening. He hugged her close and she was so safe, so cared for, in this moment. Hot tears collected on her eyelashes but she ignored them as they raced from the corner of her eyes down her cheeks.

Seth would return. He would live in England, in the landscapes she loved, and she would imagine him there, climbing the rolling green hills, following his river to the birch, in the frost and in the spring and in the splendid summers. And she was so glad.

I'm so sorry, Georgiana. You were lost. Her heartbeat steadied. *But Seth won't be.*

He raised his head but didn't release her hand. "You helped, Minnie. You don't know how much."

"Last night was terrible. Today…" How much worse would it be if he received confirmation

Georgiana had been murdered? "Today, we'll make a new plan."

His eyes centered on her and he nodded. "A plan. I don't know if I trust Colin Rivers. Even if he had Georgie's journal. He might have stolen it."

Much as she disliked Colin Rivers, the man was a well-salaried deputy director in the East India Company. Why would he steal or lie?

Moving as quietly as she could in the hotel's silent hall, she turned back to Seth. Lines were etched on his brow and beneath his eyes. Sadness. And strain. When he saw her looking, he nodded and gave her a wink.

And the crack in her heart deepened.

They could plan, but they'd never be able to prepare for what was to come. He knew that now as well as she did. How did you prepare in a world that took all your love and used it against you?

No, there was no preparing. But there may be someone along the way who could help you keep a small bit of hope alive. Maybe that was a lesson she was meant to learn. She might lose her heart, but it wouldn't be broken. It would only be taken.

Seth had said there was only one place in the world you left your whole heart. She would give hers to him and get on with the rest of her life and be grateful.

Because her heart could go home.

Thirteen

"They confirmed it, then?" Tom lowered the telegram and looked at Seth across the table in the hotel lobby. Mina and Emma sat silent, their faces pale and solemn.

Seth reached to take back the telegram from the Assam commissioner's office. "Only took two days, on account of a venture girl, Caroline. Her beau knew a man, who knew a man in the capital of Lower Assam, who expedited matters. Even the Monday before Christmas." He folded the paper into his pocket. "I got the telegram this morning. After breakfast."

Mina's eyes widened with what looked like regret. "I'm sorry I wasn't with you."

He shook his head. "It wasn't news, Minnie."

It hadn't been news at all. Georgie was lost to him the day Rivers said she was. Holding Mina in his arms that night, he'd said good-bye to his sister, the last soul belonging to him. The telegram almost didn't matter.

He found Mina's hand under the table and held it. "They confirmed the Chinese man and his companion were killed, just like Rivers said."

No one spoke, so Seth cleared his throat in the silence and continued. "I need to go there, see that she was buried proper, and ask after the little one. Find her."

And he *would* find the orphan. Finding was what he did.

But that didn't mean he'd find her alive.

"Can the child still be there?" Emma asked.

"Will Repton sent me here to find her," he said. "I can't leave until I know where she is. I can't delay any. I start the journey tomorrow."

Mina gripped his hand under the table. "Then you and Thomas must go immediately," she said quietly.

Tom nodded. "Certainly, Mina. Just as soon as I'm assured of your security here."

Mina looked at Tom like he'd just slapped a puppy. "Security?"

Ah…hell.

"We are perfectly secure, Thomas," she said calmly.

Too calmly. Mina straightened in her seat, and Seth took to studying the table. No, Mina wouldn't tolerate that. She was damn stubborn about taking care of herself and her sister. Hell, she'd turned down *his* money a half dozen times and he was running out of time—fast.

But Tom wasn't keeping his mouth shut. "Mina, my conscience and my duty—"

"Your duty is to Mr. Mayhew and his travel arrangements," she said. "It is rather clear what needs to be done. *And quickly*. Already the day is half gone, Thomas."

Seth kept his face blank, but he had the strangest

urge to laugh. His little officer quelling insubordina-
tion and giving orders. And always on his side.

But it was damn awkward.

"Yes, of course," Tom mumbled. "I...I'll start on
that today, shall I, Mayhew?"

"I'd be obliged, Tom," he said.

"Right, then." Tom pushed to his feet. "I'll start on
that carriage hire, and call on you after five."

Seth nodded and Tom took himself off. Mina
darted a glance at him. She was mothering him but
trying not to be caught at it. It was plain enough,
though—in the way she showed up at his door at
every mealtime to make sure he remembered to eat.
And helped him plan, listening to all his questions as
to how Georgie could be gone, how anyone could
hurt her. And the way she lay beside him at night so
he could sleep.

And all that felt less like mothering, and more like
saving his life.

He squeezed Mina's hand under the table and
willed her to look at him. He knew every eyelash,
every golden flare in her warm, brown eyes. How was
he meant to leave her tomorrow? Yet she hadn't asked
him to stay.

It was all that straight thinking. Mina knew she
needed a man who was safe.

And when *he* was thinking straight, he knew he
didn't deserve her.

"I suppose that *man* will be calling to collect his
reward," Emma said.

Seth sighed, knowing Emma was on her way to
getting good and riled over Colin Rivers.

Emma narrowed her eyes. "He is utterly vile. I would give him *nothing*."

"I don't like him much myself, Emma," Seth said gently. "But he's punished enough by not getting you for a wife."

Emma's lower lip trembled. "I'm sorry to dwell on the horrid man, Seth. He should not be spoken of in the same breath as you." She stood and hugged him hard around the neck. "I'm so sorry. You don't deserve this."

He patted her arm. "Thank you, Emma."

She crushed her handkerchief to her face and whimpered, "I'm going to the room, Mina."

"All right, dear."

But Emma was already weeping as she walked up the stairs.

Seth arched a brow at Mina. "With those ready feelings, she would've made a fine player for the stage."

Mina smiled at him. "Emma's always loved you a little, you know?"

"Has she now?" He held her eye, willing her to say the same. To say *more*.

But Mina dropped her eyes. She was wearing the same sweet woodruff-print dress she'd worn the day he met her, and her eyes were lighter today. Like tea with too much water. He leaned closer for the scent of English rose. Of Mina. He'd remember that perfume forever.

The breath he took was shaky, rattling him further. There wasn't any time at all left. "Can we leave, Minnie?" he blurted. "I'm feeling like the air's too thin." He couldn't draw it deep enough into his lungs.

She rose, and he stood slowly, his legs less than steady under his weight.

"Leave your door unlocked," she said. "I'll meet you as soon as I can without being seen."

"No—"

She left him before he could stop her. Not his room…not in the middle of the day. If anyone ever saw her enter or leave, her reputation would be good and ruined—

And that hadn't really occurred to him until now. In the middle of the night, he'd let her come to him again and again. What kind of man let a lady take that kind of risk?

He cursed under his breath. The entire lobby might have been judging him, as conspicuous as he felt leaving and climbing the stairs to his room. But Mina was on her way, and damned if he didn't need to be alone with her.

A long, quarter hour passed before she slipped into his room, and he pulled her into his arms. And no matter the risk, he wasn't letting her go.

"Minnie." Her name was all he could manage, and she seemed to understand, letting him hug her harder than he should.

"You have to go," she said softly. "Georgiana would want you to look for Aimee."

"She would." He closed his eyes. "I do have to go. I have to see to Georgiana. She's past caring, but if I don't bury her proper, it's like she's still lost. And I'm not letting her stay lost."

She nestled closer. "When you learn where they laid her to rest, you can say good-bye. She'll hear you."

God, let that be true.

He drew a long breath and spoke the words he was dreading. "Once I leave Bombay, I won't be coming back."

She smiled sadly. "I know it."

His heart was good and shattered now. And the strangest fear overcame him. Like nothing would matter after he took care of Georgie. Not his land in Matlock, not fixing up that cottage, not even the damn curse. What would matter if there wasn't anyone in the world who'd care for him? Or to care for—except Mina?

And she'd be here in India, married to another man.

"We don't have much time left." His words hurt, like they'd broken free of his chest and spilled from his lips.

She pulled him to the bed and they sat down. He never had gotten another chair. "Do you want some tea, Minnie? I still have what you left."

He started to rise, but she put a hand on his lap. "I don't want tea."

Her hand was so little. He covered it with his own, engulfing that elegant, white skin and slender fingers. Too damn big…

He forced himself to look at her. It was getting harder to every hour. She was blushing like he'd not seen her blush in days, and he touched her cheek where she looked warmest. "What are you thinking, pretty? You aren't getting shy on me?"

Her lids lowered, hiding those brown eyes he loved. And her hand moved higher on his leg, which made him smile. Mina *really* didn't know about flirting. She shouldn't be touching a man there. He caught her fingers and kissed them, lowering them to his knee.

"Seth?" She kept her eyes on their joined hands. "This is the worst time to ask."

He ducked his head to hear her whispering voice.

"You might think me horrible to even suggest it. But this is our last day together. And I hoped we might…be *together*." She lifted her face and scanned his eyes. "Do you understand what I'm asking? Seth? Were you listening?"

So damn pretty. "I'm listening." He smiled sadly. "You're spending too much time with me. You're talking in different directions now."

She inched close and pressed her face into his neck. Soft hair pillowed his jaw. Christ, he'd remember this, too—

"I want to be with you," she said.

The hand he'd moved to touch her stopped in midair. He tipped her chin to search her eyes, but she clasped his neck and he couldn't stop her from kissing him. He didn't want to stop her but…

Ah, Christ, she had the softest mouth for kissing, and her kiss was tugging at almost every part of his body. The muscles in his arms tightened, but he was careful not to touch her. Mina was the one doing all the touching.

"Please, Seth," she whispered in his ear, and now he was feeling that plea yank hard all through his body.

She pressed closer to him, crawling over his lap, the firm mounds of her breasts straining against him. Those slender fingers threaded in his hair and gripped like she owned him. She'd never done that before and… *Ah*, her mouth was hot on his ear.

No, she'd never done that before, either.

"*Wait*," he growled. He caught her slim body against him before the last, frayed thread of his control snapped, and pinned her arms so she couldn't continue all she was doing. "Wait. What are you wanting, Minnie?"

Her cheeks were flushed and her coral lips wet and plump, and he pinned her tighter—just so she wouldn't go back to kissing him like that.

No, that wasn't accurate. Just so she wouldn't move and take away the heaven of her breasts. Or stop looking at him the way she was looking now.

He groaned, but remembered he wasn't a damn ape. He could speak. If he could breathe first. "Minnie." He was still groaning a little, but at least he was forming words. "Tell me what you're wanting."

"I want you to make love to me."

His heart slammed against his ribs. Yes. Mina spoke plain.

"I'm sorry, Seth. The timing is… But I care for you and feel you care for me—"

"I do."

"—and I won't feel the same way when I marry whomever I eventually marry—at least, I cannot imagine I will—and so I wanted, just once, before you leave"—she dragged in a breath—"to know what that's like with you. With a man who cares."

His heart broke in his chest and he hid his eyes so she wouldn't see what he was feeling. *He* didn't know what he was feeling.

"And I would be less afraid," she said quietly.

And that was all it took. "Minnie," he groaned, kissing her with all the need and grief and desperation surging in his body. Christ, he'd give her anything she wanted, anything she asked. She needed him. And they were alive and together and they'd make love—

His eyes snapped open.

They'd make love. And Mina was small. As small as the other women he'd bedded.

And he had hurt them.

"Will you, Seth?" Mina sealed her lips to his again.

But the hairs on the back of his neck prickled. If he went slow, if he was careful, it might turn out all right. And if it didn't…

He trampled the thought. "All right, Minnie." He helped her to her feet, and that was disturbingly easy to do. No, she wasn't heavy. There wasn't much heft to her at all. "Why don't you…uh, get undressed?"

Her brown eyes sparkled with some new feeling. Excitement maybe. Or desire. It might be all right with her… God, let it be all right.

She was unbuttoning her jacket and blouse, and paused to look at him with a question in her eyes. "Should I unplait my hair?"

He'd never seen that. "Yes," he blurted. "Please." Why couldn't he unbutton his coat?

Hairpins were removed and he stopped fussing with his damn coat. She loosened her braid. Slim, white fingers peeked between all that glossy hair. And when it was free…

"Ah…Minnie," he groaned.

Dark hair tumbled and waved and shimmered all down her slim shoulders. Could he just stand here forever? Just stand here and look at her?

Her blouse was open, the white ribbon of her corset

crisscrossing her small waist and tenderly lifting those breasts. And that skin…as smooth as a magnolia petal, and her chemise as thin as a skeleton flower in the rain.

He wanted to look everywhere at once. And under all the worship, under all the awe, something male and hard was waking in him, demanding that body to be under his. He clamped down on the brute desire dizzying him like liquor. He had to be gentle.

God, how long had it been since he'd coupled with a woman? And now it would be with Mina—the woman he would've chosen, the woman he wanted more than any other in the world.

She took off her blouse and he jerked back a step. Damn, he'd been right. He'd suspected she was well formed. Her bosom would stir a priest to sin. She was little, with the littlest waist, but those breasts would fill even his hands—

A small panic lit in him. Touching her with all the lust he was feeling would be dangerous. She was smaller than Sofia. He wouldn't please her; he didn't know how. He had to do better, had to—

"Seth, what's wrong?" Mina held the ends of her stays together.

He dragged his eyes up from the shadowy valley of her breasts to look into her face. She had that look on her face when she was waiting for him to catch up with the thought he was supposed to be having at that precise moment.

He shook his head, pulled his lips into a smile, and tried the lie. "There's nothing wrong, pretty."

She looked like she didn't know what to do next. Which she likely didn't. He moved closer and eased her fingers off the ribbons of her corset so he could loosen the stays. Her breasts rose with every slow breath. For a virgin, she was calmer than he was at present.

"You're being very quiet," she said.

"I'm grateful."

"What?"

He looked at her. Had he spoken aloud? "I'm just… I've been learning what unwords me. You. Or gratitude. Maybe both. *Probably* both. I don't think I've ever been more grateful than now."

Her beautiful brown eyes softened even more. And that muzzled him good and tight.

He kneeled down, pulling the corset down past her hips and legs until she could step out of them. A slender ankle stretched up a slim, womanly calf, and her foot would fit in his hand—

"It's been two years," he blurted from the ground at her feet. "And only twice."

"What was only—?"

"Two women, one time each."

Her little toes curled into the carpet, like they were wincing at his confession. "Oh."

"I wouldn't want you to think I was some sort of seducer, like a lady-killer or even all that talented."

"No, I—"

"I'm not at all." He dared to look up at her. "Talented, I mean. Being the size I am." He swallowed. "All the other bits are fine, meaning the touching and kissing. You might not be keen on… the *other* bit. Not that you need to be afraid of me," he hurried to add.

But Mina looked at him with all the trust in the

world in her eyes. And eagerness and—*God*, with love, too.

Did she love him?

She smoothed his hair from his brow. "All right," she said quietly.

He took a deep breath. "All right." He rose from his position at her feet. "Will you help me out of my unmentionables now?"

Her eyes lit with amusement. She was a hard one to get to laugh out loud.

While she attended to his buttons, he devoured the sight of her long hair and the chemise that hung from her delicate shoulders and flowed over the swell of her bosom. He'd always remember this—her closeness, her perfume, the first time they loved each other.

The only time.

He blinked his eyes. They were hot and itching, and he wasn't going to think any more about that. She pulled his shirt out of his trousers but she couldn't reach to slip it over his head.

"I'll do that, pretty." He pulled off the shirt, and his bare chest was a sight she seemed to like. Her fingers stroked his stomach, tracing the hard ridges there, and up high on his chest, and then around and down his shoulders. He'd lost a little weight and his skin was tight over his muscle, but she seemed to like the look of him anyway.

Could he take that chemise off her now?

Maybe if he got naked first. He kissed her cheek and stepped back to unbutton his trousers. Best to give her the full aspect of his oversize body. She might change her mind…

Damn. She might at that.

Steeling himself, he stepped out of his trousers and stood tall to let her inspect his roger. He was already half-hard so she'd have some notion of what was to come. And the way she was looking at it, he didn't think the notion was a welcome one.

He cleared his throat and started to cross his arms, but that didn't feel natural at all. His arms hung stupidly at his side. "I know it looks a bit cumbersome, but you won't have to suffer it all that long."

Her eyes left his roger to meet his. "I… What?"

"I'll be fast about it."

"You will? Why?"

"Ah, Minnie." She was going to make him say it. "In case you don't"—he grimaced—"*like* it. You likely won't. It's more for the man's pleasure."

"Oh."

"But I'll do other things for you. And I'll be gentle."

"Oh." Again, her eyes dipped down to his roger and back. "Thank you."

It was getting bigger the longer they talked about it. He checked—he still had a ways to grow. He looked up as Mina pulled off her chemise.

And he damn near swooned. "Oh…*God*."

"Seth?"

Oh God. His eyes were clenched shut but firm, round breasts, pink nipples, the sweet cinch of her waist floated in front of him. "Yes, Minnie. Sorry." He opened his eyes and—*oh God*—smiled tightly at her. "It's just… I'm thinking you might be the most beautiful woman I've ever seen, that's all. So if I—well, I'm not going to cry or anything, but if I'm talking and not speaking a word of sense, that's why. So don't be concerned because it's nothing you're doing."

And her stockings tied at her sweet, little thighs— Christ God, she looked good. "Well, it *is* something you're doing, but not on purpose, so you can ignore the things I say." Right. He *might* start crying.

Confusion flashed across her face, but then she smiled and blushed, and even undraped as she was, she was still a lady. "Thank you, Seth. I think you're beautiful, too."

That didn't make any sense, but he clenched his teeth before he said anything more to disturb her.

Mina turned to sit on the bed, flashing a perfect, round bottom, and unrolled her stockings. "What other things will you do?"

He couldn't keep a thought in his head…not with those stockings. "Ay? Sorry?"

"You said you would do other things." She hugged her arms around her, which plumped her breasts higher and didn't help his concentration one bit.

"Other things, right." Right. What were those exactly?

He joined her on the bed and couldn't delay touching her a second longer. He wrapped an arm about her waist to ease her onto her back, and they were lying eye to eye. Her hands combed through his hair.

Christ, she was an angel—*his* angel. Skin soft as heaven but those lips were all temptation. He sank his mouth onto hers, letting her sweet tongue tangle with his. The soft mounds of her breasts brushed his chest, but he couldn't cover her.

If he weren't so damn big and heavy, he'd be more

comfortable for a woman of her proportions. But small as she was, she wasn't timid. He put his hand on her satiny thigh and she parted her legs. Beneath his hand, her soft skin was vibrating.

"You're not scared?" he asked.

Her eyes smiled at him. "You're not scaring me." And to give truth to the words, she hiked her leg over his.

He brushed the tender, curling hair between her legs and kept his hand there. She was warm, almost hot. Would she be wet? Was it too soon to check?

"You're not scaring me," she whispered, hugging him tight against her to kiss him.

God, she was sweet. Her smooth, silken legs rubbed against his rigid body. He couldn't keep a thought in his head but... Christ, her thighs squeezed him about the waist. She was—"Minnie."

Her eyes fluttered open, and that soft, unfocused gaze nearly made him spend right then and there. She grabbed his hair and pulled him down onto her mouth again. Small moans like he'd never heard in his life vibrated from her lips. Her thighs clamped tight, and she squeezed his posterior.

She liked this?

God, she liked this—thank you.

Carefully, he sank onto her, letting his tongue plunge deep into her hot mouth, and gripped her hair right back. It was the best loving he'd ever had. Even before his roger was even involved, the woman loved him better than anyone ever had.

And he'd return the favor.

He parted her and eased his finger into her.

"Oh! My!" She arched beneath him, her slender body straining under his weight. "*Seth.*"

He stroked her, again and again, watching her face with every careful press of his fingers. Her eyes unfocused. Her lips were panting. And he was hot, and getting hotter. "Minnie." He growled her name, ready to explode. He kissed her hard, and she ignited with spasms. And he clung so she wouldn't slip away. "Sweet Minnie…do you like that?"

She gasped, trying to catch her breath. It wasn't fair to ask questions but damn if he would stop. Not when she kept coming. Not if he could keep making her come.

"Do you like that?" he crooned into her ear. "Do you want more?"

"Oh yes…please…yes—"

He bent to her breast and, greedy for her, suckled, deeper and deeper, until her nails were digging into his scalp and she was crying out. And he couldn't stop touching her, teasing her, like her pleasure was his pleasure—

A spasm tightened her, twisted her, and wracked her with a violence that frightened him into stopping.

And then she melted into the mattress under him. "Oh…Seth…"

Panting harder than he could ever remember breathing, he rested on her shoulder, his face buried in her neck. She shivered, so he kept his touch gentle to soothe her sensitive flesh. But the happiness in his heart swelled to bursting.

His Mina. He'd pleasured her.

She hugged his neck, her arms light and weak, and

whispered in his ear. "Seth…thank you." Her voice held a smile. "You *are* a lady-killer."

He chuckled with surprise. And damned if he didn't want to shout from the housetops what he'd done. "Are you all right?"

She nodded and stretched under him, long lashes fluttering. "You and your wiles…"

Well. Mina had learned to flirt. His heart had melted, but other throbbing, pulsing, *pained* parts of his body were reminding him he wasn't done yet.

But she wouldn't be smiling, then.

A knock at the door jolted them both.

Goddamn! His heart was in his throat, and he'd instinctively covered Mina—her eyes wide with alarm. But any woman would be alarmed with his enormous ape body caging her.

"Mr. Mayhew, sir?" a boy's voice inquired from the hall.

Seth clenched his eyes, trying to calm his pounding heart. "A minute, lad," he yelled. Mina was shaking under him. "Oh no. I'm sorry, Min—"

But she was shaking with the giggles she was holding in, her eyes bright with stars and her cheeks pinker than he'd ever seen them.

And he wasn't at all inclined to take his eyes off her.

"Mr. Mayhew?" the hall voice asked again.

"I said a *minute*," he called.

He smiled down at her happy face. He'd remember this forever. He dropped a kiss on Mina's blushing nose and lifted off her, slow and careful, to move to the door.

"What is it, lad?" he asked through the door.

"I've a letter for you, sir."

He looked down at his naked body. His roger looked back at him. "Well, go on and read it. I'm not decent for company."

A pause and then the sound of paper unfolding. "Mr. Colin Rivers is waiting for you in the lobby."

He cursed under his breath.

"Sir? Do you have a response?"

He planted his fists on his hips and turned to Mina. The smile slipped from her lips and worry clouded her eyes. "Tell him I'll be down," he said to the hallboy.

Seth began to dress, strapping on his belt and money, but he couldn't look away from Mina in his bed. She'd pulled his blanket over herself and all her soft, brown hair covered her white shoulders. So beautiful. She might have been an angel fallen from above. His roger protested being tucked back into his trousers.

But damned if he wasn't...*relieved*.

He smiled at her and winked. "A sight a man could get used to."

She blushed deeper. He could always make her blush. "A naked woman in your bed?"

"Just you, pretty. Just you." He couldn't stop from bending over her again to plant a kiss on her lips. When he lifted his head a while later, he reached for her stockings she'd folded over the bedpost. "Don't suppose you need help putting these on?" he murmured.

She smiled and pulled them from his hand, the smooth cotton sliding through his fingers.

And he was suddenly panicked by the thought she'd leave. "You don't have to go. I'll be coming right back."

Damn if he didn't sound like a green lad, but she smiled at him. "I'll wait right here."

Mina would never embarrass him. Never leave him feeling like a fool, even if he was always a fool with her.

"I'll pay Rivers and send him on his way," he said. "He won't be lingering."

"Will you be all right? I can come with you."

He shook his head. "I don't want you near that man again."

She caught his hand. "And we'll make love when you come back?"

His heart plunged. A bit like climbing those cliffs. He pulled his lips into a smile. "You do speak plain, Minnie."

"I just want to be sure we're…in agreement."

His little officer. He might tease her, make some silly jest about having to be persuaded, but his heart wouldn't let him. Not today. Not in this. "Yes, Minnie." He leaned to catch the perfume of her hair, to press his mouth to the soft skin at her temple, to stroke the silky curtain of hair down her back. To remember.

"Seth, please be careful with Mr. Rivers."

Anger flooded him. The man was taking his and Mina's precious time away from them.

Rivers better be careful with him.

Fourteen

COLIN RIVERS FOLDED THE FIFTY-POUND NOTE INTO
his pocket without a word. From the moment Rivers
crossed the hotel lobby, the man hadn't exchanged
more than a dozen words with him. And Seth was
damn eager to leave the man now.

Rivers *was* more specter than man. It was his stillness. Maybe not all specters wailed and rattled chains.
Maybe some hid secrets they didn't want the living to
learn. In all the places Seth had been, and the people
he'd met, there wasn't one with colder blood than the
man sitting across from him.

And this man had traveled with his sister. Georgie had
been alive with him. "She drew you. In her journal."

That broke Rivers's silence, but it was a moment
before he spoke with that ruined, rumbling voice.
"She was always drawing. She was good."

Georgie had seen the darkness in him, too. The
charcoal sketch of Rivers in her journal barely
broke from the shadows in the background. His face
hadn't been more than brutal, angry scrapes of ash
and soot.

"Your sister was brave," Rivers said. "When it mattered."

Pain lanced across Seth's chest. When it *mattered*? What the hell did that mean?

Seth surged to his feet. He had to get the hell away from Rivers. There was no telling what he might do to the man feeling as disordered as he did now. And Mina was waiting.

Rivers rose, too. "Could I ask a question?"

"Ask."

"The man who sent you here, Will Repton." Rivers swiveled his stare toward him like a glinting saber and Seth tensed. "Do you think he lied to you?"

Seth could read nothing in the man's eyes. Not a flicker or feeling. He wouldn't be telling this Rivers a damn thing. "I think our business is done—"

A rustle of skirts and a flurry of movement sounded from behind. Taking his eyes off Rivers wasn't a comfortable thing, but Seth looked over his shoulder. Emma, in high dudgeon, was charging—a cyclone of ruffles and springing blond curls.

Ah…hell.

"You called yourself a gentleman!" Emma hurled something small at Rivers that bounced off his chest and dropped to the ground. Rivers didn't even flinch. His eyes never moved off Emma.

On the ground was a folded letter.

"You signed a contract!" Another letter was pitched that slapped Rivers on the shoulder. "We sailed for *three months*!"

Another letter bounced off his cheek and he jerked. Rivers narrowed his gaze and Seth buttressed a hand on the man's chest lest he get some fool notion to retaliate. But Rivers just stood there as Emma flung another letter that went wide. Then another.

Damn, how many letters had the man written?

Even under attack, Rivers was passionless. He studied Emma as if a raging female was a problem he might actually solve.

Emma heaved all the remaining letters at Rivers. "We said good-bye to everyone we loved. Forever!" she screamed. "Do you *comprehend* that? I have sisters I will never see again because *you promised*!"

She tugged at the neck of her blouse, dragging in a wheezing breath. Rivers jolted forward, his good arm raised. "Miss Adams—"

"You promised!" she screamed, halting his advance. "To marry me and give me a family and a home!"

A home—*enough*. Seth shoved Rivers away and the man staggered backward. "Go now, Rivers. Get out of here."

Rivers bowed his head to Emma—the first act of submission Seth had seen from the man. Rivers bent and collected the letters from the ground.

"Take them!" Emma screamed. "Take your lies! You said you wouldn't see me unhappy, not for worlds."

Seth pulled Emma back. "Come away now, Emma."

"*For worlds!*" Emma strained forward against Seth's hold. "I promise you, Mr. Rivers, I'll sue you for breach of promise."

Rivers frowned at the stack of letters in his hands before tucking them into his coat. "I appreciate your lust for justice, Miss Adams. But justice would be a very long path."

He turned and began to walk away. His injured arm was held stiff at his side, but Seth wasn't fooled into thinking the man diminished. Rivers seemed to no more regard his wounds than he did the wide-eyed porters gaping from their posts.

"You *will* make amends, sir!" Emma cried.

Rivers stopped but didn't turn. "Whatever promises were made to you, Miss Adams...forget them. Let Colin Rivers be dead to you. Seek another. Be a wife and mother, and pray to God each night for His protection."

"Don't you dare—"

"Perhaps someday you'll understand. I do you a kindness in releasing you." He continued to the door. "I'm leaving for England, Miss Adams, so you see... justice would indeed be a *very* long path."

Emma stood frozen, watching Rivers sweep out the front doors of the hotel and disappear into the blinding sun. She was blanched of color. "He left."

"Emma, come on now."

"He signed a contract." Emma's voice shook with rage.

"You don't want to be marrying him."

"I didn't want to sail to India either. And Mina— she sailed because of him, too. She came *for me*. The man can't do this to us. My God."

"Emma—"

"He's going to do what is honorable and right."

He'd never seen a woman so full of fury, and he understood it completely. "He's a cold bastard, that one. Pardon my language—"

"A bastard!" Emma spat.

The curse derailed Seth's next words. He managed to turn her from the door. "Emma, you saw him. There's no reasoning with him. Something happened, something bad enough to scar him."

"He exits perfectly well. He exited rather fast, actually. And that ugly scar was healed."

"He said he didn't know of your marriage contract and I believe him. He's got those scars on the inside, too."

Emma sank against him and dropped her head in her hand. When she raised it again, her eyes were steady. And her voice sounded so unlike hers, Seth's skin prickled.

"He will not get away with this." Emma's eyes were open, but she wasn't seeing anything in that room. "I need"—she blinked back furious tears—"I need to go back. Oh God, I need to find a ship. I'll go to the outfitters and"—she wiped her cheek angrily—"and I need money or…I'll beg them to credit the passage."

"Calm yourself, Emma—"

"No!" She spun to face him. "No, if he sails to England, I'll be on the next ship after him."

The next ship. If Emma was on the next ship…

Mina would be, too.

Seth's heart pounded. He hadn't saved Georgie. But he might have just been given a way to save Mina.

Fifteen

AFTER SETH HAD BEEN GONE FIVE MINUTES, MINA dressed in her chemise and made a cup of tea. Tea was familiar; waiting naked in a man's bed was not.

What was taking Seth so long? Paying Mr. Rivers for his information should not take a half hour. The door opened and she sighed with relief. She hurried to take Seth's hand. "Are you all right?"

"Don't you worry about me, pretty."

But his smile was wan and his face pale. The devil take Colin Rivers, and the sooner the better.

"Will you have some tea?" She pulled him to his chair at the table.

"You're a great one for tea and biscuits, Minnie." He sat, his eyes evasive.

Something was wrong. Rivers must have said something to upset him. "I know you prefer coffee."

He eyed her chemise and clasped his hands on the table. "Aren't you cold?"

She blinked, automatically looking at her clothes folded at the foot of the platform bed. "I knew you were coming back, so I didn't bother to dress."

Blunt, Mina. And not at all flirtatious or enticing or—

"Minnie."

He looked at her and her heart skipped. There wasn't a man alive with eyes that crinkled like that.

"Minnie…I was thinking, maybe I shouldn't love you."

Fire ignited in her cheeks, even as her heart shattered. "Oh," she said quietly. It took her a moment to know what to do next, but she jolted to action when the thought came to dress. "Of course. I shouldn't have asked. The timing is so thoughtless of me—"

"That's not—"

"I'm just not brave." She couldn't seem to speak over a whisper. "That's why I asked you, Seth. I'm a coward. India will give me a husband and a home. Even now I'm afraid." She fumbled, tugging on her blouse. "If I weren't…I'd marry you."

The chair scraped across the floor and, in an instant, she was crushed against his chest. His heartbeat pulsed under her ear and she pressed closer.

"I'm not"—he pushed out a breath—"I'm not all that brave right now, either, Minnie."

She breathed deep and pulled out of his arms, needing distance. "I have a sister. Mary." She moved to stand by the window, wrapping her shirt about her. "I wasn't brave with her, either. I left her. In London."

Seth sat on his bed but said nothing.

"She married a man without a penny to his name. He loved her, he worked, but there was never enough and nothing to save. But they were young and so happy." She paused. "Frederick died when Mary was pregnant with their son, and then she had nothing. And none of us had anything to give her."

Seth nodded. "I'm so sorry, Minnie."

"I begged her not to marry him, but she was in love."

"She's in London, with her son, isn't she?" Seth's jaw tightened. "In Bethnal Green."

Did he know that slum? And what that might mean for a penniless widow with a child?

"It's common in London," she said, "for women who need a little extra money to stand on the street and sell anything they can. And she—"

"I know it." He stood and pulled her against him, into his arms.

And she could tell him what she'd never told anyone. "Mary said it was only twice. The men frightened her." Seth's arms tightened. "They wouldn't have been gentle or kind like you. And I wanted to know what it's like to be with a man who cares for me." It was so easy to say the words. After all this time. "I'm so sorry, Seth, that I can't marry you—"

"Don't, Minnie."

"Because I love you." Seth was very still, and instantly she regretted her words. "It doesn't matter—"

He bent and scooped her off her feet.

"*Seth*—"

"Probably shouldn't be doing that," he rasped before setting her down on his bed. "I don't mean to be picking you up without a by-your-leave, Minnie, but I love you, too." His throat bobbed with a swallow. "And I'm thinking of how little time we've got left. And if you're afraid…well, I'm afraid, too, but I'd never want you to be."

He sat on the bed, and his weight dipped the mattress and toppled her onto her side. But he didn't notice the clumsy roll, his eyes intent on hers. "You really love me, Minnie?"

God, yes. She pushed up onto her elbows and nodded. And she was sadder than she ever remembered being. "I do. I love you."

Seth blinked rapidly, a muscle jerking in his cheek, but his eyes were latched on hers. "Thank you, pretty."

She stared without any notion what to say. "You're welcome," she whispered.

A small grin tugged at his lips. "And I'm real sorry we were interrupted."

That made her smile—a small, weepy smile, but perhaps that was all right because Seth smiled wider. She sat up and brushed an unruly lock of hair from his brow. "I'm sorry we were interrupted, too."

♋

She loves me.

Seth inhaled deeply. No…no, no, he had to hold his nerve. She needed him. What would Shakespeare say? "Screw your courage to the sticking place," he murmured.

Her hand paused in stroking his hair. "What?"

Little flecks of amber glowed in her eyes. So damn pretty. "Shakespeare."

"Oh."

There was so little time now. And he was going to hurt her. "I love you, too, Minnie." He said it softly, like a promise. And like a prayer.

She wrapped her arms around his neck and hugged him. "You're always going to call me Minnie, aren't you?"

I'm always going to call you mine. "Always."

"Thank you, Seth."

She whispered the words in his ear, but damned if that didn't shoot straight to his roger. Tensing all over, he set her a little farther back on the bed so he could think. Did he make love to her first?

Or did he tell her about Emma first, and what he just did?

But the way Mina looked at him…and the temptation of her round breasts under her thin chemise… the dizzying scent of rose luring him… His hands reached for her before another dilemma could enter his brain. "Minnie…"

In the next instant, she was under him and their lips reunited. And there weren't words or reasons why they should or shouldn't. There was only this woman, one precious woman in all the world that he loved. And who loved him. "I'd never want you to be afraid."

Her eyes were soft and glazed, and he clenched because she was stroking his back—damn, that was nice. "And like I was saying before"—he shifted so his weight wasn't crushing her—"it's more for a man's pleasure."

"You pleased me before."

"I'm real glad, but that wasn't… It's just I'm not normal-sized. Well, you can see that, but don't be afraid because I'll be fast, meaning I'll not be a month about it. And if you're not comfortable—and you *won't* be"—his throat tightened—"just know another man might be more agreeable to your body. Not that you're doing anything wrong," he hurried to add.

She squinted at him, her mind flipping through all his words. Then she raised one brow. "Do you think your male organ is too large for intimacy?"

Well.

So damn awkward—

"Seth, I'm not afraid of your size." She was tugging off his coat and shirt. "I'm a woman of average proportions—"

"I'm thinking you're not—"

"And you may be large and strong, but you're more gentle and careful than other men. The way you lower yourself in a chair." She untied his neckcloth. "The way you enter a room like you expect the ceilings will be too low." She unbuttoned his collar. "The way you touch me, like I'll bruise if handled." She unbuttoned his shirt and trousers. "No woman would ever be afraid of you. Will you take off your boots and trousers for me?"

He blinked, waiting for his brain to be of some use so he could speak. And when it seemed he might be waiting a time, he mutely removed the rest of his clothes and lay down.

Mina moved atop him, her body warm and light, and locked her gaze with his. Her lashes were pure black. Why did he think they were dark brown?

"Are you grateful again?" she asked.

He nodded. Those long lashes fluttered closed, and she kissed him, warm and wet and soft, until his head was swimming and he was hard and throbbing against her belly.

And he was too damn big.

Mina wanted him to be the first…didn't want to be afraid…

"Minnie." *Forgive me.* He kissed her as tenderly as he could, rolled her under him, and—*please, please, please don't hurt*—entered her in one smooth thrust. The small resistance, the tight channel, and then the heaven of her snug heat cradling him.

He held his breath.

She tensed, but the cry of pain didn't come. Or the bite of nails on his back, like Sofia. Or the squirming and hissed curses, like Raissa.

He must've hurt her—*he must have.* He eased up onto his arms to look her in the face. "Minnie?"

A dark tendril of hair spiraled lazily along her flushed cheek. Brown eyes glittered under heavy lids with what was looking like desire. And a small smile was on her lips. His hips tightened with pleasure, with lust, but he didn't dare move. Not when she was looking perfect like that.

Strong, slim legs climbed his hips to wrap his waist and urge him deeper. He groaned as he sank a little farther, but he didn't allow himself to be embedded to the hilt. "Ah, love. Be careful."

Her eyes widened; her fingers gripped his hair. Small, panting breaths fanned his face and her lithe torso was tense everywhere he touched. He didn't move…waiting. She writhed under him. Was she hurting? Was she—

"I love how they crinkle," she whispered.

Hell—she was addled with pain. He hurried to slide out of her, but she gripped his arms, so he froze.

"*No,*" she breathed. "Seth?"

"You're hurting."

"No." She looked down at her body, appearing puzzled by his words. "Only a very little. And I wasn't… I'm not." Her legs tightened, coaxing him closer.

He groaned, holding his weight off her. "I'm too heavy."

"You're not." She brushed his hair from his brow. "You're perfect."

Perfect?

"You're perfect," she whispered.

She tightened herself around him, and his body shuddered with pleasure. "God, Minnie," he growled. "That feels…"

"How does it feel?" The sultry way she watched him nearly finished him.

He was going to collapse on her. Clamping her against him, he rolled onto his back. "That feels so right to me, so much like heaven." He watched her. "I'm not hurting you?"

Shaking her head, she leaned close to him, her cheek against his. He was almost afraid to touch her, so he placed his hands on the small of her taut, slender back. And as if she knew, she moved on him exactly like he'd dreamed. And again, and again, finding her pleasure.

"Oh, Seth," she whispered. "Thank you."

God, no woman had ever loved him like this. How did she know to do this? He held her hips, wanting to slow her, wanting this to never end. But she only strained harder and deeper, struggling to capture a rhythm. He nuzzled her neck and that calmed her for a moment.

She raised her head and kissed him. "One place…
in all the world."

What was she saying? He couldn't think, not with his
heart pounding and his lungs working as hard as hers.
Holding her tight against him, he thrust gently into her.

Small, whimpering moans rose with each push. Her
panting lips hovered over his, and her golden-brown
gaze sharpened on his. Tears sparkled in her eyes, but
she was smiling. "I love you," she breathed.

"I love you." He gasped the words as the pleasure
rose between them. The sweetest he'd ever felt.

He gripped her tightly, careful not to bruise her soft
skin. "Minnie…ah, love." God, this was loving. This
was how it was supposed to be. He kissed her firm,
round breast, the nearest, sweetest part of her he could
reach. And he was going to come hard. Her body was
slick with the effort of their coupling, and a grunt of
approval escaped his lips. *Don't hurt her…don't…*

He clamped down and thrust deep and slow, the
sensation spiking—

"*Oh God!*" she cried, finding her completion and
he groaned with her.

A powerful, shuddering quake wracked him and,
before it was too late, he lifted her off him and spilled
into the sheets.

His heart pounded against his ribs, and with his
last ounce of strength, he pulled her into his arms.
And Mina flowed over him, soft and warm and fitting
against him like God made her just for him.

And He must have at that. He must have.

She was quiet. And that was all right. There wasn't
anything to say.

She breathed deep, and the sound wasn't steady. He tried to look at her but she hid her face. His hand stilled on her head, where he'd been stroking her hair. "Minnie? Are you sure I didn't hurt you?"

"You were wonderful," she whispered. "I never imagined how wonderful this could be."

"It was never going to be right," he said. "Not until you. I know it now."

She pushed up on her arms to look at him. "Seth…I don't think you hurt those other women."

He shook his head, not wanting to think about them.

"Are you certain that you did?"

"Minnie—"

"You can talk about them. Did you make love to them like you did to me?"

"They were nothing like you." But Mina waited. She was patient like that. He blew out a breath. "They weren't virgins, but I was still nervous. I was careful with 'em, too. But they, uh, thrashed around a lot more. They spoke Portuguese but I understood *muito grande* and calling for Jesus and God. And *mais rápido*—which means 'faster,' like they wanted me to hurry and finish."

Mina stared at him, her eyes softening with her smile. But he couldn't smile back. This conversation was damn awkward.

"I'm not certain they were in pain," she said. "But I am certain you don't ever have to worry about being too large anymore."

"I don't?"

She shook her head, but already he knew he never had to worry again. What mattered now was that he hadn't hurt Mina. He combed his fingers through her silky hair, and it spread down her back and tumbled onto his chest. "I won't ever worry, then."

"I'll always remember how perfect you were. I'll always remember *you*, Seth."

He blinked a few times, his eyes wet. Ah…Christ. It was time to tell her—he had to tell her. And she might hate him for it. Damn…she might at that.

"Minnie? You're going home."

She was still but, after a moment, raised her head to look at him. And still she didn't say anything. She was good about letting him talk and say what he needed to say.

"I said, you're going home." His voice was steadier the second time. "I sent Emma to buy you both tickets to England. She's gone to the outfitters and I told her to book passage on the next ship. The *Liverpool*'s leaving tomorrow."

She pushed herself up and out of his arms. He stopped himself from reaching for her. She was going to need to be angry.

"Why would you do that?" she asked flatly.

"Emma's of a mind to leave. She won't stay here, and I'm glad. There's nothing for either of you in India."

"There's nothing for us in England."

"There is—there *will* be."

"No, Seth." Her eyes grew round and she shook her head. "No, you don't understand. We can't *leave* India. We have to stay and marry men here. It's what we planned."

"Make a new plan. Nothing's too hard for my venture girl."

"I…I don't understand what you're saying, what you've done."

Before he could stop her, Mina was out of his bed and the chemise was pulled over her head and floating down to her knees. He rose and pulled on his trousers. "Minnie, listen to me."

"I have to stop Emma." She continued dressing—her blouse, her skirt. "What is she thinking?"

"She's following Rivers to England."

Her fingers stilled where they'd been coiling and pinning her hair. And the look of horror she turned on him was breaking his heart. "Colin Rivers? Why? Why would you help her do that?"

"*Don't.*" He caught her wrist. "Don't leave me like that." His voice sounded ravaged. "Please, Minnie. I can't take you leaving like that."

"Why would you do that?"

He'd never seen her with eyes so full of panic. He grabbed her shoulders before she could dart to the door and bent to look into her face. "*Minnie!*"

She flinched at his loud voice, but it worked. She looked at him, her eyes focusing on his lips.

"Minnie," he said softly. "Emma's leaving. You have to be on that boat tomorrow."

She dropped her head into her hands and he couldn't breathe. She wasn't saying anything. "Minnie?"

A sob broke from her and it shook him to the bone. He pulled her into his arms and steeled himself against the sound of her tears. And even if the words hurt her, she had to understand why he did it, why she had to go. "The tickets are bought. I gave Emma the money already."

Her head reared back. "No, Seth. We can't take that. You need it for—"

"What do I need that money for, Minnie? It was meant to find Georgie." He smiled sadly. "I found her."

Tears spilled down her cheeks.

And it nearly drove him to his knees.

"Please." His voice was a harsh rasp. "I couldn't save Georgie but I can save you. I don't want you sick, or widowed, or alone over here. Will you let me be a hero? Just this once?"

"You are a hero."

He shook his head. "Let me believe it then, pretty."

She stared at him, backing away. "I have to find Emma. She doesn't know what she's doing."

"Promise me."

"I can't—"

"You said I wasn't alone."

That stopped her. She turned back to him, her eyes wide. "You're not."

He approached her slowly, afraid she would bolt. Afraid he might never see her again. But she stood still, because no matter what he'd done to her, Mina was a guardian, a defender.

And she was always on his side.

He wasn't being fair, but to hell with fair. "You told me I wasn't alone, didn't you? That you were with me."

"I—"

"I didn't save my sister," he said brutally. "Let me save someone. Let me save you. Please—"

"*Don't*," she whispered. "We can't go back."

But she didn't move, so he waited without speaking

a word. And then he reached into the pocket of his trousers and pulled out the quartz pebble from Mina's garden. Clear and shiny and shot through with streaks of pure starlight. Her luckless charm.

And her face went pale looking at it.

She didn't move. He cupped the charm in his hand. "I kept this, Minnie."

She shook her head.

"It reminds me every day that you don't belong here, that you need to go home. I promise, I'll return it to you when I get to England. I have to say good-bye to Georgie first. And then I'll come home."

She raised her gaze from his hand to look at him.

"Let me save someone," he said. "Let me save you and Emma."

She wasn't crying anymore. "Do you promise me? That you'll come back safe, that you'll bring my charm back?" She raised her chin. His little officer. "Promise me that, and I'll go."

"I promise." Relief flooded him, and he sank onto the bed. "Thank you, Minnie."

"You're not alone."

"I know it," he said gruffly.

She huffed a laugh, or a sob. It sounded like both. "I do—I *must* love you, or I must be mad." She moved to the door, her shuffling steps slow and uneven. "Tomorrow. We're leaving…" At the door, she paused. "Please don't come to the dock, Seth. I don't think I could bear it."

"You could, Minnie. You can bear anything."

She looked at him one last time, then turned and left him.

And he fell back on the bed, his body leaden, Minnie's pebble in his hand.

...*it's nothing near a diamond.*

Just a bit of quartz from her garden in Derbyshire. And in the end, it persuaded her to go home.

It was a pure diamond to him.

Sixteen

THIS WAS THE WRONG PAVEMENT FOR PACING. A man couldn't go more than a few feet without begging someone's pardon. But he couldn't just sit in his room and wait for Mina's ship to sail, so he circled the pavement around Benson's Hotel like a restless beast in a cage.

"Damn it," he muttered, drawing disapproving scowls from a lady and gent walking past.

He should have seen her off. He turned for the port. They'd have boarded, but he might at least see her on deck.

He ground to a stop, the bodies flowing around him. She'd cried saying good-bye. Would it be worse if she saw him? Mina had a life ahead that didn't include him. She wasn't his and never had been his—except for those precious moments they'd made love. No matter what happened, she'd been his then.

And she loved him. But love and need were different things.

He might have a drink with Tom. Get good and pissed—no, he couldn't afford that now. For a man his size, the amount to do the job properly would be expensive.

Seth leaned against a hitching rail outside Benson's. He ought to find some shade. The sun—what did they call it here…the Bombay Blanket—scorched his shoulders and baked the crown of his hat. But the carriage horses clip-clopping past soothed him.

It was all right; everything was all right. Mina was going home—to her sisters, to a life in the place she loved. And she'd be fine with the money he'd secreted to Emma.

He'd rescued someone after all.

A young lady and her beau walked toward him. Amelia Radcliffe—the redhead he'd met at the zoo three weeks back. But that wasn't Secretary Turnbull. Good. Good for her. Turnbull was a bastard.

He straightened as she bustled up to him, dragging her gentleman with her. The gent was trying not to look pleased by the bold lady on his arm.

"Good afternoon, Mr. Mayhew," Amelia said.

"Good afternoon, Miss Radcliffe. You're looking very well."

She blushed prettily. "You remember me. Mina must have reminded me to you."

A stab of pain lanced his heart, but he smiled through it. "What can I do for you?"

The lady beamed back. She presented her gentleman. "This is my friend Mr. Nashe. I've told him of you and the matter with your sister." She looked to her gent and prodded him with a nod.

Mr. Nashe pulled a note from his coat. "We were coming to leave this telegram for you. I understand you received information of your sister, Georgiana, in Assam."

He cleared his throat. "That's right. I'm arranging to, uh"—his eyes slid to the lady—"to *see* to her. I don't know if you were aware. It wasn't…welcome news."

Nashe squinted at him, shaking his head. He held up a hand to stop his words and unfolded the telegram. "I don't… I'm not sure I understand. A man I came up with, we were at East India College together, you see, passed our exams together and all that—well, he's assistant magistrate in Burdwan." He handed Seth the telegram. "My Amelia pleaded with me to look into the matter for you, and I would deny her nothing. So what is a gentleman to do?"

Seth read the paper, the words not making sense. He checked the date. And his heart kicked in his chest. "What is this?" he rasped.

Nashe's smile slipped at the question. "Just as it says. Your sister left Pabna on the tenth of August. The collector there countersigned her passport. Fortunate she was recorded at all, actually. But there was a native police matter. Her servant, a coolie or some such, met a rather dreadful end. He and a native woman, robbed and done away with."

"So dreadful." Amelia clutched her handkerchief, prompting Nashe to give her arm a comforting pat.

The telegram read clear: tenth of August 1850, Georgiana Mayhew of Matlock, England. Was it possible? Did Rivers have it wrong?

Was Georgie still alive?

"But…but I checked the passport registries at East India. She's not recorded in any of them."

"If she's been in the country on Company business, the administrant is unlikely to exercise any sort of vigilance. East India clerks are shamefully inept or lazy—likely both." He smiled drolly. "I would be unsurprised if those Englishmen allowed their servants to feed them. They come very near it now—the sad babies."

Seth read the telegram again. "She entered India."

"That appears to be the case, yes." Nashe pulled another paper from his coat. "And here is more recent information."

Seth jerked to attention. "Ay? What do you have?"

Nashe smiled. "October fifth, your sister applied for a subsistence allowance for herself and a female infant. She's been out of Company employ since May, when she left her expedition to enter Tibet, so she was denied. She didn't have sufficient standing in Honorable Company."

Seth's heart hammered in his chest. "Where did she apply? Calcutta?"

"Not Calcutta." Amelia bounced on her toes. "*Bombay*, Mr. Mayhew! I daresay she is in *this very city*."

He might have managed a farewell to the lady and her beau, but the next thing he was sensible of was striding back into Benson's. He had to find Tom and Mina and—*ah hell*.

He pivoted on his heel and headed toward the Apollo Bunder and the HMS *Liverpool*. He didn't have a timepiece, but from the length of the shadows, it must be about eleven—a quarter after, maybe. There might be time. There might've been a delay, some cargo they were balancing. They might still be here.

Please…please…Minnie not yet…

He began to run, to fly. Sweat stung his eyes and the telegram in his hand wilted in his fist. *Please.* He rounded the corner. The dock was empty.

And the steamship disappeared over the horizon.

❧

How quickly Bombay shrank. The winds were strong. Mina reached for the pebble in her skirt and remembered too late. She grasped the rail instead.

"You'll see him again, Mina," Emma said.

She would. Someday. In six months or a year. Or two years. Who would Seth be once he returned from burying his sister? Who would she be?

They'd never sailed the same current.

"The sun is strong," she said. "I think I'll lie down."

"Mina, I *am* sorry." Tears welled in Emma's eyes.

"Don't, Emma—"

"He cared for you so much. That's why he paid for our passage. To send you home to wait for him. I know he loves you."

"*Wait for him?*" She gripped the rail tighter. "How would you expect us to marry?"

Emma stared at her. "I don't understand you sometimes."

"Should I marry him for love? For some stupid passion, like Mary?"

"Mina—"

"It's hot." She turned from the railing. There was nothing but ocean to see anyway. But the solid wall of the ship made her dizzy with the deep sea rolling under her feet. "I'm going down."

"Mina?"

She waited on the steps but didn't turn.

"Mr. Mayhew said I wasn't to tell you until we were at sea." Emma paused. "He gave us some money, Mina. For you, for us, for everyone."

Her heart sank to her stomach, but she faced her sister. "What money? What do you mean?"

"He wanted to take care of you, to be sure you would be all right."

Mina looked back to Bombay, but the city was the faintest shadow. Dear Seth. He would give the shirt off his—no.

Oh no, no, no. She swung back to Emma. "How much, Emma?"

Emma stepped back, her eyes wide and fixed on Mina's face. "He wanted us to be safe."

"How much did he give you?"

"Two hundred pounds."

Oh dear God. She clapped a hand over her mouth.

"He loves you, Mina."

"*Two hundred?* Emma, how could you take that?"

"He insisted. He said he wanted us to be safe; he said that he had enough." Emma's eyes filled with tears. "And we'll pay him back. Once we settle. Once I make Colin Rivers pay. And what else could we do? We have no money. How would we live?"

"You knew we would have to work, and we have a little money."

"Not enough—not nearly enough. We can help Mary and Sebastian, too."

Mina sank against the wall of the stairwell. "Oh, Emma."

"He insisted." Emma was crying. "He said he wouldn't pay for our passage unless I promised to take this money. I'm sorry."

He *would* have insisted. Seth would have pressed and pushed and refused to hear no for an answer. But so much… Did he have enough for the rest of his travels?

"I'm sorry." Emma's voice was little more than a whimper. "I didn't think it would—"

She hugged Emma, needing comfort herself. "It's all right, dear. Seth—Mr. Mayhew is too generous and kind. And we will return all that money to him as quickly as we're able."

Emma nodded against her. "Yes. When he returns to London. We will write to him. He said he'd collect his letters at the London post office."

"Let's not…speak of this anymore. Or of him. Please."

She turned and left her sister to follow her below deck. She could hear no more of Seth from Emma. They had a three-month sail to plan and prepare for a life in England—to *survive* in England. And now she would be burdened with the thought that Seth would be caught without the funds he needed.

The waves churned violently behind the ship. Yet she had the strongest urge to jump, to swim back to Bombay, to Seth.

To her heart.

❧

Seth watched the steamship until it grew faint and became nothing more than a speck on the ocean. His heart hammered in his chest from his mad race to the port, but he wasn't much sensible of anything else.

The sun was beating down on his head and he didn't have the will to put his hat back on.

He took a deep breath. And started to laugh.

She was gone. That was good—it was good. Mina didn't belong here. She was going home to her garden.

And Georgie was alive as of October fifth.

He slumped back against a wall of cotton bales. *I miss you, Minnie.* But damned if his heart wasn't coming back to life. Yes, it was all good. Mina was going to be safe at home and on the fifth of October, his sister had been alive.

There wasn't much money left to search for Georgie, not after paying Tom and all his informants and giving Emma all he could spare. He could use his passage fare, and he didn't need a hotel room. He was accustomed to sleeping out of doors, so that was no real hardship.

But would it be enough to find Georgie? Bombay could feel like a damn big city. It *was* a big city if not one Company man had seen her. Maybe she'd already left Bombay.

He pushed off the wall. Tom was waiting for him. He was a good man. A friend, he hoped. Not that he was certain that Tom shared the sentiment. Once he and Tom sat down, read the telegram, strategized, they'd make a new plan. He might even send a letter to Mina.

Or not. Probably better not to raise her hopes about Georgie, about how she'd been right here in Bombay. Right *here*…

Seth slowed to a stop. Something was niggling him. *I never thought it would lead her here.*

He put on his hat, but his feet wouldn't move in the direction of the hotel. Seth turned for the bazaar. He didn't know why, but he wouldn't hurry. Hurrying might chase all the questions away.

The bazaar was nearly empty. The heat kept the shoppers away till the evening, but the merchants were setting up their wares. *What was it? What was he trying to remember—*

"Excuse me, *sahib*." A small gathering of Indian men crossed the square in front of him, jostling him. "Pardon us, *Mahabali*."

Damn. He'd lost it. Seth yanked off his hat and wiped his brow. It probably wasn't anything.

The pottery stand where he and Mina had lingered that day was at the end of the row of stalls. Mina had liked the pottery there.

"I will make you a good bargain," the pottery seller said as Seth approached. "You like, *Mahabali*?"

Mahabali. He'd been called that before. The locals always smiled when they said it, but they could be likening him to a goat's bollocks and he wouldn't know any different. "Can't afford it, mate. Tell me... what's that *Mahabali* mean?"

"*Bali* is fat man."

Fat? The hell…?

The vendor cackled, stretching his arms high overhead. "Great, *fat* man."

"All right then," Seth mumbled as the old man's laugh grew louder. This language lesson was becoming damn awkward.

The pottery seller's neighbor, a linen merchant, leaned over to grumble. "Not *fat*." He shook his head in

annoyance at the translation. "*Mahabali* is a giant, sahib.
A *daitya*, a god who is a giant. In our scripture, this god
was very good but too proud. Vishnu stepped on his
head and pushed him into the underworld. The people
call you this because you are most big." The linen
vendor pointed a knobby finger at his head, chuckling.
"And to step on your big face is most funny."

Funny? The hell…?

"I see, mate. I wondered if they might be calling
me—" Seth cut off. The pottery table was wrong. No,
it wasn't wrong. It was *different*. It was missing the big
dish Mina had liked, the one with the thistle.

It feels like home somehow…

That's what she'd said, what he'd been trying to
remember. *Cirsium heterophyllum*, the melancholy
thistle. A common plant at home. He'd sketched it.
Georgie had, too. Was it common in India?

"You like, *Bali*?" The vendor hurried to uncover a
platter painted with pink camellias. The flowers were
flawless. Beautifully rendered.

And damned familiar.

"Wait, wait," the vendor said. "I will show you a
finer piece." He turned and presented an English cup
and saucer with violets blooming along the rim and
Seth's heart slammed to the top of his skull.

"Where?" The word wasn't more than a croak, but
he pointed at the violets, at the blue paint. Layer after
layer had been applied to get that shade. Not Prussian
blue, not any pigment that would fade. That was ultramarine or lapis lazuli. Only a painter particular about
her materials would use pigments that dear.

A painter like Georgie.

"Very fine." The vendor bowed his head. "Very beautiful, *sahib*. Your lady will like very much."

But Seth wasn't listening. He pulled out Georgie's journal and flipped till he found the drawing of the pink camellia. He showed the page to the merchant and pointed. "Do you see?"

He turned it to all the merchants and native people who had come to look at the drawing and down at the camellia platter Seth pointed to. There was always a crowd about him. He swept the book around to show them all. "My sister painted this."

Seth shoved the journal under his arm and pulled out Georgie's lost poster, written in English, Hindustani, and Marathi. *One of them will understand what I am trying to say. Please, God.*

The linen vendor read, then clapped his hands. "Ah, *Mala mahiti hota.*"

He translated the poster to the pottery vendor, who began to nod vigorously and gestured for him to hand him the poster. Flipping the paper over, the pottery vendor began to write what looked like a map. "You will go to Thana, and find Mr. Banik." The pottery vendor looked around him. "*Samira kothe ahe?* Where is Samir?"

Seth looked from one man to the next, and other voices chimed in and pointed in different directions. He searched their faces, trying to understand. Did *they* understand? "Who is Samir and Mr. Banik?" he asked again, pointing to the painted flowers. "Please."

The linen merchant stood to look at the directions on the poster. "Calm, *Mahabali*. He writes Mr. Banik's painting factory is in Thana. It is twenty or twenty-five kilometers. A carriage can go in three hours. Samir is the pottery seller's son."

A young boy was pushed forward.

"Samir, do you know Mr. Banik? *Tumhi Sri Banik na olakta ka?*" The pottery vendor demanded, and the boy nodded. "You will go to Mr. Banik's painting studio. The fat man needs him."

The young boy beamed a cheeky smile and nodded. "*Sahib*, we will go to Thana. You have money to pay for coach?"

Seth stared down at the lad. Seemed he was taking a trip to someplace called Thana.

Three hours later, along a well-traveled northern road with a lad eager to practice every word of English in his clever head, Seth alit from the carriage onto Thana's one main road. And there wasn't a word of English here. Might have been smart to collect Tom from the hotel.

Hell. He was a hired explorer, he was adaptive, and he had a miniature translator right here in Samir.

Samir darted off, stopping only to beckon him to follow. "*Sahib*. Come."

Seth nodded to the coach driver and raced after him. The lad led him down one crooked alley after another. Dizziness spun him. He hadn't been able to eat all day and weak with hunger as he was, his lungs were screaming to rest. He gripped Georgie's journal tighter and ran on.

Samir came to a sudden stop at a wooden door. The Banik painting studio. Seth's pounding heart wasn't given a second to recover. The lad flashed his brilliant smile and slapped on the door for entrance.

A paunchy Indian man in a white tunic and a sad-eyed woman in a *sari* that was tight about her softening waist stood side by side and blinked at him. "Yes?" the man said. "What can I do for you, *sahib*?"

He fumbled with Georgie's poster and thrust it forward. "Do you know this woman?"

The old man read it in silence for a long time. The woman watched him with an unreadable expression.

"She's my sister." Seth looked from one to the other. "I've been looking for her. She's lost."

"He is *Mahabali*," the boy piped, before spouting off a flurry of Marathi.

And the Indian man looked up from the poster and nodded. And then he laughed. "Come in, sir. We can help."

Rigid with hope, Seth stepped into the tiny reception room. Through a sheer curtain, the workroom revealed the backs of three men.

And a woman with short, blond hair.

"Jayna?" The Indian man called.

The woman turned and looked at him with eyes the same color as his own. And then his own eyes blurred behind too many tears to see anything else.

"Seth!"

His sister ran toward him and hurtled herself into his arms.

Seventeen

"You don't work for them any longer, Seth. It's no wonder they refused." Georgie said. "East India wouldn't extend me a line of credit, either. What did you expect them to say?"

She was taking his failure better than him. After moving Georgie and Aimee into a room at Benson's Hotel this morning, he'd visited the Company offices to ask them to credit him the upgrade for a first-class passage on the next ship to London for his sister. A director had spared him two minutes to make his case, then for the next quarter hour held forth on his reasons for refusing the request.

Seth fidgeted with his coffee. He'd not taken a sip since Georgie set it down in front of him a half hour ago. "I was their man in Brazil for twelve years. Sent back over a hundred medicinals. I had my good-for all written and signed, and once I'm in England"—with Mina, with a *chance* to be with Mina—"I'd pay them back."

And he would. He wasn't cursed; he couldn't be with Georgie alive.

"Once I'm home, some of my seeds should have

sold—at least a few. And the orchids, too. I'd get the money to pay them back, in any case. Told them I just needed a bit."

"I don't understand why they won't allow us to sail in the same class. We have enough for that."

"Women and babies shouldn't be sailing steerage."

"*Shouldn't.*" Georgie smiled. "Aren't *allowed*, you mean." She dipped her head to smile at the baby in her lap. "After our weeks choking down yak butter and sleeping in yurts, our standards far exceed steerage or second class. Don't they, Aimee?"

"Women and children sail first class," he mumbled. "And you should."

She snickered and shook her head, her short blond hair swinging.

Seemed all he did lately was stare. It had been a week since he'd found her and still he couldn't believe his eyes. Georgie was alive and safe and looking so much like the sister he left in Matlock, they might have parted from each other yesterday.

"Did you have to cut your hair that short?" His voice was gruff with feeling, but it was a miracle he managed conversation at all.

"You would have hated it months ago then. It was the best way to hide the color."

"In Tibet?"

"Tibet, China, everywhere." She eyed his hair. "Appears you've been robbing the barber for months."

He combed his hair off his brow and smoothed it as neat as he could.

"It doesn't look bad," she said gently. "But you've always been more handsome with shorter hair." She grinned and he caught a glimpse of ten-year-old Georgie. "Do you wear it long for the ladies? Did Mina sigh over her big, strapping Viking?"

He reddened and shrugged, feeling more like her *younger* brother. "Maybe you can cut it for me?"

Georgie nodded, pressing her lips against a smile. "Anytime you like."

The little orphan stared at him with curious eyes. He was still a stranger who had infiltrated the world she shared with Georgie, but she was slowly growing accustomed to him.

"Little Aimee's hair is near as long as yours." He mugged at Aimee and she smiled her toothless smile. "You said she was too small to sail before. You think she'll be all right now?"

Georgie smiled down at her. "She'll be fine."

"And you'll be fine with that reward of twenty thousand pounds waiting for you."

The smile slipped from Georgie's lips. Aimee bounced on her lap, wanting her attention. "That can't be real. Who offers that much money for the return of a child they've never met?"

"That's what happens when you rescue the great-grandniece of a titled lady."

"And the lady's a marchioness?"

"Marchioness or countess, I forget what Will told me. She's got a handle on her name in any case."

Georgie turned the baby to study her face. "Aimee is gentry. I wonder if she has a title, too?" A cloud passed over his sister's face. "She'll be well taken care of, won't she? Far better than I could do."

"I don't know about that." He reached for little

Aimee and the baby went wide-eyed with surprise at being lifted by him. "You're looking hale and hearty to me, Aimee."

The baby smiled hugely, catching his nose.

And he fell a little bit in love with her.

He settled the baby on his lap. "Posted a second letter to Will Repton, too. He's been starved for information."

"Let's hope he receives it. I sent one months ago, but I've no idea if it reached him. I thought it better to save money for the passage."

"You shouldn't have had to scrimp and save. I should've schemed out a better plan—"

Georgie grabbed his arm, smiling at him. "I wouldn't have counted on my being alive, either."

"That ain't funny," he grumbled. "I'm sorry, Georgie. I wanted Minnie to have all I could manage to give."

She sighed and shook her head. "I know. You always were hopeless when it came to women. I'm eager to meet her when we're back in London."

He smiled. That was one of his favorite fantasies. Knocking on a cottage door, the sun warm and flowers in a window box. And Mina spreading her arms wide in welcome. And then he'd get to tell her he'd found his sister and Aimee alive.

"She'll be surprised," he said. "If her ship had just left a day later—"

Georgie took Aimee back and set her down on the bed. He hadn't noticed the baby nodding off to sleep on his arm. His sister had become a mother.

"The reunion will be all the sweeter, then," Georgie said. "Lovers parted—"

"We weren't lovers." His face warmed at the lie,

but better Georgie not imagine any sort of…future for them. But if all his seeds lived, if they sold…

He sat up straight. "Don't worry. I'll get the passage for us. And real soon."

Georgie nodded, but he caught the doubt in her eyes. His sister knew him well. He wasn't a man who took care of things.

"Hullo, there? Mayhew? Are you in?" Tom's voice sounded from the hall and Seth rose to open the door.

Tom nodded at Georgie. "I'd not expected to see you, Georgiana." He softened his voice, seeing Aimee asleep.

"Come in, Tom." He motioned him to a seat. "We've got a kettle on."

"Thank you."

"I'll take Aimee to our room." Georgie took the baby and left them with a nod.

"How did you fare with John Company this morning, Mayhew?" Tom asked.

Seth shook his head.

Tom sat back in his chair. "They're impossible, the lot of them. But I'm glad they refused. Now you have no choice but to allow me to pay Georgiana and Aimee's passage."

He frowned in surprise. "No, Tom. I can't take that."

"You can and will. I know you gave a great deal to Mina and Emma. Just a bit too much, it seems."

"We'll be fine—"

"I insist," Tom said. "I've been feeling all the guilt that's my due. I should have done more to keep them here, should have protected them but…" He shook his head.

"Minnie wasn't ever yours to protect."

Tom slanted a look at him. "As you remind me often."

"I won't lie. I didn't want her here. Malaria was just a matter of time, and you never know how a body recovers from that."

Tom lowered his head and nodded. "Still, I didn't offer for her. I failed her and I don't really know *why*…or how I could." He paused. "You and Repton paid me a great deal for very little work. Don't refuse this money, Mayhew. If you do, I'll just buy the passage myself in their names."

Seth stood, shaking his head. Then pulled the man into a hug. "Ah, hell, Tom." He chuckled. "Why don't you just admit you always liked me?"

Tom chuckled but hugged him back. "You were the very devil at times, man, but yes. I admit I'm glad to know you."

Seth patted him on the back. "See? That wasn't so painful, was it?" He sobered. "Thank you. For all the help."

"It was poor help I gave."

"I'll call on Mina when I get to London and I'll not let a mail pass without sending news, all right?"

Tom looked out the window, his spectacles white with the glare. "Actually, there won't be a need for that."

"Won't you want to know how they're faring?"

"Yes, but you'll not need to send me letters." Tom turned to look at him. "There's something else I came to tell you."

Eighteen

THERE WERE AREAS OF LONDON AS DESPERATE AS THE slums of Bombay. Where people died like flies, and thieves and prostitutes lived cheek by jowl, and no police dared to venture alone. Mina and her sisters didn't live there.

They were on the other side of the street.

Mildmay Park was a bit tumbledown, but it wasn't Bethnal Green. On her first day back in London, four months ago now, Mina knew she had to get Mary and Sebastian out of there. And that had meant using a little of Seth's precious money.

They must be frugal, but there were limits to what women and a four-year-old child should bear.

"You're not eating your supper, Mina," Emma said.

The slice of eel pie was no more appetizing now than five minutes ago when it had been hot. Emma tried to cook appetizing meals for their little family with their small budget, but her talents were not for the kitchen.

"Sorry, I was a world away." Mina picked up her fork and forced down a bite.

Mary said nothing, as usual, but ate every last bite on her plate—just as she required Sebastian to do, along with his milk and vegetables. After the fright of his illness and their uncertain living, Mary approached every meal with a sort of humble reverence.

Or, in light of Emma's cooking, with humble submission.

Mina cleared her throat, the sound loud in the room. Their suppers were already conducted in monastic silence. To not disturb a sleeping Sebastian was a convenient excuse. But in truth, there was often nothing to say that would not lower them further.

Emma's voice broke the silence. "You mustn't force yourself to finish if the pie does not appeal."

"No... I... Thank you, Emma." Mina tucked into her plate and finished before her sister could pluck her plate away in a fit of pique.

She carried the plates to the sink and cleaned up quietly in the dark, the small candle on the table guttering. Thank goodness the sun was not setting so quickly now that spring had come, but the lamps would still need to be lit this evening, as they had sewing to do.

If they economized, and continued to get their needlework as they had this past month, they would be fine. But she had to find steady employment soon. She was not skilled enough for dressmaking but this slopwork she was given—this week, for workingmen's shirts—was too sporadic for her comfort.

Everything was so costly. Sebastian's doctors, especially. They could not allow the damp and chill to find him again. That desperation had sent Mary into the streets before. They mustn't allow that to happen again. But if Sebastian were sick or hungry, who could stop her?

Mina shook her mind free of that nightmare. Their situation was not that dire. Together, they would survive. *If* they stayed together. And if there were some unforeseen emergency, as there already had been… well, there was Seth's money.

Shame heated her. They *would* return his money and pay him back the eleven pounds they'd borrowed. In time. How they would manage to, she didn't know yet. But in time, they would.

They had pinched off just enough of his funds to survive, to eat, to stay warm, to shelter Sebastian. And as soon as they could…as soon as he returned—

Where are you, Seth?

She had no time for such ponderings. She snuffed the candle. But as she did every night, she let the memories of his grin, his warm arms, and his low, rumbling voice light her within. There was no dousing her memories.

Even if they were not to be together, what harm was there in remembering? Life in Mildmay Park was bleak enough. She could allow herself that little comfort.

Mary was already at her sewing, so Mina turned up the lamp and threaded her own needle. Emma joined her with pen and paper.

"Who are you writing to?" she asked.

Emma paused with her pen poised over the paper. Her chin lifted a fraction. "A Mister Ingram. He is an attorney who champions the cases of indigent women who have been ill used or abandoned."

"You are not exactly indigent—"

"My means are limited, and he is acquainted with law-persons and charges. Perhaps he could assign a solicitor or even an apprentice to…"

She had expected Emma's temper to ignite, but her sister's voice faded with doubt.

"Emma," Mina started gently, "Mr. Rivers's behavior was inexcusable, but your claim will not incite any great interest. Not when the restitution would be so paltry a sum."

Emma didn't lift her head. "I can't forgive him, Mina. I don't know why."

No, she had not forgiven. Her anger had only grown in the four months since she'd last seen Colin Rivers. "You're tired, Emma. Why don't you save that letter for tomorrow?"

To her surprise, Emma capped her ink. "Mr. Mayhew would not think hiring a solicitor a squandering of money." She held up a hand to silence her protest. "I know—we will return every single farthing. But I daresay this is not how he envisioned us living."

Mina said nothing. They'd had this argument enough.

Just once, she would appreciate support from Mary's corner. The lamplight cast a golden glow on Mary's placid countenance, but that was illusion. Mary was still pale, and was so devoid of spirit and speech, she seemed to have no opinion on any matter.

"We are living fine, Emma," Mary said.

Ow. Mina's needle sank into the pad of her finger at her surprise in hearing Mary's voice.

Mary didn't look up from her work. "Mr. Mayhew may have envisioned different surroundings, but I will be the first to fall to my knees and thank him for saving me from the workhouse. *That* was the living I envisioned for me and Sebastian before his generosity spared us."

Emma blinked furiously and put away her paper.

"There is little enough charity in the world, Emma." Mary's voice was flat. "No one will help you. The sooner you surrender your campaign of revenge, the better."

"It's not revenge," Emma said. "It's justice."

Mary said nothing, just applied herself to her needle as if she'd never spoken at all.

What would justice mean to Mary? Was there justice in a world for a woman who lost her husband before their child was born? Who could work and work, and still not feed and house her son?

"Mr. Mayhew would want me to bring him to justice." Emma sliced a strand of the thread with her knife and tested the seam of the piece she worked on. "Wait and see when he calls on us." She smiled at her. "He is sure to come any day and sweep Mina away—"

"Don't, Emma," she said.

Emma's smile fell. "He will, Mina."

Mary's hands stopped in their work. "I think I hear Sebastian." She set aside her sewing and walked into the bedroom.

Mina waited for the door to close before looking at Emma. "You've upset Mary."

"What did I say?"

Guilt and frustration flooded her. "I left Mary before, Emma. I will not leave her again."

"If you wed—"

"Mary cannot earn enough to survive on her own."

Emma bit her lip. A habit of hers when she was thinking. "But Mr. Mayhew loves you. I know he wants to marry you."

"You don't know that."

"Perhaps he will *want* to take on the care of Mary and Sebastian. And once he comes—"

"*He is already here.*"

Emma gaped, silenced at last.

Mina bent over her sewing. "He is already in England. The letter we left for him poste restante, the letter with our direction, was claimed a week ago."

"A week? That must be wrong. He would have come to see you." Emma's stare grew heavy. "He *would* come to see you. Mina?"

Tears stung her eyes, so she kept her head down. "I don't know."

Emma asked no more questions, and Mina was thankful. She had no answers to give. She was desperate to see Seth, to know that he was all right, to return his money. But nothing between them had changed. She had refused him in Bombay because she was afraid.

And in London, she was even more afraid.

❧

The children didn't run here. Seth peered down an alley, shadowed even at ten in the morning. Two hollow-eyed waifs stared back at him.

This couldn't be right. He checked the direction again. The nearest building with a number was two doors down. This would be the building.

But this wasn't at all a home for Mina.

"Are you lost, handsome?" A woman's hand gripped his forearm, the clawlike fingers red and raw. "Lord, you're a strong 'un."

The woman's hair was an unnatural black, and she smelled sickly sweet, like something verging on rot. But her eyes were the same silvery blue as the butterflies in Brazil. They must have been fine once.

He pasted on a smile. "I'm not lost, but I thank you."

Her lips twisted with what might've been scorn. "Are you lonely, then?"

Christ, London might've been Bombay. Might be worse.

Quelling his revulsion, he patted her hand, before reaching into his pocket. He only had a few tuppence to spare. "Why don't you go on and have something to eat?" He pressed the coins into her hand.

Lifeless eyes watched him a moment longer before she shuffled off.

Christ, Minnie, don't be here…please. He knocked on the flimsy door, the three soft raps a more ordered rhythm than his heart at the moment.

Mina and Emma must have been in London…six weeks? Seven? Their journey had been faster than his. Their passage on the new, fast HMS *Liverpool* had cost him dear, but he hadn't cared.

He'd taken a slower route, and on the overland portion, they'd lost a few days, as little Aimee needed a rest from the sea. Just as Georgie had predicted.

And in the end, he'd only been hurrying to discover all his hopes crushed—no, *crushed* wasn't accurate. Wilted. Withered. Rotted.

He wouldn't dwell on it now; he couldn't. There was only so much feeling a man could take at a time, and Mina was what mattered now.

He knocked again, instantly softening the force after the first rap. Too damn loud, though he'd not meant it to be. Mina would be startled enough by the sight of him. He'd lost half a stone on the voyage and Georgie had shorn his hair above his ears.

Was no one here? He pressed his ear to the door. Nothing. Faces peeked from windows and alleys. Would one of them know Mina?

Steps sounded from behind him and he turned.

"Mr. Mayhew?" Emma's eyes were huge with surprise, but her smile grew. Behind her, a woman with a young boy at her side.

And Mina.

It was Mina that burned away the gray walls and slick cobblestones and peering eyes. His Mina, looking like his angel, looking beautiful…and thin and tired.

"Hello, Minnie."

She stared with surprise, crushing the package she held to her chest, and he couldn't get to her fast enough. That perfect blush rose on her cheeks and her eyes glowed, and a smile he'd not felt on his lips for months stretched across his face. "There's a sight a man could get used to."

He wrapped his arms around her.

And he was home.

All the tension he'd carried for months melted from his body. The tension on that boat, and on the caravan across the desert from Suez, and sitting across the desk from his cultivators yesterday, hearing the bad news.

Damn, he might release the waterworks if he didn't brace himself. Her hair was soft under his nose, but he hugged lean muscle and bone. She'd lost weight, as he had. They'd both diminished being apart. "I wasn't expecting to find you here, pretty."

She hugged him tight and whispered, "You're here. You're really here and you came." She pushed him back to look at him. "Are you well?"

"I'm always well." He cupped her face. "May not be soon if you don't stop crying." God, he'd missed looking into those eyes. They warmed him like no fire could have. "I found them, Minnie. I found Georgie and Aimee alive."

Her eyes widened and she covered her lips with a shaking hand.

"They're alive and here in London with me."

"Alive," she whispered, and he braced her against him before she dropped to the filthy street. "Thank God. Emma, Mary—Georgiana's alive. *And* the baby."

Those tears weren't stopping at all, and he hugged her hard.

"How, Seth? I thought—"

"Me too, pretty."

She smiled and squared her slim shoulders, wiping her cheeks dry and smoothing her blouse with trembling hands. His little officer again. "Come inside. You must tell us everything."

The ladies bustled him indoors and his body tightened at the first sight of the room. Plank floors. A cold hearth. Chairs without cushions. There wasn't anything here of comfort. "Minnie, why—"

"Don't." She wiped her eyes. "We're fine. We're

just frugal. We're warm and we eat every day and Sebastian is well."

She pulled him down to sit beside her on the sofa. Emma and the other woman with the child—*Mary?*—sat across from them on those naked, wood chairs. He nodded at them, but he had a hundred questions. "All right, then. Who's Sebastian?"

"This is my sister Mary and her son, Sebastian," Mina said. "My nephew...he needed a great deal, actually. A place to live and medicine, and there were debts to pay."

Mary sprang to her feet, with her boy in her arms, and bent to hug Seth, startling Sebastian into clutching his mother's neck. "Mr. Mayhew, thank you. I thank God for you every day. You don't know what you did. Your money kept my son alive. I owe you everything—" Her voice cracked. "*Everything* and I'll never be able to repay you or thank you." She sobbed and buried her face into his shoulder.

"That's..." He patted Mary on the shoulder. The poor lady was quaking. "That's all right, Mary. I'm real glad of that. I'd do anything for Minnie's family. Sebastian looks like a fine boy." From what he could see of him, with the lad crushed between him and his mum.

Mina and Emma joined in on the hugging. A huddle of women. And they weren't letting him go.

Well.

His heart cracked in his chest. Wasn't a thing more he could do for them. And from how they were living, it seemed he'd not done enough to begin with.

"Minnie." He shifted to look at her. He remembered everything just right. Those lips were still the most kissable he'd ever known, and the milky skin and peach blush exactly as he remembered every night in his conjuring of her. He needed to be alone with her, needed to tell her—

Hell, he needed to tell her he'd failed. Tell her he couldn't take care of her.

Tell her Tom was coming to do that for him.

She searched his face and the smile on her face made him think she'd remembered him just the same, too. Yes, a man would go a long way to find a woman like her. But fourteen sails hadn't brought him any closer to having a wife, and now he knew with a certainty what was true.

He wasn't ever going to have one.

"Come, Emma." Mary lifted her head from his shoulder and wiped her eyes. "Let's leave Mina and Mr. Mayhew alone to talk."

Emma was slower to release him. "All right. But I want to hear of Georgiana, too."

"I'm certain we'll hear all of it later."

"Where will you go?" Mina asked.

"To Mrs. Bradford's. She will like the company," Mary said. "And we'll return in a half hour—no, an hour." She busied herself with Sebastian's coat. "An hour is the usual amount of time she likes us to visit. Emma, wrap a few biscuits."

Seth considered all the bustle that was occurring. Mina's deepening blush. The way Emma didn't seem to know where to walk. Mary thrusting Sebastian's arms into his coat. The way Emma protested that the biscuits weren't edible, and Mary snapping that it hardly mattered.

And that they were leaving for an hour.

Seth heated with embarrassment. What were the women thinking he and Mina might do? He looked anywhere but at what must be the bedroom door. But damned if his roger wasn't taking an interest in the reunion now.

But he couldn't be with Mina. Not ever again.

In moments, the women had bundled up Sebastian's things, pulled shawls around their shoulders, and were out the door. Mina latched the door and pulled him to his feet.

"Minnie, are you all right? I'd given you enough to—"

"You did. You saved us. We're fine. I've missed you." She pulled his head down to her mouth and he let her.

Her lips were as soft and sweet as he remembered. And there was no way to resist crushing her against him and deepening their kiss. Deep as all the love he'd hold inside him. Hold and never let out.

He should tell her...tell her Tom was coming...

Slender fingers combed through his hair and tightened. And damned if he didn't feel those little tugs good and low, right where he was desperate to join their bodies again. His sweet Minnie. She loved him better than any woman ever could.

Like she knew what he was thinking, her lush mouth smiled under his kiss and he tore his mouth away before it was too late.

And her eyes were shining, but her lashes were dark and spiked with tears. "I was so afraid I'd never see you again. You claimed your letter days ago."

He nodded through his grief, waiting for the air to fill his lungs. "I did, pretty. I needed—I wanted to see about something before coming. Something I'd been planning on for a long time."

Mina searched his eyes. "Before seeing me?"

He moved his eyes off her so he could say what needed saying. "I need to tell you something, and it will be a surprise, but I'm hoping you'll be agreeable because I think it the best thing for you. You'll be away from here and taken care of—"

I wanted to marry you. I hoped I could, thought I could. I was wrong.

He clamped down on all the thoughts vying for dominance in his brain. *Hell.* He closed his eyes, and sorted them. One at a time. Most important first. "You can't stay here, Minnie."

She blinked. Those long, wet lashes almost fascinating the rest of the words from his head. Almost.

"This isn't a place for you and your sisters and Sebastian. Why aren't you using the money I gave you?"

"We did. We used eleven pounds."

"Eleven—that's not enough. You should've found some decent rooms. A place that doesn't smell from the sewers and without whores outside the door. And with a fire burning and lamps and a window box with flowers. And you shouldn't be so *damn thin*!"

Mina's eyes went wide with hurt—and he wanted to smash his damn head into the wall for saying all the beef-headed things he always said.

And she didn't say a word. But then…Mina wouldn't.

He scrubbed a hand through his hair and said with

more calm, "I didn't... Minnie, I'm sorry. I didn't mean it that way."

Mina took hold of his arm and he forced himself to look at her. She held her chin up, but the hurt was still faint in her eyes. But she wouldn't cry or rage at him. He knew she wouldn't. There wasn't a woman alive who'd tolerate his blunders better.

He was grateful and humiliated by that at the same time.

"Mary says a prayer for you every night, and so does Sebastian. You're like Father Christmas to him."

He frowned and shook his head.

"When Emma and I returned, Sebastian was ill and Mary was desperate. She sold her clothes; she starved. She almost...almost went to the street again. You mustn't tell her I told you."

"I never would, pretty."

"She didn't know what else to do."

Hell. It was clear to him what Mary would have done. In London, men might not have the means to keep a wife, but one marital comfort was found too damn easy with the Magdalenes in the streets.

"The money you gave us erased her debt, paid for Sebastian's doctor, fed us, kept us safe," she said quietly. "*You* did that for us. If you wanted us to do more, I'm sorry. This was all we could imagine doing, because this was so much more than we had before."

Only when Mina stopped talking was he able to unclench his fists and breathe. She couldn't imagine another way of living? Couldn't imagine living some-place clean and where the sun could find her and with a garden where she could grow things?

"Damn it," he muttered under his breath. She wouldn't be imagining that life if she were married to him, either.

"Seth? What's wrong?"

"I couldn't come see you the day I returned. I wanted to. But I had to know something first, and it took time." He sat on the sofa, not wanting to look at her. "I told you I was collecting ornamentals in Brazil, on top of hunting medicinals for East India."

"I remember."

"All those seeds I collected...I packed them the best ways I knew how, all different kinds of ways. I left them with cultivators. Good men who knew the best way to bring those seeds to life." He pushed to his feet, but there wasn't room to pace. "Some survived, they tell me."

Mina took his hand in both her little ones. He steeled himself from taking her right back into his arms.

"How many survived?" she asked.

"Ten," he mumbled. "Ten species out of eighty. That was two years of work. Longer even, counting the sail back and the months they planted and waited. All I got was a hundred pounds for the trouble."

Mina went still, and he pulled his hand from hers. She let him.

"A hundred pounds isn't enough for fixing up my cottage and buildings, and starting a flock of sheep." He took a deep breath. "It's not enough for a family." He looked at her. "It's not enough, Minnie"—*to be safe for you. To marry you.*

It cost him, but he held her eye. His little officer wouldn't shy from a problem that needed sorting.

But she couldn't sort this problem.

He turned from her. "Seems it's always the same. All the hard searching, all the prizes for East India, and never...*enough* left."

"You have the money you gave me," she said. "All except the eleven pounds—"

He spun from her. "You're keeping that money."

"No, I'm not."

"Minnie—"

"I won't keep it. You need it and you have to—"

With a growl of frustration, he yanked her against him and kissed her. Kissed her to quiet her, to beg her to stop. He couldn't take any more of Mina's plain speaking.

She'd say what he couldn't bear to hear. That he couldn't afford to keep her or her family safe. Couldn't afford to wed her. That he wasn't a man who could. Tom would be that man.

His heart pounding in his chest, he lifted his mouth off hers. "Tomorrow, Minnie," he said gruffly. "Tomorrow you can try arguing with me over that money, but not today."

She looked steadily back at him, mutiny written plain all over her sweet face, but he could out-stubborn her any day. She might be as orderly as an officer, but he'd never been all that good at taking orders.

She was clenching her teeth, and damned if he didn't have to grin at how that angry, little face... didn't work at all. Her bottom lip pouted, and when he thought her mouth couldn't be any more kissable, she had to go and prove him wrong.

But his heart was tearing in two at the same time. *Ah...Minnie.*

"There's one last thing I have to tell you." He dragged in a breath because the words seemed to take all the air out of him. *Tell her Tom is coming. Just tell her and finish it.*

"Seth?"

He forced himself to look at her and her little mouth working to relax the pout from her lips.

"Before you tell me"—she rose on her toes, trying to meet him eye to eye—"could we just be grateful?"

He closed his eyes and breathed in the sweet scent of Mina's hair, her skin. *Grateful.* He smiled, remembering. "Are you asking me to shut my mouth, pretty?"

"I'm asking you to kiss me."

Her words might have been a bludgeon to his aching heart and, dizzy, he tightened his hold on her. Christ, she wasn't supposed to say that. "Minnie." He squeezed his eyes tight. Tom was coming. "I have to tell you—"

"Tell me tomorrow," she whispered. "I'm grateful today."

He opened his eyes and looked at Mina. The woman he loved—would always love. And the woman he didn't deserve. It was a sin. But he'd take one more day for himself.

He nodded. "Tomorrow." He rested his forehead on hers. "We have a little under an hour now. I should have been keeping count."

Mina smiled and pulled him into the bedroom. The one bedroom—and the one bed.

"Do you all sleep in here?" he asked.

"It's all right."

One bed. And the quilt was white with little posies

on them. "Minnie?" He pointed at the bed, not sure what he was protesting, but she didn't look, as she was busy untucking his shirt.

"*Hmm?*" Her hands were under his shirt and were stroking his chest. He pressed her a little closer, leaning into how good that felt, how healing. Warm, soft lips nibbled his neck, his cheek, his mouth. Blood surged to his roger, and he was ready for her. More than ready.

Her round breasts pressed softly against his chest, plumping into the most erotic sight he'd ever seen. Those eyes, that lush mouth, that bosom…all for him. She was beautiful and desirable, and she was offering herself to him.

Mina pushed and he backed into the bed, the mattress behind his knees with that quilt of sweet posies. She yanked at his trousers and he feared for his buttons. He guided her arms around his neck so he could free himself for her.

But he didn't want to love her on a bed where the little boy slept. Or anyone else, for that matter. "You don't sleep alone, do you, Minnie?"

Her eyes were soft and melting, and her tongue slicked her lips wet—and suddenly there wasn't any need to sort out the matter.

He didn't need a bed at all.

Turning, he leaned against the door and coaxed her to lean against him. She was such a little thing, and he was glad. With one hand under her lush bottom, he lifted her off the ground. Shoving his trousers down past his hips he drew up her skirts and positioned her right where he needed her.

"*Seth.*"

His name was a puff of heated breath on his mouth and, with an animal grunt, he squeezed her backside before he could stop himself. A soft layer of cotton separated him from the wet heat of her body.

Wet and ready for him. He pulled the seams of her drawers apart and guided her onto his roger where he stood. And he let the weight of her body sink onto him—and sheath him. She gasped and he nearly came without a stroke.

"Ah, God, Minnie." His roger pulsed in rhythm to her clenching body. "The nights I dreamed of you, taking myself in hand, dreaming I was with you. In your sweet body."

"I know. I missed you so." She rocked against him, straining for purchase without her feet on the ground for leverage. The silk of her inner thighs rubbing against his hips as she climbed him, rode him.

And he needed more. Needed to be deeper in her, needed all of her body against his.

Caging her, he turned them around, his hugging arms shielding her from the cold wall. Mina gave him what he wanted. Hugging him tight around the neck, her breasts cushioned him, and he nuzzled the heat of her neck, the silky skin of that delicate column. She whimpered, her nails dragging across his back as she sank onto him. And that was enough to calm the frenzy of their reunion.

Leaning heavily against her, his arms braced on the wall, he thrust into her. The pleasure so good, so complete, he never wanted this to end. Their eyes latched, hers warm and liquid, like he'd dreamed all those nights on the return back to her.

Those perfect lips parted, glistened, and a spasm of answering pleasure rippled in his loins.

"Seth," she breathed. Smiling dreamily, she dropped her legs from around his waist, driving her deeper onto him.

God…so sweet. "Kiss me," he groaned.

She claimed his mouth, sucking his tongue deep, and he couldn't move. She'd never done that before…

Only when she softened her kiss did he feel the desperate need to thrust in her, to bring her to pleasure. He pumped steadily, wanting this to be good for her. Even in this bleak, little room, even without any future for them, he would make this moment one she could be right with, one she wouldn't be ashamed of.

A moment she wouldn't regret. A moment she'd know was one of love.

"Minnie," he whispered. "I love you, Minnie."

And that was enough. She cried out with her completion and he clenched against following her, removing himself from her just in time.

Mina was pinned between his big body and the wall while he brought his breathing under control. He'd let her go in a moment. Just not yet…not yet.

Her smile grazed his cheek. "Thank you, Seth."

Something sharp lanced his heart, and he held still, waiting for his heartbeat to slow. But it wasn't slowing.

She rested her head on his shoulder. "I'd forgotten how good you feel."

"I hadn't forgotten, pretty. I'm thinking I never will."

He let her down on her feet. The room changed, darkened, chilled. He'd never be here again.

He took a step back, giving her space, denying

himself her touch. Her skirts rustled into place, and her blouse and hair were neat and orderly, like his little officer would require. Only the deep flush of her cheeks and the swelling of her lips lingered.

And he was so…*grateful* for that small proof of their loving that he couldn't find any words to tell her what she would always mean to him, how much he wanted her and how he would miss her.

And what had to happen despite it all.

Trying not to feel anything more, he righted his clothes. In the silence, Mina searched his face. "Seth?" She took a step closer and he had to brace himself into standing still. She smoothed his hair off his brow and he stiffened a little. Seemed his hair wasn't too short for her to do that.

Such a little hand…and she didn't know how much her touch hurt him.

"I can't… I wish I could arrange words like Shakespeare knew how, Minnie. So I could tell you how beautiful you are. How there's nothing in the world I'd count as lovelier, and I've seen skies like opals and orchids only God could color. And it's not just your beauty. It's the wonder. I feel wonder when I'm with you. Like I wasn't really living until I saw you." He huffed an embarrassed laugh. "But I'm the last man to know how to put pretty words together. I'm sorry about that."

He was hot under his skin, frustrated, but Mina was looking at him with a look he'd never seen before. And it made him hold very still.

The bottom lip of her smile shook a little, and her eyes were shiny. "Remember how you told Georgiana that if you draw true, pretty works itself out?"

He nodded.

"I think…when you speak true, pretty works itself out, too."

Seth took a shaky breath. It *was* wonder he felt. She was a lady in everything she said and did, to never rob him of his pride. But what did she really see when she looked at him? She said she loved him, but she was smart enough to say no when he'd asked her to marry him. He'd just hoped this time…

He'd *hoped*, and there hadn't been a good enough plan behind his hope.

He'd thought there was this time, *believed* there was. And that's how he knew with a certainty there wasn't a curse at all, and there never had been. He just didn't have enough sense to plan for important things, like a wife and family and a home with a roof that wouldn't cave in, and money in reserve to manage all the acres of land he owned.

But none of that mattered. Not now. Tom had his own plan, and tomorrow he'd see it done. And the best thing he could do for Mina would be to step aside.

"Seth? Do you have to leave?" she asked.

Confused, he looked at her. "Leave?"

Her eyes scanned his face. "You looked far away for a moment. I thought… You don't have to leave?"

He shook his head quickly.

She released a breath and smiled at him. "I'm glad."

Just one day with her. "There's someone I need to see today, Minnie. You remember Will Repton's the man who provided the funds to sail? The one to put out the call for Aimee that sent my sister into Tibet?"

"You didn't see him first?"

"Needed to see you first, pretty. Besides," he said, "Georgie already brought Aimee to see him. He's not waiting in any suspense."

"Oh." She smiled. "That will be a happy visit."

"Should be." He caught her hand where it rested on his shoulder and held it on his chest, wanting to keep her close. "He sent his carriage for me this morning to deliver me to Richmond. The coachman's waiting a few blocks away, seeing as how you live—well, *here*." To soften his words, he squeezed her hands. "Will you come with me?"

"Are you certain you want me there?"

His heart cracked. "I'd want you anywhere, pretty."

She smiled and snuggled closer, the sensation so sweet he nearly staggered.

Just one day.

Tomorrow he'd let her go.

Nineteen

RICHMOND WAS ONLY TWELVE MILES FROM THE CITY, but the city traffic made the journey a long one. Still, as slow as they traveled in Mr. Repton's luxurious carriage, Seth spoke little. But really, that was all right. It was almost too much to look at him, let alone have him speak. The sight of him seemed a dream.

He was in England and safe, and he'd found Georgiana.

And in her little bedroom, with Seth, that seemed a dream, too. Mina shifted to feel the slight tenderness between her legs again, wanting the sensation to never leave. But he *would* leave. His cottage was up north. What reason did he have to stay? And she couldn't ask him to.

Hot tears threatened to overspill her eyes, and she blinked them away in a panic. Today, she would be happy. Her heart had returned, and Seth was safe, and they were on their way to a happy reunion with his friend.

Seth held her hand upon his lap, his thumb rubbing the back of it absently as they rode. He sat beside her rather than across, and whether he knew that it was unmannerly or not, she didn't care.

She squeezed his hand to gain his attention. So oddly quiet, and he seemed to be tensing the nearer they drew to Mr. Repton's house. The carriage moved faster now that they'd left London.

"I've not been out of the city since my return," she said. "Richmond seems a very fine area."

"A very fine area." His eyes left the view of the gated lawns and tall, shady trees beyond the window. "But Repton married a countess's sister, so his situation's an easy one, I'm thinking."

A countess? Her boots were scuffed and her gloves cotton. "I didn't realize. I'm not dressed—"

He lifted her hand and kissed the pads of her fingers. Those wonderful eyes crinkled at her and quelled her panic. "Her name's Charlotte. A fine lady, like you. You'll get on well, I'm thinking."

Seth was often right about people, so her nervousness eased a bit. Still, she checked the pins in her hair. "My dress is so plain. I hope I'll not embarrass you."

His slow inspection scorched her from tip to toe. "That wouldn't ever be possible, pretty."

Her brain stalled under his admiring gaze. "You are still a terrible flirt," she whispered.

"Never flirted with you, Minnie." He leaned close and nuzzled her neck. "I'm not flirting now, either, when I tell you I can smell myself on you."

Her heart leaped into her throat. *Dear God.*

"I love your blush, Minnie," he murmured, lifting his head. "I want to be the only man to make you—" Something flickered across his face, and he sat up straight.

They were different here. In England. The joy of their reunion had been so short-lived. Georgiana was alive. He was home; he was safe. And yet, the news from his business partners seemed to have crushed something within him. There was so little bluster about him now. Fewer smiles. He hadn't winked at her once.

He even looked different. The brilliant green of the trees beyond the window framed his profile. He was such a beautiful man. His hair was so short now that the proud lines of his nose and brow and jaw were all the more pronounced.

But there was one thing that hadn't changed. He still wasn't safe.

Love didn't matter. At least, not enough.

She brushed aside that unhappy truth. Today was a happy day. Besides, she'd promised not to raise the topic of his money until tomorrow. Seth had been so disappointed. She hadn't truly understood how much he had counted upon his botanical discoveries to fund his future. But even without that money, surely he could find a way to survive? He would have the money he gave her—and he *would* take it. She just had to find the means to return it.

With the hundred he'd earned, and the two she'd return, he could start a small flock, plant a garden, sell his vegetables. Three hundred pounds was a great deal of money. It would be enough for him and even... even the right sort of wife.

She would just ignore the lancing pain that idea wrought. Because three hundred pounds would not be enough for a wife with six sisters and a nephew prone to illness. They might be fine for a year, maybe two. But beyond that, she would be a terrible burden, and together, they would feel the uncertainty of their future all the more acutely.

All too soon, the carriage was slowing and turning onto a gravel drive. The house was all brilliant-white stone and grand elegance, set back from its sprawling lawn and fountain. But cheery flowers bloomed in window boxes, and a glass hothouse like a fairy-tale castle sparkled in the back garden. "What a beautiful house."

Seth sat very still, looking out the window. "It is. A fine house."

The door opened, but he didn't step out immediately. He cleared his throat and tugged his coat into place. "Well. I suppose we're here."

She squeezed his hand, and he turned to her in question. "He's going to be so happy to see you."

His eyes cleared and, at last, he smiled. With a quick buss of her cheek, he jumped out of the carriage. She reached for his hand, but Seth caught her at the waist and lifted her gently out. He likely had never handed a woman out before.

The front door flew open and a man leaped down the stairs, smiling hugely. "*Seth!* By God, you know how to surprise a man."

Will Repton's hug nearly toppled Seth.

"Now there's a welcome." Seth chuckled and pushed him back to look at him at arm's length. "What surprise? You sent a carriage to fetch me."

"I mean Georgiana and Aimee showing up at my door. You might've sent me a letter."

Seth's grin fell. "Ah, hell—we *did* send one, Will. I'm sorry. We wouldn't have surprised you like that—"

Mr. Repton waved off his apology. "It was the best surprise of my life. The most wonderful surprise." He wiped his eyes and turned to her, smiling. "Pardon me, miss. I'm Will."

Mr. Repton was an inordinately handsome man, but she smiled easily back. Seth must have inured her to masculine beauty.

Seth offered his arm and she stepped forward. "Will, this is Miss Adams. She helped me in Bombay."

Evidently that was explanation enough. Mr. Repton grabbed her hand before Seth could finish the introduction. "Good to meet you, Miss Adams."

"I'm pleased to meet you, too. And so very glad Georgiana and Aimee have returned safely."

"Thank God for that." Mr. Repton's eyes shone again, brilliant with tears. But they were tears of joy. He pinched them away and composed himself.

Seth patted him on the back and sent Mr. Repton stumbling forward a step. "Now, how's that wife of yours?"

Mr. Repton smiled hugely. "Come in and meet— there they are."

Framed in the door stood the most beautiful woman Mina had ever seen. She had gleaming, black curls and big, blue eyes as pure as violets. But extraordinary as she was, her smile was warm and she was bouncing on her toes to greet them—even with an infant in her arms.

"Oh, Seth!" she cried as she came down the steps.

"How I've longed to see you. And, Miss Adams, is it? Welcome. You cannot know the joy you've brought to our house. With all the excitement, Will has not let me rest at all—"

"*Talking*." Mr. Repton's face flushed. "We've been awake talking."

Seth smiled warmly as Mrs. Repton reached them. "Look at you, Charlotte. And with your little lamb, there."

"This is our son, John." She blinked rapidly against tears. "He will be two months next week. How will I ever thank you for sailing to India in Will's place? I could not have endured parting with him."

"I know it," Seth said. "I was happy to do so for you both, Charlotte."

Mrs. Repton aimed her brilliant smile at Mina, and she couldn't help but smile back. "I had the most precarious time with John while enceinte. I am sure I would not have been blessed with him if Will had sailed."

"Oh." The woman's honest confession caught her by surprise. "I'm so glad you are both well. He is a beautiful baby."

"Yes, beautiful and perfect and as silent as his father, which is a lovely quality in a baby. Perhaps our next will take after me and squall for attention on the hour," Mrs. Repton said.

Mina laughed. "For your sake, I hope not."

Will slung an arm around his wife and baby, and steered them to the door, but Charlotte kept chattering. "Yes, do come in. I have the loveliest tea waiting—and coffee for you, Seth. I have not forgotten."

The butler bowed with a smile, and a maid wheeled in a teacart with an openly curious expression. As fine as the house was, this was a cheerful home.

Mrs. Repton handed the baby to her husband and poured them their tea and coffee.

"This is your lad, then, eh?" Seth intercepted the boy and turned him about to examine him.

Seth wasn't shy with babies, either. The sight started a horrible yearning in her.

"Shame he takes after you, Will, and not your wife." Seth handed the baby back to his father. "But I'm thinking he's a handsome lad nonetheless."

Will beamed, cradling the baby in his arms. "Thank you. By God, Seth, tell me everything that happened."

And for the next half hour, Seth did. Mr. Repton could barely sit still in his excited curiosity. But Seth sat oddly still in his chair, his hands clasped as he told the story.

What more was preoccupying him? This should have been such a happy day for him.

"Will?" Seth rose to his feet. "Would you mind if we spoke away from the ladies?"

Mr. Repton gave his son to his wife, and Mrs. Repton lured her attention back to the tea as the men left the parlor. But Mina couldn't stop herself from stealing a glance into the hall to see Seth again. As if he could sense her worry, Seth looked at her.

But there was no answering wink or smile. Seth merely dropped his gaze and followed Will Repton down the hall.

❦

"I've got an accounting of every quid of that two thousand, Will."

"I don't care about any of that." Will gestured him into one of the chairs by the fire.

Seth sat and studied the room. A library. The books all matched, covered with forest-green leather and gold writing. Might even have Shakespeare among them, as many books as there were. A fine home for a man with a family.

And none of that was his business.

Seth pulled out his letter case with the receipts of his spending.

"I still can't believe Aimee's alive and here," Will said. "She's going to have the most amazing future."

"I'm glad to hear that, Will. But I'm needing to talk about the remaining funds."

Will leaned forward and gripped his arm, his eyes bright. "All that remains is yours. For you and Georgiana."

"No, there was a couple hundred that was left."

Will's eyes searched his, a bemused smile on his face. "You have no idea, do you? What you've given me? What finding Aimee *alive* has meant to me?"

"But the money—"

"Means nothing." His voice broke. "Christ, it means nothing at all. You allowed me to stay with Charlotte when she needed me. I was here for the birth of my son. It was the greatest gift any man's ever given me, so I'll be damned if I'll hear another word from you about that money, *ever*."

Will's intense stare pinned him to his seat and all Seth could manage was a nod. *Was that it? Had he just been freed from years of debt?*

Will swiped a stray tear from his cheek and cleared his throat roughly. "Tell me what's next for you. Who is this Miss Adams? She's a beauty."

And just like that, his grief was back. "She is."

Will raised a brow. "And?"

The question clamped his heart like a vise. "And nothing. I'm in no position to wed."

"It's none of my business, but you have that land up in Derbyshire. I assumed you planned to marry and raise a family."

Seth shrugged, and miserable as he was, the move was jerky. "Can't afford to. I learned yesterday most of the seeds I collected weren't viable. I had more than a few, even shipped some meant to germinate on the sail in Wardian cases."

Will's gaze narrowed and his head tilted as if he'd misheard. "But...wait, I don't understand." He stood and moved to his bookcase, searching for something. "There's to be an auction at Chiswick next month. By the Penderton and Monroe nursery. I have the catalog here. I assumed most were yours. I plan to bid on a couple orchids myself, but my father warns me I'll lose to Cavendish. The duke is mad for his flowers."

"Those aren't mine. I didn't have enough viable plants to auction, and the orchids had already been named. The Skinners, my cultivators, tell me the survivors sold for a hundred quid."

But Will was intent on finding that catalog. "Charlotte?" He called into the hall. "Would you come here?" He sank to his haunches to check a low shelf. "The auction is to be held on the opening day of the Horticultural Society's Spring Show."

Mrs. Repton floated into the library with John in her arms, and Mina followed.

Seth tensed, rising from his seat as the ladies entered, and tried again. "Those prizes aren't mine, Will."

But Will wasn't listening, talking to his wife. "I had a catalog for the Chiswick exhibition and the auction next month."

Mina looked at Seth with a question in her eyes.

Damn awkward to explain his failure in front of Mina all over again.

Charlotte rocked her baby in her arms. "Yes, I filed that for you, in the decoupage box."

Will stared at the bookcase. "The *what* box?"

"The box decorated with the flowers," Charlotte said.

The bookcase held about a dozen flower-covered boxes. Will stared at the collection, his arms hanging at his side.

Seth rubbed his temples and waited. "Will, the auction could be flowers from the Barnes Expedition. He'd returned from Venezuela about the same time last year."

"This one, Charlotte?" Will held up a box pasted with tulips, and Charlotte shook her head.

"The tulips are for the spring receipts," Charlotte explained. "The one with the loose petals is for bric-a-brac, but the one with mixed bouquets has the catalog. Mixed blossoms for *miscellany*. It is labeled, Will. Do you see?" She moved to stand beside her husband and pointed to the word scripted carefully, almost invisibly, in a petal of a flower. "There. 'Miscellaneous.'"

"Thank you, sweetheart." Will smiled, his eyes lingering a time on Charlotte's beaming face.

Damned if Will didn't color a little, too. Seemed not much had changed with Will and Charlotte. The man was still all mops and brooms with his wife.

Will dug through his flower box. "I'm usually more organized, Seth. But this is a new, uh, system. Charlotte's an artist."

"Real clever," Seth murmured. He rubbed his hands together and waited, keeping Mina in the corner of his eye. She stood, quiet and composed, her back straight and her slim shoulders squared to the room.

Will had it all wrong, but Seth was interested in seeing the catalog nonetheless.

"I've already seen the lots for sale," Will said, rifling through the box. "They're at Chiswick's glasshouse already. My father's been told to keep them under lock and key, with all the interest surrounding them. There's that blue orchid with yellow lateral sepals that's extraordinary. The one with the banded column and mottled petals." He found the catalog and leafed to a page. "I want this one for Charlotte—ivory petals, a smoky-blue anther cap—but Cavendish says he won't be outbid. All origins, Brazil. The list is a long one." He handed it over. "Here, you can see. I thought they had to be yours."

Seth took the catalog.

And his stomach turned over.

The page contained an illustration of an orchid. *His* illustration.

"They lied." His voice sounded hollow in his ears.

"Seth?"

Mina's voice was faint. His mind was empty. But the betrayal was deafening…and drowning. "They lied." He flipped the pages, one illustration after the next. His orchids. His blooms from all the seeds he'd collected. All his drawings.

They'd lied to him, and… *Christ*. "They told me the seeds rotted."

"Who told you that?" Will asked.

"Jack Skinner. The nurserymen, the Skinners. My… They were my mates. Since we were lads. What are these numbers?"

Will stared. "Those are the put-up prices. They'll not be sold for less." Will shared a look with his wife, his voice subdued. "At Chiswick, the bidding usually ends at ten times that, Seth. Ten times—at the least."

His hands shook until he fisted them. The numbers seemed to float off the page at him. 30… 85…60…15…110—

110. For the seeds of the snowy, bell-shaped flowers he'd climbed into the treetops for in the Mato Grosso and nearly died harvesting. And seventy-five for the violet-plumed flowers above the Nhamundá River. He'd come face-to-face with a red-skulled *Cacajao* monkey climbing to reach her.

The room was quiet until Will asked, "What of your contract?"

"Wasn't any contract." Seth's voice came out rusty. *They'd lied.* He closed the auction book. "No contract. I don't… I've got no claim on 'em."

"You do," Mina said quietly. "Of course you do. You found them, Seth."

"Right," Will said. "No one would believe you gave the Skinners your prizes without any compensation. You'd have proof they're yours. Wouldn't you?"

Proof? He had cargo receipts for the eighteen cases of *Cattleya* and *Oncidium* species, and his trunks with the seeds. But that wasn't proof. They were only listed as botanical cargo. "I don't—my journals, I think." He raised his head. "My journals have illustrations. Those in the catalog are all copies I'd done."

"Good."

"And I've got extra seeds. *Other* seeds."

Will's head shot up. "Others?"

Anger blazed to life in Seth's chest. *They'd lied. Took what he did and lied to him, right to his face.*

"Seth?" Mina's soft voice hushed his fury. "You have the seeds?"

He nodded. "I packed them all different ways. Some in drying papers, some in waxed. In glass, and mixed in ashes to keep the mold and pests from them." He shook his head. "But they're months older now."

"If they germinate and match what's sold, *there's* your claim," Will said. "We'll get you an attorney. We'll get Ben"—he turned to explain to Mina—"my brother-in-law is Ben Paxton. He's the best cultivator in England and has a tropical stove up north, a palm house. And he's got two or three houses just for striking seeds, as well. If anyone can get those seeds to sprout and root, it's him."

Seth was getting muddled. He ought to write this down. "Wait, Will." He pulled out his Shakespeare book, embarrassed to let Will see his small notebook in his fine room of green leather books. He'd never shown it to anyone but Mina. And he was embarrassed now to let Mina see him writing Will's instructions down.

"You're thinking an attorney first?" Seth asked quietly.

"I'll send word to Ben in Hanover Square. He's

down from Windmere, with Lucy and the children. He'll want to help."

"This isn't your worry, Will."

"Of course it is." Will shook his head, smiling. "Christ...you're my friend, and you left England and all your prizes with those cheats to bring Aimee Bourianne back to me. There's nothing I won't do for you now."

Mina sat beside him. When she covered his hand with her small one, he forced himself to look at her. "Let him help," she whispered. "No one can do this alone."

Sweet Minnie. He looked into her eyes and saw what he always saw there. She was on his side.

He nodded and wrote down what Will said about a solicitor and the seeds. But nothing would change the fact that the Skinners had lied to him. And they had... because they could.

It had been damn easy.

Seth shook his head clear of those thoughts. He had to think straight, nail down the parts that mattered.

"We'll have to report the theft," Will said. "And enlist impartial witnesses to the sowing of the seeds, don't you think? So there's no suspicion of tampering?"

Seth considered that and kept writing. "Yes, I suppose. We'd want witnesses." It was a good notion. A smart one. One he wouldn't have thought of...

No, he wouldn't have thought of that.

He put down his pencil. Even if he had a claim to those flowers, he hadn't known enough to sign a damn contract. A man ought to think of such things.

Mina deserved a man who would.

Twenty

"MR. MAYHEW WILL BE HERE SOON, MINA." MARY had borrowed Emma's best indigo dress and was combing Sebastian's hair, who endured his mother's grooming with a cross look on his little face. "I hope the coffee is to his liking. I'm not used to preparing it."

"Shall I try a bit?" Mina tried to sound authoritative, though she didn't know the flavors of coffee any better than Mary did.

"Would you?" Distractedly, Mary smoothed Sebastian's shirt and patted him on his way, freeing him to dash to his toy ball. Mary faced her and waited, her hands twisting in her skirt.

Mina sipped and nodded approvingly. "Very good." As far as she could tell.

"Better than the tea we drink?" Mary asked.

"Anything would be better than the twigs-and-tea-dust we drink," Emma grumbled from her seat on the sofa, where she was sewing her piecework.

Mary arranged the tea tray for the third time. "Remember, this sugar is for Mr. Mayhew. No one else put sugar in your tea," she commanded.

"Don't fret so, Mary." Emma laid a sisterly hand on Mary's shoulder. "Mr. Mayhew is excessively kind. I know you believe him an angel sent from above, but he is just a man." She grinned. "A man who looks like a *god*."

Mina could barely attend to Mary and Emma's chatter. Yesterday, Seth had looked so devastated by his cultivators' betrayal—his friends' betrayal—that she had yet to decide on a new argument to best persuade him to take back his money.

He had been brought so low, his pride so battered, she did not want to add to his hurt.

"Remember," she said to Emma and Mary, "after his coffee, you must excuse yourselves and leave us alone, so I can speak to him about the money."

Mary nodded firmly and Emma sighed. The topic was an uncomfortable one, so she did not press for their assurances.

But Emma rarely shied from uncomfortable topics. "He will undoubtedly need that money now, for his own attorney." She shook her head. "How could anyone swindle such a kind, generous, and attractive man as Mr. Mayhew? After all his hard work and the years of traveling and risking his life?"

"I do not know," she murmured.

"You *will* help him, won't you, Mina?" Emma asked. "Mr. Mayhew needs someone as managing as you."

"I'm not managing, Emma."

"That is no insult. You *are* managing." Emma severed the thread of her needle and tested the seam of her sewing. "Thank goodness you did not wed Thomas. Two such managing people"—she shuddered—"I can't imagine a more excruciating marriage."

Mina's jaw dropped. "You said we were perfect for each other."

She rolled her eyes heavenward. "What else was I to say? We were in *Bombay*." She flipped her fabric over. "Mary, would you pass me that bobbin of green? Besides," Emma continued, her stare pointed, "it was plain you loved Mr. Mayhew from the first."

Why were little sisters always so provoking?

Mary handed Emma her thread, eyeing the tea tray lest something had shifted in the past second. "If that is true, Mina, no one would expect you to accept Mr. Grant."

Confused, Mina stared at Mary. "I should have thought you'd expect me to," she said quietly.

Mary stilled and, at last, raised her eyes to her. "Don't be so afraid, Mina. You aren't destined to share my fate. Besides"—she smiled a little—"love makes you brave. It makes you stronger than you ever imagined you could be." Her eyes drifted to her son playing on his pallet by the hearth before she straightened the cups once again.

Wordless, Mina could only watch her nephew, innocently playing by the fire. He would never know all his mother had done for him.

Yes, love had made Mary brave indeed.

A knock sounded on the door, and Sebastian turned wide eyes to it. They were not accustomed to company. She had to smile as her nephew pushed to his feet, clasping his hands with excitement.

Seth. There was a clamp on her lungs and a rolling sensation in her stomach. Her normally steady pulse began to throb.

But of course it would. Her heart was nearing.

With a hurried smoothing of her skirts, she dashed to open the door. "Good morning." Her eyes caught on the figure behind Seth and the breath fled her body. "*Thomas?*"

Thomas doffed his hat and bowed. "Forgive this surprise, Mina. I couldn't wait a moment more to see you. I just learned how to find you from Mayhew today."

"Thomas," she repeated.

She looked from him into Seth's bleak eyes.

"Heavens," Emma said from behind her. "Thomas, what are you doing here? That is… Do come in."

She backed away from the door, allowing the men to enter. Her pulse began to race as she introduced Thomas to Mary and Sebastian. Seth stood silent.

Thomas was here. He was *here*. Had he come to demand she return to India? She'd returned his bond. He had no right.

"Please have a seat." Mary gestured for them to join her on the sofa. "Mina? Won't you sit?"

Her legs seemed to have lost the capacity to move, but the men would not sit if she did not. With a jolt, she turned for a chair and sank onto it.

"I hope I find you well, Mina?" Thomas asked. "And all your sisters?"

"Indeed," she breathed. "Yes. We are well."

Mary poured the coffee and tea, prodding her with a speaking look.

"I"—Mina swallowed to loosen her throat—"I did not expect to see you in England, Thomas. Is your family well?"

The glass of his lenses obscured his eyes. "Yes, they are very well, thank you."

Panic crawled up her back and she had to clench her teeth against demanding answers, against screaming. *We do not suit! You love another woman! Seth told me you loved—*

She looked to Seth, but his gaze was on his coffee, and she needed him to look at her or…or she was alone. And she was afraid.

"Is the coffee to your liking, Mr. Mayhew?" Mary asked.

He lifted his head and graced her with one of his lazy smiles. "Best I've ever had. Thank you, Mary."

Mary's hands fluttered to her lap and back up to wrap her arms. "There is more. And sugar." She pushed the sugar bowl closer to him. "I hope—Mr. Grant, I hope your sail was pleasant."

Thomas nodded. "Tolerable. Wouldn't you say, Seth?"

Seth's eyes were on Mina, grave and steady. "Yes."

They had sailed together? Is that what Seth meant to tell her yesterday? How could he not have told her?

An awkward silence fell over the room, and she couldn't bear a second more. "I'll put on another kettle." She rose on unsteady legs and hurried from the room, not acknowledging the men standing for her departure. In the kitchen, she crowded the hob, needing the fire's warmth.

And then the truth revealed itself. She had to cover her lips from crying out. Seth had *brought* Thomas.

For her.

"I should have told you, Minnie." Seth had entered silently behind her.

"I was surprised to see him."

"I know it."

She was afraid to look at him but could feel his gaze on her. One of Sebastian's biscuits sat forgotten on a chair and she placed it carefully on the table. "I don't know why he's here. I can't go back to India." She laughed without humor. "Can you imagine another sail? Well, yes—*you* could, I suppose. But I can't—" *I can't…I can't leave you, leave my sisters, can't…*

"You're not going back, Minnie."

Her heart didn't ease with his words. "Did you bring him here to England?"

"No, I didn't"—he took a long breath—"I didn't bring him. I hoped—well, I'm thinking you already know what I hoped, but I didn't plan what happened." He paused. "He's the better man, Minnie."

A silent sob wracked her, convulsing her shoulders. Tears stung beneath her lids, and she kept her eyes on the table.

"He's come to marry you as he should've done the moment you met. And he'll take care of Emma and Mary and Sebastian. He promised me he would."

She leaned hard on the table, bracing against his words.

"He's a good man. You know that. He's got a hope about things and that's nice, that's better. That's"—he cleared his throat—"that's the man you need. Steady, sensible. Not just sensible, but smart. And he's safe."

She closed her eyes. Hadn't she said all this before? And believed it?

Love didn't matter. She'd said it again and again.

"You know all the reasons you can't marry me. You'd be unhappy." Seth kept talking and she forced herself to listen, though she couldn't look at him. "Once I had to sail again to earn our living. That's what my life is, Minnie. An explorer's life. You'd be unhappy. If you were cold and hungry, or our children were, you'd be unhappy."

She nodded, but she didn't know why or what she was doing. Love didn't matter. It didn't—"I would have taken care of you."

No. *No.* She wouldn't. *How* would she? Even Seth would not rose color this.

His breath hitched and when he spoke, his voice was ragged. "I know it. The moment I saw you, I knew it. And you'd do a job of it, too, Minnie." His voice had plummeted so she stared at his lips to truly hear. "But I can't take care of you. I'm not…ready."

He wouldn't look at her. *I'm not ready.* What had it cost him to say that to her? But she'd said the same to him.

And she'd said it first.

Shame engulfed her, hot as flames. She was cruel. She was a coward.

He turned his back to face the door. "I'm joining an expedition into Brazil. I thought it an opportune time to sign on with a crew."

Brazil? "No. No, what of the auction and your prizes? You can't leave."

"I didn't sign a contract. Didn't think I even had a need to. That's not—that's not a man who can take care of a family. Seems I can only take care of myself."

No, no, no. He couldn't leave, not again. "What of your land? And your stone cottage? And the hedgerow?"

Something like pain flashed across his face. "It'll keep a few years more."

"You have to stay. You can't keep sailing and I...I couldn't bear to have you so far away. Please. For Georgiana and Aimee, stay. For me."

He grabbed a fistful of his cropped hair but didn't turn. "Don't ask me to stay, Minnie. I can't."

"Seth—?"

"You have to marry Tom. He came all this way for you and you'll not be leaving England. He's kept a position with East India. You'll manage your own house. You and your children will never want for anything. Even if he dies on you, you'll be taken care of—"

"*Please.* Don't sail."

Seth's jaw tightened and he shook his head, making for the door. "There's no help for it, Minnie."

He had her heart. She had to protect him. He couldn't go. "*Wait!*"

He stilled, his arms hanging at his side.

"Wait...wait," she breathed. "Don't. You can't sail anymore." She caught her breath and rushed on. "If you stay...I'll marry Thomas. I promise I will. But only if you stay. Only if you take back your money."

He turned to look at her, and she nearly sobbed at the shame in his eyes. And the betrayal.

She had done that to him.

"I...please," she whispered. "I don't know what else to do to make you stay."

The door inched open and Thomas leaned through the door cautiously. "Mayhew?" He waited for Seth to look at him. "Perhaps it's best if I speak to Mina now. Would you pardon us?"

Seth straightened to his full height and turned stiffly back to her. His eyes burned into hers, grave and resolved, but she refused to buckle.

Until he set her quartz pebble on the table and spoke his next words.

"You can't be on my side anymore, Minnie."

She sank onto the chair before her nerveless legs could fail. She could not speak to stop him from walking out.

"Mina?" Thomas asked. "Are you all right?"

"He's going?" She could barely choke out the words. She looked at Thomas, trying to find an answer there. "Did you…did you persuade him to sail?"

"Sail?"

"He's going to sail. To Brazil."

Thomas frowned. "I didn't—he never said anything about that." He eyed her warily. "Mina?"

She forced herself to focus on Thomas's words.

He sat across from her. "I know I've surprised you. I'm sorry. But I think you must know why I'm here."

She sat very still, her heartbeat loud in her ears. "No, Thomas. I don't."

He blinked behind his spectacles.

"And I can't believe you know why *you're* here, either," she said. "You don't want to marry me."

Thomas stiffened. "I promised you my protection and then abandoned you. I treated you abominably. The only excuse I offer is that—"

"You're in love with someone else."

Thomas had the grace not to deny it. "Mina, I'll be a good husband to you. I'll treat you as I should have. I'll never knowingly be cruel or hurtful."

"No. No, I know you wouldn't. You're a good man, but—"

"I've come to fulfill my obligation to you, and I vow, I will keep you and your sisters safe. I'm done with India. I think I've been done for a long time now. And my family misses me. I missed them, and so I can"—he clenched his eyes shut—"do what I am *supposed* to do. Leave the past behind and move forward and marry. Will you marry me, Mina?"

And there it was. A marriage offer.

"Mina?"

From a man who was safe—

...I'd work hard to take care of you...and we'd be together; we'd be home—I'd give you my home. And I promise, I'd never leave you or our children. I never would. I'd never want to...

An answer to her oldest prayer—a husband, a house, safety. And suddenly, none of those things could induce her to accept Thomas's offer.

We'd be together, Minnie. We'd be home.

And Seth was home.

"Do you believe there is more to life than safety?" She didn't recognize the voice as her own. "More than just...avoiding fear and suffering?"

Thomas flinched, as if cornered by his own memories. He dropped his eyes. "I don't know. I believed so once. I *hoped* so once."

She had never hoped for a life that was anything more than safe, *never*. Until now.

She pushed to her feet. "I thank you, Thomas. *I do*. I know I ought to marry you. I know I should be grateful." She closed her eyes. "And I know I am failing my family. But there is someone else that I love just as much as my sisters, and he needs me, too. And I didn't know that until now." She looked him in the eye—even through those blasted spectacles so there would be no misunderstanding. "I won't marry you."

Thomas stared at her. And then a small smile curled his lips. "Mina...how could I not have known? You love him back, don't you?"

She met his eyes and couldn't find any way to deny it. God, her heart must be written on her face. "I love Seth, and I trust him. I trust we'll be safe if we are together. And I know that sounds feeble-headed but I am certain I want to take care of him. And I want him to take care of me, or I will be very unhappy."

Thomas smiled. "So you are refusing me?"

"You don't need me, Thomas." And the next realization came to her with an alarming...*grace*. "And I don't need *you*."

He moved closer and caught her fingers to lift her hand for his kiss. "You are a mighty woman, Mina."

Mighty? Was love deluding her as it had Mary? Was she making the worst mistake of her life? Was she mighty?

Perhaps, just this once, just for Seth, she could be.

Twenty-one

A MAN PREPARING FOR HIS FIFTEENTH SAIL KNEW he'd be packing regrets. But this time, maybe they wouldn't be as heavy.

Seth's wood trunk covered nearly all of the bedroom floor in these cramped rooms he'd rented for himself and Georgie. There was no room for a sister, in any case, so she stood in the door, watching him pack. And frowning.

She didn't approve of his going. He could have found some low work somewhere, to be near her and Aimee, but he couldn't deny he was damn eager to be outward-bound. A hundred days on a creaking ship was preferable to being so close to Mina and not being able to be with her.

"Are those the only linens you have?" she asked.

"They're all I need."

Georgie was pretending indifference, but he wasn't fooled. She was keeping an eye on his packing. "You might have some extra drawers sewn," she said. "You'll not find them easily in the Americas in your size."

"Finding's what I do, Georgie. Now stop worrying. You should be packing yourself."

"I'm done. They're sending a carriage after supper for me and Aimee." Georgie stared at him, her mouth turning down with sadness. "How could I have been so stupid, Seth?"

"Georgie—"

"I should've kept a little of the reward for you. If I did, just a little, you and Mina—"

"Georgie, stop," Seth said. "You did the right thing."

Georgie quieted, her lips thin as if in pain. "I should have helped you."

"I never took anything I didn't earn. I couldn't start now." Seth stared into his trunk because Georgie's chin had started to quiver.

That huge reward was turned into a trust for Aimee—by Georgie's own design—but in turn, she'd negotiated a position as nursemaid and companion to Aimee. They'd both be living in a Grosvenor Square townhouse that belonged to Aimee's guardian.

Seth continued his packing. "It's damn well how it should be, Georgie. That little baby shouldn't lose another mother. Your situation and…and the *other* one settled different than I'd predicted, but it settled better."

"How can you say that?"

"Minnie will be taken care of. Her sisters, too." His voice sounded wrong. He cleared his throat roughly. "Seems I'm not all that skilled in predicting matters."

"I'm so afraid you'll regret leaving."

His tin travel cup slipped from his fingers, and he hurried to cover the fumble. "There'll be regrets, Georgie. But none I can't shoulder."

Seth pushed to his feet and moved to the cupboard. "Besides, Minnie would've accepted Tom by now."

"We don't know that."

"Tom'll keep her safe, like she needs." Mina was capable, composed, and orderly-like, and Tom suited that. And once all of Mina's straight thinking returned, she'd wonder what she ever saw in a vagabond explorer that had no business turning his eyes on her in the first place.

She would forget him—might even be ashamed of lying with him.

Pain streaked across his chest at the thought. It didn't matter. He wouldn't be forgetting her. He couldn't shut his eyes without seeing her. She was always walking his land up in Derbyshire, his cottage in the background. Crossing that stream with her stepping-stones he planned to put in. He'd still do that little bridge, as soon as he got back in a few years. That wouldn't cost any more than his own labor if he was clever about it. Maybe there'd even be a day when she'd come and see it. With Tom and her children.

That pain wasn't easing, but there was something else growing there. Something hopeful and calm: a future for Mina. In time, maybe he'd feel less sad over it.

A knock sounded at the door. Georgie, with heavy steps, went to answer and returned with a letter in her hand. "Another note from Will Repton."

He grunted a reply but didn't look up.

"Will you not read this one, either?" Georgie dropped the letter on his bed. "He writes to me, too, you know."

Damn. He paused in his packing.

"What did you expect?" she said. "You've avoided him for three weeks. And I agree with him—you *are* being cruel to Mina."

"Don't, Georgie," he growled.

"She's desperate to see you and has no way to reach you. It would serve you right if Mr. Repton tells her where you live."

A sudden panic froze him, but he steeled his spine. "Not his business. Or yours."

"It *is* my business. I only… I want you to be happy. I know you go to Mildmay Park every day to spy on her and see that she's all right. Did you think I wouldn't notice your disappearing for hours every day?"

He heated with shame but shook his head. "I told you. She's marrying Tom."

"Only because you'll not marry her yourself."

He slammed his trunk shut. "I can't keep her, and Minnie knows it. She'll not be 'avin' a sket."

"You're not a *sket*."

He frowned at the bloody Midlands words. He was supposed to be leaving them good and buried.

Georgie grabbed his arm and he bit back a curse. *God save him from little sisters.*

"Seth, demand the Skinners acknowledge those are your prizes. You're stronger than a dozen Skinner boys—*bang it out* if you have to."

"May as well beat the wind," he mumbled. "It won't work, Georgie."

"Why won't you try?" Her chin jutted stubbornly. "I gave Mr. Repton your seeds."

His heart plunged to his boots. "Why would you do that?"

"I had to do *something*."

"The auction will be done before anything could be proved."

"He and Ben Paxton have a striking house in Richmond. Two botanists from Kew witnessed the sowing and verified the contents of your journal."

"And who gave them my journal?"

Georgie crossed her arms across her chest, and that little chin jutted higher.

Well. There was his answer. With a growl, he turned from her and opened his wardrobe to resume packing.

"I could tell Mina where to find you," she said.

"You wouldn't do that," he said flatly. And she wouldn't. They were all the family they had left, and she wouldn't do a thing that would cut him that deep.

Georgie sank against the doorjamb, all the spirit in her extinguished. "The messenger boy is waiting on the pavement for some sort of reply."

Hell. He cracked open Will's letter and steeled himself against the words. Mina was still looking for him. That wasn't news. She wanted to give him back that money—as if he'd ever take it from her.

He kept reading, and reading carefully, but only because Will was a good man. The note outlined all the work he'd done on his behalf, just as Georgie had said. They'd even found themselves an attorney who had written letters to the Skinner nurserymen and the Penderton and Monroe auction house.

And he didn't give a damn.

He shouldn't have chased dreams of orchards and stepping-stones, and a fine lady for a wife with the most kissable lips in the world. He was an explorer.

A traveler. A man without family who left pieces of himself everywhere he sailed.

Soon, there'd be nothing left of him at all.

"The boy is waiting," Georgie said. "What did Mr. Repton ask you?"

"He wants us to visit."

"Us?"

"I imagine he's keen to see you and Aimee any chance he can. You can go. Will says the carriage will wait, or he could send it back at another time."

"And what of you?"

Seth dropped the letter on the bed. "I've no time for Richmond." He opened the front door to speak to Will's servant. "Sorry, lad. Tell Mr. Repton I can't—"

"Wait, please." Georgie halted the boy and turned to face Seth. "Let's see him. He must have news."

"None that will change anything."

"For the sake of Peter, you can be the most stubborn man."

That stung. "I know it. I've never been smart."

"I said *stubborn*, not *stupid*." She swung open the door to the boy, muttering beneath her breath. "Mr. Mayhew and I *accept*. Please tell the coachman we'll be just a minute."

He frowned at his sister but she met his glare with an identical green-blue one. "He may have news about your discoveries. And Mina."

"It's too late."

"If there's a chance you might find the means to wed her, you have to take it." She grabbed his hand. "You love her, Seth. This could be an opportunity, and a man like you recognizes that when it arises, doesn't he?"

DISCOVERY OF DESIRE 313

Opportunity.

Well…hell. His sister knew him too well. And he didn't have the fight in him anymore. "I suppose…I could hear what he has to say," he grumbled. "See where the tide's at."

"The tide," she murmured, a sparkle lighting in her eyes. "*Julius Caesar?*"

He shrugged. "Can't tell anymore if I'm in the shallows or the flood."

Georgie smiled. "So go and see. Like the scholar of Shakespeare that you are."

Twenty-two

"SEVEN HUNDRED POUNDS." WILL HANDED HIM THE letter from the attorney and Seth sat down beside Georgie to read it.

"I don't understand what he's written." Seth flipped the letter over. It was a long one, and the language as hard as Shakespeare.

"I had to read it myself several times," Will said. "All it took was a strongly worded letter from the attorney, and the Skinner nurserymen have decided to offer you seven hundred pounds for possession of all your seeds and orchids."

Seven hundred. His heartbeat jumped in the second before his reason took over. He could fix his cottage, but he couldn't take care of Mina and her family for that. And there was no getting around it. He had to take care of Mina's sisters or she wouldn't feel safe. Marrying Mina meant marrying her whole family. He set the letter down on the table. "I suppose that's a lot of money."

Will, Charlotte, and Georgie weren't saying anything. And when he looked up to check their faces, they were all grim.

No, that wasn't accurate.

Will was looking horn-mad.

"If you accept the seven hundred, Seth"—Will snatched the letter off the table, crushing new creases into it as he brutally folded it—"then you forfeit your share of what's earned at the auction."

"But I gave the seeds to the Skinners to cultivate. They may not all have survived. How many do they even have? I gave them eighty species but—"

"You did a job packing those seeds then, because the catalog lists nearly eighty."

Hell. Seth nodded, trying to do the math. "And with the put-up price…?"

"If everything sells, eight hundred and eighty is the opening price," Will said. "But the bids will be higher."

"But how much higher?" he asked. "There's no telling. Seven hundred sounds like a good offer."

He looked to Charlotte Repton, the only friendly face in the room. Her smile dimpled. "It is a contemptible offer, Mr. Mayhew."

He blinked.

"More coffee?" she asked.

"Uh…no, thank you."

Will leaned forward in his chair, giving the letter in his fist a hard shake. "You have a choice, Seth. Seven hundred or a percentage of what's raised at auction—less the commission to your agents. And the agents would be the Skinners and the auction house."

"Is that percentage in the Skinners's letter?" Seth asked.

Will shook his head, frowning. "No. You'll have to fight them for any percentage. And they're counting on your not going to the trouble, the bastards." He looked contritely at the women. "Pardon my language, ladies."

Charlotte only beamed wider and leaned over to whisper to Georgie. "I rather adore men in a righteous passion. Fortunately for me, Will is often in just that state over any manner of things."

Georgie smiled uncertainly at Charlotte before turning back to Seth. "Seven hundred *is* a great deal of money. But Will and Charlotte would know better than us how the auction might play."

Will nodded. "I realize seven hundred is more than most men make in a decade, but I think you will make far more at auction. You should demand fifty percent as the discoverer of those plants."

Seth looked down at the letter. Mina was marrying Tom. Even seven hundred wasn't enough compared to what Tom was offering. A house in London. A salary for the rest of his life. A widow's pension. Shelter for her sisters.

Gambling on fifty percent—if he could get that—of some unknown number would be about the stupidest notion a man could have. Wouldn't it?

He sat with the focus of the whole room on his next words, and his skin heating. "I don't know any law-yers," he said quietly, as if the volume would somehow spare him a little of his shame. "I don't know if I have enough blunt to even hire one. Don't know where to start exactly."

Hell, Georgie would know that about him by now. And Will and Charlotte, they said they were friends—they *were* friends. And if he wanted his life to be different, he had to start asking for help.

"What do you think I should do?" Seth raised his chin to look at them. "It's not right what the Skinners did. But I don't know much about money. Never had enough of it to bother learning."

Will sat forward, his smile growing. "Neither did I. Fortunately, Charlotte had her own man of business when we married. He's a good man and works for the family. I don't think he'd mind taking a meeting."

A meeting with a man of business. He'd never done that before. "If I made any money, I'd want a beneficiary. If something happened to me, I'd want to make sure my...my wife was taken care of."

My wife. He almost didn't dare say the words.

"He could arrange that, and it's a good thought," Will said. "What is it, Seth? Something else is troubling you."

"Minnie. She's marrying Tom Grant." He could barely push the words out his lips.

"*Tom Grant?*" Charlotte cried. "*Who* is Tom Grant? And *honestly*, why has no one informed me of this?"

"He asked her three weeks ago," Georgie explained.

"Didn't Minnie tell you in one of her letters?" Seth asked.

"*No!*" Charlotte huffed. "No, she did not. I am not even *acquainted* with this Tom Grant. I cannot credit her accepting anyone but you."

Seth shrugged a shoulder. It was all he could manage. "He's what she wanted. A stable man. A husband who'd provide."

Georgie leaned forward to take his hand. "Maybe you can provide now?"

"But how do I know?" He shook his head. "She

would've said yes." She *would* have because Mina knew love didn't matter.

But if he had more than love…

He had land. A lot of land. And if *all* his prizes sold for as much as Will and Charlotte expected they might, he'd have money. He could fix his cottage and buy a flock of sheep and he could provide damn well for Mina, and Mary and Emma and Sebastian and all the other sisters he'd not even met yet.

He might have Mina for his own.

His fists were clenched, the nails digging into the flesh of his palms, and he eased them open. But if she'd already said yes to Tom—*hell*. He gripped his temples and shut his eyes to think. Had he missed the current? Lost his ventures? Lost his venture girl?

No. No, this was opportunity. This was the time to be bold or he'd lose her forever. There was never any curse, no fate, no luck, never any damn signs—he didn't believe in signs. Even if the first time they met…

The first time. The flowers on her dress, the sweet woodruff. Only ever saw them in the woods behind his cottage. Only ever saw them one other place in the world. And that was home.

And the pottery vendor with the platter of melancholy thistle. Mina had steered him there, had said it felt like home somehow. That led him to Georgie.

And the Rio Gurupí, where he'd found his Wilhelmina orchid, and Mina's charm—*It's no charm,* she'd said. *And it's nothing near a diamond.*

The Rio Gurupí…*the River of Pure Diamond.*

Had there been signs?

You have the sign.

His heart calmed, and he opened his eyes. There *had* been signs. But only one sign meant to simply be read: *CLAIMING W. ADAMS*.

Seth raised his head. "All right, Will. I'll fight them for a percentage. I'll go to auction."

Georgie jumped up and hugged him. "Thank goodness, Seth. You won't sail?"

He breathed deep and shook his head. "I think... maybe I can earn enough. I always planned to work. I'll work every day, so Minnie and I have enough for our babies and grandbabies. I think it'll be—it *will* be enough."

"It'll be more than enough." Will grinned. "And you love her."

Seth nodded hard. "I do. I love her." The words were more breath than sound.

"Then you'll fight the Skinners for your claim," Will said.

"Not fifty percent," Seth growled, his voice still not working. "*More*. I found 'em. Maybe if my mates were of a mind to tell me the truth, to be fair, I might've taken half." Something hot and steely was curling its claws around his spine. "I'm owed more and I'm taking more."

"That's damn right!" Will winced, darting a glance at Georgie and Charlotte. "Pardon, ladies."

Georgie waved off the apology, but Charlotte had turned sheep's eyes on her husband.

"Do you remember the day you asked to go to India in my place?" Will said.

Seth shook his head. "Not really. I remember you were so depressed over leaving Charlotte, you could barely draw breath. You barely seemed to want to. I never saw a man so heartsick. I nearly turned heel, it was so awkward—"

"Yes, well." Will frowned. "Seems you remember that well enough."

"Thought you might start weeping—"

"*All right*—"

"I'd seen that look in other explorers," Seth said. "Men who didn't have the heart to keep living. It's when I knew you wouldn't make it out of India. Knew you'd not survive the trip."

Will fell silent, studying him. "Is that why you went in my place?"

Seth looked up, surprised by the question. "Georgie was lost. She's my family. And you had a wife. I had nothing in England."

Will hugged Charlotte against his side before turning back to him. "You have something now, Seth. So I'll remind you what you said. You told me to go get my family." Will leaned forward and grinned. "So go get yours."

Twenty-three

SHE RATHER HATED SEWING.

It was a sulky thought, but Mina was prone to sulky thoughts these days. She stretched her stiffening wrist and shook out her fingers, taking a moment to glance out the window at the wall across the narrow alley. A short slant of sun lit their neighbor's wall on its way to setting for the day. What time was it? Six? Six thirty? They'd been sewing since half past seven this morning and, without Emma, she and Mary had long exhausted their conversation.

"Shouldn't Emma be home by now?" she asked Mary. Once a week, each of them volunteered at the Mother's Meeting Club in Cabbage Court. The kitchen always needed help in serving the poor. And until recently, Mary and Sebastian had been among the needy.

A light rap on the door and Mina was on her feet. *Thank goodness, Emma.* She breathed a sigh of relief. "Here she is."

Emma's cheeks were pink, and her blond curls haphazard under her bonnet, but she wore an enormous smile. "He's going to help me."

"Who?" she asked.

"Mr. Ingram. He has agreed to take my cause against Colin Rivers."

Mina sighed in frustration. "Is that where you were? You were supposed to be at the Mother's Club with Mrs. Bradford. It's too dangerous to wander alone in the City."

Emma raised her chin a notch and unbuttoned her coat. "You ought to be pleased. You're forever going on about our finances."

"Emma—"

"Mr. Ingram says if Mr. Rivers will not answer for his abandonment, we will flush him out."

"Like a snipe, I suppose?" she said.

"Like a cad who ought to take responsibility for his actions. He will certainly not like to be embarrassed in front of the directors of the East India Company. They will not like to keep a man of such dubious character in their employ."

"So you will charge him publicly? Shame him?"

"If he will not do the honorable thing. I should expect him to do the same to me had I done the same." Emma stared, her cheeks paling. "I really thought you would be pleased, but *nothing* pleases you of late."

Hurt, Mina dropped her eyes back to her sewing. And, yes, she *loathed* sewing.

The stitches blurred, but she would not wipe the tears from her eyes lest Mary and Emma see her cry. No, nothing pleased her, and the scold was the closest Emma had come to mentioning Seth's abandonment of her.

It was her own fault. She should have demanded that Seth give her his direction but he had promised to the day after their visit to the Reptons' three weeks ago. And that was the day Thomas had surprised her.

Three long weeks. She didn't even know if he was still in England. East India would give her no information. And the butler at Lord Bosham's town house in Grosvenor Square had not let her see Georgiana, but had promised to tell her she had visited.

No one would tell her where he was and she could not see him. If only she could see him again…

How could she berate Emma for chasing a man? She was chasing her own.

A knock sounded on the door and all four of them— Sebastian included —raised their heads in surprise.

Emma went to the door. "Who is there?" she asked through the door. Mildmay Park was no place to open doors wide.

"It's me. It's Seth."

Seth? Mina's stomach plummeted and only the ribbing of her corset kept her upright in her seat. *Oh dear God—Seth!* He hadn't left. It wasn't too late.

Emma looked back at her, wide-eyed and frozen, so Mina jumped to her feet and hurried to unlatch the door. "Wait," she breathed, though he could not hear her. *Wait wait wait*—a sob of panic was rising against her throat, and she fumbled with the lock. Had she imagined his voice?

The latch turned, the door swung wide, and there he was, filling the entire door. And his wonderful eyes locked on hers. And crinkled. "Ah, Minnie," he said quietly.

And his voice was so full of relief, that for a moment, all she could do was stare in confusion and wait for her heartbeat to ease. She was not even angry, though the wait had been long and so unkind. Because Seth was never unkind.

"You're here." She finally managed to breathe the words. And there were so many more words she needed to say.

"I'm here," he rasped. "I'm sorry I didn't come back and come sooner. It wasn't right but I'm needing a minute to talk to you, Minnie." His lips thinned. "No, that's not accurate. I shouldn't have said a minute. Maybe eight minutes or nine—"

"Come in," she said. "I wanted to talk with you, too."

Seth angled his broad body into their abode. He nodded at her sisters, and *for him* they put down their needlework and beamed welcoming smiles.

"Ladies, would you mind if I speak to Minnie alone?" he said.

Mary lurched to her feet and made to collect Sebastian. "Yes, of course." Mary's voice was unnaturally high and cheery. "We'll go to Mrs. Bradford's again, shall we?" Her skirts swayed with the speed in which she bundled her son and Emma into their coats and out the door to their neighbor.

Seth stood in the middle of the small parlor, his arms hanging at his sides. It was unnatural to not see him smile or hear him laugh. And she wanted that more than anything else in the world. "I'm so happy to see you. I was so afraid you'd gone and—"

"Minnie, would you mind if I talked first? On account of how all my words are about to jump out of my head? And if you're holding me to that eight minutes, I'm afraid I'll not get through them if you're saying things back, which I'm thinking you do, and have a right to—"

"You can go first."

He nodded, rubbing his big hands together. "Minnie, I was thinking you shouldn't marry Tom with any haste. It's peculiar, I know, after what I said before. But I don't want you to marry him yet, on account of my still wanting to marry you."

Oh. Oh dear.

Yes. It ached to even think the word. But yes, please…please, yes. But did he know how hard it would be with her family? How long they may have to wait? Did he love her enough to wait?

Seth's gaze dropped for an instant, and when he looked at her again, there was wariness in his gaze. "But I can't—ah, Minnie, I can't ask you to marry me right now."

The ache deepened, but she wasn't surprised. She was too practical to be surprised. She only nodded because she'd promised not to interrupt. And really, she didn't know what she could say. Sewing for hours had apparently deadened her brain.

"I don't expect you to trust me on everything, not without knowing my plan, which I'm still working on. Because I know a lady like you deserves a strong plan."

A plan?

"And Tom Grant *is* a good man." Seth hurried through his words. "But I hope I can be better for you, and I just wanted to say that before you and Tom got too far along in the matrimonial arrangements. Because my plan just needs a little more time. So I'm asking you to wait on marrying Tom. Just until I can sort out my plan. Would you?"

Seth had a plan.

He searched her eyes, looking uncertain. "Would you wait for—you can talk now, Minnie. I didn't need all my minutes."

She blinked and fixed her smile, because, really, what could she say but, "All right."

"All right?"

She moved closer. "All right."

"Ah…Christ," he groaned, staggering to the sofa.

Alarmed, she reached for him but he sat down hard, the sofa scraping on the floor to hit the wall. He bent at the waist to rest his head in his hands, clutching thick tufts of blond hair between his fingers.

"Seth?" She knelt in front of him. "What's wrong? Are you all right?"

He shook his head. "Just a minute, pretty."

She waited but stroked his shoulder, needing to touch him.

He lifted his head and smiled shakily. "I'm all right now. I didn't know if you'd agree." He swallowed. "You said you *would* wait on marrying Tom, didn't you? Just so we're both talking plain."

She released the breath she'd been holding and took his face in her hands—his perfect, kind, indecently handsome face—and kissed him. She'd wanted to kiss him the moment she heard his voice through the door. "Yes, I'll wait."

"And you'll wait to hear my plan?"

"I'll wait," she whispered. "I'll wait for as long as you need me to wait."

"Good…good, thank you." Clumsily, he caught her arms, pressing them against her sides. The tremor in his hands battered her heart so she kissed his brow, his eyes, his jaw, his chin, until his grip eased.

He took a deep breath. "Minnie, do you need me to tell Tom you're waiting? It's awkward, I know, but—"

"Oh. No, you don't have to tell Thomas anything." She straightened to smile at him. "I already told him I would never marry him."

His eyes widened. "Why would you do that, Minnie?"

"Because I want to marry you far too much." She smiled. "I think I was waiting for your plan."

He pulled her into a corset-crushing hug. "Ah, Minnie. I swear to you, I'll do everything I can to marry you. I just need to sort out my plan."

His plan. She itched to ask him what that plan was, to *help* him plan. But something told her he needed to do this alone.

This time, she couldn't manage anything.

"Can I say what I wanted to say now?" she asked.

He grinned and turned her about to sit on his lap. But he rested his head on her shoulder and nuzzled her. A long breath heated her neck. "Go on and say anything you need saying, pretty."

"I know you'll make a good plan for us, Seth." She took a steadying breath. "But I'm afraid I'm going to complicate it a little."

His arms tightened but he held still.

"I love you so much. And I want to marry you"— she pulled back to look into his eyes—"but first, I have to let you know that I can't leave my sisters just yet. We're fine now, but the income the three of us make allows us to lease these rooms and feed ourselves. I can't leave them yet. I can't leave until…" *Until Mary and Emma wed, or they find stable employment, or some miracle occurs.* "I can't leave them, Seth."

He watched her, his fingers lightly drumming on her back. "Right," he said. The word so…simple. "Right. I already knew that, pretty."

He did?

His eyes dropped to her mouth. And the next instant, he stole her breath by gripping the nape of her neck and kissing her as if he'd just remembered they'd been apart—apart that horribly long and inexcusable time.

His lips gentled, and he was caressing her mouth so softly, so sweetly. Seth. Her gentle man. So giant and powerful and handsome. And yet it was his generosity and honor and gentleness that bound her heart to him.

She held him closer and thrilled as his kiss changed, moving more urgently on hers, growing wet. Her body was beginning to simmer everywhere their bodies melded together. She shifted on his lap, needing to relieve the untouchable yearning there.

She yanked her mouth away, needing to be able to think. "Don't ever go to Brazil. Whatever your plan is and whatever happens, don't go to Brazil."

He was panting hard, the high planes of his cheekbones ruddy with color. He swallowed. "All right," he said solemnly.

"And don't ever sail again."

"All right."

Her eyes filled with tears. "All right?"

"All right, Minnie."

He cupped her face and kissed her, his lips nudging and pleading, and she let herself enjoy the sweet attention—but only for a moment.

"And one more thing," she said. "Take back your money so you can fix your cottage, and plant your orchard, and buy sheep." She drew a breath. "That was four separate things, I realize now."

His eyes narrowed—and crinkled, bless him—and at last, *at last*, there was a smile in them. "Minnie," he said hoarsely. "Keep that money and buy some sugar for your tea and coffee a man can actually drink, and take a jarvey every now and again, and buy yourself some new dresses, and take Sebastian to the sweetshop."

"But it's not our money."

"Settle it on your sisters for when the suitors come calling."

"Their suitors…?" *That would be wonderful, actually.* He kissed her and she couldn't argue anymore. When he lifted his head, she asked, "What will you do now?"

"Since you're to be had, pretty"—he grinned wickedly, his lids lowering as he stared at her lips—"I'm thinking I'll start my plan in earnest."

His voice rumbled deep in her breast. And lower. And teased her where she was most sensitive and in need. "I'm to be had," she whispered.

So handsome. And rugged. He must not have shaved today. Dark-blond whiskers covered his bronzed cheek. She slid her tongue against the coarse grain.

The powerful body beneath her jerked, but he tipped his head back, giving her full access to his strong neck and hard jaw. And desperate to taste him, she slid her lips over him, suckling him, reveling in the slightly salty taste of his skin and the rumbling growl of pleasure vibrating under her mouth.

"Ah...Christ," he groaned, writhing beneath her. "I want you, but your sisters...?"

The curtains were drawn against the dark night, but the door wasn't latched. On shaking legs, she pushed off him, pulling her skirts from his grip so she could stand and lock the door.

Mutely, he stood to follow her, but she didn't want him against any door again. Faint with desire, she could barely stand upright, so she was relieved it only took her hand on his chest to push him back to the sofa.

"What do you want, Minnie? What do I do?" he asked hoarsely.

She pressed him down and he sat, his knees parted wide, and her eyes latched to the jutting bulge of his trousers. "I'm to be had," she whispered as she straddled a hard thigh and unbuttoned him. "Are you?"

His lips twitched with a grin. "When did you learn to flirt like that?"

Wanting him near, she leaned atop him, pressing her breasts against his hard chest. "I never flirted with you, remember?" She suckled his lower lip, tugging gently with her teeth, and his hard body tightened like granite. She kissed him hard, both inflamed and frustrated by his unyielding body. "Would you like me to flirt with you?" she asked, her words husky.

His eyes were closed but he nodded swiftly. "Go on, Minnie. Flirt all you want."

No, she'd never been bold before. But Seth made her bold, made her a warrior. She yanked at the fabric of his trousers and the soft cotton drawers beneath, and dared to take the length of him into her hand. To claim him as her own.

"Ah…*God*." His voice was loud, but she no longer cared if anyone could hear. Steel arms crushed her against him, and his kiss pressed and nudged and rolled in light circles. And she mirrored that rhythm with her hand on his hot flesh. He groaned his encouragement, and she learned what pleased him.

"Do you like this?" She squeezed him gently, and his heavy lids lifted.

"How did you know?" he asked in a hushed voice.

She smiled…until he shifted to sit up straight and kiss her softly.

"How did you always know, Minnie, how to love me like you do?"

His eyes were clear and intent on her, and her heart swelled with too much feeling. "It's so easy to love you, Seth."

He blinked, and the surprise on his face made her still with wonder. His eyes crinkled, nearly closed with emotion. And he moved her hand off him and onto his shoulder so he could maneuver her leg over his hip and position himself against her.

And she nearly swooned at the feel of him entering her so slowly.

"My…*God*," he breathed, his teeth clenched as he ground into her. "Only a lady could say something that sweet to me."

She gasped as he filled her.

"A lady from the ground up. I knew it. I knew it the instant I heard your voice, heard the way you defended your friends."

The pleasure, the heat of him, was almost too much. "Please…" She eased from the sensation, but strong hands moved her right back in place. And a spark, like lightning, almost like pain, coursed up her spine and through every nerve of her body. "*Seth…*"

"Ah, pretty," he murmured. "Easy…just like that."

Trembling, she took a moment to recover. But he watched her, and no one had ever looked at her like that—not just with love. But a promise to take care of her. To take care of her body and her heart.

She'd never known how much she wanted that.

She hugged him hard and, giving over to the bliss of their bodies, plunged hard and firm to feel him deep inside her. "I love you so much."

A rumbling growl vibrated in his broad chest, and he held himself still.

"I'd do anything, Minnie." He panted hard, his breath hot on her hair. "I'll give you more than love, I swear it." He thrust up into her, and her body seized with pleasure. "I'll take care of you," he said through gritting teeth. "Like you need, like a man—"

She kissed him, needing his mouth, his tongue, and there were no more words. Wave after wave of electric pleasure coursed through her with every plunge. It didn't end. It only grew more wonderful, more perfect—

"Ah, God!" Seth arched his powerful body under her, and she held tight to stay with him. But he gripped her hard, forcing her hips down, forcing her to come until she cried out. And then he was lifting her off him fast and crushing her higher against his chest. Something wet and slick slid down her thigh, and only then did she realize he'd spent outside of her.

And she never doubted that he would. Because he was so good and so careful with her, and he would never hurt her.

His arms loosened to let her slide back to his lap. She brushed back the damp tendrils of hair from his brow. "No matter what happens, Seth," she whispered. "No matter"—*if we can't be together, if we can't marry*—"no matter the plan, I'm the luckiest woman in the world to be loved by you."

The flush on Seth's cheeks and nose deepened, and he smiled. "Always on my side." He kissed her lips lightly, but when he raised his head to look at her, his eyes were questioning. "Do you trust me?"

She nodded hard, sorry for every hurtful thing she must have said to him. "I trust you. I do."

"Good." He pulled a card from his pocket. "I'm inviting you to see my flowers."

"Your flowers?" She took the letter from his hand and unfolded it. "The Horticulture Society's Annual Floral Fete." She looked at him, his handsome face calm. "But this is the auction of your prizes."

His gaze flickered away, but he nodded.

Her heart cracked for him. He must not have been able to prove any claim on them. She hugged him tight. "I can't wait to see them. You can tell me how you found each one."

"Each one? There's quite a number. Can you listen to me run on nineteen to the dozen, all day long?"

She smiled wider. "All day long."

He flushed and shifted her closer. Looking shy and

pleased, even though he'd lost so much. But she'd take care of him now. And he'd take care of her. *Please, God. There had to be a way…*

Seth sat back and smiled at her. "Charlotte tells me Opening Day at Chiswick Gardens is a highlight of the London Season. Meaning all the Quality show in their fancy dress and hats and it's all a fine rout. Invitation only, they tell me."

The card she held was very white and very thick. "And we are both invited?"

He pointed with his chin at the one she was holding. "That's my invitation. You keep it—I won't need it to get in."

"But—"

"Imagine me, rubbing elbows with all the Fashionables."

"But, the invitation—"

"Wear your prettiest frock, Minnie. I like that lavender one a lot"—he frowned—"but you were wearing that when you said you wouldn't marry me, so maybe wear something different, all right?"

He kissed her and seemed happier than she'd seen him in a very long time.

"I won't wear the lavender." Though, really, the lavender was her only gown for such an event.

It didn't matter. She would be there for Seth and she would be mighty for him. Because he would be watching all his hard-won prizes auctioned from him. Not even a heart as large as his could forgive such a betrayal.

Twenty-four

THREE THOUSAND.

That was the number Seth had been chasing in his head the past week. And now that the Opening Day of the Horticulture Society's Flower Show at Chiswick had arrived, along with the auction that would determine his future happiness, that number seemed to be echoing in every corner of his brain. *Three thousand… three thousand…three thousand.*

A madman's babel. He might be brainsick. Or a lunatic. Maybe he'd drive *himself* to Bedlam. But three thousand was a good, round number—where twenty-six was not.

Three thousand pounds was enough to mend the cottage and outbuildings, and furnish the rooms, and plant oats and an orchard, and keep Mina, all six sisters, and Sebastian fed, clothed, and housed for twenty-six months.

And after that…hell, the rest was faith. And strategy. Mostly strategy, he supposed, and he had the faith on account of Will and his man of business, Mr. Marlowe. They'd said his plan was sound. Three thousand, and he could propose to Mina. Three thousand, and he would be the happiest man in the world.

"Nervous, are you, Seth?"

Seth jerked at Will's voice. Though why his friend's presence would startle him was damn stupid. Will and Charlotte had been wandering the manicured lawn at Chiswick with him since he talked his way past the gatekeeper.

"Can't tell," he said. "Nervous or excited or on the verge of apoplexy. I can't tell—can't pin the feeling down in my head."

Charlotte handed him a plate of shortbread. "Then have a biscuit. You'll feel more yourself."

Seth nodded and took a biscuit, but he didn't have the stomach to eat. "Thank you." He smiled at her gown, all frothy, yellow ruffles. "Aren't you shaming these daffodils today, Charlotte? They might wither up seeing as how you outshine them."

"You are full of such sweet nonsense, Seth." She beamed, her blue eyes dancing. "Which flower do you think Mina will come dressed as?"

He didn't let his smile droop, but Mina wouldn't have a dress as fine as Charlotte's. Or any of these other women's. She had that lavender ball gown she'd worn in Bombay…and he'd asked her not to wear it. He probably shouldn't have done that.

Someday, he'd make it up to her. He'd buy her a dress for every color flower in the world. And a lady's maid to dress her hair, and another to press her linens, and a cook to mash her tea.

But first, three thousand. After that, he'd find a way to hire a maid for Mina.

Where was she?

He surveyed the grounds. A dozen or more white tents covered every spare patch of lawn. The ladies twirled in their wide skirts, sparkling in their pearls and gems and satins. The flowers in the conservatory weren't any match for this level of finery. These were hothouse aristocrats. No, Mina wouldn't have a gown like those.

"I've never seen so many fine ladies in my life," he muttered.

"Yet you've not seen the *finest*, have you?" Charlotte teased.

He smiled, still scanning the crowd for his heart. "I didn't expect Minnie to be tardy."

Charlotte tilted her head and studied him. "Tardy? No, I told our coachman to deliver her late. I wish for Mina to make an entrance." She smiled at Will. "I no longer make entrances, as Will dislikes to be late. You will learn, Seth. A lady requires significant time to present herself suitably to the world. I have even adjusted my morning toilette so I may breakfast with my husband. But there is no help for it. Will rises at an ungodly hour. I have had to adjust, lest I rush my maid, and I cannot be seen as a dowdy..."

Seth nodded dumbly as Charlotte chatted on. She might be the one person of his acquaintance that could outtalk him.

"...imagine the entrance she will make." She bounced a little. "Oh, I *cannot wait* to see her." Charlotte clapped her gloved hands together, signaling the end of her monologue.

Seth was still nodding but stopped when he saw

Will's amused and knowing grin. "An entrance is it?" He needed to add something to the conversation.

Fine ladies did such things, he supposed, so he'd better get used to that. And he didn't think getting used to anything Mina did would be any hardship at all.

Will narrowed his eyes suspiciously at his wife. "Charlotte? I know that smile. What did you do?"

She blinked those violet eyes innocently. "I cannot know what you mean. Do you accuse me of something?"

Will held the suspicious look on his wife, and her composure broke in the next second with her smile. "You mustn't make me confess, Will. At least not in Seth's hearing."

Will grinned and pulled Charlotte into his arms. "Whisper your secret to me, then."

The lady cupped her hand over his ear and confessed, and Will's smile widened. "That was a wonderful idea, sweetheart. Thank you."

Charlotte blushed under her husband's nuzzling kiss, and Seth had to avert his eyes. He might only be a hired explorer from Matlock, but he knew enough to know that sort of public loving wasn't proper.

And Will and Charlotte weren't looking as if they were stopping anytime soon.

He cleared his throat loudly, and they broke apart slowly. Damned if he wasn't envious of all they had. They were in love and had a fine, healthy baby, a home with a library full of books, and not a day's worry over money. And Charlotte had herself a dress prettier than the daffodils.

"*There* you young people are." The grandest lady of

his acquaintance, Marchioness Wynston, appeared, her
footman trailing her with a small dog in his arms. "I
am vastly relieved. No one will persuade me London
Society does not grow more tiresome with each pass-
ing year."

Marchioness Wynston was a favorite of his. Great
aunt to little Aimee, rich from several dead and
devoted husbands and sons. And the bona fide Worst
Flirt in England.

They got on like a house on fire.

"I offer every thanks to you, Mr. Mayhew, and
you, William, for presenting two examples of masculine beauty for my weary eyes to rest upon. You have
salvaged what would otherwise be an excruciating
afternoon. I am rather accustomed to William's brooding beauty, of course, but I am finding the novelty
of another handsome explorer today quite delightful.
You polish up rather nicely, Mr. Mayhew."

Seth grinned. "Put on my best, knowing I'd be
seeing you, m'lady. You're looking as splendid as ever."

"Lies do make the angels weep, young man." But
the grand lady smiled at him under a bonnet of sweeping plumes. "But yes, my chapeau is much admired.
One does make an effort, as there is no place so
ridiculously fastidious as a London flower show. I only
attend today for the auction. I am desperately curious
to see how wealthy the cattle make you today."

His heart stuttered. Wealthy? Damned if "wealthy"
wouldn't be the answer to every one of his problems.
"I just hope they're inclined to buy."

"Have no fear, young man," Lady Wynston said.
"I see a number who will scrape and claw to prove

themselves sufficiently deep of pocket to possess one of your rare plants. I do not even need to turn my head to spy them, which is fortunate, as this fashion for high collars impedes me in every way. I blame the Queen, naturally, and her unfortunate chin, but that is neither here nor there.

"Look there. Elmore is quite the orchid enthusiast. I've no doubt he'll bid on them all. And I shall begrudge him any win, as he is the very devil." She fanned herself, her eyes sweeping the crowd. "And there is Louisa. How fortunate for you. She will no doubt spend a great amount, though she has no particular interest in the botanical arts."

"Then why would she?" Seth asked.

"She is one of those creatures who is *not happy with her husband*, Mr. Mayhew. And has not been going on five and twenty years now, much to the detriment of her husband's purse. But she is well in the right there—the man is odious." She hoisted a brow. "And where is your sweetheart that I have yet to meet? Everyone speaks of her with such rapture."

"I expect Minnie will—"

"Minnie?"

"That's the name I call her."

"*Minnie?* Good heavens, why? I will not call her any such thing."

He grinned. "I wouldn't like it if you did, m'lady. That name's mine alone."

She fanned herself, looking coyly at him. "How thrillingly possessive. Where is this Wilhelmina?"

"Charlotte says she's to make an entrance," he said.

"Ah, naturally," she murmured approvingly.

"Oh, there she is, by the gate," Charlotte exclaimed behind him.

He turned, eager for the sight of her.

Only her face and shining hair were visible in the crush of people milling and flowing in front of her. But their eyes met, and Mina's smile stirred up the madman's chant: *three thousand, three thousand, three thousand…*

She wended her way toward him. The bodies in her path parted like a curtain to let him see her.

But he'd never seen her like this.

A begonia. That was the flower she'd come dressed as. Her dress was coral red but shimmered gold like a dragonfly's wing where the sun lit her. Her skirt floated around her like a cloud beneath her tiny waist, and sweet roses trimmed her bosom.

No bonnet on his Mina, nothing to hide all her beauty. He'd never seen her hair like that—falling in long, twisting curls from the crown of her head like a princess.

She was a rare one. And extraordinary. And like his Wilhelmina orchid, revealing herself in all her glory the very moment he turned toward her. And he'd found her. And the most wondrous thing of all…she'd found him right back.

Thank you, God. You weren't done with your gifts, were you?

He couldn't stop the huge smile from stretching across his face. "Excuse me. I see the lady now."

He hurried to join her, seeing Mary, Sebastian, and Emma then, too. But he wasn't ever inclined to take his eyes off Mina.

Her eyes widened when she saw him coming. Damned if she didn't blush. His step might have gained a little swagger at that.

"My goodness, Seth," she whispered. "You look so handsome."

He was wearing the same coat she'd seen him in a dozen times before, but she looked at him like he'd come from a tailor on Piccadilly. He opened his mouth to speak. Then had to try again. But he had to take her hand first to settle his heart. "I…uh…"

She moved closer and took his hand with both of hers. And there wasn't anything that needed saying.

"What are you grateful for today?" she whispered.

"Everything," he said, his voice hoarse with feeling. "All of it. You in that dress. Your blush. The way you look at me." He lifted her hand to press his kiss to her palm. "Thank you."

But it wasn't just Mina he was thanking.

He raised his head to smile at Mary and Emma. "Ladies, forgive me. I'm real pleased to see you all. There's not a happier man in all of London."

"We wanted to be here," Emma said. "I think it disgusting what those nurserymen—"

"*Emma.*" Mary placed her hand on Emma's arm. "Undoubtedly, we share your sentiments but they serve no purpose here."

Mina tightened her hold on his hand, a flicker of something like pain sweeping her face, and guilt pierced him like an arrow. But he couldn't tell her about the eighty-five percent. Not yet.

If he made the three thousand, he could surprise her. Watch her composed, capable, orderly self toss off all that seriousness and whoop with joy at the future she and all her sisters were going to have.

Three thousand. And nothing and no one would ever take her from him again. And if he didn't…

Well. He couldn't think on that right now.

"What a beautiful day this is," Mina said, as they strolled from her sisters and deeper into the garden behind Chiswick House. They walked along the stream, leaving the crowd behind.

"The skies could be storming and streaked with lighting, and I wouldn't count any other day finer than this one. You look so beautiful, Minnie."

She smiled, resting her cheek against his arm for just a moment before they drew too much attention. And when she raised her head, her eyes were wet. "This dress was a gift from Charlotte. Can you even imagine such a thing?"

Seth fished for his pocket handkerchief to dry her eyes, his heart too full to say anything. He was grateful to Charlotte, but he wanted to be the one to give Mina what she needed. And more. Give her what she wanted, so an act of kindness wouldn't make her cry like this. Because his Mina was meant to be calm and composed and—

A sob burst from her. "I don't understand it. A woman like Charlotte, giving me a gown like this. *And* she sent her maid to do my hair. *And* slippers to match." She blinked against tears. "*Slippers. Look.* And now I'm going to cry again."

He fumbled with the handkerchief, and she accepted with a watery smile. Mina was feeling a lot today.

Well…hell. So was he.

"Aw, pretty." He drew her into his arms, keeping

his back to the flower show attendees to give her a little privacy.

She sniffed, burrowing deeper into his coat. "I never expected… Charlotte said the idea came to her the minute she met me." She pulled a little ways out of his arms, which he didn't like at all. "Oh! I think I should thank her again right now."

He didn't let her go. "Not just now, Minnie," he murmured. "I'm thinking she won't mind your giving me a little of your time first."

And Mina, without a worry to wrinkling her fancy gown, or upsetting her careful hair, or even drawing the attention of the high born all around them, slid her arms around his waist and crushed herself fully against him. "You're right. I'm sorry," she breathed. "I'm not thinking clearly. I couldn't sleep at all last night."

For an instant, he was so muddled, his arms lifted off her.

The sight of a lady in that dress pressed against him—the white shoulders, the dark fringe of eyelashes against her cheek, the expensive silk—jarred him. It was a little like looking through a cracked mirror.

He loved her. This was his Minnie.

Yet this lady, this fine and beautiful lady, held him like *this*. Like she wasn't embarrassed by what she was doing or embarrassed by him. Like holding him was the most important, and the most natural, thing she should be doing. If he never had another moment like this, he'd still count himself the most blessed man on earth.

And it came to him in another jolt of surprise: he was loved completely.

He was the furthest thing from cursed a man could be.

She checked his face, looking bashful. Maybe because he was staring down at her, dumbstruck. "I am so excited to see the flowers you found, Seth," she said. "I like to imagine you finding them. You, striding through the jungle, with perfumed flowers dangling from the canopy of the forest like a necklace of jewels. And you walk by every one, no matter how beautiful they are, because you're looking for that one splendid orchid that's hiding."

He bent his head closer and kissed her, because he needed to do that more than he needed his next breath. "How did you know, pretty?"

She shook her head, smiling. "Don't tease. It was just a daydream." She grew serious. "I know finding them and harvesting the seeds was so much more difficult than I could imagine. Only you would be strong enough to do such a thing."

God, she always saw him as so much more than he was. But wasn't there a little truth in that? The Skinner brothers wouldn't have survived a week in the jungles he'd traveled. And they'd thought they could just take his hard work. All the time and sacrifice and waiting. All the fear and all the passion. And all his pride.

And he'd almost let them.

The bitterness tightened and coiled up and down his abdomen, his hips, his jaw. Then he drew it into his lungs and exhaled it from his body. Mina deserved the best man he could be. He may not be rich or even all that smart, but he wouldn't be anything so useless as angry. He could at least give her that.

He bent down and, keeping his back to the world behind them, kissed Minnie long and gently. The way she seemed to like best.

He could give her that, too.

"Ladies, gentlemen," a member of Chiswick's staff announced, "the auction of ornamentals is to begin in the pavilion. You are invited to take advantage of the opportunity to acquire some of the highest-quality specimens."

To his surprise, the liveried man gestured to where he stood. "And we are joined by the plant hunter, himself. The explorer, Mr. Seth Mayhew."

The lofty audience acquiesced to his presence, murmuring with genteel approval.

"Seth?" Mina's voice was concerned, but her warm, brown eyes glowed up at him. "Are you ready?"

He straightened and smiled down at her. And he stood even taller with her on his arm. "I'm ready, pretty." He smiled. "I'm finally ready."

Twenty-five

THE INTERIOR OF THE PAVILION WAS COOL FOR AS many bodies as it held. Ladies in their wide gowns and gentlemen in their elegant schemes of black and white filled nearly every seat. She and Seth sat in two of the few empty chairs near the back wall, beside the intimidating Marchioness Wynston.

At the front, a long table displayed an array of stunning orchids and vibrantly colored blooms. Through an opening in the tent, she could see a line of labeled pots holding a veritable jungle of Seth's other flowers. How would Seth bear this?

She slipped her hand into his. Seth was perched on the edge of his chair, his attention riveted to the front of the room, but he lifted her hand for a kiss before settling it back in his lap.

Her free hand sought her charm in the pocket of her gown, and the sight of the red-orange silk jolted her again. Her first red dress.

She arranged it carefully around her, unable to resist stroking the lustrous fabric. The gown was the most beautiful creation she'd ever seen and, after Seth's two hundred pounds, the most generous gift anyone had ever given her.

She would sell it tomorrow—it was the height of fashion. And as beautiful as it was, she couldn't keep something so valuable. Not when the dress would fetch what she could earn in a year.

Her family and Seth would need every shilling.

"You look most charming, Wilhelmina," Lady Wynston said.

She had to swallow before speaking to the marchioness. "Thank you, my lady."

"Who is your modiste, my dear?"

"Oh, I don't… I could never afford such a service. Mrs. Repton gave this to me as a"—her voice broke—"a gift."

Lady Wynston arched a brow, but her faded blue eyes were warm and smiling. "Then I greatly approve her choice, my dear. Clever Charlotte—such an excellent notion for today. My dear, you would have found the Society far less welcoming had you chosen more modest attire. The *ton* cannot separate a girl from her dress."

Lady Wynston wasn't at all what she expected of the Upper Circles. But then, neither was Charlotte.

Mina sat a little taller in her chair. She wore an exquisite gown, and no one would fault her appearance as Seth's particular friend. She would not want to add to the hardship of his day. Not that Seth seemed at all depressed or even angry. He seemed rather nervous, actually. Even excited.

A rumble of eagerness swept through the tent. One of the gardeners was carrying in a glorious basket with a towering arrangement of fuchsia-and-coral-mottled orchids. Her breath caught at their otherworldly beauty and, to her horror, she had to blink rapidly to hide the tears in her eyes.

Seth must have seen the emotion, for he smiled down at her. "It doesn't pain me to see them, Minnie."

Her throat tight, she could only nod and smile weakly.

"I remember the moment I first saw those blossoms. The excitement of seeing them and knowing they were rare, thinking no one in England had ever seen such a thing. It doesn't pain me to see 'em sold. There isn't a man or woman who can ever own what nature creates anyway.

"For a simple man like me, the finding is enough." He dipped his head to whisper in her ear. "Until I found the rarest flower of all right on a wharf in Bombay"—he lowered his voice to a deep croon—"and I'm still not flirting with you, pretty."

That drew a real smile from her. She hadn't realized how much she'd dreaded this moment, how sad she was feeling for him. And he was trying to comfort *her*.

"No matter what happens today, Minnie, we'll be fine, won't we?"

She forced herself to hold his smiling gaze. And lied. "Yes, Seth. We'll be fine."

He lifted her hand to kiss it again, but Lady Wynston tapped his lap with her fan. "Cease your lovemaking, young man. The auction is to start, and I find the sight of young lovers far too diverting."

Mina heated with embarrassment and straightened in her chair, but Seth would not release her hand. She would not let him feel her shake. With a centering breath, she clamped down on her jangling nerves.

The auction master stepped up to his pulpit, and the room quieted.

"Welcome ladies and gentleman," the auctioneer said. "The first offering…"

And Minnie clenched her eyes shut. Species and origins and flower parts were presented in Latin, and then it was time.

"Will any gentleman start the bid at forty pounds?" the auctioneer asked.

"One hundred," a voice at the front said.

Her eyes flew open.

"One and twenty," a voice called at the right.

"One and forty." A hand flicked to her left.

She looked at Seth, who sat stiffly upright, his body all rapt attention. "Seth," she whispered in his ear. "They didn't start at forty."

He turned a stunned face to her, a smile tugging at his lips, and whispered back, "No, they didn't."

"*Two hundred*," a voice called from a few rows ahead.

She swung her eyes forward, her head pivoting from one bidder to the next. Until—"Goodness," she breathed. "Did he say four hun—?"

"*Five* hundred," a bidder called from the right.

Her stomach plunged, but she looked at Seth and said gently, "It doesn't matter, Seth."

His eyes were tracking the bidders. "It does though, Minnie."

"*Six*," a voice in the front barked.

Six? She swayed and leaned against his shoulder.

That caught his attention. He bent to look into her face. "Minnie? What's wrong?"

Wrong? She shook her head and tried a wobbly smile. "No, nothing, Seth. My head is just a little swimmy."

"*Eight hundred.*"

Her jaw dropped and her head spun to stare at the bidder, who was stroking his side-whiskers serenely, as though he'd not committed enough money *for a flower* to feed her whole family for the rest of their lives.

But she could not fall apart in front of Seth. She could be mighty—she *would* be. Straightening her spine, she grasped his large hand between both of hers and smoothed her expression.

And then Seth surprised her by kissing her temple. "My God, I *do* love you, Minnie."

Something warm and bracing flooded her, and she whispered back, "I love you, too."

"Eight hundred and fifty." The auctioneer was holding up his gavel. "Will no gentleman advance the bid? And twice...?" He raised the gavel higher. "And...*sold* to Lord Putman for eight hundred fifty pounds. Congratulations, my lord."

"Lud, eight hundred fifty," Lady Wynston murmured, plying her fan. "For a pretty stalk of petals. I should think that proof of a violent insanity if I had not witnessed Cavendish spend similar amounts in the past. I am rich, of course, but the *very* rich are a different breed entire."

Mina nodded mutely, and Seth flopped back in his chair, a huge smile on his face.

"And that was the first one!" he roared, and burst into laughter.

And she nearly heaved up her breakfast porridge.

"Wilhelmina, dear girl?" Lady Wynston hoisted a

brow at her. "You are looking entirely bloodless. I will endeavor to amuse you."

Amuse me...? But her attention was diverted back to the front. Another gardener set down a short trellis covered with a climbing vine bursting with crimson blooms. And her heart sank.

They were glorious.

"Gentlemen, we begin at fifty pounds." The auctioneer rapped his gavel to begin.

"Do watch, Wilhelmina." Lady Wynston raised her fan. "Seventy," she proclaimed in her queenly voice, before turning back to her. "The *ton* are as easily led as wagon horses, dear girl, and they will not let an ancient woman best them in any matter. It is my joyful calling, making such *superior* gentlemen"—she raised her fan—"*ninety*—feel their inferiority. And they resist with such zeal." She raised her fan, advancing the bid another fifty pounds. "Actually, I do rather want these flowers."

She nodded mutely as the bidding intensified. Two hundred...then, three...four and seventy... five hundred—

"Six hundred," Lady Wynston intoned.

A richly dressed older woman cast a withering stare at Lady Wynston and tipped her own ivory fan a fraction. "Seven."

Seven?

Lady Wynston sighed. "There never existed on earth a more disagreeable animal in female form than Lady Gertrude. She must be made to pay dearly." She raised her fan.

The auctioneer nodded at her. "Eight hundred, to her ladyship."

"Eight hundred?" Mina repeated weakly.

"Indeed." Lady Wynston sniffed. "Do watch Lady Gertrude, my dear. Her dour face proclaims she will not have these flowers for a shilling—"

"Nine hundred," Lady Gertrude declared.

"—and yet she bids," Lady Wynston said.

The auction master raised his hammer. "Nine hundred once…? And two times…? And…"—he nodded to Lady Gertrude—"and to Lady Gertrude for nine hundred. Congratulations, my lady."

Lady Wynston sniffed. "*Wagon horses.*"

And to Mina's horror, it continued for the next several lots. The numbers rose higher and higher, and Seth was jotting down each winning bid.

She squeezed his arm gently. "Seth, perhaps you shouldn't take an accounting."

"Have to, Minnie. I can't keep all these figures in my head."

"No, I think—"

"Minnie." His voice rumbled low and sweetly, and it stilled her tongue. "Don't you worry about me, pretty. I just need a moment…"

His pencil stilled and his eyes widened. He showed her the numbers. "Is that sum right, pretty?"

"Seth, it doesn't matter—"

"It does, Minnie. It matters."

His eyes implored her to look, so she did. And whether the calculation was correct or not, she could not add to know. Her eyes were locked on the sum. She breathed deep, her voice wavering. "Eight thousand pounds, fifteen shillings?"

And the auction was only on lot fifteen of eighty.

Hot tears sprang to her eyes, and Seth jumped to his feet, reaching for her hand to pull her up. "I'm sorry, pretty," he said roughly. "You've had enough of this."

She nodded hard, rather than speak. If she spoke, she'd burst into tears for his loss.

Seth handed his accounting to Will and whispered for him to keep track. Outside the tent, the spring sunshine was blinding, coloring the grass, trees, and sky the most head-spinning colors.

"Can you wander a little ways, Minnie?" Seth asked, putting a supporting arm around her shoulders.

She blinked her eyes to focus and breathed deep. Seth needed her to be strong. "Of course." She smiled—convincingly she hoped.

But Seth grimaced at the attempt. "Ah, pretty, it's all right."

He guided her through the throng of aristocrats beside the stream, and deeper into the garden until they found themselves overlooking a secluded, serene garden. Tiers of flawless green lawn surrounded a circular pool of water with an obelisk rising from the center. A picturesque stone pavilion rose opposite where they stood, but the most impressive element was the symmetrical arrangement of orange trees in their large Chinese urns circling the water.

The garden was the loveliest place she'd ever been. And yet, even with the man she loved beside her, and wearing the most beautiful gown, she was so... disappointed. In her life. In the world. In how *hard* it all was. And the worst of it...was how afraid she was of what came next.

People had no choice but to ignore the fear, or they

would never leave their beds. But she was standing in a garden, in the loveliest place she'd ever been, and she had a brand new fear.

Because the only thing she felt was disappointment.

Seth held her hand and pulled her nearer the pond. "This is the Orange Tree Garden. It's been here since the seventeen hundreds."

The orange blossoms scented the air. She'd never seen oranges growing on their branches. "They don't seem real, do they?" she murmured.

"I thought they were pretty." He swallowed, suddenly seeming shy and nervous.

Dear Seth…he wanted her to share in his pleasure of this garden, this day, his flowers. And she couldn't smile for him.

"And I thought it the right place to tell you my plan," he said.

She stilled. "Today? Here?"

"I thought here was pretty."

Her heart ached in her chest. His plan. For her, for them, for their future. It was going to be hard for them to be together. How long would they have to wait? How would she bear not seeing him every day?

"Minnie"—his smile broke out across his face—"I need to make sure I say this just right and not talk in six different directions."

She took his hand. "I love all the ways and directions you talk."

His eyes crinkled with his smile and—*oh God, thank you*—the ocean-green of his eyes sparkled, and the sunlight was soft on her shoulders, and the citrus trees were like perfume. And the auction didn't matter at all. Or the Skinners, who had betrayed him.

She was grateful. And she was peaceful. And all the fear shrank back into the shadows. Love *did* matter. Because love made you mighty. Mighty enough to remind you that fear wasn't really...*real*.

But love was.

"Minnie—"

"Seth, first"—she clutched his hand—"may I talk first?"

He closed his mouth and nodded, a small smile on his lips.

She straightened her spine and spoke, clear and firm. "We have one hundred seventy-nine pounds, and I think I should move with you to your cottage in Derbyshire because I don't ever want to be apart from you. And I'll work at one of the mills in Chesterfield. My sisters will have to come, I'm afraid, but they'll work, too.

"And we'll be fine. If we're together, we'll be fine. We'll take care of each other." She breathed deep. "And no matter what your plan is, I only need to be with you. All I want—all I *need*—is to be your wife."

Seth stood oddly quiet, his chest rising and falling with his slow, deep breaths. His smile had faded.

Blunt, Mina. And managing. And she spoiled the telling of his plan.

"I just...I would be so honored to marry you," she whispered.

He stared at her, his lips parted with what looked like...surprise? He blinked and moved closer. "*Honored?*" He searched her eyes. "You'll marry me without hearing my plan? Just like that?"

Her face heated. "I should have let you speak first, but yes. Just like that." She took a shaky breath and hurried to add, "I'm sorry. I *am* managing—I still want to hear your plan."

He cupped her face in his hands, and kissed her so gently on the lips that for one perfect, heady minute, there was no thinking of anything but the warmth of his mouth on hers. Lifting his head, he looked down at her with a deep glow in his eyes that she'd never seen before. Like a shaft of sunlight piercing a tranquil lagoon. He was so beautiful—

He dropped down to one knee, and she blinked with surprise.

"I'm ready now, Minnie." His voice was low and rumbling, and she couldn't stop from smoothing his hair back from his brow, needing to touch him. "I'm ready." He held her hand and smiled, and his eyes crinkled.

And she smiled back.

"I never thought I'd find a woman with so much kindness and passion and courage when she knew people needed her. When *I* needed her." His hand began to shake. "I never even let myself dream I'd find such a lady and hear her say she loved me and would marry me, just like that, just…just for me."

Her own breath was hitching—just like his—and she bent down to rest her head on his hard shoulder so she wouldn't sway.

"And I never let myself hope, never, ever believed that I'd say these words and mean them as much as I do." His voice was hushed and warm on her neck. "You're my home, Minnie."

She wrapped her arms around him and held him tight.

He hugged her back, nearly crushing her. "I'm afraid to ask."

"We don't ever have to be afraid," she whispered. "Just ask."

"Minnie…will you be my wife?"

"Yes."

"Will you honor me—?"

"*Yes*," she said, laughing. Oh God—she was laughing! She moved to look at his wonderful face. "Yes, I will marry you and love you the rest of my life and I'm not afraid of anything anymore." She kissed him, because she just couldn't wait another second. "I love you," she breathed. "And we *are* going to be fine."

He smiled and rose to his feet in one smooth, strong movement. The solid wall of him was momentarily disorienting until he pulled her back into his arms. "We *are* going to be fine. I didn't tell you my plan."

She shook her head. "You let me talk first."

He grinned and nuzzled her neck. "I did, didn't I?"

His lips were making her head swim. Oh, dear. The man was distracting. "Seth? Tell me your plan."

"Eighty-five percent," he murmured, his lips at her ear.

She opened her eyes, trying to think. "What do you mean?"

He lifted his head to look at her. "That's most of the plan, pretty. The Skinners offered seven hundred pounds, but that wasn't going to be enough for a family. Well, it might be enough for a mean sort of, hardscrabble family, but with my land expenses and your sisters, it wasn't enough even for hardscrabble.

"So I hired a solicitor. And I paid a visit to the

Skinner nurserymen. And for once, I'm thinking my size served me well. I'm not accustomed to forcing matters or claiming a grievance, but they were denying me...well, *you*.

"So when they asked me to take a seat, I just stood. And something about my standing over 'em like that seemed to put them in a cooperative frame of mind. Or so the solicitor said. And I said I had proof of all those prizes—and I do. And I told 'em they were wrong and I'd not stop fighting 'em till they behaved right." He smiled. "So we're getting eighty-five percent."

She stared at him, not understanding exactly what he'd said. Had he actually said—"Eighty-five percent *of the auction?*"

His grin widened and he nodded.

Her legs gave way and she would have fallen had Seth not held her up.

"Eighty-five percent, Minnie." He laughed. "And I was thinking I'd need three thousand minimum, but you saw what those plants were selling for. So even though I never was all that skilled at math, I'm thinking eighty-five percent has just made us rich enough for a lady's maid for you, and a library full of Shakespeare's plays in green leather books, and a pianoforte for our children. And those stepping-stones we're going to put in across our stream."

She blinked, and nodded, and tried to breathe. "Yes...Shakespeare's...stones."

"And you never have to worry another minute about any of your sisters being sick or hungry or cold. I promise you that all the rest of my days. I want to take care of you, Minnie, and that means taking care of all your sisters. And I know there's a number of them, but I'm up to the task. I'm even thinking it'll be fun to have all your family in Derbyshire with us. If that'll make you happy…?"

A sob wracked her body, and hot tears spilled from her eyes and down her cheeks. "Thank you," she breathed, hugging him tight. "Thank you."

He held her closer. "I know you don't like surprises."

"No, I'm fine," she squeaked.

"I had a plan for three thousand pounds, but we're set to make quite a bit more than that, so you'll need to help me."

"I will." They'd stay together. And her sisters, too.

"Got so many plans crowding my brain, pretty. I might start talking all over the place like that little frog. I was thinking, for Mary, there's a handsome widower by the name of Henry Danner who's the baker in Matlock. I'm thinking he'd be a good man for her. A nice man. He bakes bread still for his mother-in-law, if you can credit it. The man must be some sort of saint, I'm thinking. And he's got a nice lad, too. A couple years older than Sebastian, so an older brother at the ready. No one says a bad word about the man."

She smiled, shaking her head. "A baker?"

"A handsome baker. Wait till you see. Mary won't be able to resist. I'm a little nervous about your meeting the man actually, but I'm thinking we'll be married before you clap eyes on him, so it'll be safe enough."

She laughed. "Yes, we'll be very safe."

He dipped down to look her in the eye. "Will you leave London with me?" he asked. "Will you make your home with me in Derbyshire, in that cottage?"

Seth's arms were wide-open and there was no place in the world safer. She hugged him tight and nodded. "Anywhere. I'd go anywhere for you. I'd sail to the ends of the world and back."

"Ah, Minnie, I promise you'll never have to." He pulled back to smile down at her. "Besides, I'm thinking you already did."

Twenty-six

SETH'S KNEE WOULDN'T STOP BOUNCING. FIVE MORE miles to their new home, and the carriage was feeling smaller and smaller.

Mina sat pressed against him, her head on his shoulder and a peaceful smile on her lips. Mary, Emma, and Sebastian sat across from them, their eyes looking bright and excited as they watched the landscape outside their window, but they weren't talking much.

And damned if he could stop.

"There's work still to be done, ladies. But the walls and roof are solid, and the house is warm."

He couldn't seem to take his eyes off Mina's face. Would she love the cottage as much as he did? She liked Derbyshire, he knew that. Her cheeks had been round with a smile ever since they passed Ambergate. But the house was a woman's domain, so he hadn't done much in the way of furnishings, and he wasn't as done with the repairs as he'd wanted to be.

"You'll likely notice the cracked glass pane in the kitchen window." *What the hell was he doing mentioning it?* "But I'm mending that. It's just the glass was late, as it's coming from Manchester. And don't worry too much about that one hawthorn tree that's got the limbs growing all akimbo. I'm transplanting that to the south garden as soon as I get myself the right shovel."

She kissed his cheek, which made his heart ease a bit. "I love hawthorn trees."

Good then. Good. "We'll not all be underfoot, either." *Why weren't they saying more?* He cleared his throat. "There's room, I'm thinking, for all of us to be comfortable."

"We're so close to our old home," Emma said. "I simply can't believe it. And I can't wait for our sisters to move in. Our aunt will be sad to see them go, but they were becoming such a burden, even with the older girls working at the mill."

None of his family would ever work at a mill again. Not ever.

"So close to home." Mary's voice cracked. "And to be out of The Smoke. I prayed every night to leave London and be able to raise Sebastian in the clean, country air."

Ah…hell. Mary was tearing up again. She had to stop thanking him for every little thing. It was damn awkward. Once she got settled, she'd be all right. He'd put her in the path of Henry the Handsome Baker right away.

Mina was the woman he wanted most to make happy. But she'd seen Will and Charlotte's house. Would she be disappointed in their home?

Trying to act easy, he looked out the window. Just a few clouds. It had rained this morning, but the sun was promising to shine. Would be really fine if the sun was shining when they got home.

Mina held his hand and leaned her little head on his shoulder. "I'm so excited, Seth. I can't wait to see the river and the birch."

He smiled. "We'll have a picnic. The first fair weather day, I promise."

Her eyes lit with happiness.

"Are you eager to see the cottage?" he asked, not able to contain himself. He might have asked her that a dozen times already, now that he thought on it.

"I'm sure the cottage will be wonderful and cozy," Mina said. "You mustn't worry, Seth. We grew up in a house with seven girls, our parents, and our grandmother. And you saw how we were able to live in London. We don't require much room."

He smiled. There was another surprise he had for Mina, and she'd have it soon enough. The carriage turned onto the drive to their cottage, and he watched her face as the house came into view. And he wasn't disappointed.

Her jaw dropped open and he almost lost the thought he was having when it got replaced with the idea of kissing those lips. But he could hold a couple thoughts in his head at a time.

Especially as the kissing thought was damn near ever present anyway.

"Seth. What...what is that?"

"That's home, Minnie."

She stared. "You said it was a cottage."

Confused, he pulled his gaze off her to see what she saw. "It *is* a cottage. Just a big one. Four bedrooms on the ground, six on the second story, and four big ones on the third. One of those is meant to be a nursery, I'm thinking. Fourteen altogether.

"And see that littler cottage across the pasture? Mary and Sebastian will be real comfortable there." He leaned close to whisper in Mina's ear. "Emma's a bit of a feisty one, but maybe if we left her down on the ground level, she'd feel mistress enough of her own life. Enough space and peace and she might even forget the business of chasing down Colin Rivers.

"And we have a library, too. Not many books yet, but I ordered a fine dictionary and an atlas, which I think is a good start. Do you like green leather? I'm thinking we'll bind the books all the same color like Will and Charlotte do. I think that looks elegant."

She nodded, her lips parted. "That sounds... I like green."

He grinned, his heart ready to burst from his chest with happiness. "You're not saying anything. Are you grateful, then, Minnie?"

She blinked, silver tears clinging to her long lashes. "Yes...so grateful."

"And you have yourself a garden," he said.

The tears were streaming now, and he nearly busted with joy when she flung herself into his arms and wept. Which probably wasn't a good thing for a husband to be feeling with his wife releasing the waterworks, but she'd likely forgive him just this once.

The carriage pulled in front of the house, and the sun was bright and shining all around them. The neighbor lad had mowed down the grass, and the fresh, clean scent welcomed them as they stepped out of the carriage.

Emma's jaw was dangling. "This isn't at all a cottage, Seth. This is a country house. There are columns!"

He studied the house. "Only four columns around the entries."

"But you have"—Emma dashed to the corner of the house and bent to look at the south facade, then ran back to join them—"you have *four* entries. Sixteen columns. And glass windows on every floor. A cottage doesn't have *columns*."

Mina was wiping her eyes, but there was a smile on her lips. Thank God.

She took his hand. "Where is the stream?"

He grinned and bent down to kiss her. "Right where I left it for you, pretty."

Cottage or country house. It didn't matter.

He was home.

Epilogue

"I'M WANTING TO START ON THE ROCK WALL REPAIRS between our land and Gribbin's next week."

Seth stood over his desk in their library, the plans for the south pasture scrawled on the foolscap before him. Mina allowed herself the sheer pleasure of watching his smiling face, the tousled hair that he'd not combed since his morning ride, the way his tailored coat clung to his broad shoulders. She would have to write to Charlotte and Will and thank them for giving her the name of their tailor in Derby.

"I planned to hire one of the Stuart boys for the week, Minnie. They're good lads and the only ones skilled at stonework around here. I really only need one of them, though."

"Could you not hire them both?"

"I might," he murmured, drumming his fingers on the table as he did when he was thinking. "I might if they work three days, rather than the week. That could work. With the weather so fine, it might be best to do the work as fast as we can anyway."

"That sounds sensible. I know you didn't want to have to choose between them."

He grinned and winked at her.

Seth was such a generous man to his workers. Still, she couldn't deny that these past nine months, to her near-daily surprise, they worked harder and longer for him than she'd ever expected hired men to work. Perhaps that was because Seth worked right alongside them.

She deferred to his instincts when it came to his farm workers, but Seth left all the household staff and accounts to her—and thank goodness for that. She really *was* a managing sort by nature.

A cacophony of voices and pattering slippers rose in the hall. The library door burst open and her youngest sister, Melisande—called Missy by all—along with Emma, Diane, Sue, Karen, and Mary, with Sebastian, invaded the room. The women were engrossed in their own conversations and battles, yet without fail, whichever room Seth inhabited during the day was where they chose to congregate.

All the Adams girls were in love with Seth Mayhew.

"Seth?" Fourteen-year-old Missy leaned over the corner of his desk, her voice suspiciously sweet. "Mrs. Baxter says we are in danger of running out of your drinking coffee, and I know how you rely upon a dish of coffee each morning to invigorate your spirits."

He grinned over his papers at Mina, sharing an amused glance with her. "Whatever would I do without your monitoring the coffee inventory, Missy?"

Missy popped upright to her feet. "I would be

happy to go to the village for Mrs. Baxter to purchase your coffee."

"Would you now?" he said, smiling. "But wouldn't you need someone to drive you in the carriage? You can't walk alone."

Missy cast a jaundiced eye over her older sisters, all settling down with their books and sewing. "I suppose I *would* need a carriage, as no one will walk with me, *because they are so very lazy.*"

Mina bit back her smile. Missy was the one sister who could never sit still. She could fatigue a cattle dog.

"Minnie?" Seth darted a pointed glance at Mary. "Is there anything we need from the village?"

"I don't believe—"

Seth mouthed the word *bakery*.

Right! "Mary?" Mina started innocently enough. "I wonder if you wouldn't mind driving Missy to the village?" She smiled. "And while you're there… would you mind very much visiting the bakery and buying some of those lemon tarts I've had such a taste for lately?"

Mary gaped at her. "*More* lemon tarts? Mr. Danner will think us gluttons. No, Mina, I think it better not to overindulge. Besides, I'm starting a new shirt for Seth today. You *do* like this plaid fabric, don't you, Seth?"

Seth shrugged, grinning. "I'd like any fabric you chose, Mary."

"I know you don't like any pattern that's too remarkable. I think you'll look very fine in this one." Mary shook her finger at her. "No lemon tarts today, Mina."

"But I love them so, Mary." What a liar she and Seth had become in service to Mary's romantic life

After all these months her sister still hadn't seen through their scheme to throw her in the baker's path as often as possible.

Mary shook her head. "No, Mina—"

"Actually," Seth said, "I sure have been craving a Bakewell tart, myself."

Mary's head swung about, the protest for Mina frozen on her lips. "Oh." She put down her sewing. "Oh. Well, tomorrow, Seth *will* need his coffee. I'll go now, shall I?"

Oh…honestly. Her sister would happily spend a life in servitude to Seth. Her gratitude to Seth for saving her and Sebastian from the city hadn't lessened an iota.

Seth winked at her as Mary bustled Sebastian out the door, and called for Missy to collect her cape. He must have seen the guilt on her face, for he came to sit beside her and take her hand onto his lap. "Henry'll thank me. The man is good and smitten."

"Are we doing the right thing?" Mina whispered. "What if Mary doesn't wish to marry again? She doesn't seem to notice him at all."

"She will. Don't worry. And you *do* like those lemon tarts."

Still studying his plan for the south pasture, Seth pulled her close into the circle of his arm, and she rested her cheek on his warm shoulder.

Their library shelves were still rather empty. She had a new, green-leather-bound book with gold lettering to give him for his birthday next week.

She would tell him then that he was going to be a father. Somehow, she knew Seth would laugh at his book and cry happy tears for their child. He'd likely keep her up late listing names for their baby, perhaps with a nickname that only they were allowed to use. The book would go on a shelf in the library and be forgotten until much later. And that would be exactly right.

Because as Seth reminded her every day, in all the big and little things he did, home wasn't a library of books, or a garden with her mother's peas, or a stream with stepping-stones across it. Home wasn't a place at all.

It was a person.

About the Author

Susanne Lord lives beside a beautiful pond surrounded by hawthorn trees and wildflowers. When it's quiet and no one is about, she can pretend she is taking her exercise on the grounds of an ancient family estate. When it's not, she's reminded her family is not of the landed gentry, the pond is in the middle of Chicago, and the only adventure in her day comes in the form of emails marked "urgent" at her advertising job. She is an active member of Chicago North RWA. When not working, writing, attending theater, or reading, she travels to England, where she enjoys getting lost in the woods.

In Search of Scandal

London Explorers

by Susanne Lord

A daring explorer

All of London is abuzz with the tale of Will Repton. The lone survivor of a massacre in Tibet has returned to England a hero, but the traumatized explorer has no time for glory. Another dangerous expedition awaits. Nothing can deter him from his quest, and no one can unearth his secret—until Will meets Charlotte Baker.

Is no match for an adventurous heart

Vivacious Charlotte Baker also has a mission—to find a man whose bold spirit matches her own. When she meets Will Repton, she immediately recognizes him as her soul mate, and she's naively willing to turn her back on the rules of propriety to ensnare him.

Will is torn between his fascination with Charlotte and his vow to finish his quest. He knows what it is to risk life and limb—but what if his most perilous adventure doesn't lie across an ocean, but within his own lost heart?

"Beautifully written, deeply romantic, and utterly magnificent." —*New York Times* bestselling author Courtney Milan

"[A] delightful debut... Passionate characters and personal adventures come alive." —*Booklist*

For more Susanne Lord, visit:

www.sourcebooks.com

How to Impress a Marquess

Wicked Little Secrets

by Susanna Ives

—— ❧ ——

Take one marquess, responsible, worldly, deadly dull but concealing an artist's soul

Add one rebellious, brilliantly creative but lonely young lady who craves love, home, and family

Combine with ill-assorted guests at an ill-fated house party hosted by a dowager with a poison tongue and a penchant for scandal

You'll be shaken, you'll be stirred, you'll laugh, and you'll swoon—most of all you'll be tossed into an intriguing Victorian love story that you'll never want to leave

—— ❧ ——

"I have never, ever laughed so hard or swooned so much while reading a historical romance."
—*Long and Short Reviews* for *Wicked Little Secrets*

"Will touch readers' hearts. Ives delivers on every level." —*RT Book Reviews* for
Wicked, My Love Top Pick, 4.5 Stars

For more Susanna Ives, visit:

www.sourcebooks.com

Wicked, My Love

Wicked Little Secrets

by Susanna Ives

——— ✌ ———

A smooth-talking rogue and a dowdy financial genius

Handsome, silver-tongued politician Lord Randall doesn't get along with his bank partner, the financially brilliant but hopelessly frumpish Isabella St. Vincent. Ever since she was his childhood nemesis, he's tried—and failed—to get the better of her.

Make a perfectly wicked combination

When both Randall's political career and their mutual bank interests are threatened by scandal, he has to admit he needs Isabella's help. They set off on a madcap scheme to set matters right. With her wits and his charm, what could possibly go wrong? Only a volatile mutual attraction that's catching them completely off guard...

——— ✌ ———

Praise for Susanna Ives:

"A fresh voice that reminded me of Julia Quinn's characters." —Eloisa James, *New York Times* bestselling author

For more Susanna Ives, visit:

www.sourcebooks.com

The Girl from Paris

Paget Family Saga

by Joan Aiken

— ❧ —

Ellen Paget's life is irrevocably changed when she accepts a position as governess for the radical Comte and Comtesse de la Ferte, in whose Paris salon Ellen is introduced to the most illustrious artists, writers, and philosophers of the day. The charming Benedict Masham, second son of an earl and an old family friend, makes it his business to look out for Ellen's welfare. That would be nice, if it wasn't so annoying to Ellen, who wants to flout convention and spread her wings in Society.

Ellen soon sheds the stifling conventions of her proper English upbringing, and contends with the questionable affections of a beguiling writer, whose attentions to Ellen dismay the steadfast Benedict.

When tragedy and scandal force her to beat a hasty retreat back to England, it takes all of Ellen's ingenuity and fortitude to solve the mysteries of the past and present—but can she do so in time to save her father and brother from the machinations of those who mean them harm?

— ❧ —

Praise for *Mansfield Park Revisited*:

"Delightful and charming." —*Becky's Book Reviews*

"A lovely read—and you don't have to have read *Mansfield Park* to enjoy it." —*Woman's Own*

For more Joan Aiken, visit:

www.sourcebooks.com

A Scandalous Adventure

Victorian Adventures

by Lillian Marek

They're hiding a scandalous secret

When his monarch's flighty fiancée disappears, Count Maximillian von Staufer is dispatched to find her. His search leads Max to discover not the princess, but a look-alike who could be her double. Desperate to avoid an international crisis, he conceives a plan that will buy some time—and allow him to get to know a beautiful Englishwoman.

And time is running out

Lady Susannah Tremaine and her young friend Olivia are staying at the Grand Hotel in Baden, where so far the most exciting part of the visit has been the pastries. But when a devastatingly handsome royal Germanic officer asks Olivia to impersonate a missing princess, Susannah finds herself drawn into a dangerous world of international intrigue as she tries to protect her friend—and her heart.

Praise for *Lady Emily's Exotic Journey*:

"Captivating…fabulously intriguing locales…a roller-coaster ride of adventure." —*RT Book Reviews*, 4 Stars

"Richly detailed romance with unexpected characters readers will love." —*Fresh Fiction*

For more Lillian Marek, visit:

www.sourcebooks.com

Lady Emily's Exotic Journey

Victorian Adventures

by Lillian Marek

From sensible, sheltered girl

Safe in the embrace of her loving family, Lady Emily Tremaine longs to feel more intensely alive. Surely the magic and mystery of Assyria and the fabled ruins of Nineveh will bring about the transformation she seeks.

To the woman his heart desires

Scarred by his past and estranged from his noble grandfather, French adventurer Lucien Chambertin desires neither a home nor the chains of emotional attachment. He seeks only to explore the far reaches of the world. But he did not know the world contained the likes of Lady Emily—whose curiosity and sense of wonder match his own.

Praise for *Lady Elinor's Wicked Adventures*:

"This lively Victorian adventure has a wonderfully different and colorful backdrop that is sure to charm readers along with the quick pace, mystery and likable characters." —*RT Book Reviews*

"Marek keeps the pace at a pleasing trot and fully commits to the romance of travel in the Victorian era." —*Booklist*

For more Lillian Marek, visit:

www.sourcebooks.com

A Gift for Guile

The Thief-takers

by Alissa Johnson

Never Trust a Thief

Once a famous officer of Scotland Yard and now a renowned private detective, Sir Samuel Brass has better things to do than shadow a reckless hellion in her misguided quest for atonement. But when the daughter of a notorious criminal—and a former thief herself—returns to London to right an old wrong, Samuel is drawn back into the dangerously exciting world of Esther Walker-Bales.

Beautiful and conniving, maddening and brilliant, Esther is everything he shouldn't want. She's a liar. She's a con. She's a thief. And God help him, but he'd do anything to keep her safe.

Esther knows she's put herself in terrible danger, but nothing will stop her from making amends that are long past due—not her family's enemies, not old fears, and certainly not the domineering, interfering, and undeniably handsome Sir Samuel Brass. Yet whenever he's near, Samuel makes her long for a life that can never be hers…and wish she was worthy of being saved.

"Sweet, sexy, and completely irresistible."
—Cecilia Grant, author of *A Lady Awakened*

"Witty, quirky, and altogether fun."
—*Publishers Weekly* Starred Review

For more Alissa Johnson, visit:

www.sourcebooks.com

A Talent for Trickery

The Thief-takers

by Alissa Johnson

———— ✌ ————

The lady is a thief

Years ago, Owen Renderwell earned acclaim—and a title—for the dashing rescue of a kidnapped duchess. But only a select few knew that Scotland Yard's most famous detective was working alongside London's most infamous thief…and his criminally brilliant daughter, Charlotte Walker.

Lottie was like no other woman in Victorian England. She challenged him. She dazzled him. She questioned everything he believed and everything he was, and he has never wanted anyone more. And then he lost her.

Now a private detective on the trail of a murderer, Owen has stormed back into Lottie's life. She knows that no matter what they may pretend, he will always be a man of the law and she a criminal. Yet whenever he's near, Owen has a way of making things complicated…and making her long for a future that can never be theirs.

———— ✌ ————

For more Alissa Johnson, visit:

www.sourcebooks.com